Advance Praise for
The Heiress of Pittsburgh

"*The Heiress of Pittsburgh* is a twisty, fulfilling legal thriller in which the city of Pittsburgh takes center stage alongside a cast of memorable characters. The hold that the past has on the present—loves lost and found, the complex relationship between remembering and speaking the truth—are the themes that add power to a truly gripping story. Loved this book!"

—Scott Turow, internationally-renowned author and lawyer whose legal thrillers have been translated into more than 40 languages

"A whole lot of the Burg and a whole lot of other good things in *The Heiress of Pittsburgh*—family histories, courtrooms, neighborhoods, loves lost and found, styles of remembering and speaking. A complex, intriguing narrative about a place and people I connect with intimately. Thank you for writing and sharing."

—John Edgar Wideman, acclaimed author and PEN/Faulkner Award recipient

"Gormley's skills with language, dialogue, and narrative bring his wonderful, unpretentious, and utterly genuine characters to life. This is a book for all who love the authenticity of a regional culture and the grace of a writer who can bring it to life."
—Maxwell King, bestselling author of *The Good Neighbor: The Life and Work of Fred Rogers*

"Gormley takes us on an emotional journey through Pittsburgh, bringing out the secrets of family and the importance of neighborhoods, always showing us how the choices we make can make a difference."

—Franco Harris, legendary Pittsburgh Steelers running back, Pro Football Hall of Famer, and four-time Super Bowl Champion

"'Did you ever wonder what makes a place like Pittsburgh, Pittsburgh?' the hero of Ken Gormley's debut novel asks. The author sure knows. Part courtroom drama, part family saga, part teen romance, *The Heiress of Pittsburgh* is a generous, warm-hearted paean to the Steel City."

—Stewart O'Nan, aut *..., Alone*

D1113485

"Gormley has written a moving and compelling story which captures the heart and essence of the real Pittsburgh and its people with unmatched authenticity."

—Lee Gutkind, founding editor, *Creative Nonfiction Magazine*

"We all want to write that first novel about our home town . . . about the one that got away . . . about mystery and loss, sacrifice and truth. Ken Gormley just waited 30 years to do it. Take a look, people."

—David Conrad, film, TV, and stage actor

"*The Heiress of Pittsburgh* features an entertaining cast of characters along with many twists and unexpected turns. Ken Gormley's novel provides a window into the bygone culture of the ethnic melting pot that existed for more than a century in the steel valleys of western Pennsylvania. It is a compelling and enjoyable story."

—Art Rooney II, President, Pittsburgh Steelers

"*The Heiress of Pittsburgh* is a love story that contains all the unique flavors of Pittsburgh—the history, the folklore, the stories inherent in each neighborhood, its colorful residents, and the tale of the heyday of the industrial three rivers region. The charming hero, lawyer Shawn Rossi, bears the weight of the city's underbelly while striving to bring justice to his beloved birthplace. Gormley illuminates this journey with humor and an ample dose of humanity."

—Constanza Romero Wilson, widow of Pulitzer Prize-winning playwright August Wilson; Tony Award-nominated costume designer

"*The Heiress of Pittsburgh* is an inspirational, multigenerational epic about leaving home and finding it again, with a deep love for Pittsburgh on every page."

—Nick & Rachel Courage, founders, Littsburgh

The Heiress of Pittsburgh

Ken Gormley

MILFORD
HOUSE
an imprint of Sunbury Press, Inc.
Mechanicsburg, PA USA

MILFORD HOUSE

an imprint of Sunbury Press, Inc.
Mechanicsburg, PA USA

NOTE: This is a work of fiction. Names, characters, places, and incidents either are the product of the author's imagination or are used fictitiously. While, as in all fiction, the literary perceptions and insights are shaped by experiences, any resemblance to actual persons, living or dead, events, or locales is entirely coincidental.

For information about special discounts for bulk purchases, please contact Sunbury Press Orders Dept. at (855) 338-8359 or orders@sunburypress.com.

To request one of our authors for speaking engagements or book signings, please contact Sunbury Press Publicity Dept. at publicity@sunburypress.com.

FIRST MILFORD HOUSE PRESS EDITION: October 2021

Set in Adobe Garamond | Interior design by Crystal Devine | Cover by Lawrence Knorr | Cover art and interior map by Matt Kambic | Edited by Abigail Henson.

Publisher's Cataloging-in-Publication Data
Names: Gormley, Ken, author.
Title: The heiress of Pittsburgh / Ken Gormley.
Description: First trade paperback edition. | Mechanicsburg, PA : Milford House Press, 2021.
Summary: *New York Times* bestselling author Ken Gormley delivers a powerful courtroom drama about the decent, largely-forgotten qualities that once were the bedrock of the simple towns that built America. *The Heiress of Pittsburgh* reawakens hope that the precious qualities of past generations can be reimagined to create a dazzling new future. But only if success is boldly redefined.
Identifiers: ISBN : 978-1-62006-524-2 (softcover).
Subjects: FICTION / Legal | FICTION / Literary | FICTION / Family Life / General.

Product of the United States of America
0 1 1 2 3 5 8 13 21 34 55

Continue the Enlightenment!

This book is dedicated to my beautiful and amazing wife, Laura, whose love has made this and every other creative undertaking possible. Although she was born in the small town of Ringwood, New Jersey—375 miles from Pittsburgh—she has exemplified the most special qualities on display in this book, inspiring me daily through her extraordinary character and steady adherence to life's simplest (yet richest) virtues. The book is also dedicated to our children, our children-in-law, and their growing families (including soon-to-be grandchildren!) Wherever and whenever they may be born or settle—as a matter of geographic location or temporal distance—they will always be the heirs and heiresses of Pittsburgh.

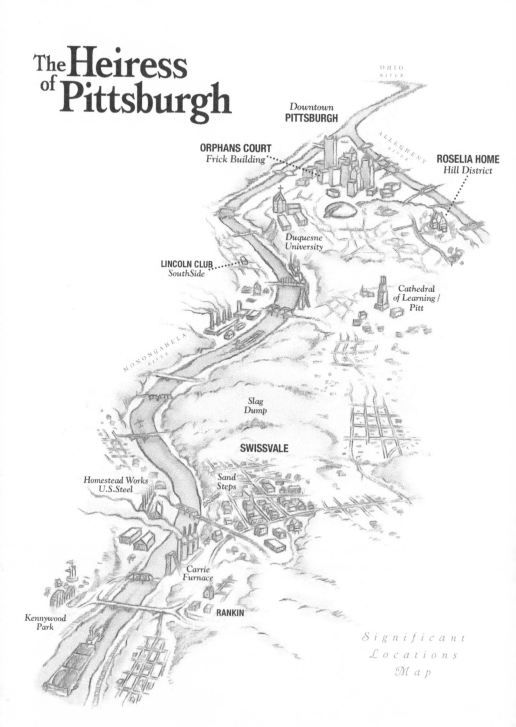

The Heiress
of Pittsburgh

OHIO
RIVER

Downtown
PITTSBURGH

ORPHANS COURT
Frick Building

ROSELIA HOME
Hill District

ALLEGHENY
RIVER

Duquesne
University

LINCOLN CLUB
SouthSide

Cathedral
of Learning /
Pitt

MONONGAHELA
RIVER

Slag
Dump

SWISSVALE

Homestead Works
U.S.Steel

Sand
Steps

Carrie
Furnace

RANKIN

Kennywood
Park

Significant
Locations
Map

September 2008 (North Braddock, PA)

THE EXHUMATION

"Beautiful job! You cracked her open real nice," a cemetery worker hollered at his partner.

Another worker wearing a bandana jumped into the muddy pit with his hammer and chisel and pounded away at the vault.

My client, Choppy Radovich, stepped closer to the hole and nearly lost his footing. I could see that his limp had become more pronounced with the worsening of his "*arthur-it is*," as he called it. His leg had been blown to hell during the D-Day invasion of World War II, leaving him with a herky-jerky limp and the nickname "Choppy" that he wore like a badge of honor.

Choppy inserted a fresh chew of Copenhagen under his lip and eyed the grave. "You mind if I grab holda' your arm, Shawn? I never figured turning eighty-six would be such a pain. I don't wanna sprain my only groin in this-here mud."

A flock of ring-necked pheasants skittered across the edge of the cemetery before getting spooked by the backhoe's engine and taking flight.

My co-counsel, Bernie Milanovich, had known Choppy for years through the Croatian community, which had deep roots in this town. (Lots of names ended in "ich" or "ach" around here). Bernie chewed nervously at his mustache, causing the white hairs to appear darker at the edges. Although he and I ran separate little estate firms in downtown Pittsburgh, we'd joined forces on dozens of cases over the years to assist each other when needed. I always tried to say yes when Bernie asked for help. But in this case, I should have stayed a thousand miles away.

Choppy was a model client, but he was also the grandfather of my first girl-friend, Marjorie, who had walked out of my life decades ago. I should have known this was a horrible idea. But something inside me told me I needed to do this for Marjorie's family.

"*Wipe off that lens!*" Bernie shouted at the video crew. "You think the Superior Court wants to look at close-ups of water molecules?"

The proprietor of the local Serbian funeral home darted around like a nervous wedding coordinator, supervising the exhumation. "Good work, boys," he said. "Let's get that sucker pulled up."

The muddy hillside of the North Braddock Catholic Cemetery provided a perfect vantage point from which to survey the region's past, or at least what remained of it. High above the bend in the Monongahela River, which flowed south to north toward the city, I could see ancient grave markers, Roman Catholic crucifixes, Byzantine crosses, and other tributes to the dead that were stained with mill soot but otherwise nicely preserved. Instead of pointing skyward toward heaven, these memorials sloped downward to provide a sweeping view of the Edgar Thompson steel plant—the last operating mill in the valley, where Andrew Carnegie had created his steel empire in the 1880s—and the silenced blast furnaces of the Carrie Furnace, which had once supplied molten pig iron to the adjacent mills. In these communities, most local families had found work, constructed simple homes, and built livelihoods during the industrial migration of a past era.

Even though I'd left this place to get a law degree at Harvard, where I'd experienced a different realm, I somehow couldn't escape my roots.

The lead worker, his bandanna drenched from the rain, hooked up a block-and-tackle then cranked up the dirty concrete box until it rose one, two, three feet into the air. He swung it onto the ground with a *thud!*

"Don't crack the lid, fellahs!" Bernie stepped amidst the workers. "We want these bones and teeth in one piece. Right, Your Honor?"

Senior Judge Warren Wendell, the presiding judge, looked around uneasily.

Over a period of two decades, the vault had leaked and collected brackish water. Inside, a bronze-colored casket bobbed in the dirty water like a Halloween apple. A pungent, offensive odor—the smell of rot and mud and death—swept into the air. The guy with the bandana jammed a kerchief against his mouth.

"Just a little water seepage," interjected the funeral director, waving his hand. "Even the deluxe model gets a little moisture after twenty years of this Picks'burgh weather."

He inserted a crank at the casket's base and began turning it.

Choppy limped forward to eyeball the perpetrator who had wrecked his daughter's life and ruined his family's future fifty years earlier. He clutched my arm and squeezed it. "Lookie here, Shawn. I know things got screwed up with you and Marjorie back when yinz two were younger. Maybe you could patch things up when she gets back here for her testimony. You were always good for each other. The Lord works in funny ways. Maybe this-here trial was meant to be for a reason."

A dozen ethnic dialects in this region had been mashed together to produce a distinctly Pittsburgh jargon. "Wash" was pronounced "worsh," "downtown" was "dahntahn," "rubber bands" were "gumbands," and "redd up" meant to "clean." Choppy spoke the lingo with a natural flair.

I put my arm around the old man. There was something special about Choppy. He was a true "mill hunky," as he proudly identified himself. Choppy was open, direct, and straightforward. Whatever he said, you could take to the bank. His granddaughter Marjorie, though, wasn't such an open book. But that was a different story.

"We'll get our proof from the DNA," I whispered to the old man. "Marjorie won't even have to waste her time flying here from California to testify. It will all work out," I said. Choppy pretended he didn't hear me.

The cemetery crew used the chisel to pry open the coffin. As the lid rose, rain doused the coffin's moldy silk liner. One worker covered his mouth, suppressing an urge to gag.

"*Jesus H. Christ!*" Judge Wendell exclaimed, making the sign of the cross. He hurriedly lit a Kent cigarette and sucked down a bolus of menthol smoke. A light-skinned Black man with graying hair, the judge was known for maintaining his cool under fire. Now, his eyes opened to the size of quarters. He seemed interested in viewing the decedent, whose alleged act of sexual gratification a half-century earlier had spawned this messy will contest and consumed a week of his Orphan's Court calendar.

"That's one ugly biddy!" exclaimed the worker with the bandana, peering inside.

"Who the hell is *this*?" Bernie pointed at the imposter.

The undertaker whipped out his cemetery map, certain that they must have dug up the wrong plot.

The woman in the coffin wore a purple chiffon dress discolored by green mold and a white wig that had jarred loose. Her wrinkled face with its hooked Eastern European nose had become eerily wax-colored from embalming fluid and the passage of time. "That's the grave wax," the deputy coroner whispered to the judge. "The technical term is adipocere."

"This sure as hell ain't Ralph Acmovic, the guy we're looking for," said Bernie.

"That *bastard,*" the Serbian funeral director cursed, adding a foreign expletive while smacking the coffin. "Looks like my uncle did it again. He swore he straightened hisself out after he got busted."

Bernie grabbed the undertaker by the rain slicker. "What the hell are you saying? Where's Ralph Acmovic, you duppa?"

"He could be anywheres," the funeral director said, wriggling free. "Probably dumped over the hillside. Who knows? My uncle lost his license back in the '70s for doing this crap. Hey, look, I ain't going to jail like him. We cleaned up our act, Bernie," he said, raising his right hand. "Swear ta' God."

"So, who the hell's *this*?" Bernie demanded.

We all stared at the corpse. Even 30 years after death, she would have benefitted from a radical nose job.

"*This here* looks to be one of my great-aunts," the funeral director said sheepishly. "She bears a family resemblance—sort of. I'm guessing my uncle wanted to give her a nice send-off, you know, to make it look good for the family? He probably dumped this Acmovic guy over the hill into the slag heap, reused his casket, and kept the cash. It's not the first time a Serbian would have pulled a fast one on a Croatian and done something like that."

The deputy coroner and his assistant began packing up their bone saws, scalpels, and plastic gloves, pleased to have a good story to take back to the office.

As the cemetery workers fired up their backhoe to lower the coffin back into the grave, three spectators at the top of the hillside drifted toward us. A young muscular guy holding a golf umbrella, wearing a McCain-Palen button on his lapel, escorted our opposing counsel from Philadelphia. She smirked as she walked past us. A third person—a rodent-like man with moles on his face—gave Bernie and me the finger behind his back. With that, the trio climbed into a Lexus.

Choppy stared blankly at the waxen face of the corpse. I put my arm around him and hugged the old man. "Sorry it turned out this way, Choppy," I said. "But we still have some legal maneuvers up our sleeve, don't give up hope." He nodded his head slowly. Then he broke down, his shoulders shaking like the flanks of an exhausted workhorse, expelling deep sobs that seemed unnatural for a man who'd lived to reach the age of eighty-six after having witnessed so many of life's injustices.

I turned away, ashamed that Bernie and I had brought him to this place.

Judge Wendell blessed himself hurriedly, then turned toward Bernie and me.

"Well, you gave it a shot, gentlemen," he said, tugging up the collar of his trench coat. "We're starting trial on Monday at ten o'clock. Unless you have the good sense to withdraw this lawsuit, so this family doesn't get hurt even worse." He glanced toward Choppy, who stared at the empty hole. Then the judge walked away.

Once the last Jeep had pulled out and I'd walked Bernie and Choppy to their cars, I spun around and dragged myself up the hillside. Clumps of red mud clung to my wingtips. I cursed and tried to kick it off against a tombstone inscribed with the words "*Tu Spokiva*" ("here sleeps"); this was obviously the Slovak section of the working-class dead.

Ordinarily, I would have made a detour to the cemetery section that included the Rossi and McFadden plots—the sacred place where my mom, dad, and their families were buried. Today, I blessed myself and blew a kiss in their direction.

At the top of the hill, I reached a thornless honeylocust tree next to a familiar stone marker. I fell on one knee. "Hi, sweetheart," I said. The red mud soaked through my trousers—another pair of pants that would need to be dry-cleaned.

I closed my eyes. My fingers traced out the words etched into grey marble:

"*Christine Kendall Rossi. Beloved wife. Best mom in the world. 1958–2006*"

"I'm here, sweetie," I whispered, stroking the marble like a precious pearl. "Your mom and the girls made *haluski* last week. It was a wild scene. The house stunk from cabbage for days. You would have *loved* it.

"Oh, you probably saw the whole thing, right? I know you're watching with those eagle eyes of yours. I'm trying to spend more time with the girls. Honest, Christine."

I stood up, kissed one of my palms, and placed it against the cold, wet stone.

"Don't get the wrong idea about me handling this case, okay?" I patted the marble. "I just feel like I should do this for the family. Choppy's one of the great mill-hunkies of all time; you know that. They're good people. There's nothing more to it than that."

I blessed myself and stared at the stone marker as if, somehow, it provided a portal through which Christine could see me.

"Just keep an eye on your husband, promise me, sweetheart? I need *lots* of bucking up right now. Being a parent without you here is a lot harder than I imagined. So is coping with this case."

September 2008 (Courtroom, Pittsburgh)

OPENING ARGUMENTS

In the lexicon of the town where I grew up, a "mill hunky" was a term of endearment, even though it might have sounded like a dirty ethnic slur to outsiders. Of course, if a person didn't speak the vernacular that coursed through the streets and Insulbrick-sided houses of our gritty neighborhood, it was easy to take it the wrong way, like somebody hearing poetry in an unfamiliar language.

My hometown of Swissvale was located in the Monongahela River Valley—referred to by locals as the Mon Valley—where steel mills and factories belched fumes and flames into the sky. Dozens of factory towns dotted both sides of the river, creating a smoky, fiery gateway to downtown Pittsburgh a few miles away. A writer once described it as "hell with its lid off," and that was fair. But these towns, too, were America's original melting pot, home to a rich stew of memorable characters, many of whom were my friends and relatives. Like most residents of Swissvale and other nearby mill communities, I was a mongrel, a "Heinz 57 variety," a blend of Irish and Italian with a drop of Slovak blood splashed in for good measure. My ancestors had come to Pittsburgh in the late nineteenth century and scraped out a living in one mill or another so that their offspring could have a better life. The lucky ones could even get an education.

My first name, Shawn (spelled with a "w"), was an odd compromise designed to placate my mom's Irish family, who thought it sounded Gaelic, and her "buttin-sky" Slovak neighbors, who insisted that this spelling (rather than Sean, the "mick" version) would work better with the bosses who handed out jobs. My last name, Rossi, was safe: It was a common surname in these towns, a clever decoy that had been shortened from "Rosario" to hide the fact that it was pure Italian-Catholic. As my Grandmother Rossi said, "The rosary part was a dead giveaway."

Through this accident of ancestry, I'd come to be born into a lower middle-class world with no pedigree or family tree worth noting. Yet somehow, I'd loved that lack of distinction. It seemed remarkable to me that such simple genetic materials could be brought across the ocean by immigrants looking for jobs in dirty mills, then shaken up like a phosphate to produce something so exotic and wondrous.

Even the Irish and Italian families, like ours, considered themselves "mill-hunkies." The same was true for Blacks, Jews, Germans, and anyone else toiling away together in the mills and factories. It was a lighthearted term of affection—a familiar way of greeting each other. It described people who worked hard, joined unions to earn enough money to make ends meet, put their families first, and exuded pride in their ability to surmount all obstacles. It signaled a unique brotherhood and sisterhood that went far beyond blood relationships.

From early in my childhood, I remembered driving with my mom before the sun rose to take my dad to work at Kopp Glass, which produced glass signals and lighting fixtures for the railroads and mills. The red brick factory was located along the tracks where Swissvale met Rankin—two adjoining mill towns on the river's north bank. When time allowed, we'd stop en route at St. Agnes's Church to give thanks. Here, my parents joined men in blue work shirts and women wearing babushkas as they proceeded up the aisle with hands folded to receive Holy Communion before Mass. Early Communion was a special dispensation allowed by pastors in mill towns like ours so that workers could begin their days under God's protective eye. The early shift took full advantage of it.

I remembered, too, riding downtown with my mom and dad at Christmastime, along the river, past the fiery stacks of the Hazelwood Coke Works and Jones & Laughlin steel mills, and parking near Horne's Department Store to look at the sparkling holiday displays in the windows. Then we'd get three tickets for the Nutcracker matinee at Heinz Hall, the fancy concert hall donated by the ketchup-and-pickle moguls whose factory was just across the Allegheny River. I'd close my eyes with music dancing magically around me and think: How could there be a greater place to be born?

In school, we would proudly recite the history: George Washington had proven himself here as a young officer during the French and Indian War in 1755 when he saved the British troops from annihilation in the Battle of the Monongahela. From the start, this triangle of land had been viewed as a strategic location. Here, the Monongahela and Allegheny rivers converged to form the Ohio at "the Point" downtown, creating a major artery of commerce, trade, and navigation. It remained a booming economic engine throughout two World Wars and multiple industrial revolutions.

By the time I'd graduated high school in the early 1970s, jobs in the mills were still plentiful and paid more than most other options. Still, my parents advised: Get the heck out of the heat and stench of the Edgar Thompson mill, the Carrie Furnace, the Union Switch & Signal, and this whole world of blue-collar servitude and find a safe suburban life built around a golf course and nice strip mall.

So, when I'd decided to aim for law school, they'd been elated. "We'll always be grateful for our little community; people look out for each other here," they'd said, before quickly adding: "But a law degree will give you a pathway out of the Mon Valley, and you'll achieve *more* for your family than we were able to give you."

I remember learning in a philosophy course that "geography is fate." That was especially true in towns like Swissvale. Despite my parents' admonitions, this hard-scrabble town of 1.3 square miles, with a population of 8,000 citizens and a business district that was barely two blocks long, was in my blood. Its inhabitants not only tolerated the fumes and gritty particles pouring out of the mills, they even saw a certain beauty in the fiery industrial world along the river because it represented jobs and security.

As my Aunt Kate would say in her classic Pittsburgh accent, "If the porch don't need *worshing dahn*, people *ain't workin'*." And that about summed it up. For sure, there were downsides to living in a mill town. It was tough, dirty, dangerous, and cramped. The smoke could get so thick that it deposited black soot on laundry hanging from clotheslines no matter what time of day. Professional men had to bring a second shirt to change during their lunch breaks to eliminate the stench and grime. The mills dumped truckloads of sediment from the blast furnaces— smoldering residue resembling volcanic rock—into giant slag dumps that rose like mountains next to our neighborhoods. Factories regularly dumped waste into the rivers even as families held picnics and fished for carp along the banks. It was an environmentalist's nightmare.

But the mills provided a steady paycheck and enough extra cash to start a bank account to afford a family vacation, a daughter's wedding, or even college tuition. More importantly, earning money wasn't the sole motivator. People in these towns were proud. They made the steel that built the products that developed the whole country and protected it, allowing every other big shot in America to succeed. And their pride had rubbed off on me.

———

While the deputy clerk organized papers for this day's trial session, I allowed my eyes to wander out the seventeenth-floor windows of the Frick Building. It provided a magnificent view of the city of Pittsburgh below and the small towns dotting the three rivers.

For years I was happiest at my two-person estate litigation firm, Rossi & Associates, where I could quietly help people in these little communities. When I'd started thirty years earlier, I'd knowingly passed up the perks of big firm life by telling myself I could pick cases that gave me fulfillment and still earn a respectable stream of income. Increasingly, though, I doubted that decision. Work was becoming more of a struggle now that Christine was gone. I found myself neglecting my daughters so I could work harder while earning less. The luster of my practice, which I had once considered so noble, was wearing off. This case had been a perfect example: I'd somehow been dragged into this nasty court battle between Bernie and a nasty lawyer from Philadelphia. Even worse, I was now sitting at the counsel table representing Marjorie Radovich—the *one* person I vowed never to go near again, literally or figuratively.

Bernie smacked my arm. "Why don't you take another antacid and relax, Shawn?" he whispered. "I wish our Marjorie friend would show up, too. We'll have to manage till she gets here."

"I know this woman too well, or at least I did," I countered. "Don't count on her showing up."

Marjorie had largely ignored the steady stream of emails and questions sent to her by my law associate, J.V., whom I'd assigned to deal with her. We had to build our whole case on interviews with Choppy and Marjorie's mother, Lil, relying on their memories and stray letters they could find in dresser drawers. It wasn't ideal in terms of case preparation.

I swept flakes of dandruff from the shoulder of my suitcoat. It was a bad omen to start any trial with dandruff all over your coat; it telegraphed to your opposing counsel "*nervousness!*" and "*personal distress!*"

I locked my eyes on the courtroom door. If Marjorie showed up, should I be watching for blond hair or some other color now that she was middle-aged?

"Don't get your head all screwed up thinking about the past," Bernie whispered. "Put that stuff behind you, Shawn. Let's focus on winning this case for these folks. They need your help."

Jimmy LaPaglia, the deputy clerk, entered the courtroom. Deputy clerks were permitted to dress in business attire like the lawyers. Jimmy, a natty dresser, took full advantage of it. Today he wore a brown plaid suit with a snappy yellow pocket square in his coat. He stood erect and bellowed in his sloppy Pittsburgh accent, "All rise! This court's now in session. Senior Judge Warren Wendell presidin'."

Judge Wendell climbed up to the bench and stretched out his arms to loosen his robe. Proudly parochial, he was a classic Pittsburgh trial judge, required to stand for election by the voters every ten years to keep him honest, delivering justice for the people of Allegheny County.

"I have before me a petition to open the decree of distribution in the estate of Ralph Acmovic, Sr.," the judge said, flipping through his file. "Number eighty-seven of 2008, petition of Marjorie Radovich *et al.* This estate was open years ago. The trust is now worth about six million dollars. However, our lead petitioner argues she's the biological daughter of decedent, so she claims she's entitled to half of the trust proceeds. She says her existence was *purposely* hidden by the greedy half-brother." He cast a questioning glance down at Ralph Acmovic, Jr.

"Our attempt to resolve this case using some newfangled DNA testing was an unfortunate waste of time. Hopefully, we don't plan to dig up any more corpses. Is that correct, counselors?"

"No, your honor," I said.

"No, your honor," Bernie echoed.

Bernie shot daggers at our opposing counsel. She scowled back at him. They'd already had plenty of tussles during pre-trial skirmishes.

"Are you prepared to commence, Mr. Rossi?" Judge Wendell asked.

I took one step forward toward the bench, trying to dislodge the chalky Tums tablet that had stuck to the roof of my mouth. Out of habit, I clicked my gold Cross pen three times, "Ready, Your Honor." *Ready or not, I thought.*

I dreaded this trial, mainly because I wasn't sure what I felt about seeing *her* again.

"We call Lillian Marie Radovich," I announced in a firm lawyerly voice that drifted from my mouth with practiced self-assuredness. "Mother of the principal petitioner."

September 2008 (Courtroom, Pittsburgh)

LIL'S STORY

Marjorie's mother, Lil, ambled to the witness chair. In her youth, she doubtless was a pretty young woman. But those days were long gone. Now, lines of sadness and worry were etched into the folds of flesh on her face.

Lil shifted her large frame in the witness chair before untying a loose-fitting scarf around her neck.

"Mrs. Radovich," I began, "can you state your full name and address for the court?"

She pressed a finger against the shunt valve at her throat, avoiding eye contact with the judge. "Lillian Marie Radovich," she stated.

"I'm sorry, Your Honor," Lil continued. "I had part of my vocal cords taken out a year ago. The doctors gave me this-here '*trake*.' I apologize if I sound garbly."

She released her finger from the valve where she had her tracheotomy. It emitted a gust of rattly breath like a whale expelling air through its blowhole.

"No problem at all, young lady," Judge Wendell said, raising a hand and dismissing her apology. "My Aunt Vanie had one of those operations. It sounded like she was burping up soda pop every time she talked." He chuckled at that. "I'd give you an A-plus; you speak the Queen's English," he added graciously. "Just take your time. This court won't let *anyone* embarrass you. Here in the halls of justice, we don't take kindly to people making fun of folks with disabilities."

I stepped back toward the witness chair, glancing at Bernie with feigned modesty, having accomplished my goal of eliciting sympathy for our client in the first twenty seconds.

"Now, Mrs. Radovich. Are you familiar with a man named Ralph Acmovic, Sr., the decedent in this case?" I asked.

"Yep. I mean, I *used* to be," Lil said. "He's dead."

Lil kept her finger poised over the shunt as if dreading the following forty questions. She stared at her mother, whom everyone called "Aunt Peg," slouched in her wheelchair in the front row next to Choppy.

Aunt Peg and Choppy had been a perfect Pittsburgh couple whose devotion to each other was stronger than the steel that poured out of the mills. Choppy was first-generation Croatian, and Aunt Peg was first-generation Slovak. They'd met at a gathering at the Sokol Club—a Slovak social club and gymnasium in Homestead—dancing all night to Eastern European music, then getting married six months later.

They'd bought a home where their daughter, Lil, had been born just as Choppy packed off to serve his country in the war. After he'd returned, they'd dreamed of boundless opportunities—perhaps even a cottage at Conneaut Lake—as Choppy rose in the ranks at Carrie Furnace. But Lil's unplanned pregnancy at age 16 had shot that plan to hell. Instead, they'd taken out loans and incurred debt that only seemed to spiral upward each year, especially when Marjorie went to college and (in later years) when Aunt Peg fell ill. They shouldered these burdens quietly, hiding the harsh financial facts from Lil and Marjorie. They'd dedicated themselves, year after year, to staying afloat.

Choppy and Aunt Peg had recently celebrated their 65th anniversary. Aunt Peg rarely went out in public; the messy adult diapers and the undignified way she chewed her food embarrassed everyone. For Choppy, though, this will contest was an exception and required her attendance. Aunt Peg was belted securely into her wheelchair so she could watch and listen to every word. Even though Aunt Peg's cognitive skills were impaired because of a stroke, as I glanced over, I could swear she winced in anticipation of her daughter facing this questioning.

"When did you first become acquainted with the decedent, Ralph Acmovic?" I asked Lil.

"When we worked together that summer at the Switch—I mean the Union Switch & Signal in Swissvale," she said. "It was good income. Everyone in Swissvale tried to get in there. I got hired 'cause my uncle Jake was a shop steward. I think we met in June of '57 or something like-gat. We both did piece work over in Section B."

"How old was the decedent at that time?" I asked.

"Pro'lly nineteen or twenty," she said. "He was a couple years older than me. I was still fifteen. I was gonna be a junior at Swissvale High. I was lucky to get the job at the Switch. It paid good money."

"Did you come to have—let's just call it—an 'intimate' relationship with Ralph Acmovic during that summer of 1957?" I asked.

"Objection!"

Our opposing counsel, Constance Drew-Morris, stood up on her 4-inch heels and delivered the objection with a sharp tone. "The word 'intimate' is ambiguous and subject to multiple interpretations, Your Honor," she said. I recoiled from her pronunciation of the word "your." It sounded more like "yer," just as "water" sounded like "wooter" when people from Philly uttered them.

Drew-Morris was the newest partner in the Philadelphia satellite office of Sidney, Welles & Rupert, a successful boutique firm specializing in estate litigation with headquarters in New York City and branches in a dozen other cities. She attended Penn Law, where she was managing editor of the Law Review and Order of the Coif, known for out-performing even the best male competitors who stood in her way. Drew-Morris was reportedly separated from her husband, a former Penn classmate who now practiced banking law in New York City, which allowed them to keep their respective distances. She was only thirty-two, a dynamo known for chewing up attorneys and spitting them out. As the lowest person on the firm's totem pole of partners, she drew the short straw and was assigned all the cases in Pittsburgh, Cleveland, and other places deemed to be in the boondocks.

"Overruled," Judge Wendell said. "You may answer the question, Mrs. Radovich."

"Yes . . . I mean . . . he was handsome as all get-out," Lil said. "He had shiny blond hair and a good build. All the girls noticed him. We messed around in the stock room in Section X while the foreman was having lunch at the Sportsman's a couple times."

"Messed around?" I asked.

"Yeh, nuzzling and feeling up, usual stuff like-gat," she said.

"*Objection!*" Drew-Morris was back on her feet, but not before Lil continued with: "That was *before* he had sexual relations with me at Kennywood Park against my will."

"I have no idea what the witness means by 'nuzzling and feeling-up,' Your Honor," Drew-Morris cut in. "Counsel's trying to sneak in evidence improperly. He's never established an ultimate sex act."

Bernie stood up. Our law firms had won many estate cases together; he was unmatched when it came to arcane evidentiary maneuvers.

"Perhaps Ms. Drew-Morris needs to read up on her *fornication and bastardy* cases so she'd be more up to date on this subject," he said, raising an eyebrow in her direction.

Drew-Morris smacked her fist against the counsel table. "This is unacceptable, Your Honor. This man's purposely throwing around sexual innuendos to make me feel uncomfortable." She pivoted on her heels. "He was looking at me funny during our pre-trial conferences, too. If you do it again, Mr. Milanovich, I'll have to slap a *complaint* on you," she said.

She glared at Bernie as if to indicate, "You're a *marked* man."

"Overruled," said the judge. "We'll see where the evidence takes us."

Drew-Morris sat down with a subdued *huff.* She was too polished to allow the judge to see her get ruffled. Instead, she ripped a page from her yellow legal pad, scribbled down some words, then lifted a finger.

From the back of the courtroom, her paralegal, a young man in a business suit, made his way toward us. His neck appeared tense, like an Olympian preparing for a world-record pole vault. It was the same muscular guy who'd been holding the golf umbrella for Drew-Morris at the cemetery.

Drew-Morris handed him the folded paper as she said in a stage-whisper, "Fax this to New York. Get it done *now*."

The paralegal accepted the sheet as if it contained orders from the battlefield. He turned and gave my co-counsel and me a death stare.

Before I could whisper to Bernie not to take the bait, Bernie put two fingers to his mouth and blew a kiss in their direction.

"*I saw that!*" Drew-Morris cried out. "Let the record reflect that opposing counsel was blowing *kisses* at my legal assistant and me. It's a continued pattern of *sexual harassment!*" She glanced at the court reporter to make sure she was typing this into the transcript.

The judge grabbed his gavel and banged it repeatedly to restore order as the paralegal sprinted out the door.

"Let's try to maintain some professional *decorum* here," Judge Wendell said, holding up a hand as if to stop a runaway truck. "We're in Orphan's Court. Do all of you understand the significance of that? We have different rules in Orphan's Court, and I'd ask you to respect that tradition. We don't tolerate loud disruptions or shouting around here. Do you all catch my drift?"

The judge leaned over the bench, stared directly at Drew-Morris, and whispered, "Because all of our clients are *dead. . . .*"

September 2008 (Courtroom, Pittsburgh)

ORPHAN'S COURT

The Orphan's Court of Allegheny County was a vestige of the magnificent era that had once defined Pittsburgh—an era of steel mills and coke ovens and Eastern European immigrants shoveling paychecks into local savings and loans, an era that now teetered upon extinction.

Due to the collapse of steel in the 1980s, J&L Steel, the Hazelwood Coke Works, and the phalanx of U.S. Steel plants that had hugged the banks of the Monongahela River for decades had largely disappeared. In blue-collar towns farthest from the city, the shuttered mills left behind derelict neighborhoods, vacant storefronts, and empty Eastern Orthodox churches. Ethnic fraternal organizations no longer existed to serve the next generation's needs because the next generation had left for jobs in other cities. In place of the old mill sites closer to downtown Pittsburgh, state-of-the-art medical centers, high-tech university research facilities, expansive sports complexes, and dazzling office towers built of glass and new brands of specialty steel had slowly risen up in their place.

Just as the city had been getting back on its feet and recent college graduates could look forward to good-paying jobs instead of fleeing the area, the global economic meltdown wreaked havoc once again. By early 2008, banks had begun calling in loans, and unemployment skyrocketed—an all-too-familiar story. As President George W. Bush scrambled to calm the financial crisis in the final months of his presidency, many businesses and institutions in this town braced themselves for the next body blow.

It was one of the reasons Marjorie's family had decided to file this lawsuit. Even though Choppy didn't broadcast it, he'd confided in Bernie and me that they could be "in a little trouble" if they couldn't pay off their mounting bank loans and debts. In his eyes, this lawsuit was a chance to achieve justice for his family and be repaid for the enormous financial burden Lil's pregnancy, decades earlier, had placed on all of them.

Orphan's Court, located in the magnificent granite Frick Building, was their best hope. This granite edifice, built by Henry Clay Frick to intentionally choke off light and air from the adjoining building owned by his ex-business partner, Andrew Carnegie, had stood in this spot since 1902. It had escaped demolition during two renaissances that had swept away much of Pittsburgh's old grit and grime. Nestled on the highest floor, Orphan's Court occupied a secretive world known only to lawyers with a penchant for this obscure litigation art. Quiet and solemn, it looked and smelled like a courthouse with hallways paneled in Carrara marble, stained-glass windows, and heavy bronze doors at the entrance of each courtroom.

This court was far from the chaos and shouting litigants that were hallmarks of the criminal and civil divisions across the street in the Allegheny County courthouses. The media rarely scrutinized or covered it. Here, judges could allow a little extra latitude and relax the rules of procedure to seek the fullest measure of justice. Orphan's Court handled only the most grave, personal issues such as wills, estates, probate, guardianship, incapacity, orphanage—matters that touched the beginning and the end of life and defined the breadth of human existence.

Although I'd never taken a course in trusts and estates during law school, I'd worked as a summer law clerk for attorney Tim Mulroy, who'd assigned me to draft wills for his family and friends in the no-frills Irish neighborhood of Garfield. I'd loved it from the start. I learned that people avoided talking about their wills or estate plans at all costs. It scared them to think about "what happens when one of us dies?" and "what happens to our kids and grandkids?" Most of our clients were elderly, so this meant speaking of such private matters required absolute trust, and I found I was good at it. It also was more rewarding than doing boring corporate work.

When it came time to prepare bills, Tim often would say, "We'll just skip the fee on this one. I'll log in more hours on *other* cases, so the firm earns plenty of money. That's how we'll work it." He would smile and add, "On my tombstone, I want it to say that I helped my own people. That's my definition of success."

That became my definition of success, too. Orphan's Court became the place where I spent most of my legal life.

"Let's take a quick ten-minute break," Judge Wendell announced, checking his watch. "I look forward to hearing the rest of your witness's testimony, Mr. Rossi. Every plaintiff deserves her day in court."

"Thank you, Your Honor," I replied, nodding toward Lil to relax. "I agree completely."

As Judge Wendell slid into his chambers to catch a smoke, my associate, Jaime Vascov, hustled up to the counsel table, a hand pressed against her swollen belly. She was eight months pregnant and showing every bit of it. Known to everyone in the courthouse as "J.V.," she was famous for her tenacity and willingness to speak her mind.

"Here's the last batch, boss," J.V. said, pulling out a stack of legal memos from her capacious briefcase. A few crayons, a banana peel, and a granola bar wrapper from her boys' breakfast spilled onto the floor. She deftly swept them up.

"Jeez, Shawn, you look stressed out and haggard," J.V. added. "You should take some Advil next break."

"Thanks, J.V. That makes me feel better about myself," I told her. "Maybe I'll just take some cyanide instead."

As quickly as she'd appeared, J.V. whispered "good luck" and slipped out the door. A pink message slip was at the top of the papers. I slid it toward Bernie. "It's another message from Marjorie. She says she needs to wrap up 'an important transaction' before she can come here. I told you—I think she has *no intention* of showing up."

Bernie crumpled it up. "I wish we could just grab some DNA from that little runt Ralph Junior. One strand of hair would prove he's the half-brother; I'd bet anything. It's absurd the PA appeals courts say we can't collect DNA samples in civil cases without the person's consent. Privacy my rear end. This family suffered an injustice. They deserve to have the truth come out."

Bernie had represented Choppy and Aunt Peg since he'd done a simple will for them fifty years earlier through the Croatian Fraternal Union. When Bernie took on clients, he dedicated himself to them for life. Now, he raked his fingers through his mustache; it looked like a paintbrush dipped into off-white paint from smoking too many White Owl cigars. "We're gonna have to beat them with or without the DNA stuff, Shawn," Bernie finally declared. "I know you're up to it."

———

"Go ahead, Mr. Rossi. I think your witness was talking about some alleged hanky-panky at Kennywood, as I recall," Judge Wendell stated.

I jerked my head up. "Thank you, your honor." I checked off several non-existent items on my notepad—to display total command—then plunged back into the direct examination. Lil wasn't good at spontaneous thinking. So, Bernie and I had helped her rehearse her answers over and over until she had memorized them. Now, she delivered the story flawlessly:

Lil had met Ralph Acmovic, she said, when work let out on the last Friday in July of 1957. She remembered that afternoon perfectly, she said, because it was two days before her sixteenth birthday. Her parents never allowed her to date older boys—"especially Serbian boys"—on account of what Choppy called the Serbs' "general feeling of goddamned superiority" towards Croatians. "But this was *the* Kennywood Park picnic for everyone at the Union Switch & Signal," she clarified. "I'd earned my own money there, and Ralph Acmovic invited me."

Acmovic had picked her up that afternoon at the Union Switch gate, driving his father's enormous green Buick. "It was a gorgeous car," Lil added, tentatively sipping a glass of water. "A 1955 Super."

He was a thin and handsome boy with a Serbian hook to his nose and distinctive blond hair, she said with a dash of wistfulness. A pack of Lark cigarettes was stuffed into the boy's sleeveless shirt pocket. "I really didn't smoke," explained Lil. Yet she partook this day, "what with it being the Kennywood Park picnic day and all," with the sun shimmering on the river as they drove across the Rankin Bridge. Lil had heard that Ralph's father had plenty of money as the owner of a factory in North Braddock. But Ralph never said much about his family. With a cocky grin, he'd bragged that he intended to build his *own* fortune, and he wanted nothing to do with the Union Switch or his father's grimy work. After he joined the Marines for a couple of years, he said he planned to come back to Swissvale, open his own real estate office, and become a multi-millionaire.

"He told me he was good with numbers," she testified, "and even better with people, especially ladies."

Lil looked up at the judge to make sure she was clear to proceed. He nodded.

The Buick had glided into the enormous cinder-paved parking lot at Kennywood, she explained, where Ralph had picked a space in the most distant corner. Together, they'd walked the empty rows of the parking lot holding hands and sopping up the excitement of attending the Union Switch picnic, where they'd stay until dark.

"For the record," I interjected, causing the judge to lift his head. "I'd ask the court to take judicial notice that Kennywood is a family-owned amusement park that's been in operation since 1898."

"So noted," he said, giving a "thumbs up" from the bench.

Every person within a hundred miles knew this landmark. Kennywood Park was a Pittsburgh institution, carved into the hills overlooking the fiery stacks of the Edgar Thompson mill and the Monongahela River. Popcorn and cotton candy, roasted lamb in the picnic shelters, big band music, shrieking roller coasters, the clattering Jack Rabbit rollercoaster on wooden tracks, the wooden Howdy Doody figures that measured children's height—all these sights and smells, every Pittsburgher knew, could blend on hot summer nights to produce the ultimate pleasure.

On this particular Friday of July 1957, Lil explained, she and Ralph Acmovic had felt that pleasure with full force.

"Where did your sexual intimacy with the decedent take place?" I nudged Lil forward in her script just as we'd rehearsed at the Radovich's house in Swissvale days earlier.

"It started in the Old Mill," Lil said, her windpipes seeming to constrict. "It was the old boat ride with dragon heads on the front." Lil took an asthmatic breath, dabbing a tissue against her shunt valve. "There was a big paddle wheel that pushed water along and moved you through this dark tunnel. I guess you could call it kind of a canal, like the ones in Venice, maybe?"

Judge Wendell nodded and took a brief note. The judge had probably ridden the Old Mill a hundred times in his youth.

"How long did the ride last?" I asked.

"About ten minutes," she said. "There were all kinds 'a romantic scenes lit up inside the tunnel. Couples holding hands, pictures of Niagara Falls an 'at. He told me this was the place lovers went. I believed him. I mean, I was only fifteen."

"What happened then?"

"He gave the ride operator fifty cents to let us have our own boat. As soon as it knocked open the doors and drifted into the tunnel, he started trying to get intimate—the real thing, y'know. Not even a kiss or some regular necking. He just slipped his hand under my skirt. I'd never done that before." She covered her face, looked up at the judge, then gulped down some water. "He touched me in my private places," she stated hurriedly. "I think he said he loved me. He said he'd marry me as soon as I graduated high school. He promised he'd buy us a house and pay for my college."

"Objection," Drew-Morris said, standing up. She was careful not to sound too aggressive after her last outburst. "I move to strike this entire testimony about these *alleged* events in the Old Mill, especially the references to *'private places.'* The whole thing assumes facts not in evidence. It amounts to rank speculation."

Judge Wendell blinked his eyes, nonplussed. He'd lived by his wits for nearly eight decades in the Hill District, being chewed up by ruthless coroners and district attorneys before becoming the first black jurist on Orphan's Court. A Penn-trained lawyer firing off objections didn't rattle him.

"Well, that's an interesting point, Ms. Drew-Morris," Judge Wendell said, leaning down from the bench. His own voice took on an avuncular tone. "I suppose if this were a hypothetical on a law school exam, that argument might fly. But this lady is trying her best to tell us what happened, and we should respect her right to do that, shouldn't we?"

Drew-Morris started to speak, caught herself, then clamped her mouth shut. She knew that smart-mouthing a 78-year-old judge and having it recorded by the court reporter might not play well in the court of appeals.

"Now, Ms. Drew-Morris," the judge continued in a genial voice. "Let's allow the witness to tell her story." He cleared his throat. "I'd like to let Mrs. Radovich finish her testimony, or we'll be late for lunch, and I get a tad cranky if I don't get to my booth at Mitchell's by noon."

Bernie chewed on his pen and winked at me, stifling a chuckle.

"Did your sexual encounter continue after you left the Old Mill?" I asked.

My witness closed her eyes, pressing her finger against the shunt. "We got corn dogs and cans of pop for supper to have a picnic, only the pavilions were all filled. So, he says that we should go to his car, and that's what we did. It was getting dark. I remember the Ferris wheel and Noah's Ark an 'at were all lit up with colored lights. We walked through the parking lot and climbed into the back of his old man's car—the green Buick. Then we counted lights on the roller coaster and ate our corn dogs and made out. It was big as a living room back there. It even had a lighter so we could smoke our cigarettes. He started rubbing me again, you know, down there. But this time, I mean, he just *kept going*."

"Did you resist?" I asked.

I looked into the face of the woman. Her cheeks seemed ready to explode at the question as a tiny wattle of fat shook at the base of her neck. "All's I remember is my brain kinda went fuzzy, y'know," she said. "I was a young girl, and he was handsome as get-out. God, I wish I'd known how to make him stop."

Lil's shoulders started shaking, and her face turned red. "I didn't know what to do. I never said a *thing* to make him believe he had the right. He just took advantage of me while I tried to count the roller coaster lights," she said, sobbing. Her throat produced ungodly noises as she pressed her finger over the shunt.

"And I was only fifteen years old," she said, pulling out an Albuterol inhaler and administering a quick blast into the hole in her throat.

"*God Almighty!*" Choppy stood up in the front row of the spectator benches. "My daughter needs medical attention!"

I glanced up at the judge for guidance. He held out both hands as if to say, "Whatever you want, Mr. Rossi."

"I need to keep going," Lil choked out the words. "I want this to be *over*."

My witness's brown hairdo tilted sideways. A black streak of eyeliner dripped from her lashes.

"How long did the sexual intercourse last?" I asked gently.

"About two or three minutes. He couldn't hold off," Lil said, laughing and sobbing simultaneously. "He was in a big rush to make sure the Kennywood Police didn't catch us. He jumped up front and drove that big Buick back across the Rankin Bridge without saying a damn word. But he got what he took me there for."

Before Drew-Morris could object, I blurted out the next question, "Now, Mrs. Radovich, I noticed you hadn't used the word 'rape.' Is there a reason for that?"

Drew-Morris opened her mouth but had trouble formulating an objection.

"I was afraid to call it that," Lil answered, "'cause it scared me to use that word. I kept feeling guilty that maybe I led him on somehow. But now that I'm grown up, I know that wasn't true. So yes, I feel that's what it should be called—rape. *Absolutely*."

"Objection!"

"Denied," said the judge. "She's permitted to express her impressions without this court reaching a legal conclusion on it."

"Now, Mrs. Radovich, you just testified under oath that decedent Ralph Acmovic 'got what he took you there for.'" I stood up and directed my eyes to the judge. "How do you know that? Can you be more specific?" I asked.

Lil groped the side of her chair and stared at me, chin quivering. "Well, it's pretty easy to tell. Nine months later, my daughter Marjorie was born. You think I could help noticing *that*?"

Lil slumped backward; I feared she was going to pass out.

"That rat-bastard done it!" Choppy shouted. He stood up, pumping his fist in the air. "It was that Serbian jag-off, Ralph Acmovic, who knocked up my daughter. She deserves to be compensated for her pain and suffering after what that ignorant punk done. And my granddaughter deserves compensation, too!"

Drew-Morris tried to fire off a string of objections while the judge's deputy pounded the gavel and ended testimony for the day.

———

J.V. met me at Crazy Mocha after receiving my urgent Blackberry message. I ordered two large herbal teas because J.V. was banned from caffeine until the baby arrived.

"Lil's testimony was powerful. It went just like we practiced," I reported. "But Choppy lost his cool, and then Drew-Morris flipped out."

J.V. blinked her eyes as if to indicate, 'What did you expect, boss?' "You may as well get ready for more of these fireworks," she said.

"Hey, J.V.," I continued, dumping extra sugar into my tea. "Do you think it was crazy for me to take this case? I mean, not only is it a loser, legally speaking, it involves my *ex-girlfriend*. Christine's only been dead for two years."

"So what?" J.V. asked. "You're just a lawyer handling a case."

"Besides being stupid, isn't it disrespectful? Christine gave me two beautiful daughters, and we had a perfect life together. Maybe I should tell Bernie I need to get out."

"What does Christine's passing have to do with handling this case?" J.V. asked, one eyebrow expressing puzzlement. "I'm not following why this is freaking you out, boss."

"Marjorie and I never really resolved our issues when we broke up, okay?" I lowered my voice so the people at the next table couldn't hear. "She did a number on my mind and screwed up my self-esteem, I admit it. That finally went away when I met Christine. She turned my life around, and I haven't thought of this other person for nearly 30 years. Now here I am, representing her and her mother, who's talking about getting raped in the Kennywood parking lot and getting pregnant with Marjorie. It's so strange, J.V. Why *shouldn't* it freak me out?"

J.V. scrutinized me. "Do you think you still have feelings for her?" she asked pointedly.

"Feelings? Absolutely not!" I smacked my hand on the table so hard J.V.'s tea sloshed over the rim.

"Maybe you should go have some beers with Uncle Billy and talk about it," my associate said solicitously. "You probably need to have a guy discussion about some of this."

Billy Keefe was one of my best childhood friends; he also turned out to be J.V.'s uncle. That's how things worked in Pittsburgh.

I waved my hand to dismiss that idea. "Other than winter months, that guy barely sleeps," I said. "Running a landscaping business is no picnic. I'm not going to pester him."

"Well, I think you're blowing all of this out of proportion, Shawn. Marjorie was your first love, right? We all have bittersweet feelings about our first romances. You're just stressed out." J.V. patted my hand. Her eyebrows rose in sympathy. "Go home and ride your exercise bike, tire yourself out, and get a good night's sleep. Tomorrow's another day."

I nodded and gulped down my tea, nearly choking on the pool of sugar at the bottom. "Thanks," I said. I slid a tip under my mug and stood up to leave.

Images of Christine and Marjorie crept into my head and began throbbing like a horrible nightmare. I fished two Advil out of my pocket and slugged them down with a final sip of water. "See you tomorrow," I said, rubbing my temple.

I had some sort of problem. It was stirring in me again.

CHAPTER 5

Spring 1978 (Pitt Campus)

ROLLING DOWN A MOUNTAINSIDE

I'd met Marjorie one afternoon during my junior year of college when I'd taken my new puppy, Plutarch, to the lawn at the Cathedral of Learning in the center of Pitt's campus to teach him to play Frisbee. Plutarch had locked the Frisbee in his jaw and wouldn't let go. So, I'd dropped to my knees, grabbed the other end of the Frisbee in my mouth, and pulled backward. I hadn't even seen Marjorie. She was lying on a blanket behind me, studying. I kept backing up and growling through my teeth at Plutarch, showing him who was in charge. That's when I backed into Marjorie, knocking over her Diet Coke.

"That's pretty ridiculous," Marjorie said, eyeing me up with the Frisbee still clenched in my mouth. "But kinda cute."

It turned out Marjorie had grown up just a few blocks away from my house on Commercial Street, yet I'd barely known her because we'd attended different churches and schools. She was two years younger than me—just a freshman when we met. But from that moment, I was hooked.

My friends didn't consider me a ladies' man, and they joked that Marjorie must have suffered from bad eyesight. Like many guys from my neighborhood, I was a hodgepodge of physical traits: light skin, favoring my mother's Irish side, and dark "Eye-talian" eyes like the Rossi side. I'd allowed my brown hair to grow longer than my parents liked—typical for guys in the '70s—so it would vaguely resemble the style of rock stars, or so I thought.

As my senior year came to a close, I tried to spend as much time as possible with Marjorie, certain that this was the start of something far more significant. It was hard to fathom what life would be like when it was time to move on from college and take the next step. I just knew that, somehow, she had to be at the center of it.

"Marjorie, babe. Your boyfriend's here," shouted Rocco, the manager at George Aiken's diner. "Go ahead and clock out. Never mind that there's seven minutes left till close."

"Thanks, Rocco," she answered, deadpan. "Just subtract it from the eight hundred hours you already owe me."

Marjorie looked up at me and gave a tentative wave.

She wiped down the counters and dumped chicken and lime Jell-O into the trash to prevent Rocco from trying to sell it to customers the next day.

"See ya tomorrow, Marjorie babe," Rocco said. "Another day, another dollar!"

"See ya, Rocco. No charging my customers for free refills of coffee."

As she leaned over to pick up her pay envelope, I could see Rocco slide his hand behind her snug uniform and, with a deft motion, quickly grab her rear end as his eyes seemed to roll around with pleasure.

Marjorie immediately jerked her body from his grasp, straightened her uniform, and disappeared into the kitchen. A minute later, she returned with a massive carving knife reserved for the biggest chickens with tough bones. Marjorie stared at Rocco, who had taken his spot at the counter, now shoveling some dinner into his mouth. As he was in mid-chew, she raised the carving knife and slammed it down the center of Rocco's chicken dinner, sending splinters of bone, meat, plastic plate, and cheesy macaroni all over her boss.

The entire establishment of patrons looked up. A few regulars in overalls applauded and pounded their tables.

"You touch me again like that, Rocco," Marjorie stated in a calm voice, "and I'll do that to your breastbone. You got it, *babe*? This day's been lousy enough," she added, flinging her timecard onto the counter, "without a *pervert* like you making my life more complicated."

Marjorie was tougher than most women who had just turned 20; she could handle herself in the diciest situations. Yet, this little episode reminded me there were secret parts of her I still couldn't fully fathom, no matter how close we became.

I knew it probably related to her early childhood and the mysteries surrounding the identity of her father. But this was a topic that was generally off-limits. So, I tried to remain patient and told myself that my girlfriend would eventually share these personal details when she felt the time was right.

———

"You should quit working for that pervert," I said, feeling guilty that I hadn't knocked Rocco's head off.

"I overreacted," she said. "It just brought back a bad memory." There was a long pause. "Truthfully, I probably should've done everyone a favor and stabbed that lech through the heart. He's been hitting on every college girl who works there," she said, pushing the blonde hair out of her face. Marjorie tried to get comfortable, perching herself on the edge of my bed.

My two-story apartment, which my roommates and I had dubbed "the Semple Street Coop" (pronounced like "chicken coop"), was in a run-down area abutting the University of Pittsburgh campus. Outside my second-floor window, as dusk settled over the city, I could see smoke and iron ore particulates blowing out of the furnaces of the J&L steel mills, igniting themselves into a blaze of dramatic colors.

"One of these days, they'll find Rocco hanging in the meat cooler, and there won't be a single witness who'll testify," she added. "Those mill guys are my pals. They'll be the first ones to help me string him up." She stuck her tongue out the side of her mouth as if depicting Rocco in his final state of repose hanging from the cooler.

"Remind me not to get on your bad side," I told her.

I smacked an envelope against my hand and handed it to Marjorie. "Oh yeah, I talked to someone in the admissions office. It's mine, all right. Pitt Law School's still offering me nearly a full ride," I said, taking Marjorie's hand and squeezing it. "We'll have to discuss it in more detail, but that might be a better option."

Marjorie reached into her bag and pulled out a quart of Boone's Farm Strawberry Hill and two paper cups. Boone's Farm was our tradition for special occasions. Tonight, we skipped the formalities. Each of us just slugged down a shot of the cheap, unnaturally sweet wine.

"C'mon, Shawn," she said. "How can you turn down an offer from Harvard? Get serious, dude."

"Being apart for three years would be absolute torture, wouldn't it?"

"*You're* the one who got admitted to Harvard Law," Marjorie was quick to remind me. "C'mon—you just won the lottery in terms of a massive educational opportunity, Shawn. We'll figure out how to make it work."

"How are you so sure?" I demanded. "What if I screw everything up?"

Marjorie looked at me sideways. She downed another shot of Boones Farm. "It's like driving through the Squirrel Hill tunnel at sixty miles per hour for the first time," she said. "Maybe you just need to conquer it, Shawn."

Marjorie had been born to a teenage mother during a time when becoming pregnant out of wedlock was the worst sin imaginable—like a black mark stamped on a person's forehead. She'd spent all twenty years of her life trying to scrub that stain off.

Still, this didn't stop her from having big dreams. Marjorie liked to note that all the blast furnaces in the valley—Carrie, Eliza, Dorothy—were named after women, a sign of strength. Despite the odds stacked against her, Marjorie was determined to conquer the world beyond Swissvale. And she encouraged me to do the same. "Some of the greatest success stories came from people of modest roots who shook up the world," she reminded me. "We should be able to do that too, Shawn."

When Marjorie entered Pitt, she registered for classes in the newly formed "CS," or computer science, department, taking strange-sounding courses like FORTRAN, WHAT 4, and COBOL. Computer science had seemed like an odd choice for a female, especially one from Swissvale, but Aunt Peg would reply to her skeptical neighbors, "This girl is going further than any of us could have ever gone. We'll let her do it *her* way."

Marjorie snapped the strap of my sleeveless undershirt. "Yo, Shawn, you can do it!" she said. We'd recently gone to see *Rocky* at the Student Union, a boxing flick filmed in Philly starring an unknown palooka named Sylvester Stallone. Marjorie said that my sleeveless undershirts were now "hot."

"I just worry I'd be eaten alive by all those Harvard preppies," I said. "Their brains are as big as cantaloupes."

Marjorie slipped her arm around me and squeezed me.

"Get serious, Shawn," she said. "Your parents worked hard to get you to this point. Just revel in the moment, dude. Don't even *think* of wimping out."

It was true that my folks had done everything to make opportunities possible for me. My dad had attended Duquesne University at night when I was a kid so he could study physics, chemistry, and materials science, enabling him to get a lab position at Kopp Glass—far better than the jobs wearing overalls and work boots. My mom never had enough money to go to a regular four-year college, but she'd taken classes at a community college once I was born and was able to help me with my math and biology homework. Everything my parents did had a purpose. Vacations, when we had them, were for visiting family and learning facts about new states. My morning paper route taught me the value of keeping a schedule and saving every cent I earned in a college account at Pittsburgh National Bank. It was all part of my parents' master plan, which featured giving up things now to get something better later, mainly through more education.

When Marjorie and I had first started dating while my dad was still alive, she'd told me that she sometimes dreamed of having a "normal" mom and dad who would look "just like *your* mom and dad." I could understand why she felt going to Harvard was an important thing for all concerned.

"I guess I didn't think things like this happened to people like us, Rad," I confessed to what was bugging me. "Maybe this is a dream or something."

"It *is* a dream," Marjorie said, waving her hands through the air as if whisking away smoke. "And a beautiful girl just walked into it, so get ready." She grasped the zipper on her uniform and tugged.

There was a faint scratching sound on the door. Because he was a miniature Dachshund shaped like an oversized sausage, Plutarch was able to worm his way into the room. My roommates said the name didn't fit a wiener dog. But some names are a matter of timing and fate: I'd aced the course on Plutarch and the early Greek philosophers just before I'd gone to the pet store, so this puppy was stuck with it.

"Can you unzip this thing, Shawn?" Marjorie leaned back, laughing at the timing. "I'm tired of wearing chicken grease all day."

Marjorie never fully paid attention to how sexually arousing she could be just by undressing in front of me. She seemed unabashed about these things, which made her even more alluring.

After changing into a T-shirt and gym shorts, she dug into her bag and slid out George Benson's *Breezin* album. She loved music and would spend an afternoon digesting the latest issue of *Rolling Stone* magazine. To feed her habit, she'd taken a part-time position in the business office of the *Pitt News*, which allowed her to get free promotional albums—shipped to the newspaper for music reviews—and back copies of Rolling Stone. This *Breezin* LP was a good find.

Marjorie cued it up on my stereo. Benson was one of our favorites—a local boy from the Hill District. As we tucked ourselves in a spoon position, listening to "*So This is Love*," Marjorie placed my hands on her stomach.

"Maybe I could figure out how to transfer to Tufts or MIT. I mean, *eventually*," Marjorie mused aloud. "Doc Cliff says this computer stuff is catching on in Boston. MIT has a killer program in complex data structures. Maybe I'd have a shot at getting in as a transfer student."

"Hey, that would be amazing, Rad," I said. "The two of us living together in Boston and being together whenever we wanted?"

"Not immediately." Marjorie cut me off before I could get carried away with such tantalizing thoughts. "It would freak my mother out if I told her I was thinking of moving right now while she's laid off," Marjorie continued. "We'll hold that idea till later. Hopefully, she'll get settled into work again, sometime soon."

Outside my window, the flames of the J&L mill were visible in the distance. I could see Marjorie's silhouette and one finger on her temple as she put on her game face but mentally ticked through the list of her mother's health problems—both physical and psychological—that would cause Lil to become unglued if Marjorie tried to leave. Like me, Marjorie was an only child. Given her mother's delicate emotional state, it would be extra hard for her to escape the demands of home. Marjorie's face flushed scarlet.

"Don't worry, Rad," I said, trying to take her mind off it. "Everything will get worked out soon enough. If you want some distance from your mother, we'll just move to the South Hills as soon as I finish law school and you get your degree. We'll figure out how to get you some space."

Marjorie smiled. "Good plan," she laughed, appreciating the subtle joke. "My mother's *totally* afraid of driving through those tunnels."

Downstairs, my roommates had dragged in a case of Iron City beer and begun an all-night game of Risk. Someone cranked up Bruce Springsteen's new "*Born to Run*" album, causing it to reverberate through the walls, drowning out George. I stomped my foot against the floor. "Keep it down, *animals!*"

To make sure this moment didn't slip away, Marjorie got up and slid a different album from its jacket, dropping it onto the turntable. It was the title cut of the

"*Main Ingredient*" album that she'd just pulled from the pile at the *Pitt News*. Even though the song never made it onto the commercial radio charts, it had become our new anthem.

The needle hit the vinyl and found its groove, enveloping us in the soaring sound of electric guitar and drums. The lyrics obviously had some heavy meaning that ordinary listeners like us were supposed to decipher, but even the song's title stumped me. It was called "*Rolling Down a Mountainside.*"

"Oh yeah, I even talked to that philosophy prof I told you about—the one who recommended me for the Ph.D. program?" I added. "When I told him about the Harvard offer, he stared at me with these glassy eyes and said, 'Good lawyers with Harvard degrees make a lot more money than philosophy professors, son.' Geez, what kind of loyalty is that? I thought he'd be standing up for his profession. Anyhow, I understand this is a big deal, Rad. You're right—I'm lucky as heck. I guess I'm just afraid of leaving *you.*"

Marjorie pushed back my hair and kissed me, making a soft, smacking noise. "That's really sweet, Shawn," she whispered. "You want the truth? I'm *way* more afraid of it than you are. But just hearing you say that makes me feel like we can do this."

Marjorie pressed her hand against my face and stroked my cheek. It felt incredibly sensual. "This is probably one of those times when we just have to go for it," she continued. "To hell with trying to plan out every detail. We'll just have to figure it out as we go. Isn't that what Choppy always says?"

Spring 1978 (Swissvale Home)

CROATIAN FEAST

Choppy squeezed the trigger on his drill. I held both hands up to prevent the flying shrapnel from spraying into my eyes.

"This here is gonna be a damn masterpiece," he said. He bore down, sucking on the chew under his lip. "Now we're cooking with gas! It'll be a helluva surprise."

In his basement workroom, Choppy had mastered the art of building, ripping apart, and re-assembling an endless array of machines, household gadgets, and junk—a true "Swissvale mill-hunky Renaissance man," as his buddies called him.

Choppy's given name was "Stepan (Steven) Radovič," with an accent over the last consonant to make the tongue press against the teeth, so it formed a nice "itch" sound.

He had begun working at sixteen when he'd landed his first job at the Carrie Furnace. He'd started by loading the skip car that took ore up to the blast furnace. Then he'd advanced to "second helper" to "monkey boss" to "keeper"—the top man on the cast house floor. "Making steel is part art, part magic," Choppy would tell us. "You have to have the exact amount of coking coal, the right kinda' pig iron, the exact temperatures and specs for everything. There's a lot of skill that goes into making something as strong as steel that can hold up giant skyscrapers. Everybody's gotta do their part." Choppy had taken that work seriously. He'd also transferred his skills to every aspect of home life.

After he'd fallen in love and married Aunt Peg in the 1940s, they'd lived initially in a two-bedroom house in Homestead with her parents to save every nickel of Choppy's earnings. Once Lil was born, they'd purchased their own home on top of the hill on Homestead Street, right where Swissvale merged with Swisshelm Park above the river. As Choppy liked to explain it, "Every mill-hunky's definition of success is to move out of the hell-hole next to the mill and move uphill—as far away from the smoke and stench as possible—just like the mill bosses. When we got this house, I felt like the king of the goddamn Mon Valley."

He renovated and rebuilt every inch of this place that became home. It was his pride and joy, along with his family. He especially felt fulfilled in his workshop.

Today, polka music blared from his radio. Choppy was listening to the Tamburitzans—an Eastern European song and dance troupe—on *Croatian Hour*, his usual Saturday afternoon program. "Did I ever tell you about the time Dutch Burns outsmarted them mill bosses that time?" Choppy asked me, holding the drill upward like a pistol.

"No, sir, Mr. Radovich," I said.

"Jesus, you've been dating my granddaughter for two years, and it's still 'Mr. Radovich?'"

"Yes, sir, I mean, Choppy."

The old man spat into his mayonnaise jar.

"All week long at lunch, old Dutch Burns would leave through the guard station with this little piece of his bathroom faucet in a wheelbarrow and say to the guard, 'My boss told me I could weld this-here faucet during my lunch break. I'm just takin' it to my car.' The guard would check out the slip, say 'okay,' and wave him through.

"This happens day after day. All the guys are asking, 'How long can it take for Dutch to fix a lousy bathroom faucet?'"

Choppy spat into his jar. "But I knew that guy since we was in kindergarten, Shawn. I knew exactly how his brain ticked." Choppy grinned to expose his chew. "That sneaky SOB was taking out *wheelbarrows*. After a week of pulling off this trick, he collected a whole garage full of them and doled them out to the guys for their landscaping projects!"

There was no end to the ingenious use of materials "borrowed" from the Union Switch and local mills. Many of Choppy's friends welded together their own jack-stands so they could do car repairs in their garages. Stan Galovich next door cut lengths of stainless steel and milled them into handsome carving knives that he gave out as gifts to friends' wives at Christmastime.

But Choppy's most prized possession was his "Auto-Croat"—a motor-driven spit for cooking pigs that was welded onto a metal drum sawn in half; his coworkers at the Carrie Furnace had built it as a gift for his tenth anniversary at the mill. Choppy dragged out this huge contraption every summer to host friends and neighbors in the backyard for a picnic with a roasted pig, a keg of Iron City beer, and horseshoes—"the goddamn essence of a prosperous life," he told us.

"I don't know if the Pope would buy your argument that all this stuff is a loan," Marjorie interjected, patting her grandfather's hand. "But even Pope Paul the Sixth couldn't say it isn't being put to good use."

Choppy inspected his latest work of art. It was a bird feeder attached to a copper pipe that could be installed outside Aunt Peg's kitchen window—a surprise gift for their wedding anniversary.

"Look alive. Here she comes!" Choppy threw a sheet over it.

Aunt Peg came halfway down the basement steps, yelling, "C'mon, kids. The food's getting cold!" She eyeballed Choppy. "Enough of that ogling, Romeo. Wash your hands and get up here. Shawn's joining us for dinner. You probably didn't even remember our anniversary's tomorrow, did you?"

Choppy shrugged his shoulders. Then he looked sideways and winked at us.

"That's okay," Aunt Peg went on, "you're still the only husband I have, so I got a bottle of homemade *Slivovitz* from Mary Palko. C'mon Marji, help me with the drink orders. Maybe I'll put on a dress and let your grandfather kiss me—if he's lucky."

Upstairs, the smells of a sumptuous feast filled the rooms.

Marjorie's mother, Lil, clomped into the dining room carrying a bowl of hot beets. She was wearing a pair of Kelly-green culottes, short enough to reveal jiggling layers of fat on her thighs.

Marjorie rolled her eyes. "I'll take the bowl, mother. Don't you want to run up and get some *clothes* on before supper?"

"I thought this outfit was cute," Lil answered.

Marjorie picked up a spoon and drummed it against the table. I knew that murderous look in her eyes. She had limited patience with her mother, especially now that she'd gained a little independence at the Pitt dorms and no longer needed to put up with her mother's "cluelessness." Marjorie often complained that her mother acted more like a "simple" big sister than a parent.

Part of the problem, most likely, was that Lil's educational growth was stunted. After she'd become pregnant with Marjorie in tenth grade, she dropped out of high school. At Aunt Peg's insistence, she eventually got her GED and, after working at the Union Switch for over a decade, now wanted to be a medical assistant. Choppy and Aunt Peg had taken out a fresh loan on the house so Lil could enroll in a good program, buy a car, and work part-time at a nursing home across the Homestead bridge. Marjorie was skeptical about her mother's latest career plan. She'd whispered to her grandparents that this might be throwing "good money after bad."

"Maybe Marji's right, sweetheart," Choppy said, eyeballing his daughter's outfit. "Why not throw on one of my jackets? If the neighbors come to the door, they might think you're a *hooker*."

I always enjoyed visiting Marjorie's house. Unlike mine, where it seemed calm and ordinary, there was always plenty of melodrama here.

Marjorie's mother plopped into her chair. "Johnny Milsap from the Switch said he might pick me up after dinner and give me a ride in his new V.W. Bug over to Kennywood," she said. "Then maybe we'll get Klondikes at Isaly's on the way home."

"For God's sake, honey, don't you ever learn a lesson?" Choppy asked, dropping his voice to a whisper. "Why do you think these perverts want to go to Kennywood at your age? If that Johnny Milsap shows up, I'll get my bolt cutters out and show him how they work."

Marjorie's jaw clenched. She flicked her eyes toward Choppy as if to admonish him to cease and desist discussing private family matters in front of me.

Marjorie never explained why she called her grandmother "Aunt Peg," just as she never fully explained her family genealogy and left much of it a mystery. Yet, Aunt Peg was the undisputed matriarch of the family, and it was clear that her bond with Marjorie was special.

"Time to sit down!" Aunt Peg said, stifling this conversation with a wave of a potholder. "Will you say grace, hun?"

Choppy obliged with a quick prayer so he could begin digging in. The dinner was his favorite—pigs-in-the-blanket, or "hunky hand grenades," as Aunt Peg called them, a Slovak delicacy made of ground meat wrapped in cabbage leaves simmered in tomato sauce.

While passing the warm bread, I seized on the opening. "Did Marjorie tell you I got into Harvard Law this week?" I tried to raise the subject casually. "I really didn't expect to get that one. It's a great honor and all, but I'm not sure I want to rack up that much debt."

Marjorie's mother nearly swallowed half a stuffed cabbage.

"Harvard? Isn't that in Connecticut?" Lil asked.

"It's in *Massachusetts,* sweetheart," Aunt Peg corrected her.

Marjorie pushed away her plate. "Shawn's scheduling a meeting with his pre-law advisor on Wednesday. Nothing's decided yet, okay?"

Aunt Peg looked at Marjorie with loving eyes but a raised eyebrow as if to say, "Be nice to your mother."

"I'm not opposed to Shawn going to Yale," Lil continued. "As long as Marji's here to help with our doctors' visits, we can make do."

Marjorie glared at her mother and squeezed her fork as if choking it. I could see Aunt Peg kicking her leg under the table. Choppy got up abruptly and kissed Aunt Peg on the cheek as he excused himself. He wiped his mouth with a napkin and grunted, "I got chores to do." As he walked past me, he whispered, "Meet me in the workshop as soon as yinz are done."

Aunt Peg did her best to salvage the conversation and steer it back in a fruitful direction. "That's a big decision to make, going off to Harvard," she said, forcing a smile. "It certainly throws a wrinkle in things." She glanced at Marjorie, then back at me, hopefully. "How's your mother feel about it?"

"She's fine with it," I said, chewing on my stuffed cabbage to buy some time. "She just closed on our house and moved in with my Aunt Kate in Aliquippa. It's been a year since dad passed away." I took a quick sip of water. "Mom thinks it's good for her to get a fresh start, same thing for me. So, she's okay with it. She said it's a question of what place would make me the best lawyer, but *also* what's the right thing for Marjorie and our future too. She's a big fan of your granddaughter, you know."

Aunt Peg smiled. She knew my mom was an ally.

"My good buddy, Billy Keefe, says I should only go to Harvard if they give me a full ride and free housing," I added. "Otherwise, he says stay here where the cost of living is cheaper."

"That's why Billy is doing landscaping work with his political science degree," Marjorie said, laughing. "I know he's been your friend since you guys were kids, but let's face it, he's risk-averse."

"I don't know," I defended my friend. "Billy said he went with landscaping after he decided that it was easier to cut down trees and mow grass than to make sense of the American political process. He may have a point there."

"Well," Aunt Peg continued, "*selfishly*, it would be great if you'd stay at Pitt." She took a deep breath. "But this may be your big chance, Shawn-boy. This could be a golden-plum opportunity for *both* of you kids. You have to look at it that way."

She patted Marjorie's hand as if acknowledging this was a tough pill for everyone to swallow.

Outside the dining room window, Choppy wrestled with the garden hose to spray down the sidewalk, a nightly ritual that seemed to do nothing but move mill dirt from one piece of concrete to another. On this night, Choppy kept spraying at a single spot with a vengeance while the hose knotted itself like a writhing boa. He finally threw down the coil of rubber, placed a finger over his nostril, and blew a projectile of mucus onto the sidewalk—a "Polish handkerchief," as he called it.

Aunt Peg rapped on the window, "Get a tissue!" she stated through the glass, waving her hand. "Are you some kinda *Magarac*?"

Choppy nodded obediently, just as he'd done a hundred times whenever he'd been caught in the act. He was used to being called a jackass in Croatian.

Aunt Peg removed a tissue from inside her sleeve and dabbed her mouth. "Look, Shawn-boy, just getting *into* Harvard is a helluva honor. And you, young lady, you could be running U.S. Steel one of these days with that computer degree. I'd prefer nursing, but, who knows, maybe computers will catch on one day." She twirled Marjorie's hair with her fingers.

"In our day, a person's *background* limited how far they could go," she continued, "but now, you two kids can have the moon if you want it." Aunt Peg took a breath.

"It's just a surprise, that's all." Aunt Peg put the tissue over her mouth. It sounded like she was stifling a sob. "I just start to worry when things are unsettled; that's my nature." Tears started to stream down Aunt Peg's cheeks.

Marjorie jumped up. She pushed aside a chair and went to her grandmother's side. "It's okay, Aunt Peg," she said, massaging her grandmother's shoulders. "Don't get upset. You'll start *me* crying, too." My girlfriend took a deep breath to pull herself together. "Shawn may need to go to Boston for a couple of years to further his education, okay, but it's just temporary. I may want to go up there, too, at some point." She glanced at her mother but continued. "Don't worry about any of this, though. Whatever Shawn does, we still plan to end up here, so we'll all be together. Right, Shawn?"

Marjorie nodded her head vigorously at me.

"Absolutely," I said.

By now, Marjorie was starting to sprout her own tears. She reached into Aunt Peg's pocket for a spare tissue.

Aunt Peg squeezed Marjorie's hand. "I know all that, sweetheart." She stood up, straightened her housedress, and composed herself. "I'm wrong for getting so emotional. Old ladies do that sometimes." She clutched her tissue. "This is a great thing for Shawn, and whatever he does will turn out perfectly for both of you." Aunt Peg kissed my forehead. Then she loaded her arms with dirty plates and hustled out to the kitchen, where I could hear her blowing her nose.

In the meantime, Lil had slid an eight track into the tape player on the credenza—the latest sappy album by Rod Stewart. She plopped down in her chair and glanced out the window, still checking to see if Johnny Milsap might show up in his VW Bug.

"Harvard's tops in the country, right, Shawn?" she asked while lighting a Virginia Slim and inhaling contentedly. "If you get in with one of those big firms, maybe you'll be able to buy *us* a big mansion in Fox Chapel after you buy one for yourself and Marjorie. I want one with a pool and tennis court!"

She coughed—*hack, hack, hack*—so severely it sounded like she might hawk up an entire lung.

Lil grabbed onto our hands and clutched them to her bosom. Rod Stewart's *Tonight's the Night* seemed to be throwing her into a hyper-emotional state. "Yinz two kids, maybe you got born under a lucky star. Maybe this is your time."

She swiveled toward the window, tears beginning to spill from her eyes.

"I never had any of these golden-goose opportunities, cause, uhm, *other* things happened in my life." She glanced at Marjorie, who seemed mortified by her mother's presence. "But you two can be big-time professionals and hit the jackpot, *irregardless* of what happens to the rest of us."

The emotion in the room was getting too intense for me. I extracted my hand and offered a quick excuse.

"Uh, I think Choppy wanted to see me," I said and headed for the basement steps that led to the workshop. There, Choppy was seated at his portable bar wearing his Steelers cap, a shot of *Slivovitz* already poured for each of us, polka music blaring so the ladies upstairs couldn't eavesdrop.

"I heard some of that drama up there," he said, shaking his head. Choppy clinked our glasses together and gulped down the clear liquid. "Peg wants great things for you, Shawn, believe me. It's just that ever since Marji was a little girl, Peg's been waiting for her to find the right guy. Naturally, she'd like our granddaughter to have babies and start a nice family of her own. I mean a *real* family. That was something Lil never had."

He brushed an invisible speck off his shirt. "We both think that person is you, that's all, Shawn. We don't want to wait till we're planted six feet under in Braddock Cemetery before you two get on the stick and give us some great-grandchildren." He chuckled at that imagery.

"Anyhow, after what we've been through with Lil, Peg sometimes worries she could lose all that." Choppy lifted his eyes as if making sure nobody was listening through the floorboards. "We'd be devastated if we were too late to be part of Marjorie's family and *her* life. You understand that, don't you, Shawn?"

"Anyways, Pittsburgh's the greatest place in the world to be, right?" he continued. "Not that I'm trying to influence your decision. I just want you and Marji to think about all the angles."

He poured another shot for each of us. "And I got a personal interest in this, too. Let's face it, one mill-hunky in the family is never enough. It takes two to watch each other's backs."

Choppy looked at me with a face that communicated sincerity, honesty, and a touch of genuine sentimentality. "Keep that in mind, whatever you decide here. Will you do that, son?"

CHAPTER 7

September 2008 (Courtroom)

LEGAL MANEUVERS

Judge Wendell flipped through a thick file. There was a certain erudition about him, the way he raised his eyebrows and scanned the papers.

"Ms. Drew-Morris, I see here you filed a motion for directed verdict, saying this case is legally flawed because petitioners can't prove Marjorie Radovich is the biological child of Ralph Acmovic, Sr." The judge scratched at his temple. "Are you sticking with that motion, or can we expedite things and proceed?"

"We're *absolutely* sticking with it," Drew-Morris said as she stood up and slid her Blackberry into its clip. "This family's paternity claim is a sham. My client's grandfather worked hard to earn his money, and he never intended these people to have it. It would dishonor his memory to take away even a *penny* of it."

"We'll file a response to the motion in the morning," Bernie said with a wave. "It's typical Philadelphia double-talk."

Drew-Morris shot daggers at my co-counsel. Philadelphians had a natural rivalry against Pittsburghers, whether related to sports teams, the proper way to make cheesesteaks (Cheez Whiz dumped onto hoagies was considered sacrilegious in Pittsburgh), or who had the better weather.

"I'll take it under advisement," the judge said, pushing aside the motion for another day. "I don't know who's really entitled to this trust fund, but I'm going to ensure we hear the full story so we can achieve justice here."

Judge Wendell's story was legendary among the local bench and bar. He'd grown up in Rankin, one town down the Monongahela River from Swissvale in the heart of the smoldering steel empire built by Andrew Carnegie. Judge Wendell's original home on Third Street—just a few blocks from Bernie's boyhood home—was in a neighborhood of Slovaks, Croatians, Blacks, and other newcomers to the region who toiled side-by-side in the mills. Except Judge Wendell's parents weren't millworkers. His father, Dr. "Brue" Wendell, a transplant from South Carolina, was the town doctor. His mother, Vervy, was a registered nurse who assisted in their home office. Together, they delivered without discrimination Black babies, White babies, Caribbean babies, or any other bundles of joy who entered the world in Rankin.

Judge Wendell himself had reddish hair as a boy and splotches of freckles under his eyes—a light-skinned, mixed-race combination, or a "meriny," as the locals called it. His mother had some mixed blood, or at least that's why she'd told Wendell he'd turned out so pale looking. In some communities, a meriney was looked upon with suspicion by both Whites and Blacks. But not in this mill town. Here in Rankin, where the smell of sulfur blew off the mills, and freight trains rumbled steadily down the tracks behind his house, young Warren had known nothing but "a beautiful, diverse, welcoming place," as he would tell Bernie. He was still in grade school when his father died and his mother moved them to the Hill District, but he still had those vivid memories.

On Sundays, some families attended the Russian Orthodox church with its distinctive "teardrop dome." Others, like Bernie's family, worshipped at the Croatian Catholic church overlooking the river, while Warren's family attended the Mt. Olive Baptist Church up the street. On summer Sundays, with the windows propped open, one could hear from the neighborhood alleys the black gospel choir and the preacher's call-and-response in one direction competing with sacred organ music and Croatian hymns from another direction.

Dressed in their Sunday finery, folks would leave church and visit on porches for coffee and lemonade. The Wendell family's back porch along the red brick alley behind Third Street was a bustling gathering spot. "Black, white, or purple," Bernie would say, "they were all welcome."

"It was a hard-working, blue-collar place," Bernie would reminisce, "where people stood up for each other, just like they watched each other's backs in the mills. It was about work ethic, Shawn. And simple values. And being trusted by each other. That was the life Warren and I knew—at least until his father died from a sudden heart attack and his mother felt she needed to move them to the Hill District, which we never understood exactly why."

Following a stint in the service at the tail end of World War II and graduating summa cum laude from Morehouse College, his father's alma mater, Warren had worked in the J&L mill by day and attended Duquesne Law School at night. He was able to help support his mother while earning the highest grade-point average in his class. The day he passed the bar exam, Warren walked directly into the Red Lion tavern downtown, where lawyers congregated after trying cases in the courthouse and sat at the bar drinking shots and beers to celebrate. With his reddish hair and light skin, he didn't look the least bit conspicuous. After imbibing for several hours, he finally said to the bartender, "You don't serve colored people in here, do you?" The bartender snorted as if he'd heard a good joke. "Hell, no!" he bellowed. "What kind of joint you think this is?" "Well, you just *did*," Warren had said, slugging down his final shot and dropping twenty dollars on the bar before he walked out.

As a young trial lawyer in the mid-'50s, when Pittsburgh was still *de facto* segregated, Warren had hung out his shingle and successfully sued the city for refusing to admit Blacks to the Highland Park swimming pool, then helped to desegregate Kennywood amusement park. He'd also challenged racially restrictive covenants in deeds—a trick that allowed private property owners to keep "undesirable people" (i.e., Blacks and Jews) out of their neighborhoods. Attorney Warren Wendell had been a solid champion of fairness and equity for *all* people as he established his legal practice. Two decades later, he had become one of the first Black judges elected to a court in Allegheny County after enlisting the help of the Italian, Croatian, Polish, Slovak, Irish, and other ethnic organizations that enjoyed sticking it to the WASPy Protestant blue bloods accustomed to controlling the political apparatus on Grant Street. As a senior judge, he was now semi-retired and handled a reduced caseload to suit his scaled-back schedule. By virtue of his scrappy political upbringing, though, he was still adept at negotiation and diplomacy.

Judge Wendell tidied up his paperwork, then tapped his gavel. "We'll adjourn until tomorrow morning," he said, handing a pile of folders to his deputy clerk. "You may want to review petitioners' brief that spells out where all this money came from before you invoke honor and righteousness, Ms. Drew-Morris," he said, peering down from the bench before he exited. "I'm not sure who's entitled to that trust fund, legally speaking. But it's not as if your client's family has clean hands here; that's all I'm saying."

———

As best Bernie and I could piece together from our private investigator's reports, which we'd slipped into our reply brief, the wealth that had accumulated in Ralph Acmovic's trust fund had been acquired in the underground world of Pittsburgh's economy, the seedy flip side of commerce that had co-existed with Carnegie's steel mills during the early 1900s.

Ralph Acmovic's father, a first-generation Serbian immigrant named Branko Acmovic, had earned enough working 80-hour shifts at the Edgar Thompson mill to invest in his own electroplating business in North Braddock in the shadows of the smoldering mills for which he served as a supplier. In the early 1940s, as the urgency of World War II had descended on the Mon Valley, Branko's dream had taken off. Electroplating—a process by which copper and brass electrical connectors were plated with silver to produce higher conductivity and better efficiency—was suddenly in demand as war-time orders poured into the mills.

For "personal friends" who could be discrete, Branko's business was strictly cash only. Like many other small business cronies in the Mon Valley, this enabled Branko to keep a chunk of the proceeds hidden from the IRS's roving eye. Soon,

Branko added a new layer of ingenuity to his business practice; he began ordering extra 1,000-ounce bars of silver from the U.S. Mint, stashing them in a deep, water well on his farm in the Laurel Mountains. Silver was a necessary raw material for electroplating; if he ordered small excesses at a steady clip, nobody noticed the hefty consumption of precious metal by this nondescript electroplating factory in the smoky world of North Braddock.

It turned into a neat scam. When he needed cash, Branko would take a night-time drive to the farm and fish out a dozen bars or ingots, then transport them to a Serbian cousin in Monessen, who ran an under-the-table jewelry business. Everyone made out handsomely. Branko sold the silver a dollar below "spot price," for which the cousin paid him in crisp hundred-dollar bills.

It was the American dream, with a crooked little tax-evading twist.

But fate played a cruel trick on Branko; by the time his wife had died of lung cancer, he had nobody on which to spend his fortune. Ralph, his estranged son, had fathered a son (Ralph Jr.) and a daughter out of wedlock (according to whispers in the neighborhood). For the most part, the son had thrown away his life in taverns and wasted away from cirrhosis of the liver. When Branko died in his sleep with tens of thousands of dollars stashed under his mattress, nobody cared except the undertaker, who made out handsomely when he removed the corpse.

It was through these unexpected events that Ralph Jr.—who had been thrown out of his father's house as a teenager and despised his grandpa as a baby rodent might despise the rat that begat it—had awoken one day and discovered he was a wealthy man. He soon began receiving quarterly checks from a multimillion-dollar trust fund that he hadn't known existed, using the money to purchase seedy massage parlors throughout the Mon Valley. He'd learned to slip small cash-filled envelopes into the hands of every police and code enforcement officer with the power to shut him down for "morals" violations, thus protecting his soft-core sex businesses from the district attorney's office.

Ralph Jr.'s current business strategy—which required only limited brain-power—boiled down to making sure that he never failed to write a check to his take-no-prisoner lawyers, thus ensuring that the sheer weight of the payments ended up crushing his opponents.

His large retainer check cut to Drew-Morris now seemed to be paying off.

———

As Bernie and I left the courtroom with another oppressive brief to write by morning, J.V. shoved us into the stairwell, shooing away a lawyer who was trying to sneak a smoke. Her cheeks were flushed.

"I called the mortgage company like you asked and I finally heard back from a loan officer," my associate said. "It's lot worse than we thought. They're calling the note due on Choppy and Peg's house, like in the next week. They said it's going into foreclosure soon. They can't hold it off any longer."

Bernie sank down on the steps. He'd known there were problems, but Choppy had obviously hidden the extent of them from us.

"The loan officer bared his soul. They're in the middle of an economic melt-down," J.V. said. "The S&Ls were overvaluing their portfolios, and now they're getting called on it. The big lender in Charlotte that holds the paper on Choppy and Peg's house is calling these things due. The timing sucks."

Bernie smacked the wall. It was the curse of working-class life. Whenever money was tight, folks would take a second mortgage or refinance. The savings and loans were always happy to oblige, appraising houses for more than they were worth to front the cash, then packaging and selling off the paper to bigger banks. Everyone made a profit except the homeowners, who fought to stay afloat.

In Choppy and Peg's case, the second mortgage 50 years earlier when Lil needed to go to a home for unwed mothers was only the start. They'd then refinanced it four more times to help Lil get a certificate as a medical assistant, pay for Marjorie's tuition at Pitt, and pay for Aunt Peg's ongoing medical care. Now, they literally owed more than the house was worth. Choppy's pension had taken a big hit earlier in 2008, too, with the economy in shambles. People on fixed incomes like them were drowning as if sinking into a pool of sludge. Once they started going under, they couldn't pull themselves out.

"Someone probably should tell Marjorie how bad things are, so she gets her butt back here for the trial," J.V. said, holding her hand against her belly and breathing heavily. "I keep telling the mortgage people to hold off—if the Radoviches win this case, there will be plenty of cash to pay off the mortgage. But the clock's almost run out; we're talking weeks before they post it for sheriff's sale. Marjorie needs to know how dire things are becoming. She needs to understand that if she testifies, we may have a chance."

Bernie pulled himself up slowly. He shook his head. "I'll talk to Choppy to-night," my co-counsel said. "But we have to respect his wishes. He's told me a hundred times he doesn't want Marjorie knowing any of this. He's a stubborn coot—he says he doesn't want to be a financial burden on her. And he's looking into moving into one of those government projects in Turtle Creek if that's what he needs to do. It's not ideal, and it probably will take a big toll on Peg if these bank problems force her to leave their house. But they're proud people. That's their wishes, and that's how we have to leave it."

"Wait a minute." I wasn't following this logic. "How does winning this case make it any different?"

Bernie's mustache twitched. "It's *way* different," he replied. "At least in Choppy's mind. Folks like him would rather die before they take money from family to pay off their debts—especially their children. But he feels they're entitled to this money from the Acmovic trust. As he sees it, that Acmovic guy raped his daughter and screwed up his granddaughter's childhood and should pay for it. Lil and Marjorie are co-petitioners. As far as Choppy's concerned, this money belongs to the whole family, so that's a different situation."

J.V. kissed Bernie on the cheek. "I'll keep stalling as long as I can," she said. "We've got to get Marjorie to understand she needs to show up. Her testimony is our best hope for winning a verdict. The DNA strategy didn't work. It's hard to imagine a court ruling in our favor without first-hand testimony by Marjorie to corroborate her mother's story and hopefully some tangible evidence if she can locate it. With Aunt Peg legally incompetent, I can't see any other path. The court of appeals wouldn't let a judgment stand, based on a single witness who has a big stake in the case."

I lowered my head, feeling as if the whole situation had become hopeless.

"Hey, your feet are swelling up," I said to J.V., pointing toward her shoes. "Let's get you out of here. We'll figure out a plan later. Bernie, tell Choppy we're sorry as hell. Get some rest, and we'll figure how to deal with it."

I led them to the elevator, weary from another contentious day. When we reached the ground floor, the doors opened, and two lanky men stepped forward, wielding television cameras and microphones.

"What's your response to the allegation that you sexually harassed a female lawyer from Philadelphia, Mr. Milanovich?" one shouted.

Bernie nearly bit the foam covering off the microphone. "What the hell are you talking about?"

"Attorney Constance Drew-Morris just filed a complaint against you with the State Employment Discrimination agency," intoned the reporter, speaking directly into the camera and flashing his teeth. "Do you deny the charges?"

"What, she's suing me for sexual harassment for blowing a kiss at her and that toady paralegal?" Bernie demanded. "That's a load of bull!"

The cameraman, dragging loops of cable, moved his tripod within an inch of Bernie's body. Bernie saw his opening and gave the man a swift kick in the knee, causing the cameraman to buckle over.

"Hey, don't you know about the *freaking* freedom of the press, man?" A young college intern with a press badge came after my 75-year-old co-counsel.

Just as Bernie opened his mouth to spit out a profanity, J.V. shoved her hand against his back, propelling him toward the door of the Frick Building. "No comment, no comment!" she shouted. With her purse strapped across her swollen belly, my associate powered her way past the camera crew like a small tank.

"Pregnant woman! Get out of the way, gentlemen. My doctor says putting pregnant women in claustrophobic situations can send them into premature labor. Either of you guys wants to *test* that theory and deliver this baby?" J.V. asked with a defiant look.

"I didn't think so."

CHAPTER 8

September 2008 (Law Office)

J.V.'S THERAPY SESSION

"These crazy antics won't help your blood pressure, J.V. C'mon, prop up your legs. We're gonna have to start boiling water in the kitchen, for God's sake. I'm not a licensed *midwife*," I said.

My associate sunk back into the couch, tossing a stray sock off the cushion. My corner office had once been the executive boardroom of Koppers' corporate headquarters until the mills collapsed and a dozen Fortune 500 companies fled the city. It provided a dazzling view of downtown Pittsburgh and all three rivers, but it needed a good cleaning.

"I'll get a copy of the complaint Constance filed against Bernie," J.V. said. "It's the oldest trick in the book—slime your opponent before he can do damage to you. This woman's hiding something, Shawn, I can sense it. Plus, this disaster with Choppy's mortgage company is really depressing me. Can it get any worse, boss?"

"Take a break and decompress," I told her. "You need to watch out for yourself and that baby. I'll handle this other stuff. For now, let's take a breather, and I'll tackle it in the morning."

J.V. untied her Nikes and gave her toes a quick massage. On her wrist, I could see a tiny collection of blue tattoos. Two big shooting stars followed by two smaller stars—an artistic display of devotion to her husband and their two boys, she'd told me. It was one of the things I admired so much about J.V. She always seemed to know what was most important in her life. Her husband and two kids were at the top of the list, and they even warranted their own tattoos.

"Hey, did it hurt getting those things?" I asked, pointing at the blue stars.

"Not really," J.V. said, still catching her breath. "It just felt sort of scratchy. You should try it."

"Liza's been talking about getting one," I said. "I think it's unsafe and probably leads to infections. Maybe you can talk her out of it."

J.V. laughed, knowing it was impossible to talk my youngest daughter out of anything. "I'm glad you made Bernie go home," she continued, getting back to the topic at hand. "He's under a lot of stress, poor guy. This sexual harassment crap will only make it worse. We've got to look after him."

J.V. was the best associate I'd ever hired in all my years of practice. Raised in the scrappy Hazelwood/Greenfield neighborhood, she was a competitor in a moot court competition I was judging at Duquesne Law School. When I congratulated her and asked about her background, I learned that she was the niece of my best friend from Swissvale, Billy Keefe, whom she called "Uncle Billy." That was quintessentially Pittsburgh—everyone was somehow connected to everyone else. J.V. had other options, but she'd joined our firm after graduating at the top of her class from Duquesne's night program. She'd quickly turned into a dynamo who cranked out the work of three junior associates and wasn't afraid to tackle any dog-and-cat case that walked through the door. At home she was equally formidable, hustling her two boys to camps and soccer games and running a busy household with her husband, Kalvin, who worked in the IT department at Community College and had a second job at the Apple store.

Because Kalvin was Black and not all communities in Pittsburgh embraced mixed-race couples, he and J.V. had moved from their trendy townhouse in the mostly White community of Upper St. Clair to a renovated row house in Lawrenceville on the edge of the city's Strip District. "Once Kalvin got pulled over by the police just for driving back to our neighborhood from the Shop 'n Save one night, I knew it was time to leave," J.V. told me. "The suburban folks were nice, but they just didn't get the mixed-race family thing." The old blue-collar neighborhood of Lawrenceville was becoming gentrified and had become popular with millennials. It was much more welcoming of J.V., her husband, and children, so they'd set roots down there. "The older couple next to us invites the boys over to bake cookies," J.V. reported happily, "and Gen X-ers stop by to play cornhole in our backyard with us." Selfishly, I felt it had worked out perfectly; she was only ten minutes from our office.

After Christine's death, I'd left my old firm and started fresh. It was just me, J.V. (who did all her work on a laptop), and my semi-retired secretary. I liked this small operation. Fewer people equaled fewer headaches.

These days, J.V. had also become my therapist. Ever since Christine's death, she was one of the few people I could talk to frankly; and she never hesitated to speak her mind. J.V. genuinely worried about me and the girls; she regularly texted them about things that would concern a vigilant mother—school, grades, food, boys. It gave me a sense of comfort.

My associate pulled out her newest piece of technology—an iPhone—and scrolled through messages while listening to voicemails on an earbud. Her husband called her the "queen of multitasking."

A classic mill-town mix—a little bit Irish, Slovak, Croatian, and German—J.V. was big-boned with broad shoulders but ordinarily stayed trim by running on a treadmill in her basement. Now that she was pregnant, she was huskier, and her face grew red like a mood ring when she got excited.

"Constance is a bully who's ready to roll over people to advance herself; they're the nastiest breed," she said. "It's what's giving the whole gender-equality movement a black eye. She's up to something here, Shawn. She overreacted *way* too much to Bernie's kissy-face stuff. It was stupid but harmless. There's some other motive driving that woman. We can't submit to her."

My secretary, Ann McNulty, who insisted on being called *Mrs.* McNulty, strode into the office carrying a pile of faxes and pink message slips. When she saw J.V.'s swollen legs propped up on the coffee table, Mrs. McNulty pitched the papers onto my lap.

"God's sakes, Mr. Rossi. You should be horsewhipped for letting this poor girl anywhere near the office like this," Mrs. McNulty said while tucking a pillow underneath J.V.'s calves. "I'm calling her doctor and reporting you."

My secretary threw open the curtains. She eyed a Kit-Kat wrapper on the floor and gave me an incriminating look.

"I'm catching the bus home, so my family doesn't forget what I look like," she said.

Mrs. McNulty fluffed the pillow behind J.V.'s back and kissed her carrot-top head. "Goodnight, sweetheart," she said and then turned to me. "The bug man's coming in tomorrow. I saw another roach the size of a giraffe in here. We wouldn't have an infestation problem if you didn't drop candy all over the rug, Mr. Rossi."

"Goodnight, I love you too, Mrs. McNulty," I said. After twenty years, the stress of the job was obviously getting to her.

J.V. typed with one finger on her iPhone. "Hey, Carmen Gentille dropped off a pan of her eggplant parm. Did you do another free will, Shawn? Our firm's gonna go broke if you keep doing legal work without charging people." She laughed. We both knew I'd been doing this forever.

"She needed some help after her husband died," I said. "Carmen grew up with my dad. That eggplant parm is better than a fee of five hundred bucks. I'll split it with you."

"Deal," J.V. replied.

I retrieved a ginger ale from my mini-refrigerator and lined up two glasses.

"Here's to the end of another God-awful day in the practice of law," I toasted J.V. "I'm not sure why we pay rent for this fancy place. Some days I think I should hang it up and get a new occupation."

"Don't even say that, boss." J.V. waved a finger to chastise me. "What about Mrs. Debrovnic, who needs that living will for her husband at the nursing home? Or Mr. Kochick with that tangled title on the house? Or Noreen Gallagher and those ladies at church you're helping to set up trusts for their grandkids? You've got your own Pittsburgh melting pot going on here, Shawn. It's pretty cool."

"That and a dollar will get me a cup of coffee," I retorted.

"Oh, yeah," J.V. said, handing me two pink message slips. "Your congressman buddy, Jim Dobbs, called at 2:45. He was just checking on you. He told me the House oughta be recessed by the weekend. He'll call you when he gets back to North Carolina. He wants you and your friend Stick to come down to Florida next month for a Jimmy Buffet concert. Apparently, he has backstage passes. He said you were lots of fun when you were in law school, boss. Your friend Stick says that you guys even had a wild spring break trip to Florida, too. Is that really true? You should do fun things like that again, Shawn. Also, Britt and Liza called. They asked if they could order hoagies from Rudy's. I told them it was okay if they did all their homework. They took money from the house envelope. They were complaining that their Mimi and Pap were making them do homework before they watched Extreme Makeover."

"Thank God for Christine's parents," I said, blessing myself.

I stared at the photos of Britt and Liza on my desk. My girls were now 16 and 14, respectively. In this picture, they were little girls—long before Liza had dyed hair or a nose piercing. "Damn," I muttered. "I guess I need to update those things."

"You'd be better off just hanging out with them, Shawn," J.V. said. "Leave the trial prep to me."

The flesh beneath J.V.'s eyes had become bloated like tea bags from the stress of baby-brewing. I walked over and pushed the orangish hair away from her temple. There were a handful of gray hairs at the roots, probably from working two thousand billable hours for me for eight consecutive years.

"*You're* the one who ought to go home and get some rest, sweetheart." I touched her forehead; it felt too warm. "I'll finish the brief tonight. You already did most of it. I've got this Radovich case totally under control."

"Under control, my rear end," she said before I could finish. "Your whole life is a mess, Shawn. You need family time with those girls. Let someone help you for a change."

J.V. pulled out a Trader Joe's power bar and ripped it open, a sign she wasn't going anywhere.

I swiveled in my chair and stared at the pile of cases on my desk. It had been a long time since I'd taken a proper break. My mind jolted back to an image of Christine and me sprawled out on the couch with the girls during a Sunday "movie night" at home, relaxing, eating popcorn, and laughing at our favorite scene in the "*Father of the Bride,*" where two Dobermans chase Steve Martin, and he falls into the pool. These activities weren't fun nowadays. It seemed cruel that God had found me the perfect wife, then taken her away before we'd been able to realize even a fraction of our plans.

These days, dinnertime was the worst. The hours from seven to nine reminded me too much of Christine, sitting down for our family dinner and cleaning up dishes together. To avoid the pain of that memory, I stayed in town many nights, working and eating sandwiches at my desk. I understood this meant my in-laws (and sometimes J.V.) were left to take over duties with the girls, but I knew I couldn't give them the emotional support they needed, and I didn't want to be perpetually sad in front of them.

"You know you two were lucky to have each other, Shawn," J.V. said, intuiting that I was slipping into a funk. "Don't ever minimize that. Where would you be if you hadn't ever met her?"

"I know," I said. "But the whole thing just seemed so short."

Christine and I had met accidentally at a black-tie benefit hosted by Presbyterian Hospital three years after I'd returned to Pittsburgh from Harvard. My breakup with Marjorie had been so traumatic that I didn't even go on dates. A big night out was drinking beers with my buddy, Billy Keefe, at a local dive so we could commiserate about being single with no prospects. Billy had just launched his landscaping business, so he had as little time to meet women as me. My boss, Tim Mulroy, handled trusts and guardianship cases for the hospital. As always, he was looking for ways to introduce me to clients and create opportunities for me. "All the bigwigs will be there," Tim said. "Make sure you introduce yourself and bring plenty of business cards. And have some fun, Shawn. You're too serious these days."

I'd spotted Christine standing in the corner of the Grand Hall of the Carnegie Music Hall wearing a simple blue gown. She was sipping champagne alone because her boyfriend, a hot-shot young neurosurgeon trained at Johns Hopkins, had received an "emergency page." ("A common occurrence," she had said, slugging down her champagne.) Christine and I had chatted for an hour, and then we'd gravitated to the empty balcony of the Music Hall and sunk into a row of velvet-covered seats until the party shut down.

I could still remember that night vividly: Heavy snowflakes had smacked against the windshield as we'd sat in my old Mustang till two in the morning, parked in front of the botanical gardens at Phipps Conservatory like teenagers who'd shaken their chaperones. We'd discovered we had a remarkable number of things in common, even though Christine came from the fancy neighborhood of Fox Chapel up the Allegheny River, which (compared to Swissvale) might as well have been on the opposite end of the solar system. But that added a strange allure to our chemistry. When Christine had heard the story of Marjorie's dumping me and taking off for parts unknown, she'd slipped her arm around me and told me, "You're an amazing person, Shawn, don't forget that. You'll be okay after you're nursed back to health." That had been the first time I'd felt warmth and security since I'd come back from Harvard three years earlier.

After a Pittsburgh police cruiser had crawled past us and shone a flashlight into the car window to see if we were making out, Christine had admitted that while she *liked* the young hot-shot doctor, she didn't exactly *love* him. "He's like lots of people in Fox Chapel," Christine had said matter-of-factly, scooting closer to me. "They're *wonderful* people, but their neurons are so busy thinking about money and social status and other serious stuff, something else gets lost. Am I talking gibberish, Shawn? I realize I don't know you that well, but I feel I can tell you this."

Christine's black hair had swished against my face, creating an exciting sensation. "I'm not interested in a lifetime of snooty cocktail parties. I want a *family*, Shawn. I want a house that's crazy with kid activities and people who *really* live together. That's enough excitement for me. I'll chuck everything else for that."

The following week, Christine had broken up with the hot-shot doctor, and I took her out to Aliquippa to meet my mom for our first official date.

That October, we'd tied the knot with a raucous Swissvale-style reception at the Irish Centre, where my mom and her Swissvale neighborhood friends had danced till midnight. My buddies drank shots of Corby's while they sang Slovak drinking songs and paid dollars to dance with the bride.

"And Christine's parents were an incredible catch, too," J.V. pointed out. "It's not as if you were exactly the ideal son-in-law from a social *status* point of view."

I chuckled at that one. At first, Christine's folks had found it hard to explain to friends why their daughter was marrying an Italian-Irish-Catholic mongrel who worked at a small firm in the rinky-dink Lawyers Building instead of pulling down a six-figure salary at one of the blue-stocking firms like Reed Smith. And why—their friends would pose the question tactfully—were we buying a house in Swisshelm Park, a middle-class ethnic melting pot on the edge of the Mon Valley? No matter how many questions people fired at them, though, Christine's parents defended me as a "good son who has his head screwed on straight."

"Why are your folks so good to me?" I would frequently ask Christine.

"Because you have *great* judgment when it comes to picking wives," she'd say with a poker face.

I loved Christine so deeply; it was hard to believe this was possible. She had burst into my life like a beautiful fireworks display, erasing the loneliness and making me feel as if I'd found my soulmate.

J.V. sat up on the couch and pressed gently on her belly to check if the baby was kicking.

"And you and Christine worked together to make the ideal work-life balance, Shawn," she said. "You were ahead of your time on that. You were darn millennials before we even existed. That's something special, boss. Most people never get that for a single minute."

J.V. was right on that front. As our friends were scrambling around working 60-hour weeks and trying to cope with the new two-career norm facing our generation, Christine and I had decided to invent our own plan. Instead of having two Lexuses or BMWs, we bought one used minivan, and I caught the bus to work. My boss fast-tracked me to partner in my sixth year even though the other name partner, Jim Kennedy, thought it was "premature." I felt like I was on top of the world.

Two months later, Tim stepped up to give an opening argument in Orphan's Court, then crumpled over and dropped dead of a massive heart attack in front of the judge's bench. It shook me to the core; I was sitting at the counsel table five feet away when he died. I considered quitting and finding a new occupation. My mentor—and role model—had been erased from my life for no reason. But Tim's close friend and frequent co-counsel had lectured me that quitting was a cop-out. That person was Bernie Milanovich.

"Are you so self-centered that you aren't thinking about the system of justice that Tim cared about every day?" Bernie had put it to me.

So, I pulled myself together, finished the case, and won a big verdict for the client, who was Tim's childhood friend. Much to the dismay of the other partner, I declined the fee; I knew that's what Tim would have done.

Each day before I left for work, Christine had kissed me and reminded me what Tim's mantra had been: "Put your family first, and the rest will follow." Those became the words we decided to live by, too. Once two beautiful, healthy babies arrived two years apart, Christine switched to part-time, and we paid her a "salary" out of my pay each week to acknowledge that her work was *just* as important as mine. We set up a simple office in our house so my clients could visit for wills and powers of attorney *after* we ate dinner together. This arrangement allowed me to take over "bath time" with the girls so Christine could take a few night courses to pursue her master's in nutrition and dietetics. It had worked out well.

Of course, I was earning less as a new lawyer than nearly all of my classmates from Harvard; but we patched it together. By the early 1990s, Christine felt ready to create a consulting business using her newly minted degree. Before long, big downtown corporations were leaving messages at her "home office"—a phone next to the washer in the basement—offering to pay a hefty retainer to set up in-house wellness programs.

She'd limited her hours so we could immerse ourselves in kid activities. Between my coaching the girls' soccer teams and Christine being appointed to the finance committee at their grade school for five years, we had been going full tilt and loving it.

"Remember that boss," J.V. said. "You packed into fifteen years what most couples would accomplish in fifty. And you put the emphasis on the right things. Kalvin and I have already learned a lot from that."

J.V.'s eyes were scanning mine for a reaction. She was trying to keep me in a positive zone.

I got up and rubbed a finger against my temple. My mind was starting to get confused and agitated—a common occurrence when we had these talks.

"I've gotta ask you a question before you go home, J.V." I stood up, pacing back and forth in front of my associate, working up the nerve to say it directly.

I paused. "My head's been screwed up recently thinking about something," I finally said.

It wasn't an easy topic to broach. Sometimes, after Christine's death, I walked the streets at night to sneak a cigarette, which I craved even though it burned my lungs and tasted so repulsive I wanted to vomit. I'd zip up my jacket and walk seven blocks from Swisshelm Park to the streets where I'd grown up, noticing the shabbiness of the aging homes and businesses. I'd veer into the heart of my old neighborhood, past Grana's Market (now closed), Gatti's Pharmacy (now a seedy check-cashing business that also sold lottery tickets), and Rocco's Bar (long gone). When I ventured toward the hillside overlooking the mills, I'd look for the Sand Steps that once sloped precipitously down to the river and provided a perfect spot for young lovers like Marjorie and me to share private time. Those steps were unde- tectable now because the area was filled with sticker bushes, empty beer cases, and ripped green tarps that homeless people and a few drug dealers used as makeshift shelters to hide from the Swissvale police. Surely, I'd think, I could have given Christine and my daughters a better life somewhere else where the future looked bright instead of so desolate. Why hadn't I become a partner at a fancy firm in a big East Coast city like New York or D.C. so we could live in a gated community and own a summer place at a beachside resort?

I'd ask myself over and over, "Why am I so stuck on this place? Should I leave now, if it's even possible before I do permanent damage to my family?" Without Christine, though, I had no one who could help answer those questions.

Increasingly, images of the past were rising from deep in the recesses of my mind, then swirling away like phantoms. And it certainly didn't help that I was now handling a case that brought Marjorie creeping back into my life like a ghost I'd believed I'd shaken a long time ago. Returning to the courtroom each day to work on the Radovich trial made me more, not less, anxious.

"Do you think it's wrong for me to think about *other* women?" I blurted out. "Tell me honestly. I mean, isn't even *thinking* about this stuff equivalent to being unfaithful to Christine?"

"*What* other women, Shawn?" she asked. "You keep bringing this up. Are you having a fling with someone on the Q.T. without telling me?"

"I'm just asking *if* I had feelings for someone else," I said. "It's all hypothetical. Wouldn't that be the same as cheating on Christine?"

"Don't be crazy, boss," she said. "Maybe if it was a *week* after the funeral, people would raise their eyebrows. But Christine's been gone for over two years now. Nobody would fault you for feeling like a normal guy. I've even talked to Britt and Liza about it. They'd be fine with you dating."

"I'm not talking about *dating*, for God's sake," I said, frustrated.

J.V. looked at me with a poker face.

"I'm talking about having feelings for someone who I knew even *before* I was married to Christine; *that's* what I'm saying," I said. "After all the horrible stuff the girls and Christine's folks had to go through, wouldn't that be a kick in the teeth if it turned out there had always been a *second* woman in the picture? They'd say, 'He was biding his time all along. What an unfaithful jerk!' And I wouldn't blame them."

J.V. rubbed her calf to ease the swelling.

"I don't think I see it that way, boss. I'd need to know the facts," she said. "You're not saying there was an *actual affair* during the marriage?"

"God, of course not," I said. "I'm just *asking*: Isn't rekindling an old flame like saying, 'Hey, I had conflicting emotional allegiances all along?'"

"Old flame?" J.V. loosened her waistband to give her belly some extra breathing room. "Is there someone, *in particular,* we're talking about here?"

J.V. glanced toward my desk at a pile of deposition transcripts from the Radovich case in preparation for the next day's testimony. My discussion in the coffee shop must have given her a suspicion.

"Look, I'm just posing hypotheticals," I said.

"Well, it's possible you're just yearning for that time when you were 21 or 22; everybody does that," J.V. responded. She looked like she was evaluating how to handle this topic gingerly. "If you *are* having feelings for an ex-flame, do *you* feel there's anything wrong with it?" she asked.

"I'm so freaking mixed-up I couldn't tell you," I said. "I probably need to see a *real* shrink."

J.V. rearranged the pillows on the couch. She blinked her puffy eyes; her attention span seemed to be evaporating.

"I don't think you need a shrink, boss," she said, trying to focus on me. "You just need a little TLC. That's okay. We all do. Maybe you should talk to one of those Spiritan priests at Duquesne. They're such a kind, compassionate bunch. You always seem to feel better when you go up there to attend Mass and shoot the breeze. This kind of emotional roller coaster you're experiencing is probably just part of the grieving process."

My associate wriggled her toes. "You have another pillow, Shawn?" She yawned at me, glancing at her phone to see if there was a message from home. "I'm feeling super-tired here."

"Just keep that leg up," I said.

"Promise me we'll figure out how to win this case so Choppy and Peg don't lose their home. It's all they really have to show for their whole life of sacrificing for others. I don't think I'll be able to sleep again if that happens, boss," J.V. said. She blinked her eyes, trying to stay focused. "And we've gotta stand up for Bernie on this sex discrimination thing. It's plain sick that she's doing this, and we need to figure out what's driving her."

"I promise," I said. "On both counts."

"By the way, would it offend you if I said you need to get this place sprayed and cleaned up?" J.V. asked this question dreamily. Her eyes transfixed on another sock under my desk.

"Oh, yeah," I said. "I'll get the cleaning company here as soon as the trial's over. That's on my list, pal. Now stop babbling and give yourself a rest."

Before I could retrieve a second pillow to prop up her leg, J.V. had begun snoring loudly like a she-bear that had fallen into deep hibernation. I walked over and stroked her cheek. She was out cold.

I draped my jacket over J.V.'s shoulders to ward off the chilly evening air that had slipped into my office. Then I tiptoed over to the phone and called a cab to take my young associate home before heading home myself to see my daughters and assess my shortcomings as a parent. I would at least make sure they logged off their computers and got into bed, at which point I would retreat to my home office and work long into the night, as I did most nights since Christine had died.

September 2008 (Courtroom)

DAUGHTERS' SOS

"*Listen up*, counselors," Judge Wendell said, examining a copy of the morning *Pittsburgh Post-Gazette* and shaking his head. "In light of the media coverage regarding the allegations Ms. Drew-Morris filed with the state employment discrimination agency," he said, clearing his throat, "I'm between a rock and a hard place. I'm no fan of sexual harassment, and I don't tolerate any kind of bias in my courtroom. But I'm *also* not pre-judging any case." He aimed his eyes at Drew-Morris, then at Bernie. "Unless and *until* these charges are proven in a court of law, we're proceeding with the Acmovic case as scheduled. I don't want *any* talk about sexual harassment in my courtroom. In fact, I'm issuing a gag order. That matter is off-limits. Anyone who *mentions* it will face the wrath of this court." He waved his paper to make his point. "I'm insisting that you attorneys fulfill your oaths and play nice together in the sandbox."

Bernie swiveled his chair and glared at Drew-Morris. The night before, Channel 4 had splashed a horrible headline across the TV screen, "**70-year-old Lawyer Accused of Sexual Assault,**" with footage of Bernie getting in the face of the cameraman. We'd gotten our hands on the complaint, quizzed Bernie, and discovered Drew-Morris's angle. It turned out that Bernie's courtroom stunt was only the tip of the proverbial iceberg. Weeks earlier, Bernie confessed that he'd gone to the president judge and accused Drew-Morris and her paralegal of manipulating cases to earn fees for their firm. But it got worse. Bernie had also told the president judge that Drew-Morris was greasing the skids for this scheme by having an extramarital affair with the register of wills.

"You accused her of having an *affair?*" J.V. had nearly blown her cork when she'd heard this. "Spreading falsehoods about a sexual relationship *can* be a form of harassment under federal and state law, Bernie. Do you have any proof?"

Bernie had pushed back. He didn't have any *concrete* proof, he admitted. But he was "nearly positive" for reasons he couldn't share with us.

"Oh, great," J.V. had groaned.

"I had a damn good reason for turning over that information to the president judge," Bernie had stated emphatically. He'd discovered that Drew-Morris had worked out a plan with the "creepy" Register of Wills, Rick Rankin, to delay sending out notices to opposing lawyers on her estates' disputes so they'd miss the statute of limitations and she could enter default judgments and claim the fees. The chief victim of their dubious arrangement was a young lawyer, Alison Varanti, who lost multiple estates, causing one of her clients to sue her for malpractice. Now her solo practice was in shambles. "I had a duty to do what I did," Bernie had stated, clenching his jaw. "I don't give a rat's duppa who was engaged in extra-marital hanky-panky. But this young gal is having her career wrecked. That's not okay."

Unfortunately, the elderly president judge had confronted "Rick-the-creep" about those charges and let slip that Bernie was the person who told him. Of course, Rankin and Drew-Morris had immediately denied the affair and gone into attack mode. "Constance is ambushing you first with this sexual harassment charge, so anything you say about her affair will be discredited and look like payback." J.V. had said, throwing down the complaint. "You played right into her hands, Bernie."

Inside the courtroom, Bernie had now sunk into his chair at the counsel table, seething.

"I received counsel's reply brief, and it makes some cogent points," the judge announced. "So, I'm denying respondent's motion for directed verdict as premature. Are you ready to ask some questions, Ms. Drew-Morris?" Judge Wendell asked, tapping his gavel to get our opposing counsel's attention. "I'm going to be eligible for enrollment in the nursing home if we don't keep these proceedings moving."

"Yes, Your Honor," she said promptly, casting a smug glance at Bernie.

As Drew-Morris strode up to the witness box, she appeared ready for battle. Bernie and I had been dreading this moment: In most courtrooms, we would finish presenting all our testimony before the other side could ask questions. But Orphan's Court followed more relaxed rules. As Judge Wendell liked to say, it played a unique role in "fairness and equity," which meant he went at his own pace and created his own rules to suit the situation. Now, he had given Drew-Morris a chance to quiz our witness. It was one thing to prep someone like Lil Radovich to follow a script. It was another to subject her to cross-examination by a smart litigator with the feral instincts of an attack dog.

"*Mrs.* Radovich," Drew-Morris began, pivoting on her heels. "First, can we talk about that *name*? Enlighten me, ma'am. Have you ever been married?"

"No, not rilly," Lil said, loosening the scarf around her neck.

"So, you're really not *Mrs.* anything, are you?"

"Marjorie's friends called me that growing up," Lillian answered, glancing at Bernie and me for help. "I guess you could call it a term of respect."

"I see, *Ms.* Radovich. Did you ever tell your daughter's friends that you weren't married to Ralph Acmovic Sr. or anyone else?" Drew-Morris asked.

"No, but . . ." Lil sputtered.

"What physical evidence can you provide that establishes that the decedent fathered your child?" Drew-Morris asked.

Marjorie's mother stared desperately toward Bernie and me. "We never found no actual documentation. I was at a home for unwed mothers. They probably didn't keep papers like-gat. It wasn't a regular hospital."

"So, it's safe to say, *Ms.* Radovich, that you know of *no* tangible evidence that decedent Ralph Acmovic Sr. fathered your child?" Drew-Morris demanded.

"No, that's *not* safe to say," Lil said, the wattle beneath her neck shaking violently. "My daughter Marjorie's 'tangible evidence.' Isn't she evidence of what he did to me?"

Drew-Morris took a step backward as if shocked by these words. She strode toward the witness box until she stood face-to-face with Lillian Radovich, eyeing her coldly.

"Tangible evidence that you were promiscuous, yes. Tangible evidence that at the age of fifteen, you had sex with a young man or a *dozen* young men. Who knows, *Ms.* Radovich?" Drew-Morris said. She had taken on the posture of a hardened litigator. "Let's face it. You made your own reckless choices. Your daughter *abandoned* your family years ago by moving across the country and staying there, even though she's had ample opportunity to change that equation. But now, you both see an opportunity to salvage something of your unfortunate lives by extracting money from *my* client and his deceased father's trust. You figure a court will sympathize with you and—what the hell—there are six million dollars in the kitty, why shouldn't you help yourselves to some of it? Isn't that what it comes down to, *Ms.* Radovich?"

Lil appeared momentarily faint. Her head jerked backward against the hard wood of the witness box, causing her eyes to roll sideways into their sockets as she gulped for air.

Choppy pushed himself out of his chair. "Why don't you go back to *hell* where you come from, lady?" he roared. "My daughter's entitled to *all* the money for what that bastard did to her, don't you get it?"

Judge Wendell banged his gavel sharply. "Are you through with this segment of your cross yet, Ms. Drew- Morris?" He raised one eyebrow hopefully.

"Just one more question, your Honor." Our opponent sidled over to her table, pushing a button to check messages on her Blackberry. Then she spun around.

"Can you tell us, *Ms.* Radovich, why this daughter of yours—who still hasn't deemed it important enough to show up in this courtroom—has had nothing to do with the decedent, Ralph Acmovic Sr., all of these years? If she and her California brood care so much about the decedent, why didn't they exhibit a shred of interest in this man before he left a trust fund worth six million dollars?"

As Lil tried to speak, her throat filled with air like the gullet of a trapped lizard.

"*Objection*, Your Honor." I stood up to full height. "She's badgering the witness."

I could detect that my opponent's sucker punches had done damage. I could see it in the way Judge Wendell's face had lost its playfulness, turning dark, reflective, and sober. It was the oldest litigator's trick for poisoning a parochial Pittsburgh judge's mind. Drew-Morris had succeeded in making the judge view our client as a carpetbagger who had abandoned Pittsburgh and wanted to use the legal system to extort money from a local citizen, however unsavory that citizen might be. I worried that it might be an effective strategy—mainly because it might be true.

I sank back into my chair and didn't even try to salvage our witness's testimony. Bernie sat mute, effectively neutered.

Just then, my Blackberry began vibrating. The message said "S.O.S." My heart sank. I held the phone under the table, waiting for the other shoe to drop.

In another minute, the device spewed out a more extended message:

"Dad-o, it's B. Liza was saying vile stuff." I read it glancing downward as inconspicuously as possible. *"She's a freak. I can't take it anymore. Will you be home tonight?"*

P.S. I've been wishing mom could be here while we're starting our new school. She was always great with that stuff. Do you think it will EVER get better, Daddy?"

Messages like this usually signaled a fight was brewing between the two girls. I shoved the Blackberry into my pocket, pulled Bernie by the sleeve, and whispered, "I've gotta sneak out early; it might as well be now. I'll get the other witness summaries from J.V. Our *star* witness isn't showing up. We might as well face it. Think of some half-baked excuse for the judge. Tell him it's a personal family matter. Maybe tell him the girls have the flu, okay?"

Bernie nodded solemnly. He understood the drill.

————

I'd only been at home for a few hours to keep an eye on things when J.V. appeared, out of breath. She flicked on the lights of my home office to snap me out of my reverie. "Can't stay boss," she said, sweat glistening on her brow. "I'm taking my kids to Muppets on Ice. They're locked in the car. I'll probably get cited for reckless endangerment by Children and Youth Services." She dumped a stack of case summaries onto my lap. "How are the girls doing?"

"I talked to Britt, and she wants me to ground Liza, but that would make things worse," I said. "I'm keeping them apart, for now, then I'll talk to Liza when she's in the right mood. Thanks for the delivery."

"Don't be too hard on Liza. She's a good kid. It's tough without a mom," J.V. said. Before ducking out the door, J.V. shouted up the steps: "Hey, *girlfriends,* be good for dad tonight. You've got him all to yourselves!"

Upstairs, I could hear *"Beautiful"* by Christina Aguilera blaring from Britt's room. *"Move Ya Body,"* a senseless hip-hop song blasted from Liza's room across the hall so loud it shook the foundation.

I climbed the steps and pounded on both doors.

Britt emerged with a hair straightener and shouted over the noise, "Hey, Dad-o. Perfect timing! Jarrod's coming in fifteen minutes. Can I have money in case we go out for food?"

"Your grandparents already picked up pizza," I said.

"I know. But what if me and Jarrod want pizza from *Mineos*?" she asked.

"Jarrod and I," I said automatically.

"Whatever."

I held out ten dollars in my clamped fist, forcing my oldest daughter to pry it out.

Having just reached the age of 16, Brittany had turned into a beautiful young lady who reminded me exactly of Christine when she stood with her feet planted firmly and her toothbrush pointed toward me.

"Are you sure you wanna hang out with these public-school kids?" I said, switching subjects. "I feel guilty that I made you and Liza leave your friends at the Academy. The tennis team at this new school isn't even ranked. I don't want our neighbors calling the police 'cause we have troublemakers hanging out here. Get me their names, and I'll check their rap sheets."

"Chill out, Dad-o. That isn't fair. Since when did you become so *judgy*? These guys are cool. You'll like 'em—especially Jarrod," she said.

"Yeah, he's the one I'm *most* worried about," I answered. "I'm not 'judgy'—I'm a dad, okay? I don't like seventeen-year-old boys taking my daughter out in their cars. What happened to hanging out in the living room and playing Twister?"

Brittany unclamped her hair. "Don't worry, old dude." She kissed me on the cheek. "Your daughter's pretty responsible. I'll make sure we outrun the Swissvale police. Jarrod's car is faster than yours."

Liza barged out of her room, hoisting Zoey, her Abyssinian guinea pig that smelled horribly because she never changed its cedar chips.

"Keep that *pig* away from me," Brittany threatened, pointing her straightener at it.

"You touch the pig, and I'll dump your makeup in the toilet." Liza moved closer to her sister. She had recently dyed a swath of her hair pink. She looked more volatile than usual.

"C'mon Punkin," I said, stepping between them. "Can't we keep it calm for once?"

"Did you give Britt money, Shawn?" Liza asked, glaring at me. "What if I want to go play laser tag?"

"Don't call me Shawn," I corrected her for the umpteenth time. "To you, my name's 'Dad.'"

Liza belched. She wiped her sleeve across her mouth. "*Right.*"

"That's what I'm saying, dad," Brittany said. "She's *totally* inappropriate. Why don't you take her to a shrink and have her institutionalized?"

"Okay, no one is going anywhere if you're acting like this," I declared. "We're having a family meeting right *now*."

"She's the one with issues," Brittany said. "Jarrod's here. Can't we talk tomorrow?"

"Hopefully, I'll be gone by then," Liza retorted, holding up the guinea pig toward Britt's face, its feet spread as if it was preparing to be launched into space.

Brittany pushed the rodent away. "If mom was here, she'd wash your mouth out with soap," she said.

"Right, *sistah*," Liza said. She glared at me and marched back into her room, slamming the door.

In the driveway, a horn blared. Brittany dabbed her eyes with her sleeve, careful not to get makeup on it.

A red GTS appeared outside the window. I wasn't about to tell Britt, but I'd already had the Swissvale police run Jarrod's plates. Unfortunately, I thought, only half-kidding, the boy's record seemed clean.

Brittany held me by my shirtsleeves. "God, Dad-o. That girl's mentally disturbed," she said, giving me a quick hug. "Any parent would have trouble with her. Don't take it personally."

I kissed my oldest daughter on the forehead. "Don't worry, sweetheart. It'll be okay," I said. "Just have a good time tonight. And tell that boy to behave, or I'll deck him, okay?"

I retreated into my home office and sunk into the chair. I faced another night of reading J.V.'s witness summaries about the complicated, depressing story of Marjorie's early life. Just the thought of all this made the acid reflux come roaring back.

I dropped my head into my hands. "God, what am I doing?" I asked myself. "I'm totally failing at this dad thing." I knew these girls were growing up. They had their issues—especially Liza since Christine died—but how could I blame them, given the screwed-up circumstances life had thrown at them?

I found myself pulling out my old vinyl albums to play them in the dark as a form of self-administered mental therapy. When I finally dragged myself to bed and fell into a distracted sleep, I kept replaying the day's events in my head. Images of Britt and Liza encircled me as they bickered with each other while (in my dream) my wife, Christine, whispered gentle words of advice and encouragement, trying to buck me up to perform my parenting duties correctly.

After that, though, the nightmares started coming again. But this time, they weren't about Christine. They were about *her*. And as much as I didn't want Marjorie, of all people, creeping back into my life at this moment, I couldn't stop it.

CHAPTER 10

Fall 1978 (Harvard Law School)

IVY BARRIERS

I'd found an apartment in the low-rent area of Somerville—far enough from the border of Cambridge to be unattractive to people who wanted a Harvard zip code but close enough to make the walk easily.

While wandering around Inman Square looking for paint, I'd stumbled across a pet shop. For no particular reason, I'd selected a soup bowl-sized box turtle that seemed sturdy enough to survive even in the most unsanitary surroundings. I'd named my new pet Walter—in honor of Vice President Mondale (who reminded me of a turtle)—and picked up a pint of strawberries at the Star Market on the way home. The only food turtles ate, according to the clerk, were worms and strawberries, and I had no interest in splitting a tub of worms if we both got hungry at night.

After dropping off my purchases, I played Springsteen's "*Jungleland*" at full volume, then picked up the phone and dialed my mom. "Just checking in," I said, keeping an eye on my watch to make sure I didn't overspend on long-distance calls during my first week.

"Is everything okay, sweetheart?" mom asked. "Did you get a spare key made in case you lose one like I said?"

"Yeah, mom. It's a cool apartment. Trash pick-up is included in rent here. How's Plutarch?"

Mom laughed. She knew it was a leading question. "He peed on the carpet at first," she said. "I think he was resentful you left. But your Aunt Kate and I have been spoiling him rotten. Now he's acting like he owns the place."

"Perfect," I said. "Glad to hear he's adapting. Hey—I'd better go. It's time for my first big Law School event." I signed off with a telephone kiss.

After showering, I picked out a tight shirt that (hopefully) showed off my biceps, then headed out to the dean's orientation party. As I cut through the back streets of North Cambridge, I could smell persimmons, wisteria, and other unfamiliar New England trees. The houses, too, were unlike those at home: stately, Federal-style homes landscaped with azalea bushes and Solomon's seals and surrounded by stone walls.

I felt almost guilty that Marjorie was back in Pittsburgh while I was embarking on this amazing adventure. Every other neophyte law student in the country would have killed for this opportunity. Not only was I attending Harvard, but I still had my girlfriend, and we were doing great from afar. It was the best of all imaginable options.

Inside the Law School Yard, a gathering of entering 1Ls had already assembled. A classmate handed me a fizzy drink and clinked his glass against mine as "*American Girl*," by Tom Petty and the Heartbreakers, blared from a house party across the street at Lesley College.

"How did you, ehm, enjoy the dean's speech?"

"I missed it," I said, sipping iced lime punch.

"You must be from Pittsburgh, ehm, right?" asked my classmate, a guy with frizzy hair wearing a yellow oxford shirt that covered a decent-sized gut. Through his spectacles, he was checking out my "*Pitt Sugar Bowl Champs*" T-shirt—a gift from Marjorie.

"I, ehm, stayed at the William Penn Hotel once to see the Bears play the Steelers. It was one of the dirtiest, ehm, cities I ever saw," he said.

I spat some Copenhagen juice on the grass.

"The Steelers are the greatest team in football history," I interjected.

"Oh, my name's Lanny Marsh," he continued, undeterred. "I'm from Highland Park. It's a suburb of Chicago. Have you heard of it?"

"Not really, Laniard," I said, deliberately mangling his name.

Before I had a chance to ditch him, a gorgeous woman in a polka-dotted outfit sashayed up to us. Her light-brown hair was cut into a chic style. Perched atop her head was a pair of sporty sunglasses.

"I thought I spotted you over here, Lan," she said, raising her drink to click his glass. "So, you made it here in one piece with the U-Haul?" She glanced my way for a second, then ignored me.

"Yeh, ehm, nineteen hours straight. I went through *three cases* of Tab," Lanny said, turning to me eagerly to verify his connection to this goddess with shapely legs. "We both, ehm, attended the University of Chicago. Four years of *hell* together. Right, ehm, Erica?"

She swiveled around and thrust out her hand. "Erica Welles," she said. I felt her fingers compress my knuckles.

"Good to meet you," I said, trying to squeeze back. "I'm Shawn Rossi. It's spelled Shawn with a 'w.' The Irish side of the family in Pittsburgh tends to Anglicize the hell out of everything."

I asked myself, "*Why the hell did I say that?*"

Whenever Erica shifted her position to sip her punch, the slit on her sundress provided a nice view of her legs. I couldn't help staring.

"What college did *you* attend, Shawn-with-a-w?" she asked, trying to act interested.

"I went to Pitt," I said, pointing at my shirt. I tried to flex my biceps as inconspicuously as possible. "This is an authentic Sugar Bowl jersey; it's licensed by the NCAA."

"Seriously?" She shifted her feet to take another sip. "I didn't know there was a college named *Pitt*."

"I hear that city is the *armpit* of the world," Lanny guffawed.

"Hey," I said, stepping closer to them. "I still have a girlfriend there. Don't say it's an armpit."

Lanny kept jabbing to stay relevant in front of Erica. "Only insecure people cling to junky places and old relationships," he said. "You don't need that when you move to Harvard."

Erica looked at me and rolled her eyes. "My boyfriend Joel is in med school, and he's still back in Chicago," she said, looking impatient. "He misses me; I miss him. But Joel and I maintain an *open* relationship. This is the seventies, Shawn-with-a-w. Relationships aren't meant to stunt a woman's growth."

"Okay, I get what you're saying," I said. "I mean, ten years ago girls couldn't even be at a place like Harvard—"

"*Girls?*" Erica looked like I had slapped her. "Do you see pigtails and lollipops around here?" She took a step toward me. "I don't know about that girlfriend of yours, but these are women up here. If you're hunting around for cute little *girls* to amuse you, you should rethink things."

"I didn't say that." I stepped backward.

Erica came within an inch of my face and sized me up. "Oh, I get it. You look like one of these big talkers who's never even been *intimate* with a female, right Shawn-with-a-w? That rock-n-roll haircut doesn't fool anyone. You probably wouldn't even know *how* to have a relationship with a *real* woman, would you?"

She stared at me with a self-satisfied grin. I stared back, not allowing my facial muscles to flinch. The relationship between Marjorie and me was admittedly complex, given her background. But I wasn't going to give this Erica person the satisfaction of knowing that she'd just plunged a sword into my vulnerable spot and hit her target.

I tucked in my Pitt T-shirt, pushed Lanny out of my path, and marched away.

There were some things that I hadn't even told my best friends about Marjorie and the complicated nature of our relationship. I certainly wasn't going to share these private details with a conceited Ivy League person like Erica Welles.

The night Marjorie and I had almost thrown away our self-restraint was the Friday before I'd left for Harvard, just before Marjorie had turned in her dorm keys for the summer.

There was something naturally soothing about lying in an all-girls dormitory, kept inviolate by heavy metal fire doors that could be accessed only by a special passkey. Here, the noises and daily routine always fell into a comfortable pattern unmatched on a raucous male floor.

Marjorie and I had split a bottle of Boone's Farm Strawberry Hill, drinking the pink synthetic-tasting wine out of Steeler mugs as she flipped through the *Rolling Stone Record Guide*. "Look at this, Shawn," she pointed at the page. "They only gave *two* stars to Average White Band's *AWB* album. Talk about a *travesty*."

"I can't worry about AWB right now, Rad," I said. "I've gotta think about our future. What if I sell out at Harvard and become a tragically boring corporate lawyer? You'll probably dump me for a laid-back architect."

She laughed. "No chance, dude. I like guys who see opportunity and go for it."

"Really?" I said, sliding my hands onto her shoulders and pulling her close.

Outside, the day was transforming itself into the night in a swift transition of colors. Marjorie pushed my hands away, and I stood up. "They're almost ready to go on," she said. "Are you ready to play the Streetlight Game and try your luck?"

"Are *you* ready?" I asked.

"I've told you. The day you beat me is the day you can take advantage of me," Marjorie said, one eye squinted.

The Streetlight Game was always best when we were alone and even better when we were swigging Boone's Farm wine.

We both hung off the edge of the bed. As soon as the first acorn-shaped streetlight on telephone poles along Fifth Avenue came on, I blurted out: "I wish my three years at Harvard would be over tomorrow so we could get married and lay around together for a week."

Marjorie quickly took her turn: "I wish. . . ." The two-mile row of streetlights exploded into a bath of yellow electricity, illuminating the street all the way down to Children's Hospital before she could complete her sentence.

"Ahhh," I said, making a growling noise. "You *lost*, Rad. So, what happens next?"

I enveloped Marjorie in my arms and fell back onto the narrow single bed.

Her warm flesh squeezed against the top of my breastbone. It made me twitch with a sudden tingling of ideas, all of them bad, all of them the subject of a half-hearted apology to my conscience with a capital "C."

As we kissed, I stripped down to my sleeveless T-shirt. My eyes adjusted to the half-darkness. Because of her family "circumstances," there was an invisible barrier that I never crossed. Marjorie had never directly given me orders, except for the first time I'd stayed over at her dorm. She'd said only, "You wouldn't do anything to make me lose my trust in you, would you, Shawn?" "You know I wouldn't," I'd answered. And I had stuck to that promise, even when our hormones were surging and the self-restraint was killing both of us.

"Nice haircut. I like how they layered it," Marjorie said. "Get over here, Robert Lamm," she continued, suggesting (maybe due to the wine) that I now looked like the lead singer of *Chicago*.

Swissvale folks considered Marjorie a "tease." But I knew her flirtatiousness was just a front. When you grew up suspected of being a "bastard" in a mill town like Swissvale, she'd later admitted after we'd been seeing each other for a while, you couldn't help being gun-shy when it came to *any* sort of intimate relationship. It posed too great a risk, she said, of repeating the nightmarish events that had brought her into this world.

"Wait a minute." Marjorie rolled off the bed and moved through the semi-darkness. She closed the drapes to her seventeenth-floor window, then checked the deadbolt on the door. Next, she cued up a romantic *Michael Franks* album on her Kenwood stereo.

Then Marjorie did something she didn't normally do—she clicked off the tiny nightlight above her desk—and began covering my mouth and face with hot, pro-longed kisses. Suddenly, she kicked off her cottony PJ bottoms.

"Hey, wait," I said, grabbing her face. Her thin, blondish-brown hair swirled around me sensually. "We can't do this," I whispered. "I mean, I really *want* to, but we can't."

I remembered what my mom told me after Marjorie and I had started get-ting serious: "If you had a sister, Shawn, you'd want her boyfriend to treat her with respect. Remember that with this girl, Shawn. She's a lovely person. Never do anything to hurt her."

"I can't get pregnant now," she whispered in a voice that sounded much deeper than usual, almost guttural. "It's the right time, Shawn."

"Don't you think we should talk about this? I mean, it's kind of important." I tried to sound gentle, rational.

"Stop *thinking* so much about it, Shawn," Marjorie said, pressing hard against me. "Let's just make love. Can't we do that? Stop being so damned cerebral about it."

"But we should probably talk," I tried to say, just as the telephone began ring-ing, freezing us in place. It rang eighteen, twenty times. Marjorie finally pushed herself away from me.

"Dammit," she said, feeling her way to the dresser guided by the light on the stereo. After two more rings, she snapped the receiver off the wall.

"Yes?"

There was a long pause.

"Of course, I will," Marjorie's voice grew louder, taking on an angry edge. "Yes, I'll take her shopping right after she gets her hair done, mother. But I have my calculus test on Monday. Summer semester's almost over. I can't do the laundry and vacuuming until I pack up. No, for God's sake, *please* don't come down to get me early."

Marjorie stood stiffly against the wall. From her dark silhouette, I could see she looked down as if she was trying to direct this conversation into a crevice of the floor. "I'll get it done before dinner on Tuesday night. Yes, I *know* Aunt Peg is making *halupkis*. But some of it will just have to wait, okay? I have an exam to study for. I love you too, mother, but I just have to go."

She hung up. There was absolute silence. Finally, she clicked on the tiny night-light, the moment of passion abruptly over. Marjorie's eyes filled with tears that fell onto the floor and her bare feet. She tried to hide her face by cracking open the drapes and staring out the seventeen stories over Fifth Avenue.

"What did your mom want?" I asked quietly.

"Nothing," she said. "She just called to say 'Hi.'"

"Oh, that's good," I said.

"She *always* picks the best times to call. It's like the woman has sonar. It's like she's a goddamn fruit bat," she said.

I stood up, stepping toward her in the semi-darkness. I pulled Marjorie against me. Even though her muscles were tight, she felt incredibly soft and sensual, this beautiful blond-haired creature who had just tried to seduce her boyfriend before he packed his gear and shipped out to law school.

"Don't worry," I'd whispered into her ear, staring out over the streetlights that swept down Forbes Avenue in a graceful after-dark display. "This wasn't meant to be the night, that's all, Rad. I mean, we've got our whole life together. It was just meant to be some *other*, more special night."

Fall 1978 (Somerville, Mass.)

WOMEN AND GIRLS

After the dean's orientation party had fizzled out, most of my classmates drifted into the Langdell Law Library to begin reading cases, or they slipped into the old mansion-like dormitories with names like Hastings Hall, or walked the paths that Oliver Wendell Homes and other legendary graduates of Harvard Law School had once walked.

I swiped a strawberry for Walter from the demolished food tray, wrapping it up in a napkin and pocketing it. After a couple of glasses of punch, it seemed pointless to try to study. And that fizzy stuff was disgusting. I craved a beer and the company of some normal people.

One of the other stragglers was a first-year named Andy Stickman, or "Stick," a lanky guy from the University of Nebraska with a scruffy Allman Brothers T-shirt. "It's autographed," he said, pointing to a black scrawl across the front. "I got a backstage pass at the Civic Auditorium in Omaha. Best day of my life. That's how I aced the LSAT the next day."

The two of us also ran into a guy from Georgetown named Jim Dobbs, a former debater with dirty blond hair and a handshake like a hydraulic pump. He'd grown up in North Carolina, where he was a high school basketball star. But he'd torn his ACL, so he couldn't play college ball or go pro. After law school, Dobbs said his ultimate goal was to be elected president by age 42, beating JFK by a year. I didn't usually hang out with wildly ambitious people. But this place seemed to be filled with triple-type-A personalities, so there was no choice. We discovered that all of us lived in Somerville, so we headed in that direction.

"Did you guys notice that they don't allow cars in Harvard Yard?" I asked as we navigated through unknown streets with twilight descending on the outer campus, making this walk with two fuzzy figures seem even stranger.

"So what?" asked Dobbs.

"Didn't you hear that saying '*Pahk yah cah in Hahvahd Yahd*'? It's a *fraud*. There aren't *any* cahs in Harvard *Yahd*, get it?"

"Lighten up, Pittsburgh-boy," said the blurry figure of Dobbs. "*Everything* about these Ivy League schools has an element of fraud, and that includes *us*. Get used to it."

At Beacon Street, Dobbs led us into a grimy neighborhood bar called O'Henry's, where the light bombarded our eyes. "*Takin' It to the Streets*" by the Doobie Brothers was blaring from a jukebox. "Let's grab a booth, gentlemen," Dobbs boomed. The bar patrons swiveled around, scowling. One of the regulars bashed his sixteen-ounce Knickerbocker on the table, screaming at the TV screen, "Damn jerks. Up *youhs!*" The Red Sox were just playing the Yankees. Everyone in Boston hated that team, Stick explained.

I stuck in a chew of Copenhagen in my lower lip; if you were from Swissvale, it was an inescapable vice.

"So, did you get admitted under some sort of affirmative action program?" Dobbs asked me with a chortle, crunching a peanut left behind on the table. "I didn't realize they let people from Pittsburgh into this place."

"At Pitt, we considered guys like you *jag-offs*," I said, laughing off the comment.

As it turned out, none of us had a proper Harvard pedigree. Even Dobbs had come from a working-class town outside Raleigh instead of one of the affluent suburbs that typically stocked the Ivy League schools. "Statistically, it's bound to happen," said Stick. "We're probably the people the admissions committee picked while they were drunk during their office Christmas party."

Stick shared that his dad worked for Caterpillar Tractor outside Omaha and his mom was a third-grade music teacher, which is how he'd learned to play guitar and piano. Dobbs's father worked as a bank teller in Raleigh, where his mom ran a daycare center, and his younger sister had just shaken up the town by quitting her job and joining the U.S. Coast Guard.

"Is this your girlfriend?" Dobbs pointed at a photo as he flipped open my wallet on the table. "Whew! What a pretty blondie. How come you ditched her?"

"I didn't ditch her at all, Dobbs. Cut me a break here. And stop pawing through my wallet. Having two people who want to advance their education is the way to go these days. Someday you'll understand. Do you even *have* a girlfriend?" I asked, snapping shut my wallet.

"I have more girlfriends than I can keep track of, Pittsburgh-boy," he said, lifting his chin.

"You guys are as bad as my *sisters*. Quit yelling and shaking the table," Stick admonished. He lifted his long neck and held up his hand. He was trying to balance a saltshaker on a grain of salt, and we were screwing up his efforts.

"So, Rossi—does your old man work in one of those steel mills that smells like rotten eggs?" Dobbs continued, looking for another pressure point. He was a debater who couldn't help himself. "I always wondered how they produced such a stench."

"Not exactly," I said, setting down my beer. "My dad was a material science guy who did thermal design for Kopp Glass—only he died a year ago of malignant melanoma." I wiped my mustache against my sleeve. "Some guys said it was caused by chemicals in the lab, and we should sue them. But what the hell would *that* get us? It wouldn't bring dad back."

Dobbs shut his mouth. He looked chastened.

"But lots of my family *did* work in those smelly mills," I said, "and I'm honestly proud of it. My girlfriend's family were mill hunkies, too. One of her great-uncles shot a Pinkerton during the Homestead Steel strike. He's considered a hero in the Mon Valley. Families like ours *built* Pittsburgh, which built the whole goddamn United States, including the part where you came from," I told Dobbs, struggling to prevent my words from slurring together. "Remember that."

"Well, I hope that girlfriend doesn't dump you, now that you've left her behind," Dobbs interjected, flipping open my wallet again. "It would be a shame to lose her. It sounds like she has some unusual genes."

"Nobody's dumping anyone, okay?" I said, taking a slug of beer. "If you didn't interrupt every two minutes, Dobbs, maybe I could finish a sentence."

He gave me a death stare. I finally laughed and threw a crumpled napkin at his face.

As we ordered a fresh round of Knickerbockers, three women dressed in pleated shorts and crisp Lands' End blouses walked through the door.

"Harvard *chicks*," a patron grunted.

I recognized a face at the center of the trio. Erica Welles. She'd already changed into a new outfit.

"It's nice to see that *some* Harvard Law women are cool enough to buck the usual stereotypes and visit a local watering hole," Dobbs said, bowing graciously. "Care to join us?"

Erica inspected the three of us, her jaw clenching when she came to me. "Thanks. We're just catching a cigarette before we grab dinner in Porter Square," she said to Dobbs, totally ignoring Stick and me. "It's Jim, right? We're getting together a group for lunch at Ames Inn tomorrow. Meet us there at noon?"

"I'd be honored to join you *women*," Dobbs said, winking in my direction. He leaned toward Erica. "By the way," he whispered, "are you the classmate who did modeling in New York?" Erica waved him away as if acknowledging that many people made that mistake but not disabusing him of the notion.

I grabbed Dobbs and pulled him aside. "Are you kidding? Modeling in New York? How could *anyone* buy that lame pick-up line?" I slurred.

Dobbs measured the arc of my gaze. "Oh, I get it. You've got the *hots* for her. I'm sorry I didn't notice."

He glanced in Erica's direction. Then he lowered his voice. "I bet you could still have a fling with her if you acted like a sensitive male instead of a Pittsburgh neanderthal."

I pushed Dobbs against the wall. I was six feet tall—but he was even taller than me, which irked me. "I don't have the hots for *any* of these Harvard women. I called her a 'girl,' and she tried to rip my throat out. I was just trying to give her a compliment."

"*I was just trying to give her a compliment*," Dobbs said, imitating me. "Don't you know there's a sexual revolution going on? You've got to get with it, man, or you'll never get to first base with her."

"I've got a serious girlfriend back in Pittsburgh, okay, *big man*?" I said. "I'm not interested in getting to first base with *anyone*."

Stick stepped between us, having pumped some quarters into the jukebox. "Chill out, dude," he said to me, jabbing a finger in my stomach. "You're supposed to be having fun."

"Yeah, don't be so defensive," Dobbs said, looping his arm around me as if sharing the advice in confidence. "You're in the big leagues now, Pittsburgh-boy. There's nothing wrong with trying to trade up for a better deal. Everything's subject to renegotiation in a place like this."

"Thanks, but no thanks," I said. "I'll handle this Erica woman my *own* way."

I marched up to the bar and ordered a gin and tonic. When it arrived, the drink was in a cloudy plastic mug, a slice of lemon floating topside in it like a dead fish.

"Ooh, *gross* man." A skinny townie seated at the bar pointed toward my crotch area. "Are you having your period or something, *dude*?"

I looked down. A red splotch had spread across my pants where Walter's strawberry had squished inside my pocket.

"That's hilarious," I said. "You must have been the funniest guy at Somerville High, *dude*. You could probably have a future in comedy if you got those teeth fixed."

Erica was intently conversing with a woman with hexagonal-shaped glasses who was smoking an imported British cigarette.

"Excuse me," I butted in. "About that 'girl' comment earlier. I really didn't mean it, okay? I mean, I get it that you're a *woman* and all." I glanced over at Dobbs. "I sometimes get tongue-tied in front of attractive women who look like models from New York." I offered her the gin and tonic. This time she didn't refuse it.

"I guess we just express ourselves differently in Pittsburgh than you folks in Chicago, Erica," I said. "Sometimes we're a little rough around the edges, but there's no harm intended."

"Apology accepted, I *think*," Erica said with an inscrutable smile. She patted me on the shoulder. Her fingers gently stroked the collar of my Pitt T-shirt.

"That's a nice shirt. Is it cotton?" Before I could answer, she blurted out "*Oops!*" and dumped the drink down my shirt, causing the bar patrons to howl.

"*Check it out!* That preppy babe just gave that dude a *bath!*"

I stared at my assailant.

"Sorry," said Erica, smiling opaquely. "Could you get me another one of those, Shawn-with-a-w?"

I grabbed an order of nachos and melted cheese from a nearby table and stomped back toward Erica, ready to dump it on her head.

Before I could exact my revenge, Dobbs grabbed the cheese bowl from my hands and pushed me and Stick out the door so I wouldn't ruin my social life at Harvard forever. "Judging from the response you got to your *lame* pick-up attempt," he taunted me as we staggered onto the sidewalk, "I'll revise my prior statement. I'd advise you *not* to try to put the moves on that woman again. It was painful to watch."

"Thanks, Dobbs, you really know how to boost a person's self-esteem," I said. "Look, I never plan on talking to that person again. She doesn't exist. That's how I'm leaving it. Ivy League women and I don't seem to get along."

I sprinted through the darkness of Somerville until I found my street corner and unlocked the door to my apartment. Inside, the stench of fresh paint and leaking gas made me nauseous. I threw my keys onto the counter. My head was spinning from too many Knickerbockers.

I propelled myself into the stuffed chair that smelled of cat hair and stale beer and picked up the phone from its cradle. I considered calling my mom again, but it was nearly midnight, and I knew the sound of the phone ringing this late at night would probably worry her and Aunt Kate. I could call my buddy Billy Keefe or one of my roommates from the Semple Street Coop. But they had regular jobs and were probably already in bed. Then I realized that Marjorie had just moved into her new dorm and her roommate hadn't arrived yet. I held my breath and dialed the numbers.

"Is that you, Shawn?" Marjorie sounded sleepy. "How come you're calling? You just got there. Is something wrong? It sounds like you're slurring your words."

"I miss you," I said. "Is that a crime?"

"No, but . . ." she started to say.

"Hold on, Marjorie," I said. "I just had a couple of beers. I've gotta go try out my new john."

I navigated myself sideways into the narrow bathroom, spotting a three-inch mushroom growing out of the green indoor-outdoor carpet at the base of the commode. "*Yechh.*" I washed my hands and turned off the light.

"I'm back, Marjorie," I said. "Aunt Peg would say this place needs serious *redding up*. Hah, hah! I'll get some Lysol tomorrow at the Star Market." I fell back into my chair and exhaled. The beer was making me feel weird: It was probably stale.

"Hey, Rad. I'm already experiencing withdrawal from my girlfriend. I miss messing around while your mother and Aunt Peg are in the kitchen."

"Is that *all* you think about, Shawn?" she asked.

"Yep."

It had been a rhetorical question.

My eye detected movement across the living room. A cockroach the size of a miniature pony skidded across the floor then took cover under an empty grocery bag. I flung a *Newsweek* at it.

"I just mailed a care package with Starbursts and a box of Screaming Yellow Zonkers to you," my girlfriend said. "They should be there soon. Didn't we decide this was the best thing for *us,* in terms of our careers? You're just a little homesick, Shawn."

"Awww," I said, untwirling the telephone cord. "That's so nice that you're taking care of your boyfriend." I sunk deeper in the stuffed chair. I jammed one shoe against the floor, trying to make the room stop spinning. "How are you doing, gorgeous?"

Marjorie laughed out loud into the phone. She knew this much flattery indicated I had over-indulged.

"Hey, there's a cool song on this Boz Scaggs' album I just found—it's called *Harbor Lights* on side A. You should get it, Shawn. Just close your eyes and pretend we're in a faraway harbor in the tropics together. That's what I've been doing."

"I'll pick it up tomorrow," I assured her. "Hey, give me a couple of telephone kisses. That way, I can have spicy dreams about you for a week."

"You're crazy," she said, making a quick smacking noise.

After we hung up, I slid Walter's box into my room. His feet flailed around in midair before he pulled his scaly head and feet into his shell.

"You're not as sociable as Plutarch," I said. "Hmm, I guess I should have figured that out."

My bedroom was dark except for the faint glow of a streetlight slipping in through the curtains. I suddenly felt sick to my stomach, partly from the stale Knickerbockers, partly from knowing how far away I was from Marjorie, from familiar streets, from everything that until recently had provided a safe reference point.

I crawled into the single bed without taking off my pants or shoes. My Rocky poster was taped to the plaster on the wall, the only decoration that had survived the trip in my footlocker. With one hand, I reached over and tapped Walter's shell.

"Night, bud," I said aloud, half expecting Walter to answer back.

I shut my eyes. All I could picture, suddenly, was hundreds of miles of mountains and turnpike roads and sagging telephone wires now separating me from Marjorie, as if we were on opposite sides of the world. And it bothered me that as hard as I tried, through the fog clouding up my brain, I couldn't even reconstruct what it had felt like the last time I'd *really* kissed her.

"Tomorrow will be better," I said to Walter, giving him a "goodnight" tap on his shell.

As I fell asleep with a raging hangover gathering in my skull, the image of a Homestead millworker pounding ingots of steel with fire exploding all around him flashed into my mind. It was one of Marjorie's heroic great-uncles. But the vision of this millworker slowly transformed itself into Jim Dobbs, his dirty-blond hair hanging over his forehead, his horsey teeth bared in my face.

"I hope you can keep that girlfriend of yours," he was saying with a sly wink as three strange women dressed in pleated skirts floated past him, transported on clouds. "*It would be a shame to lose her. It sounds like she has some unusual genes.*"

September 2008 (Courtroom)

EXPECTING AT 16

Judge Wendell tapped one finger against the side of his greying hair, where it narrowed into a furry sideburn. "Are we ready to proceed, ladies and gentlemen?"

Our opponent was lining up copies of cases with which to bludgeon us. She glanced at Bernie and smirked. She knew any false move on his part, when she'd already filed a complaint against him, could pave the way for a separate charge of retaliation for additional damages. Bernie was stewing. In confidence, he'd broken down and told me and J.V. that he knew for certain that his statements to the president judge about Drew-Morris having an affair with the creepy Register of Wills was true: Rick-the-creep's wife had caught the two of them in the act, buck naked, when she came home early from bingo one Friday night. The wife played bridge with Bernie's wife at the Croatian Club and shared the whole sordid story with her and Bernie one afternoon, breaking down into tears and begging them to keep it private. "This woman felt terrible about the poor Alison girl getting hurt by their shenanigans and wanted me to fix it on the QT," Bernie had explained. "But the poor thing's a devout Catholic and doesn't believe in divorce," he'd added. "And she doesn't want to be humiliated in public. So she asked me to keep it between me and the president judge, and I promised to do that. For now."

Drew-Morris, unaware that Bernie was privy to this information, appeared to feel in total command at the moment.

"Ms. Drew-Morris?" The judge spun in his seat. "Are we really intent on fighting to the death here? I know you attorneys from Philadelphia take special pride in beating lawyers from Pittsburgh. But maybe a little peace treaty might make sense under the circumstances? There's six million dollars in this trust fund. Shouldn't we talk about splitting the baby, so to speak?"

Drew-Morris stood and addressed the court. This appearance was her first solo trial as a new partner. She seemed intent on proving something here. "There's *no* reason to discuss splitting *anything* with a sexist like Mr. Milanovich. His client's a goldbricker. Their whole case is a bunch of unproven *crap*," she said.

Judge Wendell raised a single grey eyebrow at the word "crap."

"*Excuse* me, Ms. Drew-Morris," he interjected. "Nobody's authorized to use questionable language in this courtroom. This isn't a Flyers game—we don't throw those words around in here. Am I making myself clear? Or would you like me to send a written notice of sanction to the managing partners of your firm so they can pay the fine?"

Drew-Morris shrunk backward as if blasted by chemical foam from a fire extinguisher. "Yes, Your Honor," she said meekly. "I mean no, you don't need to do that. It won't happen again."

The judge nodded, accepting the apology.

"Well, I guess I'm wasting my breath on this settlement notion. That means we've got to keep going. Does your witness need to be reminded she's still under oath, Mr. Rossi?"

Lil tilted her hairdo in the direction of the judge, a blank look in her eyes. "The witness understands *perfectly* well, Your Honor," I said with a nod.

"Proceed," the judge directed.

— —

"Can you describe the period of your pregnancy, Mrs. Radovich?" I asked, flipping through the questions J.V. had prepared. "Tell the court about the role decedent Ralph Acmovic Senior played after he got you pregnant."

"*Objection!*" Drew-Morris nearly popped a vein in her neck, but she clutched the table to restrain herself.

"Sustained," Judge Wendell said, smiling at my blatant attempt to freak out my opponent.

"Just tell the court about the events leading up to the birth of your daughter, Mrs. Radovich," I instructed Lil.

Marjorie's mother straightened her billowy dress. The past day's early recess had provided time to relax and regain her composure, helped in part by eating a turkey Devonshire sandwich at Ritter's Diner topped off with a pecan ball for dessert.

"I remember I started throwing up in the girls' room at Swissvale High. That was about in October . . ."

"Of 1957?" I asked.

"Yep—right after that summer I worked at the Switch—a couple a' months after all that stuff happened with Ralph Acmovic at Kennywood," she said.

I clicked my pen. "So, you found out you were pregnant when you started getting sick at school?" I asked.

"Not exactly. I mean, a lot of girls were getting their periods irregular during junior year. I didn't think nothing of it. I thought I had the flu or something," she said.

"Okay," I nodded.

"I was drinking lots of hot tea. But I still felt like retching my guts out. Sorry, Your Honor, I mean my intestines out," she said, turning to the judge. "So, my mother—" Lil pointed at Aunt Peg, who sat stoically in her wheelchair "—she had me go see Dr. Broughert downstreet on Schoyer Avenue to get a note for school. Dr. Broughert did some tests and had me pee—I mean urinate—in a cup. After I threw up in his waiting room, Dr. Broughert called me back into his office and told me I'd better start thinking about how I was gonna tell my parents," Lil said, tilting her chin upward, "'cause he said I was three months pregnant."

"This was October of 1957?" I asked.

She took a deep breath before answering. "Yep. It wasn't Halloween yet," she said. "I remember seeing trees with leaves the color of fire outside the doctor's office window. All's I could think about was how I was going to burn in hell. That's what Father Sanderbeck said happened to girls who were immoral before they got married. I asked Dr. Broughert *please* not to call my parents; I needed time to figger out how to tell them. I was barely sixteen; I was just a girl. I needed time to figger it out."

The courtroom was quiet, except for the ticking of the clock on the wall. Choppy lowered his head, staring at the gold band on his finger.

"I *begged* Dr. Broughert," Lil said, gulping down air. "But he picked up the phone anyways, and he dialed their number. That's how come I ran out of his office. That's when I went looking for *him.*"

Lil's face collapsed like a punctured kickball. I stepped toward the witness box to assist her. Lil put one hand over her face, waving me away. "No, no," she insisted. She wanted to tell her story in one horrible session, she said, so that she *never* had to repeat it. Fortunately, thanks to our repeated rehearsals at her home, Lil was prepared to cover all the key points almost by memory. So, she took a deep breath and shared the unpleasant details with the court, laying out the sequence of events for the record:

After she'd received the news, she'd slammed the door at Dr. Broughert's office and ran three blocks toward the gate of the Union Switch & Signal. The afternoon whistle had just begun to blow from atop the big steel shed where men had started to line up. At the sound of the whistle, workers had begun to stream out, many of them aiming for the Sportsmen's Bar across the street. Lil knew Ralph Acmovic worked in the stockroom near the front of the complex. So, she tried to find him. At the same time, she recalled, the thought of marriage had crossed her mind for the first time, and it was scary. "To be honest," she told the judge, "I didn't *want* to get married and live with an older guy for the rest of my life. I mean, I was just getting ready to start junior year at Swissvale High, you know?" But she had decided that if *he* insisted on it, she was prepared to do it. She'd known girls who'd dropped out of high school for this reason. "It wasn't the *ideal* option," Lil told the court. "But I figgered it would cause both families the least amount a' humiliation."

Lil had spotted Ralph's blond hair riding above the sea of older, balding men. She'd yanked him aside next to the red brick building outside the mill gate, staring at him, her face red and feverish. She had intended to "break the news" slowly. But instead, she'd blurted out five simple words: "Doctor Broughert says I'm pregnant." Even as she'd spoken the words, she recalled, they'd sounded strange and unreal. "I guess I'm gonna have our baby," she'd told him.

Ralph had stepped backward, dropping Lil's hand "like I had some kinda terrible disease," she said. Lil remembered that his breath when he spoke had smelled raw and harsh like Kent cigarettes. "It couldn't be *mine*," he had told her. "It's someone *else's*. Don't try to pin this on me."

"There isn't anyone else whose it *could* be," she had responded. By this point, she was feeling rattled. "Maybe I hadn't expected love," she told the judge, "but at least I'd kinda hoped he'd care about me and the baby like a nice person would do."

Instead, Ralph had turned mean, and his voice had become loud. "If it *is* mine," he'd said, pushing Lil against the brick building to keep her out of view of the other Switch workers, "just get *rid* of it."

At this point, Lil said, she couldn't even speak, and she began to cry. She had come here for support from the *other* person responsible for this mess, she said. "It wasn't just *my* problem, but he was making me feel that way."

"Get rid of it however you want," she recalled Ralph told her, almost growling. "I'll get the money from my old man to pay for it, but I ain't happy about this." He had stared at Lil and took another step backward as if she were dirty and unworthy of his respect. "It's your fault for leading me on," he'd said, his face now looking hateful. "You think a grown guy like me's interested in a high school *slut* like you? You should've known it was that time of the month. Why didn't you take precautions? How's a guy supposed to take responsibility for *that*?"

He'd looked Lil up and down one final time. Then he'd spat on the ground before walking rapidly in the direction of the railroad trestle on Braddock Avenue, up the steep set of steps that climbed to the upper hill of Swissvale. She would never forget this horrible moment, she told the judge.

"I'm goddamn *ashamed* for you," were the final words Ralph had called back at her.

By the time Lil reached home, after walking aimlessly through the alleys behind Homestead Street, she recalled that her house had appeared completely dark. Lil said that she'd hoped—in fact, she'd *prayed*—that her father would be working the three-to-eleven shift that night. "He worked swing shifts at the Carrie Furnace," Lil explained. "I thought maybe God would do this *one* thing for me and let him work second shift that night so I could talk with my mother, *alone*."

The living room had been unlit—a positive sign. Lil said she'd placed one shoe in front of the other, inching toward the steps that would take her up safely to the bedrooms so she could look for her mother. But before she got to the staircase, she said, a shadow that looked like it had two heads had blocked her way. She could see two people standing in the darkness in front of the kitchen table.

"Where the hell you been?" Choppy asked his daughter.

Lil remembered holding out one hand to her mother, hoping that she'd save her. But Aunt Peg had seemed afraid to touch it. Her father was normally one to crack jokes and play pranks on the guys at the Carrie Furnace and chastise Lil for being "too damned serious." But on this night, she said, there was no joking in his face. From the strange slant in his eyes, Lil said, it appeared like her father was looking directly through her clothes at that moment and seeing all her sins on display in one sickening glance.

"*Whore!*" Choppy had spat the word out.

Looking over at the spectator seats, I could see Choppy drop his eyes toward the floor.

"Goddamn whore," Choppy had repeated as Lil had stood there, feeling completely exposed.

Lil said that she'd spent the whole night crying in her room but only after breaking down and telling Choppy the name of the father. Through the register vent, she said she could hear Aunt Peg and Choppy walking back and forth on the linoleum in the kitchen, speaking in hushed voices, blaming themselves for the fact that their only daughter was a "mortal sinner."

"We'll have to put the baby up for adoption," Aunt Peg had said. "God knows what it takes to feed and care for an infant twenty-four hours a day." Then came the worst part. Aunt Peg had lowered her voice, then Lil had heard her say, "Lil's a little *slow,* to begin with. We both know that. We can't trust her with a baby. If it survives, we'll give it up to one of those adoption agencies. Maybe the pastor of the Slovak church in Rankin can help us. Lots of young couples want babies if they can get a healthy one."

Choppy had replied in a mocking tone. "So, we're supposed to tell the whole goddamn world our daughter got knocked up by a Serb?" He had smacked the kitchen table. "Why not post it in the goddamn *Pittsburgh Catholic?* What the hell are all the guys down the Carrie Furnace gonna say? Think I raised a hooker for a daughter? First thing I'm gonna do, I'm gonna find that Acmovic kid who knocked up Lillian and cut his pecker off."

For the next two days, Lil testified, she'd remained hidden in her room. She'd contemplated suicide by jumping off the Frick Park Bridge. An abortion, she said, was her second choice. She remembered one of the Ofcansky girls at Swissvale High School had gotten an illegal abortion from a "self-taught nurse" working out of her house in Braddock. It was a dangerous procedure, Lil knew, but she'd heard that some doctors could prescribe medicine to cut down the chances of infections or death.

Before she fell asleep, Lil thought she heard her father through the register on her bedroom floor say: "We need her to disappear. We need her to goddamn disappear."

And that's how the plan had been hatched: Lil would go to a home for unwed mothers. Her parents had no idea what costs would be involved; hiding a pregnant girl from public view for a half year until she had her baby probably wasn't cheap. To be safe, they'd already gone to the bank to fill out papers for a loan on the house. Choppy and Aunt Peg had rubbed salt into the wound by saying, within earshot of Lil, that they'd always dreamed of one day moving from their house on Homestead Street to a bigger place with a choice view overlooking the river and the steel mills. But that was never going to happen now, they had said, not with a second loan on the house. Choppy had stated loud enough for Lil to hear, "so our daughter who's barely hit puberty herself can go to a home for unwed mothers and ruin our dreams, 'cause she couldn't have followed our moral training and kept her pants on and prevented that Serbian boy from taking away her damn virginity."

Inside the personal section of the *Pittsburgh Catholic,* they'd found the Roselia Foundling and Maternity Home, located in the city's primarily Black Hill District. The Hill had once been a beautiful melting pot like Rankin—with Blacks, Ukrainian, Russian Jews, Italian, and Greeks—before the city had condemned big swaths and had begun mowing down neighborhoods and driving out families. Now, the lower Hill District had become a distressed neighborhood—lots of dangerous areas, Choppy said—but Lil would be safe here. She'd be locked up out of sight, under the protective guard of the Sisters of Charity and a six-foot iron gate until she had the baby, who could be given to a responsible couple to raise.

The Roselia Foundling Home, Peg had told her, had a waiting list of over a hundred girls from multiple counties—so it wasn't going to be easy to get in. But fortunately, after many phone calls, Peg had found a nun of mixed Polish and Slovak descent who'd agreed to help Lil gain admission and guide her through the "nightmare" of giving birth.

"I know this isn't pleasant to talk about, Mrs. Radovich," I interjected. "But what did you intend to *do* with the baby?"

Lil held a Kleenex to her mouth. At first, no words came out.

I'd never heard this part of the story until I'd met with Choppy and Lil to prepare for this case. Marjorie had never shared this private information with me. Standing there looking at Marjorie's mother, it suddenly occurred to me how easily this story could have turned out differently, for all concerned.

"The plan was always I would give the baby away," Lil pressed forward with her testimony as if horrified by the sound of her own words. "My parents made me promise before they'd sign the loan papers. But I never really wanted to." She broke down sobbing in loud throaty gusts, prompting the deputy clerk to pull out a box of tissues.

In the front row, Choppy's face had turned pale. He stood up, looking unsteady on his feet. "That was the way people done it back then, sweetheart," Choppy said, reaching toward his daughter before falling back into his chair. "Jesus Christ, Lillian."

Aunt Peg tried to stand up in her wheelchair, grasping for her husband's arm, but she was held back by her restraining belt. Aunt Peg started to cry because *he* was crying. "Jesus, Lil," Choppy repeated. "We'd give anything if we could do that whole thing over."

The judge tapped his gavel gently. "The court would like to hear the rest of this witness's testimony," he said. "Let's not prolong this woman's discomfort. Go ahead, counselor."

By the fifth month of her pregnancy, Lil continued haltingly, gripping a Kleen-ex, she could no longer hide the swelling of her belly, even under floppy shirts and loose dresses. Peg and Choppy had told neighbors that Peg's cousin in Chillicothe, Ohio, was expecting a baby but was suffering from severe diabetes aggravated by her weight and the pregnancy. This cousin, Peg and Choppy had fibbed with poker faces, had three little children. Her doctors had ordered her to stay in bed and get help around the house because her husband was constantly on the road selling auto parts. Lil, they had spun the story, had received permission from the school in Ohio to attend half days, which would allow her to help with the kids each afternoon until Peg's cousin regained her health.

That was how her family presented the story, Lil told the judge, "so that nobody had a clue about the truth." Then, one Sunday morning in November, Choppy and Aunt Peg had packed Lil into the family Plymouth and had driven her six miles to the Roselia Foundling Home. It was here, Lil said, that she would give birth four months later to a baby girl.

CHAPTER 13

September 2008 (Courtroom)

ROSELIA HOME FOR UNWED MOTHERS

Judge Wendell raised his chin, suddenly attentive.

"Is that the old Roselia Home in the Hill where Perry Como used to sing to the pregnant girls when he was in town?" he asked.

"That's the same one, Your Honor," Bernie said, standing. "It used to be the best damned operation around—far more discreet than that Booth Home up on West Liberty Avenue."

The judge nodded. We'd caught his attention: Every local pol worth a nickel knew of the Roselia Home and the great deeds it had done for Pittsburgh—especially for the "White" families who'd escaped ruination because a loving group of nuns in the Hill District had "taken care of their daughters' mistakes." This judge was an astute student of local history.

"My mother worked there in the '60s before she passed; God bless her soul," Judge Wendell said, blessing himself. "They had a heckuva group of nuns there. Those sainted ladies really cared about the kids. Let's hear more."

I nodded toward the judge, then turned and winked at Bernie. Today I was feeling in control, thanks partly to a quick haircut at Enrico's in Oakland.

"Mrs. Radovich," I continued my questioning. "Can you share with the court the details of your giving birth to your daughter at this now-defunct home for unwed mothers?"

Lil loosened her scarf. She placed a finger, haltingly, over the small hole in her neck. Then she leaned forward and continued her story:

She and her parents—Lil remembered as if it were yesterday—had pulled up at the old building perched over a hillside in the lower Hill District. The whole area, Lil recalled, looked like a bombed-out scene from a World War II movie on television. Already, houses and churches were being knocked down to make room for the new Civic Arena that the city was building. It had looked scary driving up to the Roselia Home.

Nobody had uttered a word. Lil's only memory, she said, as she was seated in the back of her parents' green Plymouth Belvedere, was that she had brought along a tote bag filled with pencils and lined paper for writing four months' worth of letters.

Choppy had kept the engine running while Aunt Peg had escorted her daughter with brisk steps toward the side entrance of the building—an old three-story mansion that was crumbling into disrepair like the rest of the buildings in the neighborhood. At the entrance, the chief administrative nun named Sister Benedict had inspected Lil up and down, then ushered her and Aunt Peg into the building and locked the door behind them.

Like the other nuns she could see walking around the place, Lil recalled, Sister Benedict wore a white, full-length habit and a round, white bonnet tied with a bow under her chin. The nun said she and the other Sisters wore white, instead of black like the regular Sisters of Charity, because their clothes had to be frequently washed with bleach to get rid of blood and baby vomit and other unsanitary messes that were part of their work here.

The interview had been brief and matter-of-fact. From this point forward, Sister Benedict had told her, Lil would be known simply as "Ruth," an alias or "house name" meant to preserve her privacy and keep her identity unknown to social workers and even to the other nuns. She had to attend chapel and rosary sessions at least once a day. She would also carry out regular chores as instructed by the nuns. It would be best to have no communication with outsiders, except her own family. "We've all made a promise not to share the details of anything that goes on here to preserve the confidentiality of everyone who enters these doors," the chief nun said. "It's essential to the privacy of everyone." And most importantly, *before* Lil was officially admitted, she and Peg *both* would have to sign a document agreeing to give the baby up for adoption because the institution's priority was to find *legitimate* homes for children born outside the holy bond of matrimony.

Lil had signed the document in her best cursive penmanship, followed by her mother in the space for "legal guardian." With that, Peg had buttoned her coat, slid one arm around Lil with a quick hug, then hurried outside to the idling Plymouth. Lil had watched through the curtains as her parents' car had disappeared in the direction of the North Side across the river, where they planned to spend the day driving aimlessly to complete their grand deception. By four o'clock that afternoon, Choppy and Peg had whispered among themselves, they would be able to return to their house and their ordinary Swissvale lives without the black stain (at least nothing their friends and neighbors could see) caused by their daughter, who had committed life's "most unforgivable sin."

In the third-floor dormitory, Lil met girls working jigsaw puzzles, playing solitaire, or writing letters to parents or boyfriends. Many of the girls, she observed, wore gold bands on their ring fingers; they seemed to be cheap jewelry from the local 5&10 store that provided the appearance of being married if they were permitted to go downtown to shop.

"I heard you were comink today, Ruth," said a soft-spoken nun who had appeared from the sun porch to help Lil unpack. "She made a lot of 'k-sounds' when she talked," Lil explained to the judge. "I guess that was the Polish in her."

The kind nun had introduced herself as Sister Maria Fidelis Jaworski. She was the nun who had helped Lil get admitted to the Roselia Home. The nun's olive-colored skin, wide nose, and rubbery ears peeking out of her bonnet reminded Lil of many of the Polish ladies whom Peg had over for coffee when Lil was a little girl.

"Thank you for looking after me, Sister," Lil had told the nun. "I been scared of coming here. I'm not sure if I'll be able to do it."

"I have a chore for you," the nun had said, smoothing out the clothes in Ruth's dresser drawer. "No use sittink around feeling sorry for what you can't change. I want you to help me feed the babies in the nursery."

When they'd arrived, the second-floor nursery was filled with cribs under which squirmed dozens of noisy, hungry babies, all of whom seemed to want to eat at the same time. The Sisters moved from crib to crib, dispensing a bottle of formula and loving attention to each infant. Here, Lil (as she said she continued to refer to herself in prayers to the Blessed Virgin Mary) had found a reason to avoid sinking into a black hole of desperation. In the confines of the nursery, she could at least change diapers and provide food and warmth to clutching little hands and find a shred of value in her tragic new life.

Ralph Acmovic had answered Lil's first letter, promising to cover whatever costs they had to incur for having this baby, even though "it was YOUR fault. You're gonna put him up for adoption, right?" After that, Lil said, she'd received only one brief note from Ralph via her parents, informing her that he'd enlisted in the Navy and that he'd be in touch "real soon."

The nuns had burned both letters in the fireplace so Lil wouldn't obsess over them. She'd never heard from Ralph again.

Humiliation, she came to realize, was part of life for residents of the Roselia Home. Yet this was a purgatory of their own creation, Ruth had concluded, no matter how much the warm-hearted nuns told them otherwise.

Some girls on Lil's floor had tried to lose their babies by mistreating themselves—purposefully tripping down the staircase or having someone strike them in the belly or standing on their feet for days to induce miscarriages. But Lil said that she couldn't do any of these things; she had felt a strange sense of warmth and love toward this tiny new life taking shape inside her belly. She could now feel it kicking. Still, she felt confused when they'd gathered on Saturday afternoons in the library to watch films the social workers were showing like "How to Change My Personality" and "Me and My Baby: Hello and Goodbye." Lil recalled falling asleep and dreaming of delivering a *real baby* with a handsome husband at her bedside, whispering, "I love you, Lil, more than anything in the world. I'm really proud we got this beautiful girl who looks just like you," as he handed her a bunch of flowers and a box of delicious Bolan's chocolates. Each time she'd have that dream, though, she'd wake up and cry for hours.

The only thing that Lil said saved her from "total despair" during those four months at the Roselia Home was working in the nurseries.

"You take care of dese-here babies and make dem strong and healthy," Sister Maria Fidelis had told her on the second day. "And you'll see what a great thing you are doing by bringink your own baby into this world. You're not a bad girl, Miss Ruth. You're part of God's miraculous plan."

The pragmatic Swissvale side of Lil, she admitted (looking away from the judge long enough to become red in the face), had trouble seeing how allowing a boy to "knock her up" in the Kennywood parking lot at age fifteen could possibly be part of God's master plan. But she humored the nun because she was kind.

Consequently, Lil spent most of her time in nursery three, working with what the nuns called the "special cases." Most of these babies came from mixed-race couples—part Black and part White, or "merinys," as some folks there called them. White couples didn't want these babies and considered them "freaks of nature," Lil explained. Black people treated them with a mixture of superstition and fear; if they adopted them, they believed, bad things might happen to them. For that reason, Lil said, those mixed-race babies were like "baby birds that other birds wouldn't go near 'cause human hands had soiled them." So, they landed in nursery three, along with babies suffering from birth defects. After twelve months, Lil knew from listening to the nuns, these "special cases" would become wards of the foster care systems in the counties where their mothers lived or sent to government-run orphanages.

"Orphanages?" the judge interjected, suddenly lifting his head and directing his comment to the witness. "Sounds harsh to me."

"That's why I spent so much time in there, Your Honor," Lil responded, nodding her head. "Sister Maria Fidelis said these babies deserved someone to love them like every other baby."

Our opposing counsel rolled her eyes. I took advantage of the judge's spontaneous comment to quickly lead Lil back to her story:

One afternoon, she said, Sister Benedict had swept through the nursery on a surprise inspection, noting, "That girl's spending way too much time with these babies. Transfer her to the kitchen." And so "Ruth" was assigned to clean dishes and chop vegetables. But after lights out, she said, while other girls were playing canasta in their rooms, the kind nun, Sister Maria Fidelis, would sneak her back to nursery three to allow her to have some purpose in life.

By March, Lil said, her stomach had swollen "to the size of a huge kickball." She'd discovered "spotting" in her underwear one night, so Sister Maria Fidelis had advised her to spend more time in bed to prevent "premature labor." "Do it for your own sake, Ruth," she had told her. "Do it for the sake of your baby."

"You don't have to call me that," Lil had whispered, trying to make sure that the other girls wouldn't hear. "I want you to know my *real* name. My name isn't 'Ruth.'"

But the Sister had pressed her finger to her mouth. "It isn't permitted that we know the name that a girl's family has given her. Pray to God instead, and I'll know *everythink* about you. That's how we'll do it."

So, Lil had spent her time praying while lying in her cot on the third floor of the Roselia Home. From the window, she could take in a glittering view of the city at night; it was much different than the one visible from her bedroom in Swissvale. Here, Lil said, she could lay with both hands resting on her belly and pick out her favorite landmarks on the city's skyline: the Gulf Building with its pyramid of colored lights—orange and blue—that kept track of the weather; the Grant Building that blinked "Pittsburgh" in Morse code (Choppy had told her this on trips to the city); and the fortress-like Frick Building where her parents had taken her by streetcar when they needed to draw up a will at the office of their lawyer, Bernie Milanovich.

Staring out the window, Lil remembered, she'd prayed that the baby taking shape inside her would find a decent life in this city sprawled out before her, outlined in twinkling lights that seemed to promise good luck. She'd take her mind off her sins and failures by reading aloud from a daily prayer book that the nuns read at the 6 A.M. Mass each morning. Lil didn't fully understand it, but she felt comforted by reciting this prayer—Psalm 43—only because it seemed to fit her dire circumstances. Now, she closed her eyes and repeated it from memory, as the judge leaned forward, listening:

"Defend me, O God, and plead my cause
Against a godless nation.
From deceitful and cunning men
Rescue me, O God."

"We're getting *way* off track, Your Honor," Drew-Morris said as she stood up. "This recitation of *Ms.* Radovich's hard-luck story years ago—caused by her *own* lapse of moral judgment—is *hardly* relevant to the question of whether her daughter has a right to reopen this trust when the law is clear that illegitimate children were *not* permitted—"

"Overruled," Judge Wendell said curtly, waving his hand. "The witness may continue. I find it highly relevant, and I'm the judge."

"Yes, sir," Drew-Morris said and sat down with a grimace.

The birth, Lil continued, had happened on the evening of April 9, 1958. After timing the contractions and finding them too close, one of the young nurse assistants had helped Lil to the labor and delivery room, a converted bedroom on the first floor. "I'll call the doctor," the young nurse had calmly told Lil. "Don't be scared, Ruth. It only takes him a half-hour to get here."

Lil could hear the nun dialing one number, then a second. When she finally got someone on the other end, her conversation seemed sharp, not at all like a nun.

"He's been drinking at the Teutonia Club again," the young nun had whispered to one of the social workers as she hung up. "We'll have to get Sister Maria Fidelis to do it."

By the time the Sister arrived, Lil had remembered her saying that she was already "six centimeters dilated and partially effaced." But the nice nun had remained calm. "Don't think about the pain," Sister Maria Fidelis had said, wiping a cold washcloth across Lil's forehead. "Just think that there will be a beautiful baby here soon that God *allowt* you to make like no other baby in the world."

The delivery room had seemed frightening to Lil, with its surgical table and instrument cabinets and bright lights pointing at her body. She recalled that the mirrors hung at a sharp angle away from her. One of the girls said the Sisters didn't want the mother to see the baby after it was born for fear that the maternal bonding process would begin and separation would become harder. Instead, the baby was usually whisked away to the nursery so the adoption process could start before the mother and baby formed a connection.

Lil recalled that the pain and the pushing had come in hard, relentless surges that hurt more than anything she'd ever imagined. "If something goes wrong and I *die*," she had shouted out, "I want you to know who I am. My name isn't Ruth, dammit. My name is Lillian Marie."

Sister Maria Fidelis had motioned her to be silent. "Save your *strenth*," she had hushed.

Lil had thrown her shoulders back, feeling like a python with a rabbit in its stomach—like she'd seen in pictures at the library—as she braced herself for another surge of horrible pain. "I said my *real* name is Lillian Marie Radovich."

"Stop it, and don't worry. God already *toldt* me that," the kind nun had replied. "Now push harder, Lillian. This baby is *comink*."

Lil had pushed and bucked up her rear end, begging the Blessed Virgin for an end to her pain and praying that the baby would come out safely because it shouldn't pay the price for her mistakes.

"You probably didn't realize *I* have a real name, too," the nun had whispered softly, clenching Lil's hand as the smell of blood and birth had begun to fill the room. "My name is Marjorie Maria Jaworski. I wasn't born with this nun's habit on;

you hear that, Lillian? Now push like you never pusht before. I can see the crown of this baby's head comink."

Lil would never forget the moment the baby arrived, followed by the liver-sized placenta. Sister Maria Fidelis had cut the umbilical cord, and then the young nurse had wrapped the pink bundle in a tiny blanket and turned to take it away. Lil had heard the baby start to make a loud, bleating noise "like the sound a baby goat makes at Idlewild Park."

"Is it a boy or a girl?" Lil had asked. She remembered that her legs and shoulders were shaking uncontrollably. "*Please*, can't you let me see just for a minute?"

Sister Maria Fidelis had grabbed the arm of the young nurse, pulling her back toward the delivery table. "It's a girl," the nice nun had said, smiling as she wiped the perspiration from her eyes. "It's the most beautiful little girl I've ever seen. Here, let Lillian holdt her a minute."

The young nurse stood frozen in place. "We usually don't want the girls to hold their babies," she had whispered, her jaw becoming tense. "It should go to the nursery. For *both* of their sakes."

The kind nun, though, had continued to speak in a calm, unflustered tone. "I'm the one on duty. It won't hurt for Lillian to hold her child for a minute," she'd said.

Lil said that she would never forget that moment, lying on the cold delivery table half-naked, enveloped in the bloody smells of human birth, her teeth chattering with cold and exhaustion. Once in her arms, the baby had miraculously stopped crying. For the first time in nine months, Lil had felt that she had done something wonderful and that God had singled her out for a special purpose. This *perfect* baby that she had produced, with her blond hair and beautiful pink face, had pushed its little fists against the hospital gown and had now searched out Lil's breast, taking hold until she was rooting and sucking like it was the most natural thing in the world.

"Her name is Marjorie," Lil had declared, tears of joy beginning to well up in her eyes. "I'm naming her Marjorie Marie Radovich."

CHAPTER 14

September 2008 (Courtroom)

APPARITION OF JOE MAGARAC

A loud chirping sound shattered the silence of the courtroom. I froze. "*Gimme More*"—a Britney Spears song that Liza liked to blare on her iPod—played somewhere in the courtroom. The judge adjusted his hearing aid. "What the heck's *that?*"

I shoved my hand into my briefcase to grab my Blackberry.

"Sorry, Your Honor, my mistake," I said.

"Let's save the rap music till after work, Mr. Rossi," the judge said with a chuckle. "I prefer not to have folks boogie-woogie in my courtroom on taxpayer's time."

"Yes, Your Honor," I said sheepishly. "One of my kids must have played a joke on me." My mind flashed with red alarms and sirens: The girls never called during a trial unless there was an emergency. Something was going off the rails at home.

"Let's power off all our devices and wrap up the testimony," the judge said. "It's gotta be painful for this lady to relive all this stuff. Go ahead and take a sip of water, ma'am. Your lawyer can continue whenever he's ready."

I squeezed my eyes shut and counted to five. Then I strolled in front of my witness and asked her to describe what had happened at the Roselia Foundling Home after Marjorie's arrival:

For the first full week after the baby's birth, Lil recounted the events, she snuck into the nursery on the second floor whenever Sister Maria Fidelis Jaworski was on duty. Breastfeeding was not easy in the first days, but she would feed her baby a bottle, bathe her, and dress the infant in pretty little gowns that reminded her of doll clothes. She'd take Marjorie out on the enclosed sunporch and pat her back to bring up burps, something she was pleased to see she could do well.

But when Sister Benedict had walked in one day and caught her seated in a wicker chair feeding Marjorie, the nun had become upset. "That's not usually permitted, Ruth, you *know* that," she had stated, shaking her head. She then told Sister Maria, "You should know better than this, Maria Fidelis. We have rules for a reason."

"She has a right," the kind nun had replied in a calm voice.

"She may have a *legal* right, but that doesn't make it a good idea," the chief administrative nun had stated, lowering her voice. "We have a responsible Catholic couple signed up for this baby. Don't confuse this girl by letting her grow close with a baby she can't *possibly* care for. It's not in the best interest of Ruth; it's not in the best interest of the baby."

"She has a right to decide," Sister Maria Fidelis had repeated. "Lillian can decide for herself."

They'd called Choppy and Aunt Peg and within hours convened an emergency family meeting in the visitors' room that barely had enough space for three chairs. As Lil recalled the story now, it was a tense situation. "You signed the papers as the legal guardian of the girl," Sister Benedict had explained, trying to remain patient. "You can't go back on the promise that you made before God and myself as witnesses. You agreed you'd put this baby up for adoption and give it a *legitimate* home. We have everything worked out."

Aunt Peg had picked at a thread on her jacket. Choppy had sucked on a chew of Copenhagen under his lip. Lil had just sat there, she recalled, saying nothing. But she remembered that she was starting to feel happy again. Her stomach had shrunk except for ten pounds of baby fat, causing her to look surprisingly healthy when she inspected herself in the bathroom mirror. Her eyes were bright again. Through some miracle, Lil said, the unclean feeling that had clung to her body now seemed to have passed.

"Can we look at the baby?" Choppy had asked.

Sister Benedict had seemed conflicted. She'd finally thrown up her hands and said, "As you wish."

But as soon as Sister Maria Fidelis had re-entered the visiting room carrying Marjorie and slid the baby into Lil's arms, Lil now recalled, the faces of both Peg and Choppy had changed. They seemed filled with wonder at the way the baby nestled naturally in the crook of her mother's arm and at the way Lil was able to expertly raise a corner of her blouse to allow the baby to nurse, like a true mother.

"We need a couple minutes *a'* privacy by *ourselfs*," Choppy had grunted, waving one hand to shoo Sister Benedict out of the room. "But we want Sister Maria Fidelis to stay."

The chief administrative nun had stared at a crucifix on the wall. Then she'd relented, blessed herself, and closed the door behind her.

Choppy had allowed his eyes to rest on Lil. Then on the baby. Then on his daughter again.

"Lillian would still be eligible for state welfare money," the nice nun had stated softly. "Probably a hundredt dollars a month. It's *hard* work taking care of a baby by yourself, but it can be done."

"What would we tell our neighbors?" Aunt Peg asked, touching the baby's foot. The baby had given a cute kick, then continued to suck at Lil's breast as if enjoying a feast.

Sister Maria Fidelis had looked directly at Peg, locking eyes. Lil still recalled this part very clearly. The nun had spoken in a gentle and calm voice. "Sometimes the girl's mother pretendts it's her baby. Or the girl's mother says her sister had a baby she's unable to care for. The real mom just acts like a big sister or cousin, and nobody knows the difference. After a while, people forget. After a while, it's just a beautiful child that's a gift from heaven, and nobody remembers the other details of how God brought it there."

Choppy had stood over Lil, the collar of his Dickie work jacket flipped up, a sign that he felt good. He'd put his hand on the blanket that was wrapped around the baby like a sausage casing and patted it. "This baby's got a *hundred* percent Croatian and Slovak genes," he said. "Look at her damn nose—not a drop of Serbian blood, thank God."

The baby had stopped sucking and turned her eyes upward, looking directly at Choppy. It was, Lil recounted, "like Marjorie knew exactly what she needed to do to stick with her family." She'd touched the old man's whiskers with her tiny fingers and made a cooing sound. At that moment, Choppy's chin had started to quiver. Then he'd blurted out: "Lookit, I didn't tell yinz about this 'cause I didn't want anyone getting upset." He had turned to his wife and Lil. "But I couldn't sleep last night thinking about all this stuff, so I went for a walk on the alley overlooking the river."

Lil explained to the judge that her father was famous for these walks when he couldn't get his mind to settle down. Nobody but the Swissvale police and men on night-turn at the mills were anywhere on the streets at that hour, and it was a good way to clear his head.

As they sat in the room, deciding their next move, Choppy had blurted out: "So, I was just on this late-night walk, minding my business, when all of a sudden I seen flames and gas coming outta those stacks at the J&L mill, right where the Sand Steps go down to the riverbank."

Aunt Peg and Lil had both nodded. They knew the spot perfectly. "It was so bright it almost blinded me," Choppy had continued. "I thought maybe it was from the tiredness. Only I could see this figure taking shape over the river. It was a guy the size of a house—I swear it. He had legs as big as railroad ties. His muscles rippled like bands of goddam steel cable. His eyes—I mean, they were hot blue like the color from a blowtorch. When he looked at me, honest ta' God, he smiled, and it looked like his cheeks were glowing from melted iron."

Aunt Peg and Lil had looked at each other.

"That's when I said to myself, 'Jesus H. Christ, it must be *Joe Magarac.*"

At this point in the story, Judge Wendell put down his pen and lifted his head. Every Pittsburgher who'd grown up in these mill towns had heard tales of Joe Magarac appearing on rare occasions—usually during an explosion that nearly killed a man in the open hearth or when a crane operator had almost fallen into a ladle filled with molten iron but escaped through a preternatural intervention. According to stories passed down in local bars and at family dinner tables, Joe Magarac had steel ribs and bulging iron muscles—some said real, some said purely mythical. According to these legends, he was so devoted to the mills of the Mon Valley that when Carnegie's deputies had threatened to move the plants to the Midwest to make a bigger profit, Joe Magarac had climbed into the blast furnace and melted himself down to produce the richest batch of steel ever, causing profits to soar and saving the Pittsburgh mills from ruination.

This part of the story had gotten the judge's attention. I nodded for Lil to continue her testimony:

Choppy had told Aunt Peg and Lil that he kept staring down at the fire forming this face over the mill and saying to himself, "Goddamn *looks* like Joe Magarac." Then he had asked himself, "What the hell could I be seeing a ghost like Joe Magarac for?"

As he had stood over his new granddaughter in the stark visitors' room, Choppy had held out his arms as if inviting the answer.

Aunt Peg had jumped in, "Having a baby is a *big-time* responsibility." She'd held Lil's hand, then gently stroked the baby's pink cheek. Lil recalled her saying, "I'd be willing to help out, sweetheart. We'll just say that cousin of mine from Ohio had the baby but had serious complications and got real sick, so the family asked us to take care of the baby. But *you'd* be the mother. You'd have to take responsibility, so your father and I don't have that worry." She'd glanced over at Choppy. "You willing to take that on, Lil? Are you sure you can handle it?"

Lil had nodded her head. Her tears had streamed onto the baby's blanket.

"We did what our pastor advised us and took out a loan," Choppy had said, turning to the kind nun. "We'll have some money left over."

The kindly nun had smiled. "We're waiving the bill," she said. "Some places charge, but we try to run this home as a charitable institution. We're here to help wonderful young women like Lilian. And beautiful babies like your little Marjorie."

Choppy's eyes had bulged out of their sockets. "Did you hear that, Peg? That means we could use the money to fix up the house. We could change up the bedrooms and bathroom on the third floor so Lil and the baby could have their own space." He turned to his daughter. "Would you like that, hun?"

Lil began sobbing. She shook her head in the affirmative.

"Of *course,* our daughter can handle it," Choppy next said, turning back to Peg. He'd pressed his hand against the baby's cheek as if feeling its warmth. "Like the Sister said, in a couple years when the baby's old enough to understand, Lil can just be the mom, and we'll all forget this 'aunt' stuff. Nobody will ever notice. And this little Marjorie sweetheart will be just like any other beautiful Croatian girl. She looks like you, Peg. She got them beautiful Slovak eyes, and her nose looks perfect. . . ."

Choppy's voice had suddenly choked up. Lil recalled that he had turned to the nice nun and stated firmly, "I'll hold my *granddaughter* while you call in that other nun," he'd said. "You can tell her we made a decision."

———

Lil poured herself a glass of water from the metal pitcher on the witness stand. As she took a sip, her hand was shaking.

"You did wonderfully," I whispered. Lil gulped down another sip, grateful for the encouragement.

Choppy now clutched Aunt Peg's hand. As he whispered something to his wife, she began rocking back and forth in her wheelchair, grinning.

I turned to scrutinize Drew-Morris. For the first time in this trial dealing with ugly family secrets and multi-million-dollar trust funds tainted by sins hidden for decades, our opponent's shoulders appeared to slump—the sign of a litigator visualizing the prospect of defeat. Lil's account had been so compelling it was hard to imagine how our opponent could undermine this direct testimony that Ralph Acmovic was the father. After all, Lil's family had stepped forward to take responsibility for the baby, despite the tough circumstances, and had never tried to extract a penny from anyone, even after re-mortgaging their own house. All of the sympathies were now on our side.

"No further questions of this witness, Your Honor," I said with feigned modesty. I turned toward Bernie. "Get me out of here," I whispered between my teeth. "Kid issues. Use a different excuse than last time."

Bernie rose. "We've completed our questioning of this witness," he announced, glancing at his watch. "By the way, Your Honor, I wondered if we could break a little early. I had a little family emergency come up."

The judge dropped his pen. "You should have said something, Bernie."

"Nothing life and death, Your Honor," he said, bowing respectfully. "My great aunt's having gallbladder surgery." That was a good one. I appreciated Bernie's originality.

The judge tapped his gavel. "Say no more," he said, scooping up his papers. "I have my own doctor's appointment tomorrow morning to check out my prostate. I'll spare you the details. Hopefully, everyone will survive intact. I'd like to see counsel in my chambers at ten o'clock."

He raised one gray eyebrow at Drew-Morris before slowly closing the *Acmovic* file.

"I think we oughtta talk settlement, okay, Ms. Drew-Morris? Mr. Rossi's putting on an impressive case, even though I had my doubts it could be done," the judge said. "He sure learned the art of lawyering."

I felt myself blushing.

"You went to Penn, is that right, Ms. Drew-Morris? Maybe tomorrow, Mr. Rossi will share his secret when we sit down and see if we can get down to brass tacks," the judge said. "These folks who got their law degrees at Harvard have a real knack, wouldn't you say? There must be something about getting an education up there that makes these Harvard lawyers so darn effective. When we get together to talk settlement, maybe he'll tell us what the special sauce is."

CHAPTER 15

December 1978 (Pennsylvania Turnpike)

THE MADDENING CAR TRIP

"Those cases were analytically tough—ehm—weren't they Rossi? Or maybe you didn't read them at all. Pittsburgh people seem lazy as hell."

I'd taken my seat in Langdell North. Inside my casebook, I was studying a letter from Marjorie. I lifted the paper to my nose to see if I could smell her perfume.

"*Thanks for the beautiful flowers, Shawn. I hope you didn't spend your student loan money on them and break the bank!*" she wrote. "*All's good here in the CS Department. I got picked for an internship at Respironics in Murrysville. Not bad for a Swissvale girl, that's what Aunt Peg said. I hope you're standing up to those Ivy League eggheads. Don't be intimidated by them—show those Harvard nerds what you're made of. . . .*"

"You're not even reading the cases, are you Rossi?" Lanny leaned into my space, trying to sneak a peek at what I was doing. "You'll probably get called on and get kicked out of class for treating this like a joke."

We had been allowed to select our seats on the first day. Laniard had picked the one right next to me.

"Don't worry, Laniard." I closed my book on the letter and card so he couldn't see. "Bradwell won't call on our row for another week. I have inside intel from some 3Ls."

As the clock in Langdell North struck ten o'clock, Professor Bradwell navigated through the swinging doors, his seating chart stuffed under one arm. Above his head, an oil painting of an early eighteenth-century English judge wearing a white wig seemed to gaze sternly down on the classroom.

"Well, I'm sure that you have *all* found these readings on the laws of adverse possession stimulating." The words seemed to fall out of his mouth like Scrabble pieces.

Stick was seated in the row behind me. His hair looked like he'd slept on it sideways. He jabbed a finger into my back and whispered: "You *stimulated* by this, Rosey?"

"Right," I laughed.

"Why don't you jokers cut it out?" Lanny hissed between his teeth, glaring at me, then at Stick. "Take a look at that judge up there. This is supposed to be a sacred profession, not a joke."

"And now," Bradwell cleared his throat. "The case of *Keeble v. Heckeringill* is one of my favorites. Who can *succinctly* state its holding? Let me see . . ." He allowed one finger to zig-zag across his seating chart. "Mr. Rossi?"

My ears began to pound; I had a sudden urge to blackout. This was a mathematical *impossibility*. According to the usual pattern that our third-year friends had shared with us, he was supposed to be six rows away, two seats to the left.

Lanny arranged his note cards on the desk and tapped them tauntingly as if to communicate: "The answer's right here, *Pittsburgh moron*. But you aren't taking this seriously and didn't take the time to prepare and produce neat case summaries like me."

My heart pounded irregularly. I started having an out-of-body experience.

"I don't think he's here today," I answered in what sounded to my out-of-body self like my own voice.

Bradwell stroked at a sideburn the size of a lamb chop.

"Oh. I see," he said, pausing. "Where might Mr. Rossi be?"

I sat back in my wooden seat, maintaining eye contact with the painting of the English judge. "I honestly don't know."

Bradwell blinked one eye. "If this wasn't *Shawn Rossi*," his razor-sharp Harvard logic was dissecting the information, "it has to be *someone else* nearby on the chart." He allowed his finger to move around several nearby photos until he asked:

"Well, could it be . . .Mr. Marsh?"

Lanny's eyebrows nearly leaped off his forehead. His upper lip raised itself, exposing his adult braces. At that moment, I could see directly into Lanny's mind: He was going to rat on me.

I took my pen and pushed it against his index cards until they teetered on the edge of his desk, ready to fall into a pile of disorganized notes, rendering all of his prep work useless.

Lanny sat back, defeated. He straightened his spectacles. "Yes, professor. What was that, ehm, question again?"

After class, I swept my books into my backpack to make a quick escape. Lanny stood up and glared at me. "You're an *A-hole*," he said. "So, what are you going to say *next* time he calls on you, Rossi? Did you think of that, moron?"

Stick interjected himself, slapping my shoulder. "Just tell him he mangled your name so badly you didn't hear him correctly. Tell him the proper pronunciation is *Rosey*—a Slovak name that had six consonants but got shortened when your family immigrated to Pittsburgh. He'll believe you. This guy's in outer space."

"What *bullcrap*." Lanny grabbed his briefcase. "I hope you both flunk out."

As Lanny vanished through the swinging doors, Stick scratched his ear. "What's that dude's problem? All this *Paper Chase* stuff is already giving every Harvard Law student a bad name, even normal people like us. We need to find a way to loosen up these folks."

I slid the yellow envelope from Marjorie into my backpack for safekeeping. "Yeah," I said. "I'm game."

After most classmates had drifted from the library over to the Hark Cafeteria for dinner, Stick and I met Dobbs in Langdell Hall's basement. We stashed our gear, then headed up the rear stairwell. A solitary maintenance man was vacuuming a room down the hallway. The classrooms were dark and empty.

"Do you remember the elements of breaking and entering from crim law?" I asked. "I think we just checked off all of them."

"Hurry up," Dobbs whispered impatiently. "I've got a political future to worry about. I can't afford to get arrested."

"Quit being chickens," Stick said, wielding a penlight. "Where's your sense of daring?"

"*Shhh!*" I said.

We flicked on the front lights in Langdell North. There, illuminated in a gold frame on the center wall, was the painting of Lord Chancellor Philip Yorke Hardwicke, an old English judge from the King's Bench in the 1700s, his white wig tilted cockily.

"What a pompous ass," I said, pointing.

"Let's get it done fast," Dobbs pressed us.

Dobbs and I hoisted Stick up by his tennis shoes and handed him a rolled-up poster and strips of masking tape. Stick unfurled it, positioned the corners, taped the poster to the frame, and jumped back down to the floor.

We stood back and admired his handiwork.

"It'll blow Bradwell's mind," I said. "He'll have to call the janitors and waste half of tomorrow's class to take it down. That should shake up the world of these uptight preppies."

Inside the golden wood frame, the English judge had been replaced by a three-foot psychedelic poster of Jimi Hendrix playing the electric guitar with his teeth.

The three of us smacked hands like victorious athletes, then flicked off the lights and crept down the rear stairwell, exiting into the shadows of Langdell Yard.

"This may be one of the great achievements in the history of Harvard Law," Stick said. "Too bad we can't put it on our resumés."

"I'm proud of you guys," Dobbs chimed in. "When our classmates start buzzing about this prank, I'll make sure they understand you helped."

Stick gave him a swift kick. Dobbs was already trying to take credit for the whole escapade.

"Don't worry, Rosey," Dobbs added, putting an arm around me as we headed toward Somerville. "I won't tell your girlfriend how you're goofing off. Your secret's safe."

"What do you mean, man?" I laughed, feeling good that I'd finally made some real friends in this place. I tugged up my windbreaker. "Marjorie will get a kick out of fun stuff like this. People from Pittsburgh aren't full of themselves like these Harvard highbrows.

"I'll share *everything* with her over break," I added, already imagining the scene, snuggled up with a bottle of Boone's Farm in her dorm room. "That's why I'm psyched for this first semester to be over. Next month can't come soon enough."

—•—

"Did you read those cases on pendent jurisdiction?" Lanny asked, hanging over the passenger seat of Erica's car. "*Dancing Queen*" by ABBA was playing so loudly I could barely hear him.

I punched the winter coat that I was using as a pillow.

"C'mon Rossi," he pressed me. "Time to get serious about exams. And I *know* you were one of the people who put up that stupid poster in our classroom. That was juvenile."

Erica kept her eyes on the road as she pulled her red Porsche out of the HoJo's rest stop and onto the snowy strip of Pennsylvania Turnpike. "Yes, juvenile," she chimed in, turning down the stereo a tad. "But kinda funny." She turned slightly toward the backseat and winked at me.

Erica and Lanny had made plans to ride back together to Chicago for Christmas break and had posted a note on the ride-sharing board for someone to split the cost of gas. I should have stayed behind and taken a Greyhound bus. It would have been far less painful.

"What, ehm, really bothers me," Lanny continued while he opened a package of brownies, "is whether this rule about pendent jurisdiction applies to *state constitutional* claims, too? What do you think, *Rosey*?"

I watched the orange reflector posts flip by on the side of the turnpike. I didn't like it when non-friends used that nickname.

"I don't know, Laniard," I finally said. "That exam's not till February, for heaven's sake."

Lanny turned around and scowled at me before taking a bit of his brownie.

"Oh, don't bother him, Lan. He's ruminating about that pretty little undergraduate of his," Erica said.

"I'm actually thinking of how annoying that song is," I replied. "Anyway, you two would be lucky to have a relationship that *meant* something, like me and Marjorie have."

"Marjorie and I."

"*Me* and Marjorie."

Erica laughed with a "*tsk*"while downshifting at the Blue Mountain tunnel and turning up the volume on her tape deck.

"You know what she's probably been doing the whole time you've been away, Shawn-with-a-w?" Erica cajoled.

"*Huh?*" I said. "Can you turn down that goddamn music?"

"That pretty little undergrad bimbette of yours," Erica said over the disco noise. "She's probably exploring her femininity by enjoying a few casual relationships on the side. Can you blame her?"

"She's probably *doing* it three nights a week," Laniard sniggered.

"*Go to hell!*" I mouthed back at them.

I rubbed a circle into the condensation that had collected inside the Porsche window and prayed I could make this trip end so these people would disappear.

"*What the heck?*" I woke up with a jolt and jammed my foot against the floor as if I were hitting the brake pedal.

We came barreling out of the Fort Pitt Tunnel, high above the rivers, as the lights of the city of Pittsburgh appeared around us, shimmering off the water. Erica must have gotten off too far east at New Stanton, and now we were coming in a roundabout way. But the delay made no difference. We were finally home!

A sense of relief overcame me. Red lights wove across steel bridges, illuminating streetcar tracks and familiar stretches of the Mon River wharf. The old Duke Beer clock shone its light from across the river. It was only 11:30. Marjorie's dorm locked down at midnight. I still had time to slip in.

As the Porsche climbed toward the Boulevard of the Allies, Erica jerked the steering wheel to the left. It was too late—I could feel the little sports car shake as it hit a giant pothole, causing the dashboard's lights to dim. Erica downshifted into third, then second. The engine coughed as if trying to shake off a bad cold. A ten-wheel semi tractor-trailer roared past us. Erica jerked the wheel again and pulled off into the emergency lane under the darkened Birmingham Bridge.

"*Crap!*" Erica said, pounding the dashboard. The car's emergency lights flashed red.

"Are we, ehm, there?" Lanny said, slouched down in the front passenger seat. He cupped one hand over his spectacles to fight off the oncoming high beams.

The Porsche shuddered and shut down completely. Now only the "check engine" light flashed on the dashboard.

"Damn potholes," I said.

Erica appeared freaked out. "Something's moving under that bridge, Shawn. What *is* it?" She pointed to cardboard and torn blankets under which were huddled homeless people from the Upper Hill.

"Probably just some people waiting to donate plasma in the morning so they can buy breakfast," I said. "They're harmless. I'll hike up the hill and look for a payphone to call Triple-A."

Erica dug her fingernails into my arm. "You're not going *anywhere*," she gasped. "I'm not staying here *alone*. Lanny, climb into the back seat, goddamnit. Shawn needs to get up here in case someone tries to assault us."

CHAPTER 16

December 1978 (Swissvale)

CHRISTMAS EVE REUNION

"*Please*, mother." Marjorie yanked me back down onto the couch. "Shawn didn't come home to watch you dust. Can't you give us some privacy?"

"It's okay," I whispered. "Hey, that sweater's pretty. I can't believe how much I've missed you."

"Did you catch that, *mother*? He's trying to say something romantic, except there are too many people in the room *spying* on us," Marjorie said.

"I haven't seen Shawn for months either," Lil replied with a pouty lip. She took a long drag of her Newport Light and stopped polishing the mantle. "We're all proud of Shawn. My chiropractor says that a Harvard grad *never* has to worry about going broke; they make more than hookers." *Hack, hack!*

"*Please*, mother," Marjorie said.

Lil's foray into working as a medical assistant had ended abruptly. She had taken a job bathing patients at a nursing home but had become upset when she witnessed a male nurse mistreating an elderly woman and reported it to the supervisor. Unfortunately, the supervisor and male nurse were dating; Lil was terminated the next day for allegedly failing to fill out her timecards properly. Luckily, the Union Switch was willing to take her back. However, the bills from her medical assistant's training now created another burden on the family's bank account, which made Marjorie extra cranky with her mother.

Lil made a pouty face again before clomping away, disappearing into the dining room where she sprayed Lemon Pledge onto the breakfront with a vengeance.

I stretched my arm around Marjorie, feeling the soft angora sweater that I'd bought her at Filene's Basement for Christmas. She had put on a cool new version of "*Little Drummer Boy*" by David Bowie and Bing Crosby to set the mood. I always loved Christmas music.

"Oh. I got you something else in Boston," I said, handing Marjorie the Coop bag. She opened it slowly.

"Oh my God, *Shawn!*" she said, bursting out laughing.

Marjorie held up the red satin Harvard nightie guardedly as if examining a stripper's outfit. Then she pitched it under the couch. "We can't let Aunt Peg see that," she said.

"I was gonna give it to you last night in your dorm," I said.

Marjorie kissed me impulsively on the lips. "Poor planning," she said. "If you hadn't driven home with that spacey intellectual snob who didn't bother to get her car tuned up," she gave me a seductive bite, "we could've done a lot more than *this* last night." Marjorie's face became flushed as she pressed herself against me while Bowie and Crosby crooned from the speaker.

"It was a pothole," I corrected her. "It knocked something loose. Triple A fixed it."

Aunt Peg hustled into the living room wearing an apron splattered with sauce. Marjorie and I sat up, quickly disengaging. Behind her grandmother was a trail of delicious odors from the Christmas Eve dinner, including "city chicken" (breaded pork on a stick), halushki (buttered noodles and cabbage), and other Slovak delicacies.

Marjorie eyed her grandmother, then exclaimed, "What the hell? Why don't you join us, too? Everyone *else* is."

"So, you're going to be a big-shot Harvard lawyer pretty soon, huh, Shawn-boy?" Aunt Peg said, ignoring her granddaughter. "I've been wearing this worry ring and counting off prayers for you every day," she said, holding up a cheap metal ring with bumps on it, popular among ladies at the Slovak church. "Are you still coming home this summer?"

"Oh, sure, Aunt Peg," I said, scooting closer to Marjorie. "I don't want your granddaughter getting away from me."

She patted my hand. "Good boy. We'll keep you."

Aunt Peg raised her eyes to Marjorie and smiled lovingly. "Did you put your mom's present under the tree yet, sweetheart? You know how much she looks forward to finding it there. She's just like a kid at Christmas."

Marjorie grimaced. When Aunt Peg asked again nicely, her resistance melted away. "I'll get it in a minute," she said, capitulating.

A fresh-cut Christmas tree, courtesy of the Swissvale Boy Scouts Troop 90, threw colored light around the room from dozens of festive blue, orange, and yellow bubble candles. On the mantel, I spotted an old snow globe with a scene of Pittsburgh inside it; as the bubble candles bubbled away, the sphere caught the light. I took in the whole sight and inhaled deeply, absorbing the atmosphere.

Choppy walked in, smelling as if he'd doused his entire body in Old Spice. "C'mon, get the hell out! These kids need some time alone," he said to no one in particular. He waved around a shot glass containing plum brandy—*slivovitz*—which doubled as his home remedy for gout. Then he ushered Aunt Peg out with a swat on the rear end.

"Don't worry," Choppy whispered to me. "I'm dropping them off at her Aunt Josie's after church while I go drink at the Croat Club. You kids need some time to yourselfs."

Choppy sucked down the remaining liquid in his shot glass, exhaling with satisfaction, "*Nostravedi!*"

"If I was you," Choppy continued, "I'd sneak out while everyone's gone and get married tonight in Ohio or some damn place. Yinz can always figure out the next step from there. Your grandmother already has a room picked out for a nursery, and I put in new weatherproofed windows—just in case."

"Sounds like an interesting plan to me," I said, my eyes clinging to Marjorie's curves.

Marjorie smacked my shoulder. "You men are *way* too simplistic." She straightened her angora sweater. "Women need *advanced degrees* today before they begin careers or start pumping out babies."

Choppy pulled his empty mayonnaise jar from its hiding place under the couch and spat snuff juice into it. "Yinz love each other, don't you?"

"Sure," Marjorie said with a shrug of her shoulders. "*Of course.*"

He scratched one ear profoundly. "Well, as my old Croatian grandma used to say: 'The two biggest mistakes people make is thinking life's *longer* than it really is and thinking life's *shorter* than it is.' Don't put your plans on hold; otherwise, the train will pull out without you."

Marjorie smiled at her grandfather. She got a kick out of his homespun aphorisms.

"Look," Choppy continued. "I had offers from management to be a superintendent. The union even asked me to run for president of Local 1253. But I turned them all down. I never gave a rat's *duppa* about moving up." Choppy jammed the Copenhagen deeper into his lip. "Greed and corruption are sons of a bitches. We'd of been financially better off if I'd sold out. But I'd rather be small and right than big and wrong. Hear what I'm saying, kids? I put other things first, including your grandmother and mother—and you." His lip quivered for a moment. "Once you find that groove that feels right, you gotta hang onto it like your life depends on it—'cause it does."

Choppy gestured out the window onto Homestead Street. Outside, Stan Galovich was clearing ice off his sidewalk next door after taking care of two neighbors' walks. He'd now taken a break to crank up Christmas music on his boombox.

"Or think about Izzy Kline acrost' the street," Choppy continued, pointing in the other direction. "His mother was getting Old Timers' disease. Fell down the steps and cracked her head open a couple times, then started a grease fire on her stove. So, what did Izzy do?"

Marjorie and I looked at each other, utterly baffled about where this story was heading.

"He found a couple women in the neighborhood who volunteered to cook the old lady meals and give her baths, so she didn't go wandering around the neighborhood naked. He even lined up five nieces to visit every day in shifts. Guess how old Mrs. Kline was when she died?" he asked.

Marjorie threw up her hands. "I have no idea."

"She *didn't* die," Choppy said, smiling broadly, pleased that we'd taken the bait. "She's ninety-five. The old lady will outlive Izzy; her heart's like a damn pneumatic pump. Maybe her life seems simple by some people's standards. But she's happy as a clam, staying in her little house on Dickson Street like the goddamn Queen of the Mon Valley. Life's about being in a place where people look out for each other. You can get all the fancy degrees and big houses you want, but you can't buy that other thing for a million bucks."

Choppy glanced around the room, starting to look as if he was becoming emotional. "How could anyone want more than what we got in this little house?" he asked. "It's the most beautiful place your grandmother and I could have ever wanted. And the special things about our neighborhood? Every night I fall on my knees and thank God that he gave all of this to us. It's more than we could have imagined. Even though I know it may not seem fancy."

"Don't worry. We're gonna capture the brass ring for *all* of us," Marjorie said, kissing her grandfather on his cheek. It made a scratchy sound like sandpaper. "It's just a matter of being smarter than people who get tripped up. Shawn and I have a master plan. We don't want to face all of the challenges you and Aunt Peg had." She glanced around, checking to make sure her mother wasn't listening from the next room. "We want the basic things, plus a lot more. We're gonna make sure we have the best of *all* worlds."

Choppy's high Croatian cheekbones seemed to sink inward. "I'm not sure it works like that, sweetheart," he said.

"*What* doesn't work like that?" Marjorie asked, staring back at her grandfather, trying to be patient.

"All of *this here*," he said, pointing a stubby finger at the tree with bubble candles, at Aunt Peg's nut roll on the coffee table, and at Stan Galovich outside, now dancing with a shovel as he and his wife Edna cleared off another neighbor's walkway together.

"All of *this here*, sweetheart," he said, his voice starting to choke up.

December 1978 (St. Agnes's Church)

MIDNIGHT MASS DEBACLE

"Outta the way, *douche-bag*. You young punks take up too much goddam space."
An unshaven man scowled as he pushed his way through the back vestibule.

Obviously drunk, the man looked to be in his fifties with thin arms and blond
hair that was prematurely white. His coat emitted a stale odor of beer mixed with
cigarette smoke and vomit. With its sharp hook, his nose resembled a weapon.

"Hey, man," I said. "Don't scuff up my good shoes."

He shoved an elbow into my gut. "Jesus Christ, outta the way, punks."

Marjorie kept her eyes fixed on the floor.

Unfortunately, Marjorie and I had to stand in the back vestibule—the worst
place to be for midnight Mass.

"Sorry, Rad," I whispered. "Next year, we'll get here early enough to get seats."

Billy Keefe was safely seated with his girlfriend in a pew in the middle of the
church. He looked back and shrugged his shoulders as if to say, "too late—I tried!"
Saving seats for more than a couple of minutes for a special Mass like this was
considered a mortal sin.

Midnight Mass at St. Agnes's was a time-honored tradition. I'd been coming to
this church since I was baptized here. Tonight, the old church built of Depression-
era marble, dark mahogany, and stained glass looked magical with red and white
poinsettias arranged across the altar. There were many memories in this place. I
squeezed my eyes and saw a picture of my dad. He was still strong and healthy,
dressed in his suitcoat and red Christmas tie, seated proudly beside mom and me,
holding a missalette in a pew toward the front of the church. I squeezed my eyes,
and he was gone.

A group of high school boys stinking of alcohol and cigarettes tramped in
through the back door. They'd been in the school playground drinking Iron City

beer and homemade "Dago red" wine that they'd smuggled out of their houses under winter coats.

"Hey, Rossi, is it true you're goin' *up 'air* to law school at *Harvard?*" a stocky guy asked me. "How come you're not celebrating Christmas at the goddamn Playboy Club in New York? I thought you'd kiss all this low-grade Swissvale crap goodbye."

I finally recognized him: "Squints" had gone to high school with me and now worked at Penn Compression Molding. Tonight, as he stared up at me, Squints' nose was as red as Rudolph the Red-Nosed Reindeer's.

I grabbed Marjorie's hand and pulled her toward the door. "Let's ditch this place," I said. "We can't hear anything, anyway." But before we could exit, we were blocked by six ushers crowding around the holy water font, trying to pry away a man who was kicking, spitting, and singing in a slurred, off-pitch voice:

"Si-i-lent night. Ho-ol-lee Night. All is white. All is bright!"

The drunk guy with white hair was fighting off the ushers while gripping the font to steady himself, intermittently hurling invectives at the Pope and Jesus Christ.

"Hol-lee virgin, so ten-der and mild!"

This drunken display was too much for the inebriated high school students, who started howling and slapping each other's backs.

"Hey! That's the pecker-head who tends bar down the Sportsmen's," a voice shouted from the throng. "You been drinkin' your own boilermakers, Ralph?"

The drunk simultaneously waved his hand and gave the finger to the crowd. Then he leaned over the holy water font where—to the horror of the Christmas faithful—he vomited.

"Oh, gross. Don't blow your cookies in there, Ralph!" one inebriated teenager shouted.

"That's a goddamn mortal sin," another said. "Get him away from the f--'n holy water fountain!"

Marjorie turned away.

A middle-aged man with a tattoo on his neck pointed at Marjorie: "Hey," he said to her. "Ain't that your old man?" He allowed his finger to dance around as if outlining the curves on Marjorie's body.

"Yeah, Ralph," he said to the drunk. "Ain't that your bastard daughter over there?"

The drunk looked up from the holy water font, trying to focus on Marjorie, until a team of ushers picked him up by his skinny legs and shoulders and heaved him out the front door, dumping him into the bushes where the pastor wouldn't spot him.

"Yeah, I think that's Ralph's bastard daughter over there with the nice bum," the taunting continued from someone in the crowd. "Go help your old man, honey. He needs a quart a' Iron City."

Marjorie's eyes looked cold and murderous. "That alchy isn't my father," she spat out the words. "I've never met that reprobate, and I never *plan* on meeting him. Let's go, Shawn. This neighborhood's nothing but mill-town trash anymore."

Outside, a fresh coat of snow blanketed the streets of Swissvale. It glistened against the soot-stained houses sheathed in Insulbrick—a cheap, fake-brick siding—along McClure Street. Under the faint illumination of the streetlight, I could see Marjorie's eyes. Instead of their usual hazel-green confidence, they showed combativeness and defeat.

"That jerk was probably right," she finally said. "Why should you come back to a crappy town like Swissvale, *especially* for a girl with a million problems? You've got options now, Shawn. I should've seen this coming. How could I be so stupid? I don't have a damn thing to offer."

"Look, Marjorie," I said, grabbing her arm. "That's crazy. . . ."

"Look, yourself," she said, pushing me away. "That old alchy's *not* my father, you understand? I've never seen that man in my life. Do you hear me?"

"I never said *anything* about that guy. How come you're being so touchy about it, Rad?" I asked, trying to sound solicitous. The whole episode with the riffraff in the church had been odd. If the old drunk had no connection to her, why had Marjorie become so freaked out by their taunting?

We walked together in silence across the abandoned trolley tracks along Monongahela Avenue before she stopped and squeezed my hand hard. "Sorry, Shawn, it must be PMS," she said. Marjorie gave me a gentle kiss as an apology.

By the time we reached her grandparents' house on Homestead Street, with the familiar slag dumps visible in the distance, the unpleasant memory of Midnight Mass had already begun to melt away. Colored Christmas lights twinkled in neighbors' windows, a festive reminder that we still had two glorious weeks together; the snow seemed to envelop us in a romantic panorama as we clasped hands.

Marjorie skidded onto the sidewalk in front of her house, leaving tiny imprints from her high heels on the virgin snow. We leaned against my mom's car, which I'd borrowed so I could drive back and forth between my Aunt Kate's place and Marjorie's house. As I bent over to kiss her mouth, her back made an imprint on the hood, like a partial snow angel.

Marjorie pulled me against her. The warm scent of her strawberry lipstick ignited every sensor in my body.

She thrust her hands into my coat pockets, pulling me toward her. "Should we go inside?" she asked.

As Marjorie removed her hand, she extricated a little piece of creased notepaper. "You writing me love letters now, Shawn?" she playfully asked while unfolding the note. The porch lamp at the Galovich house threw a weak light towards the sidewalk, just enough to illuminate the white paper.

"What's *this?*" she asked, her hands shaking as she scanned the words.

Star-shaped crystals of snow pelted the paper, making the ink run. I grabbed it from her and read: "*Shawn-with-a-w: Thanks for keeping me company in the front seat. Maybe I was a little tough on you. Even though you're rough around the edges, I appreciated your company in an odd, truck stop kind of way. Maybe I'll consider an encore when we get back to Cambridge if the right moment presents itself. Until then, enjoy that little bimbette of yours. Merry Christmas, Pittsburgh boy. Maybe you're all right, after all, Erica.*

P.S.—You're kind of thin, but I do like your biceps."

Marjorie ran up the steps leading to her grandparents' porch. She skidded again, scraping a knee against the concrete.

"Look, Marjorie, this is some kind of sick joke," I said. "I only moved to the front seat 'cause she made me after we hit that pothole. C'mon, I swear I'd never do anything to hurt our relationship."

Marjorie pushed open the front door then swung the storm door closed, almost catching my finger. She stared at me through the glass, her eyes afire with anger. "Why don't you go the hell back to Harvard?" she yelled.

Then she slammed the door in my face, locked the deadbolt, and turned off the porch light, leaving me speechless.

Winter 1979 (Somerville, Mass.)

A COLD WINTER'S NIGHT

"Just me," I yelled to Walter, hoisting my laundry bag onto the bed and kicking the snow off my boots. "It's cold as hell. You're lucky to be in captivity."

I had spent a few days hanging out with my Coop friends and catching up with Billy Keefe over some Iron City beers. I'd also spent lots of time with my mom and Aunt Kate in Aliquippa, stuffing myself with home-cooked meals and playing Frisbee in the snow with Plutarch. It was great seeing all of them again. But it was tight quarters, and Aunt Kate had planned a big New Year's party for the AARP ladies, some of whom needed a place to stay because they couldn't drive at night. I didn't want to hog the only spare bedroom, so I told a white lie to my mom, insisting I had a writing project due right after the break that required access to law books in Langdell. The truth was, I was feeling down because Marjorie didn't even want to see me. So, I ended my Christmas vacation early and caught a Greyhound bus to Boston.

Walter sat listlessly in his box amid apple and strawberry chunks. I could relate. I, too, was eating less. I wanted to save enough money to fly Marjorie up for Valentine's Day to help repair the damage from the Christmas Eve debacle. I put on "*Pick Up the Pieces*" by the Average White Band and cracked open a Mountain Dew.

The phone in the kitchen rattled with an odd sound; the bell was missing one of its strikers. I turned down my stereo.

"Hey, Rad, I'm glad you called," I started to say, assuming Marjorie was the only person who would be calling me so late.

The brief silence lasted three beats. "Hello, Shawn-with-a-w." The voice sounded more subdued than usual. "It's me, Erica. My boyfriend just dumped me for some little hussy nurse back in Chicago. I need to talk to someone, and I've tried calling a bunch of people. The guy at the Langdell desk told me he saw you at the library. You're the only one who's back from break. Look, just come over right now—*please*."

Erica lived on the other side of the law school campus in North Cambridge, an area favored by Harvard faculty and rich Ames Inn students because of its quiet streets and magnificent homes where rent was six times higher than Somerville. Erica's brownstone fronted Follen Street and featured a grand entrance with authentic gas lamps. The snow had blanketed the neighborhood in white frosting that drooped from the slate roofs and eaves, giving the Victorian and Federal-style houses a splendid wintry appearance worthy of a Currier & Ives lithograph.

I stomped the packed snow off my winter boots in the foyer. Before I had a chance to locate Erica's name on the gold buzzers next to the mailboxes, a magnetic lock clicked open on the glass security door. Her staticky voice came over the intercom: "*Come on–open–Shawn.*"

Erica's apartment was small but grand. I could hear "*You're the One that I Want*," featuring the blended voices of John Travolta and Olivia Newton-John, on a radio somewhere in another room.

"Just sit down anywhere, Shawn-with-a-w," Erica said, motioning me over to a large, flowered sofa in the center of the living area. "This stuff came from my parents' summer home. Pretty horrid. I would've preferred stripes."

I backed into a comfortable easy chair with fruit-like designs and a matching ottoman. After placing my winter coat over the heating register, I allowed my eyes to sneak sideways to look at her. Erica was wearing a light blue men's cotton shirt as a sleepshirt. On the pocket were embroidered three initials in a flowing black script: "A. M. W." The top two buttons were flung open. It suddenly felt exceptionally warm in the apartment.

"Alfred M. Welles," Erica said, following my eyes.

"What?" I turned my head, pretending to study a Central American tapestry on the wall.

"They're my father's initials—Alfred M. Welles," she said. "I wear these old things to bed. Sorry, I'm such a mess, Shawn. I hadn't been planning to see anyone tonight. God, I never expected to feel so *lousy* just because some worthless *jerk* told me I wasn't good enough for him."

I sat back in the easy chair, realizing too late that I should have probably taken off my boots. They were now dripping a dirty slush of melted snow, rock salt, and cinders onto the carpet. "*This is great,*" I thought. "*My girlfriend slams the door in my face and sends me packing my bags, and now another woman wants me to console her because her boyfriend dumped her. Can it get any crazier?*"

"I'm sorry for whatever happened, Erica," I said, folding my hands on my lap.

Erica stared straight ahead at the wall. "Joel could have just *told* me he was too busy for a relationship or that Boston was too far away," she said, her chest heaving under the blue sleepshirt. "That would've been no problem. I didn't really *need* him. It was honestly getting inconvenient to fly home on weekends and build my studying around *his* schedule. I could have lived with that but *not* with finding out that he's screwing around with a little nurse from Highland Park he met while I was in France last spring. My father always warned me I shouldn't trust med students. It *kills* me that Alfred was right. I could handle a workaholic or someone who had an occasional affair. But not *this*. They were shacking up, and the whole world knew it, *except* me. And I was thinking of *marrying* this guy? Here he's been screwing around with a nurse like some X-rated skin flick while I'm up here busting my hump for *both* of our sakes. It's just so hurtful. Why would he do this?"

"I really feel bad for you, Erica," I repeated, repositioning my boots to hide the mess they were making on the carpet.

"Did I ever tell you my father didn't even want me to enroll in law school?" she continued. "When I got admitted, he freaked out. I asked him, 'Don't you want a lawyer in the family?' He told me, 'Sure. Why don't you marry that guy you were dating at Chicago Law instead of that med student and stay here to study art or something more suited for women?' "He told me I'd never do anything with a Harvard Law degree other than hang it on the wall, once I started having babies."

Erica stopped as if processing her own story.

"Wow, what a kick in the rear. He was probably right on both counts," she continued, wiping a hand across her nose. "Let's not talk about it anymore. I don't even know why I asked you to come over, Shawn. I was just so keyed up, and I knew I'd never be able to sleep. Do you do coke?"

I stared at Erica, confused by the non sequitur and not sure I heard her correctly. From her monogrammed pocket, she removed a tiny glass vial, the diameter of an ink pen. She held it obligingly in my direction as if she were offering me a stick of gum.

"Cocaine? No, huh-uh," I said, looking at the Guatemalan tapestry. "Drinking beer and chewing snuff—those are my only vices." I tried to make a joke of it, but I could feel my heart pounding irregularly in my chest from the suggestion of a criminal conspiracy.

"Well, let's have a little party," she said. "I never had a chance to celebrate New Year's Eve while I was in Chicago. I was too busy having my life screwed sideways by this creep."

Erica walked into the kitchenette barefoot. She opened the refrigerator and bent over to inspect its contents as her nightshirt hiked up her legs.

I could see several near-empty shelves. On them were a pint of some exotic brand of yogurt, a cut lime, a bottle of unfamiliar bitters, and a bag of macaroons from Evergood's Market two blocks away on Massachusetts Avenue.

"I guess I'm not much of a hostess, Shawn-with-a-w," she said, closing the refrigerator. "I usually eat at Ames Inn or one of those simple Chinese places in the Square. Not to worry, though."

She bent over again, rummaging through a small liquor cabinet at the base of the countertop. "There!" she said, standing up and displaying a large green bottle with an elaborate corking mechanism.

"What's that?" I asked, squinting my eyes, trying to make out the identity of the drink.

"*Grolsch!*" Erica said with a conspiratorial smile. "Imported beer from the Netherlands. It's not cold, but I can add some ice."

I flinched as Erica poured a half bottle of the dark-yellow liquid into a pewter mug fit for a German king, then dropped in two ice cubes. She flounced back over into the living room, her blue nightshirt jumping at the sides to expose her bare thighs. The radio in another room was now playing "*Crazy on You*" by Heart, the heavy metal chords rippling through the entire apartment.

"Sit over here. I don't allow mugs of beer on my chairs. There's a coaster on the coffee table," Erica said with a mischievous smile. She pulled me by one hand out of the easy chair and physically transferred me to the couch. As I sat back into the soft cushioned pillows, Erica sunk into the spot next to me and watched as I took a sip of the warm beer with ice cubes bobbing on the surface.

"How is it?" she asked.

I took a long gulp. The dark yellow beer tasted warm and putrid, unlike any other I'd ever had. "Great," I said, nearly choking on it.

Erica tipped over the orangish vial and spilled the contents onto the top of her glass coffee table. From a huge book on French post-Impressionist paintings, she removed a razor blade in a plastic sheath and a crisp $100 bill, a denomination I'd never seen except in a bank. Erica chopped the white powder with the razor blade, spreading it into two congruent lines.

"Why don't you try some, Shawn-with-a-w?" she said, looking at me knowingly. "It gives you a real rush. Have some fun."

"No, thanks," I said, grasping my mug for safety. "I'll just drink this beer. It's fantastic."

Erica rolled the green bill into a tight tube. She stuck one end into her nose, then inhaled some white powder in a quick snort. "Excellent stuff," she pronounced. She made a tentative sniffling noise as if to ensure that every grain of coke had made its way up her nasal passage. "I got it from a connection at Ames Inn who knows a banker in Boston with plenty of cash for the good stuff," she said, sniffling some more. "You sure you don't want to try some, Shawn-with-a-w?"

I took a long swallow of the now tepid beer. "No. You go ahead," I said.

Erica repeated the procedure, snorting up a second line of white powder. There was a watery intensity to her eyes now as she seemed to survey me with a sense of detached amusement. "Can't you take those boots off, Shawn?" Erica said with a loud laugh. "You're ruining my damn carpet!" Then she sniffed harder to prevent a drip of mucus from escaping from her nose.

I reached down and untied my boots, one at a time, embarrassed at the mess they'd made on her immaculate rug. "Sorry about that, Erica," I said. "I can clean it up."

Erica scooted closer and looked directly into my eyes. "By the way, I probably shouldn't have written that note and called your girlfriend a bimbette," she said. "I was trying to be funny."

"Well, she read it, Erica," I said, sinking back into a pillow. "It didn't help matters, that's for sure. But Marjorie's still my best friend. I mean, we'll be fine. Me and Marjorie trust each other."

"Marjorie and I," she laughed giddily.

"Marjorie and I are gonna get married after all this," I added. "And we always get through these things. Hey, I'd better think about heading home. I've got a bunch of laundry to put away." It seemed like it was time to bolt before things got any heavier.

I got up and began lacing up my boots. Erica nodded at first, appearing grateful that I'd shown up. But as she made a motion to stand up so she could walk me to the door, she abruptly slid sideways, nearly falling off the couch. At first, I thought that she was playacting. But when I went over to help her, I could see that the color had drained from her face, and her hands were shaking.

"Whoa. I'm not feeling so good, Shawn," she said, clutching for my hand. "I don't think it's the coke. I feel really weird." Erica tried to stand up again but couldn't get her footing.

"Sit down, Erica. You'll be okay," I said, easing her back onto the couch. "You probably just got up too fast."

Erica held her head in her hands and took deep breaths. Her face seemed to twitch weirdly as she looked up at me.

"Hey, I hate to, uhm, put you in this position," Erica finally said. Her words seemed to slur as her face grew paler. "But I think I need some help, Shawn. Do you think you could drive me to the Harvard health clinic?" She motioned toward the table. "My keys are over there. I hope you can drive a stick. Something's not right."

September 2008 (Judge's Chambers)

JUDGE WENDELL'S CORNER VIEW

"Please come in, counselors," Judge Wendell said. "Sorry, I'm late after my doctor's appointment. These people take a perverse pleasure in poking around in every nook and cranny. I hope your great-aunt survived her gallbladder surgery, Bernie. Take a seat anywhere."

The judge's chambers provided a spectacular view of the city in both directions. From one angle, one could see the glittering glass of Oxford Centre with a piano bar in the lobby and a glass elevator that moved like a spider on a silk thread up and down its elegant floors. From another window, one could see the crumbling expanse of the Hill District, a predominantly Black area of the city that had slipped into decay in the 1950s and had yet to regain its vitality. The Jews had left, migrating to Squirrel Hill to establish new neighborhoods and business communities; the Italians had moved away to South Oakland. But the Black community had remained trapped in the Hill District with dreams that rarely materialized because (as the judge pointed out) grand visions became a reality only with money and political clout. The Hill District—his community—lacked both.

"Is it a major inconvenience to ask for a cold drink?" Drew-Morris asked, crossing her arms.

The judge raised an eyebrow.

"Jimmy, see if you can rustle up some Diet Cokes," he asked his deputy, who scooted out in search of government-subsidized refreshments.

The judge leaned back behind his enormous mahogany desk, propping one Florsheim shoe on a footstool. Beside him on a credenza was an award from the American Legion and a baseball signed by Roberto Clemente.

"So, let's see if I have the drift of this case, now that we got a couple days under our belt," he said, straightening the handkerchief in his breast pocket, a standard element of his wardrobe. "Ms. Drew-Morris's guy—the original Serbian grandfather—he earned his money in the electroplating business in the Mon Valley, then he started socking his loot into a spendthrift trust in 1952 because he knew his only progeny was an irresponsible son who would squander it in the beer gardens."

Drew-Morris sat in a stuffed, floral-print chair with her hands folded. She frowned at such a vivid summary.

"Nobody knew about the existence of the trust," the judge continued, "even our decedent Ralph Senior because he was too busy imbibing boilermakers at the Sportsmen's Bar and chasing after young, innocent girls."

"I *object*, Your Honor," Drew-Morris said, partially standing up.

"Nothing to object to; we're off the record," the judge said resolutely. "Like I always say, we're a little informal here in Orphan's Court. Let's just see if I have the lay of the land from the briefs. It's okay to humor an old judge. If I get it wrong, the court of appeals will reverse me."

Drew-Morris frowned and slid back down.

"So, the Serbian grandfather set up this trust providing for no distribution during his lifetime," the judge said. "After his death, the trustee Mellon Bank provided some discretionary income to son Ralph for maintenance and support. At the same time, they exercised tight controls so the money couldn't be shoveled down the drain. Right so far, Bernie?"

My co-counsel nodded approvingly. They had been in the same class at Duquesne Law night school; Judge Wendell had been ranked first in the class, and Bernie had been sixth. He greatly admired the judge's legal acumen.

"Now, when grandfather Branco passed away unexpectedly in 1976, decedent Ralph Senior started getting his disbursement checks from the trustee at Mellon Bank. It wasn't much because those folks take their jobs seriously; they're tight with a buck if they can keep it invested. Plus, they knew decedent would drink himself to death with the cash if left to his own devices, which he eventually did in the fall of 1979."

"Your Honor, I take *issue* with this mischaracterization of the facts," Drew-Morris said, crossing her arms. "I'm not trying to be disrespectful, but I need to stand up for my client and his family's reputation here. We submitted affidavits showing that decedent suffered from *bona fide* medical problems that led to his demise."

Judge Wendell coughed. "The medical reports said his liver was eaten away by cirrhosis, consistent with him being an alcoholic for three decades. Now that's how I read the facts," he said.

Bernie and I glanced at each other and smiled; the judge had certainly done his judicial homework.

"So, Ralph Junior didn't learn about this fortune until his old man passed away in '79," he said, leaning toward Drew-Morris. "At *this* point, your client Ralph Junior got a decree from Orphan's Court authorizing the disbursement of monthly trust checks by Mellon Bank, listing himself as the only remainderman. Except, he conveniently forgot to mention that this Marjorie Radovich gal—whom we've never seen but whom these gentlemen assure me actually exists—might be entitled to half the funds if she's *legitimately* the daughter of Ralph Senior. The whole trust fund is supposed to be paid out in a lump sum after thirty years, which was scheduled to occur in 2007. That's when Ms. Radovich, the daughter from California, found out about this substantial pot of money after she saw a legal notice about the trust on the internet and eventually filed this lawsuit, which brings us together today."

"You got it right on the money, as usual," Bernie complimented the judge.

Judge Wendell stretched his hands behind his head and scrutinized our Philadelphia opponent. "Would you mind if I smoke, Miss Morris?"

Before her mouth could form an objection, the judge had plucked a pack of Kent king-size cigarettes from his suit coat pocket and lit one up. He did his best to blow his smoke away out of courtesy. Bernie pulled out a Phillies Blunt and chewed on it, savoring the taste. It was impolite, Bernie knew, to allow the judge to indulge alone.

Jimmy returned bearing Diet Cokes as if to complete the festivities. He stood in front of Drew-Morris and held one out. "Ladies first," he said. Drew-Morris stared at Jimmy's exotic crocodile shoes. For as long as I'd known him, Jimmy had been open about the fact that he was gay. Fashion was his passion, and alligator shoes were a favorite staple of his wardrobe. Drew-Morris seemed wary as she accepted the Diet Coke.

Judge Wendell continued to thumb through the pre-trial briefs. "This affidavit from plaintiffs' expert Dr. Wade is pretty darn compelling, Ms. Drew-Morris," he said. "She's a *crackerjack* psychologist. The Court of Appeals respects her as much as I do. Don't you think it would be good to show a little love with a settlement offer and make this case go away?"

"I'm not worried about Dr. Wade's affidavit," Drew-Morris said, poo-pooing the idea. "We'll prove it's flawed like the rest of their case." She stuck her chin out. "I can't help it that this plaintiff was an illegitimate child who's entitled to nothing under the trust. Mr. Milanovich and his clients are hardly the paragons of virtue." She scowled at Bernie, her eye starting to twitch. "These people are just '*mill-hunks*' trying to make a buck, isn't that what you call them around here?" Drew-Morris sniggered at her joke.

The judge reared up in his chair. He didn't look amused. "You don't have a right to speak like that, *ma'am*," he said firmly. "You have no idea who these people are, so please don't utter words like that again."

Drew-Morris clenched her jaw. "Yes, sir," she muttered, clearly not repentant.

Bernie saw the opening and took it. "We'll prove paternity, Judge," he said calmly. "If we aren't allowed to take DNA from Ralph Junior, we'll prove it with circumstantial evidence. Surely, Your Honor can take into account that Ralph Junior refused to submit to a DNA test. That should create an inference of a biological relationship. He's obviously afraid the test will prove he and our client are both offspring of Ralph Senior."

"Hold on," the judge said with a wave at Bernie. "You know I'm not allowed to take that into account. Parties in civil cases have an absolute right to decline a DNA test. The legislature's been clear about that. And when it comes to the ultimate right to an inheritance, even if you could prove paternity, I'm still not sure how you get around the pile of cases Ms. Drew-Morris submitted, my friend. What about the *case law*?"

Drew-Morris cut in. "That's what I've been *saying*, Judge. Under the law, when this trust was made, illegitimate children were deemed to be *irregulares ex defectu*, sins of the flesh. They couldn't inherit under the law. It's a principle that's older than Jesus Christ, fellas."

Bernie spat cigar juice into his Coke can. "You'd probably deny an inheritance to Jesus himself, wouldn't you?" he asked, shooting a nasty look at our opponent.

Drew-Morris swiveled around. "If Lil Radovich could have controlled her sexual urges fifty years ago, maybe we wouldn't be sitting here being assaulted by *toxic* cigarette smoke and drinking warm Diet Coke."

Judge Wendell touched his Coke can to test its temperature. Then he stared at his cigarette smoldering in its ashtray; he was a gentleman, so he stamped it out. Finally, he sighed, disappointed but not surprised that his settlement conference had degenerated into a verbal brawl.

He stared toward the ceiling pensively. "And if we're going to be candid with one another, we should talk about this Marjorie lady," he said. "She's still a puzzle to me."

"And to me," I said to no one in particular.

He swiveled slowly toward us. "Is she really a victim, or is she an opportunist, like Miss Morris says? Bernie tells me she's a good-looking gal, even after two kids. Successful in the computer business. She apparently has a low six-figure salary, so she's not a poverty case. So, what's making this young lady tick, fellows? I know this is all off the record. We're still talking on *background* here. If all this glowing material you put in your brief is true about this Marjorie lady, where's she been all these years? And why hasn't she stayed closer with her mother and grandmother, and why hasn't she shown up to testify at this trial? It's bothering the heck out of me."

Bernie wiped the lens of his bifocals with his handkerchief. "Nothing fishy at all, Judge. She's just facing, let's call it, some *complicated* circumstances. She'll eventually be here to explain."

"What's *your* assessment, counselor?" The judge spun his chair directly toward me. "Bernie reports you knew this Radovich lady from your youth back in Swissvale. How *legitimate* is she? My apology—that's probably a poor choice of words. I meant to say, is she the *real* deal?"

I glared at him wide-eyed. J.V. had encouraged me to start drinking Starbucks to "pep me up" instead of drinking my usual decaf tea. Now, my eyes felt bigger than quarters after downing a double shot hazelnut latte.

"I haven't spoken to Ms. Radovich for decades, Judge," I said. "This is a purely professional relationship. I want to make that clear *on the record*."

Drew-Morris stood up. "Mr. Rossi's the *last* person qualified to tell the court about his client's 'pure intentions,'" she declared. "He *knows* this woman intimately and has a contingent fee agreement giving him forty percent of any award she wins. That makes him *inherently* biased."

Judge Wendell raised his hand into the air. "Now hold on," he said, waiting for silence. "Attorney Rossi is a well-respected member of the bar here in Allegheny County. We're proud as heck of him. He attended *Harvard* Law School; didn't we establish that? I think we determined you only made it into *Penn*, Ms. Drew-Morris." He raised an eyebrow with mild amusement.

She returned the volley. "I *work* for a Harvard lawyer," she said. "They're arrogant as hell, I mean *heck*."

"Well, I guess we're all entitled to our opinions," the judge said. My heart was pounding wildly, stimulated by the extra shot of Starbucks. "But *I'm* interested in the story behind the story, okay? Mr. Rossi has known this Marjorie Radovich phantom for years. I mean, I can't really fault young, ambitious people for wanting to leave the Burgh. After all, since the mid-'80s, we've been the number one home of belly-up industries and senior citizens on fixed incomes in the United States, I get it. But, if she *really* cares about her family and winning this case for the Greatest Generation, what explains her behavior? I know she visits every summer with the kids, but that's it. She's *continued* to stay away and leave these elderly folks to fend for themselves. What explains that? And why hasn't she shown up for this trial if it's so important to her? They invented *airplanes*, you know."

Bernie shrugged his shoulders.

"Can *you* tell us, Mr. Rossi?" the judge pressed his point. "I mean, I'd like to know what's driving this woman so I can make informed decisions. Mr. Rossi?"

That exact question had been nagging at me at night as I tossed around in my bed, wondering why Marjorie kept sending J.V. excuses about having to finalize a "big closing" before she could travel to Pittsburgh. I kept visualizing how the two of us would react when we stood eye to eye in the same courtroom, facing each other for the first time in eons. I suspected that Marjorie had agreed to file this lawsuit at Choppy's insistence to placate her mother and to get her a small settlement but that she had no intention of returning to testify if she could run out the clock. After all, she'd spent a lifetime avoiding uncomfortable situations and facts.

My Blackberry began vibrating in my pocket with a message. I slid it out and sneaked a peak.

It was from J.V. "When R U returning to office?" it said. "Some things I need to talk about."

I snapped out of my reverie and slid the phone into my pocket. "I'd like to know, too, Judge," I replied. "But I can't help you out. That particular woman is a mystery to me. You'll have to ask *her*."

September 2008 (Courtroom)

NAME OF THE FATHER

Judge Wendell tapped his gavel one, two, three times.

"For the record, we had a brief settlement conference in my chambers that was regrettably a waste of the court's time," he announced. "Ms. Drew-Morris, you can finish questioning the witness. Try to wrap it up before the Monongahela Incline shuts down for the night."

As Drew-Morris stepped up to the witness box to complete her cross-examination of Lil, her demeanor had become surprisingly gentle, almost compassionate—if that was possible.

"Your story earlier this week was *very* compelling, Ms. Radovich," our opponent said to Lil. "You must have gone through quite an ordeal to give birth to that baby all those years ago. I've never had a baby myself," she added, tucking in her tummy and smoothing her suit. "But I can imagine that it takes a *tremendous* amount of courage for a sixteen-year-old girl to do what you did."

Lil was looking more comfortable in the witness box. She loosened her scarf, relieved that she'd finished what she thought was the most grueling ordeal of her direct testimony. "Thank you," she said, helping herself to a big sip of water. "I just wanted to do what was right for Marjorie, I guess. I still feel like-gat."

"I'm sure you do, *Ms.* Radovich," Drew-Morris said, lightly touching the edge of the railing. "Now, maybe you can help me out here. What *date* did you say your daughter Marjorie was born? Let's see. Was it April ninth of fifty-eight? I can't always read my own writing." She rolled her eyes at her inadequacy, smiling at the witness woman-to-woman.

"Yes, ma'am," Lil said, trying to be helpful. "Don't worry. Anyone can goof up." She took another gulp of water.

"So, if the baby was born on April ninth, do you remember when your last period was?" Drew-Morris asked.

Marjorie's mother looked up as if she'd been bludgeoned.

"You know, your last *menstrual* cycle, *Ms.* Radovich," Drew-Morris continued in a sharper tone. "Can you tell the court when your last period was before you got pregnant?"

"*Objection.* Argumentative," I said.

"Overruled," the judge responded, scratching his chin. "I'm afraid it's relevant, Mr. Rossi."

"I *honestly* can't say," Lil said, her face puffy and pink. "It must of been in the beginning of July. I went to Kennywood with Ralph Acmovic at the end of July, so I must have had my period sometime before that. I didn't pay much attention."

"Sometime before late July. Fine," Drew-Morris said. "So, during the summer of 1957, did you have any sexual relations with any *other* boys besides your alleged encounters with the decedent?"

Choppy stood up defensively. "Are you some kinda hired gun?" he blurted out. "*Your* guy knocked up my daughter. Don't you get it, lady?"

Lil slid down into her chair, her enormous blue dress bunching up around her.

Drew-Morris plowed ahead. "It's *not* a difficult question to answer, *Ms.* Radovich. *Did* you have sexual relations with any other male during that summer of 1957?"

Lil looked toward her parents for help. Aunt Peg appeared to be catching a cat nap in her wheelchair; her chin had slumped down into her blouse. I'd warned Lil that the cross-examination might go in this direction.

"I went down the Blue Dell Drive-In on Route 30 a couple 'a times with Jake Zidanic that summer," she said, struggling to complete the sentence. "It wasn't a big deal."

"And what did you *do* at the Blue Dell Drive-In?" Drew-Morris asked, tapping her pen against the witness box.

Ralph Acmovic Jr. leaned forward in his chair, smirking. He dusted a piece of lint off his sleeve.

"We just messed around a little, you know," Lil said.

"Like *nuzzling* and *feeling up*?" Drew-Morris said, glancing at the judge to make sure he appreciated the irony.

"*Objection*, Your Honor," I said, raising my hands.

"That was the witness's *own* term, Your Honor," said Drew-Morris. "I'm entitled to an answer."

"I guess," Lil said, sucking down several labored breaths. "It was so long ago, I just—"

"So *long* ago?" Drew-Morris said, cutting off the witness mid-sentence. "No longer ago than the events at Kennywood *allegedly* involving the decedent that you so *clearly* described under oath."

"Yeah, but I—" Lil started to say.

"Well, if you were 'nuzzling' and 'feeling up' with Jake Zidanic at the Blue Dell Drive-In and your last period was just *before* that, isn't it possible that Mr. Zidanic was the father?" Drew-Morris said. "I mean, a girl as sexually active as you must have trouble remembering all the details, but according to my math, it lines up."

"But I *didn't,*" Lil said. She tried to stand up in the witness box but teetered like an unsteady bowling pin.

"I'm saying that based upon the *dates*, it's perfectly possible that Mr. Zidanic could have fathered the child in July or August of 1957," Drew-Morris said.

"But I said I never . . ." Lil tried to keep speaking.

"I don't need excuses," Drew-Morris said. "You've answered my question quite clearly, ma'am."

I squeezed the arm of my chair until my knuckles turned purple. I was beginning to hate my opponent with every fiber in my body.

"Now, Ms. Radovich, there's something *else* we need to talk about."

Lil turned pale as if staring directly into the mouth of Hell.

"You stated under oath that you recall signing a birth certificate at the Roselia Foundling and Maternity Home, shortly after your daughter was born. Correct?" Drew-Morris asked.

"*God,*" I whispered, looking at Bernie.

He scribbled a quick note onto his legal tablet: "*Stay cool, pal.*"

"That's correct. I signed that birth certificate," Lil said, blinking her eyes.

"Now, do you remember *whom* you identified on that official document as being the father of your illegitimate daughter, Marjorie Radovich?"

"Jesus, Bernie," I whispered. "We've gotta *do* something."

My co-counsel's mustache twitched as if he was experiencing a mild seizure.

I sprung from my chair, raising both hands to signal "time out."

"*Your Honor,* if I could just have a minute to consult with my client. This raises some extremely sensitive issues which—"

"*Excuse me?*" Drew-Morris said, advancing toward the judge. "This isn't a football game where we huddle every time Mr. Rossi wants to coach his witness and get her to spin her testimony." She opened and closed her fist. "I have a right to get some answers from this witness without interruption, or I'm filing my *freaking* appeal to the Superior Court this afternoon. Excuse my bluntness, Your Honor."

Judge Wendell winced at the use of the word *"freaking"* in his courtroom. Otherwise, he seemed unfazed by the dust-up.

"She's entitled to her answer, Mr. Rossi," Judge Wendell said with a shrug of his shoulders. "I've got no discretion on this one, Bernie. I have a reputation to maintain with the Superior Court."

Drew-Morris moved toward the witness. "Repeating my question, *Ms.* Radovich. *Whom* did you identify on the birth certificate as the father of your illegitimate child?"

Marjorie's mother stared at me as if she was being lowered into a vat of boiling oil.

"I'm not sure," Lil said. "I remember the social worker helping me fill it out. We both certainly knew who the father was; I can say that for sure."

"You both *certainly* knew?" Drew-Morris repeated carefully for the record.

Ralph Acmovic Jr. wiped a piece of lint off his suitcoat.

Drew-Morris pedaled backward on her spiked heels, keeping her gaze fixed on the witness. She gave a hand signal toward the rear door.

The paralegal, wearing his athletic-cut suit, strode up and handed Drew-Morris a brown accordion file.

Drew-Morris slid out a document, grasping the piece of paper between thumb and forefinger. She slapped it onto the witness box.

"Are you familiar with this document dated April 9, 1958?" she asked the witness.

Lil studied the paper, her brow furrowed.

"For the record," Drew-Morris prodded her, "this is a certified copy of the Certificate of Live Birth maintained by the Department of Vital Statistics."

Bernie drummed his fingers against the table.

"As you can see," Drew-Morris continued, "this is the *actual* document prepared by the Roselia Foundling Home and filed with the state at the time your daughter was born. I obtained it from the Department of Vital Statistics. Maybe your lawyers thought we couldn't find this, but we located it in the State's archive in the mushroom mines in Butler." She unsheathed a gold pen from her breast pocket. "Is that your handwriting, Ms. Radovich?"

"Yeah, but—," was all Lil could say.

"Can you please read what you wrote in the space marked 'Name of Father'?"

Lil squinted at the paper. "It says 'Identity Unknown.' But I *remember* filling out. . . ."

Judge Wendell scrutinized Bernie and me as if we'd betrayed him. We had found this archived version of the birth certificate months earlier. We probably should have disclosed it ourselves. But our client had drawn a blank as to why Ralph Acmovic's name wasn't on it, identifying him as the father. She was certain she'd shared the name with the social worker.

Drew-Morris loomed over the witness as Lil hyperventilated.

"You've taken the oath to Almighty God, *Ms. Radovich*," she said. "You *swore* in these proceedings that you knew the identity of the father all along. Now we see that the *actual* record says the father's identity was *unknown*. Tell the court: How do you square your testimony with the *true* facts?"

"I'm sure there's a good explanation," Lil said with a deep, bosomy sob. "I told my lawyers it was probably some kind of mix-up."

"So your *lawyers* have seen this document, too?"

Lil shrunk back. Bernie and I receded into our chairs. This was not good.

"Oh, wait!" Lil sat up, her eyes becoming larger. "I'm starting to remember—I think I told the social worker it was okay not to put Ralph's name on there. That's it! I think the social worker said that was the best thing to do because the baby was going to be adopted!"

"But she promised me she took down every bit of information, including Ralph Acmovic's name as the father," Lil added. "She said it would be kept safe in case that ever became important."

"How convenient." Drew-Morris moved within an inch of the witness, shaking her head as if with pity. "The Roselia Home shut down 40 years ago. You know that, don't you, *Ms.* Radovich? That place doesn't exist anymore. So there's no way anybody can check out your new story, is there? Did your *lawyers* tell you to make up this tale?"

"No, they didn't tell me to make it up . . ." Lil stated evasively, recoiling from our opposing counsel.

"The bottom line," Drew-Morris continued, lifting her eyes toward the judge, "is that you have no tangible proof that Ralph Acmovic Sr. was the father of your baby, right? In fact, this evidence shows you *didn't* know the identity of the father. And now, the court reporter has a transcript of your admission that you and your lawyers *hid* this proof from the court and *concealed* the fact that you signed a document that would undermine your case."

Lil looked at Bernie and me. Her eyes shifted nervously.

"I don't know anything about hiding evidence, honest I don't!" she said, pressing her finger against her shunt valve and gasping for air through the hole in her throat.

"So, what *else* are you hiding from the court, Ms. Radovich?" Drew-Morris continued.

"I don't *know*," Lil sobbed louder. "I really can't tell you."

Drew-Morris stood in front of the broken witness, delivering the final blow with a deep, commanding tone: "So you've shamed and disgraced yourself a *second* time, *Ms.* Radovich. One time in the Kennywood parking lot wasn't enough. Is that what you're telling us?"

I remained frozen in my chair with this final, brutal series of questions and responses. I recognized that our client's entire testimony—in fact, our entire case—was now decimated. Even worse, Bernie and I were now in hot water for hiding relevant evidence from the judge.

———

When I dragged myself back to the office, J.V. was sitting amidst a blizzard of papers and files at the conference table, typing furiously on her laptop. "Marjorie hasn't returned my calls or emails again," she said, her belly and face looking so swollen I worried a sneeze would trigger labor. "I was believing all her excuses, but I'm giving up hope that woman is coming to testify. So, I've got an idea for a new legal theory. It might get the judge's attention. I've got a few more cases to research, but I'll have the memo ready for you tomorrow morning. You can use it when you get Dr. Wade on the stand."

I shook my head, too exhausted to respond, and walked into my office. Before I could sit down, the phone rang. It was Bernie.

"Judge Wendell called," he whispered. "He said he wants to talk to us. Privately. Meet me at the Lincoln Club at nine."

"The Lincoln Club?" I made sure I heard correctly.

"Yep," he repeated. "And don't tell *anyone*."

"I was afraid of this," I whispered back, peering into the adjoining office where J.V. sat, making sure she couldn't hear anything. "We're in deep trouble for failing to disclose that birth certificate. I knew it was a big mistake."

September 2008 (Lincoln Club—Part I)

JUDGE WENDELL'S SHOT

The Lincoln Social Club, where Bernie and Judge Wendell met regularly to play cards and escape into a zone of privacy, was located on a brick alley off Carson Street on the South Side of Pittsburgh. On rare occasions, they allowed me to join them there. From the early 1900s until the late '70s, the Jones & Laughlin mill had been booming nearby, supplying this club with blue-collar patrons carrying fat wads of bills in their pockets. As one shift replaced another, regulars had arrived here searching for beer and relief from the stress and danger that had filled the long buildings that supplied their paychecks.

When I pulled up on this night, the alley was pockmarked with inoperable parking meters and bent street-sweeping signs, proof that the public works department didn't care enough to send trucks down this way any longer. Now that the mills were gone, this neighborhood had slipped into decay. College students and millennials preferred the craft beer houses and eateries ten blocks up Carson Street in the rejuvenated section of South Side.

But Judge Wendell still frequented this place or the Froggs Club, a private Black social club in the Hill District. Particularly after he had attained senior status and had scaled back his caseload, he liked the camaraderie and the opportunity to get out of the house to relax in a private place.

Inside the Lincoln Club, chairs were upended to allow for dry mopping. A group of men played cards at the bar, their cigarettes and snuff cans resting on the counter. The bartender, Petey Koehlar, dried glasses with a towel and straightened big jars of red pickled eggs and sausage sticks on the counter. I ordered a shot and sat down with Bernie and the judge.

Only three of us were in the dining room. As guests of Judge Wendell, we could stay here until the building collapsed.

"Can I get *yinz* anything else, Judge? Mr. Milanovich? How's about another round of Rock n' Rye?" the bartender asked.

"You twisted my arm, Petey," Judge Wendell said. He didn't look particularly angry. "Three of those suckers and a couple more beers. You're a sweetheart no matter what your missus says."

I shifted uncomfortably in my seat. It was understandable that he wanted to talk to us about failing to disclose that document. But, it was dicey to do it this way. *Ex parte* conferences with judges about pending cases, we knew, were a risky business. Orphan's Court was a bit more lenient because of its historic connection to the courts of equity. Yet, having private conversations was still a dangerous game. Any meeting in a social setting without the other side present could be wildly misconstrued and twisted into a violation of the Rules of Professional Conduct, even for a semi-retired judge. It was no coincidence that Judge Wendell had suggested—when he had called Bernie at home earlier—that we meet at the Lincoln Club. Secrets were safe in this place.

"Looks like this Obama dude is starting to pull ahead with a decent lead," said the judge, continuing his small talk. "If a Black guy wins for president, I'm gonna have to do some break dancing in the streets in front of the courthouse."

"McCain's a decent guy," Bernie offered. "I like his view on guns. But that Sarah Palin gal is *nuts*."

Neither of them looked flustered. Something strange was going on here.

Petey delivered the next round of shots and beers; no payment was permitted. The judge had represented the owner of this establishment forty years earlier, *pro bono*, in a debt collection case that saved his bar. Now everything was "on the house" for perpetuity. It would have been an insult to offer money.

Petey cleared off the empty glasses. When he leaned over, I whispered in his ear that I needed a glass of buttermilk to coat my stomach and absorb the nasty shots of Rock n' Rye.

"So, about that birth certificate you failed to share with me . . ." the judge began.

"We didn't do it to mislead anyone," Bernie jumped in, standing up. "We were stuck. Lil was positive the people at the Roselia Home recorded the name of the father. It just didn't end up on that birth certificate. And we couldn't find anything else."

"Don't have a brain aneurism on me, Bernie," the judge said, motioning him to sit down and lower his voice. "I believe your client's story. That birth certificate didn't prove anything one way or another. No harm, no foul. Drew-Morris was just making a show for the court of appeals. But she lucked into finding that document. It gives her something to hang her hat on and makes your case even harder to prove."

Judge Wendell accepted a fresh tray of Iron Citys that materialized out of thin air. This time, he slipped Petey a twenty-spot, nodding toward the other room.

Petey hustled into the adjacent area, placing a white poker chip in front of each patron at the bar, indicating a free drink.

"I feel if you give us a little more time to search the old Roselia Home files, we could find something proving what Lil said is true," Bernie insisted. "The proof's *gotta* be somewhere."

"Incorrect assumption, my friend," the judge said, smiling obliquely. "If you had another *lifetime,* you'd never find it, at least without destroying the confidentiality of *thousands* of girls who stayed there." He looked around.

"What do you mean?" Bernie demanded. "What makes you so sure?"

Judge Wendell liberated another king-size Kent from its pack, tapping it against the table to shift the tobacco leaves into the proper configuration.

"When the issue of the girl's birth records came up in the briefs, I made a few calls myself," the judge continued, smiling with an odd tinge of sadness. "I mean, I had a *duty* to do a little due diligence, nothing personal, you understand? I had info that a couple of the old nuns from the Roselia Foundling Home might still be alive at their retreat house in Greensburg. Those Sisters of Charity are a tight-lipped bunch, but I have my own sources." He took a pensive puff. "I found the nun your Marjorie gal was named after—that Slovak sister."

"Sister Maria Fidelis Jaworski?" Bernie said, waving his hand dismissively. "We found her months ago. She's obviously been robbed of her memory due to Alzheimer's. She didn't remember the Roselia Home or any of the patients there. I'm not sure she knew what she had for breakfast that morning. That poor Sister can't confirm or deny anything."

"You're right," the judge said. "But one of her great-nieces who was visiting took me down the hall to visit another Sister who worked with her at the Roselia Home."

"Another Sister?"

I liberated a Kent from the judge's pack and fired it up. It tasted disgusting, but I was desperate for a jolt of nicotine.

"Yes, it turned out to be the other nun who was there at the time—Sister Benedict. Remember her? The chief administrative nun at the Roselia Home?" The judge looked around. "There she was, in the flesh."

I coughed smoke out of my nose.

"We looked everywhere for her," Bernie said. "That's impossible. There was no record of that nun."

The judge smiled. "That's because she changed her name back to her given name, way back in the '70s. Lots of them did that. They considered it *hip* to take their real names. Her name is now Sister Mary Jo."

"Sister Mary Jo?" Bernie and I looked at each other.

"I spent an afternoon with her at the motherhouse," the judge continued. "She gave me some good intel about how things worked at the old Roselia Home. She's sharp as a tack. But I can't share all of that info with you right now." He shifted his eyes away.

"Let's just say it wasn't uncommon at all for the Certificate of Live birth to leave off the fathers' names in these situations," the judge said, lowering his voice. "It was up to the mother and the social worker to make that decision. But the information about the identity of the father would have been preserved in the intake interview and the history of the girl. Those were handwritten notes that got locked up in a safe in the basement. Nobody had access to the safe but the Sisters, so the girls and their families could make a clean break. Those nuns were all about looking out for the well-being of the girls and their families. They were disciples of God; they're amazing ladies."

"So the records still exist somewhere?" I asked, taking a slug of Iron City.

"Maybe they do, fellahs," the judge said, shrugging his shoulders. "Who knows? The point is, the secrets of hundreds of girls are locked away in those files, wherever they are. Who knows if they're even legible anymore. Ink fades; it was a half-century ago. One way or another, those files were kept secret for a reason. I couldn't authorize you to start hunting for them, especially at this late date. But that doesn't mean Sister Benedict didn't know anything. That sweet old nun is ninety-three. Those Sisters of Charity live forever. I asked her about this case. She told me she remembers Lil Radovich being there, very clearly."

"She does?" Bernie and I spoke over him.

"She said she also recalls something about the identity of the real father. She was there for the intake interview. The Sister said she remembers this case vividly because she allowed herself to be a real stickler for the rules. Lil was originally putting the baby for adoption, and an adoptive couple had been located, so she was trying to make sure nothing interfered with that." The judge lifted his eyes toward the ceiling. "But the good Sister told me she was overjoyed when she learned from Sister Maria Fidelis that Lil decided to keep the baby and her parents were so supportive of the decision. That made all of her concerns melt away. She said she'll never forget that beautiful ending. She said she learned a lesson in humility and never again second-guessed girls who changed their minds and wanted to keep their babies. Lil and her family taught her that God always had a way of making sure everything worked out for the best."

"That's wonderful, Warren!" Bernie smacked his hand against the table. He looked toward the adjoining room, where patrons lined up at the bar. He quieted down.

"That means we can subpoena the Sister and get her to connect the dots and confirm it was Ralph Acmovic," Bernie whispered. "This is too good to be true!"

Judge Wendell stamped out his cigarette and lifted his eyes. "That's the main reason I wanted to meet," he said, an uneasy look creeping over his face. "Sister Benedict can't testify," he said. "All those nuns made a promise never to reveal what went on behind the closed doors of the Roselia Home. They pledged to protect the privacy of the families and *everyone* involved. And it would reflect terribly on the whole order if they disclosed any of this. They were doing the Lord's work out of sheer compassion. Sister Benedict got extremely upset when I asked about you fellows getting a statement or putting her on the stand. The poor thing started crying. She's in a wheelchair and barely gets around. It was too much for her to handle. She told me their whole life was devoted to ensuring confidentiality for the girls and their families. They don't want anyone pawing through those private files or forcing them to disclose confidential information, as much as she'd love to help. So, that's where it stands."

"What do you mean, that's where it stands?" I stood up, not even caring that someone might hear me. "We need that nun to testify or Choppy and Peg are going to lose their house, and Lil will be screwed over a second time. How's *that* fair, Judge?"

Bernie pulled me back into my chair and motioned me to keep my voice down. "Don't forget we can't be seen in here," he whispered.

Judge Wendell appeared genuinely contrite. Even sad. "Listen, fellahs, I understand this isn't something you wanted to hear," he said. "Believe me. I'd tell you if I thought there was a way to get the Sister on the stand. You'll have to trust me here. Your best hope is to get this Marjorie woman to testify and pray she can salvage things. Or else someone else with firsthand knowledge. If you tried to subpoena the nun," the judge concluded, sliding a bill under his glass as a hefty tip, "I'm guessing she'd literally die before she'd get on that stand to testify."

September 2008 (Courtroom)

HAIL MARY PASS

Bernie had called my home at dawn. Marjorie still hadn't shown up to testify, and her mother's whole story had been shredded by Drew-Morris. This, he said, combined with the judge's edict that we couldn't subpoena Sister Benedict, meant that we had no choice but to resort to a "Franco Harris Hail Mary pass" to keep our case alive. Like most Pittsburghers, Bernie believed that the "Immaculate Reception" in the NFL playoffs of 1972 was a magical event that could be replicated in other settings if one prayed hard enough and had faith. In contrast, I'd prayed we wouldn't have to call this witness. Now, we had to hold our breath and take the chance.

Walking inside the courtroom, I felt like a criminal under the hot lights. As Judge Wendell entered, Bernie and I looked the other way, avoiding his gaze so that nobody would notice our guilty faces. In hindsight, the meeting at the Lincoln Club seemed foolish and reckless, not to mention pointless. I arranged my papers until the judge uttered the words "proceed counsel." Then I stood up, a sudden sense of trepidation taking hold of me. I had no choice but to go forward.

I called Edna Galovich, widow of Stanley Galovich, to the stand.

Edna had lived next to Marjorie's grandparents on Homestead Street for a half-century. She cast an endearing smile toward Judge Wendell as she wriggled into the witness chair, trying to find a comfortable angle for her bony frame. Her lipstick was bright red, a brilliant contrast to her milk-colored skin and hollow cheeks that reflected a lack of appetite except when it came to her favorite Betsy Ann "meltaway" chocolates.

Edna gave a secretive wink in my direction; she still thought of me as "Marjorie's boyfriend."

"Could you state your name and address for the record?" I asked her.

"Edna Rita Galovich, 406 Homestead Street, Pittsburgh 18, Pennsylvania," she said clearly.

I smiled at the use of the old postal zone instead of zip code to denote Swissvale. Old habits really did die hard.

"And how long have you lived at that address next to the Radovich family, Mrs. Galovich?" I asked.

"Fifty-four years. We moved there in 1954. I've known Peg my whole life, even before we got houses next to each other. She's like a second sister," Edna said, gazing lovingly at the old lady who was fiddling at the belt that restrained her in her wheelchair.

"My husband worked at the Carrie Furnace with Choppy, only Stan's been dead since 1991 from lung cancer, never smoked a day in his life, rest his soul," Edna said. "You seen him laid out at Nied's Funeral Home. Remember how Godawful he looked, Shawn?"

"Yes, Mrs. Galovich," I said. "Now, can you please tell the court, was there any *common knowledge* in the neighborhood concerning Marjorie Radovich's family history, specifically, the identity of her father?"

"*Blatant* hearsay!" Drew-Morris said, standing up. She was regaining her brashness.

Bernie took two steps toward the bench. "Your Honor," Bernie said, fingering the chain of his gold pocket watch. He avoided direct eye contact with the judge. One never knew what Drew-Morris could read on our faces. "There's a well-established 'pedigree exception' to the hearsay rule relating to a decedent's personal or family history. This witness lived next to the petitioner's family for fifty-four years. She's certainly qualified to tell the court what neighbors knew about Marjorie Radovich's family lineage."

"I'll allow the witness to testify under the pedigree exception," the judge said, flapping his arms to loosen his robes. He didn't seem edgy in the least after our *ex parte* meeting. At least one of us was calm. "For the benefit of the *omniscient* Court of Appeals, this testimony is coming in not for the truth of the matter asserted but to see what the nebby neighbors knew about the true identity of the child's father. I'm curious myself. Let's hear it."

Drew-Morris glared at us.

"Oh *yes*," replied Edna. She leaned her skinny frame flirtatiously towards Judge Wendell. "Everyone in the neighborhood knew about poor Lil's pregnancy. Peg and Choppy tried to keep it under wraps. But it's impossible to hide a plump, crying newborn once it takes up residence next door. At first, they pretended the baby belonged to Peg's sister in Ohio; but that didn't last long. Lil was obviously the mother. My gosh, she was breastfeeding on the porch! Peg was helping with all the other duties. And I must say, Marjorie was the most adorable infant I ever laid eyes on. I still remember that first day I saw her naked in the sink, getting her first little bath; she was just as beautiful as when I'd see her sunning herself in her bikini as a grown woman."

I felt my face turning red.

"*You* know what I'm talking about, right, Shawn?" Edna asked me.

I cleared my throat. "Let's stick to the questions, Mrs. Galovich. Was there any discussion concerning the identity of Marjorie Radovich's father, ma'am?"

"I object *again*," Drew-Morris said.

"Of course," Edna beamed. "I heard *many* times that the father was that Serbian Acmovic boy. I never seen him around the house. He abandoned poor Lil and Marjorie, but the men who drank down the Sportsmen's bar across from the Union Switch knew *all* of the juicy details."

"So, you're referring to Ralph Acmovic Senior, the decedent in this case?" I asked, finally making progress.

"Yes, I heard his name repeated a hundred times. Marjorie even had that man's *ears*. I saw him on the Sherman Block whenever I walked upstreet to the bank. He became a regular alchy, that Ralph Acmovic, always prowling the streets going from beer garden to beer garden. Those ears were *unmistakably* the same ears that got stuck on Marjorie's head; you could have taken them off his big Serbian noggin and pinned them right onto hers."

"I *object!* That's *triple* hearsay," Drew-Morris declared, raising her voice.

Bernie didn't bother to stand.

"*Commonwealth v. Pearl* back in 1907," Bernie directed his comments to the judge, "allows a certain amount of flexibility when it comes to family resemblance. The law presumes that 'likes produce likes.' After all, Your Honor, we asked defendants, but they weren't able to provide us with any baby pictures of Mr. Acmovic to compare them."

"I'll let it in on the basis of *Pearl*," the judge made a checkmark on his notepad. "Let's not take it too far, Bernie. Ears are probably the limit."

"Yes, Your Honor," Bernie said with a respectful nod. "We'll stick to ears."

Drew-Morris threw up her hands. "Next, they'll be comparing petitioner's *bottom* to Ralph Acmovic's," she said.

"Their bottoms were entirely *different*," interjected Edna.

Judge Wendell raised his hand. "Are you through with this witness, Mr. Rossi?" he asked.

"I am, Your Honor," I said, glancing at my co-counsel as if to signal, "I think that's as good as we can do."

"Thank you, Your *Honor*," Drew-Morris said, her voice unable to hide the sarcasm. "I guess *I* get to ask some questions now?" She flipped through her legal pad.

"Now, Mrs. Galovich, how long were you privy to this 'common knowledge' that decedent Ralph Acmovic Senior supposedly fathered Marjorie Radovich?" asked our opponent.

"From the *start*," Edna beamed, directing her attention at Judge Wendell. "I knew that little Marjorie from the day Lil brought her home."

"*Really?*" Drew-Morris said, suddenly interested. "There must have been lots of juicy gossip that a smart lady like you would pick up in a close-knit little town like Swissvale?"

"There certainly *was*," Edna said, squirming in her seat. "Being a housewife and mother wasn't like it is today. We didn't have cars or shopping malls back in those days. We couldn't *help* knowing one another's business. Frankly," she said, batting her eyes at Drew-Morris as if passing along some maternal advice, "I think women were *much* better off back then."

"I'm sure you do," the Philadelphia attorney said with a sugary smile. "So, can you tell Judge Wendell what *other* interesting stories you heard about our petitioner Marjorie Radovich over those fifty-four years? I'm sure a woman like you who's so *important* in the community must have heard *all kinds* of good stuff. Who *else* did people say was the father?"

"Oh sure," Edna said, taking on a confidential tone. "Bastard children weren't accepted too well in towns like Swissvale. It was a shocker for a while. Oh, yes, all kinds of rumors."

"Like what?" prodded the Philadelphia attorney.

Edna leaned toward the judge. "Some people said the baby was *Peg's* daughter if you can believe that!" she said. "They said she had a fling with a priest over at the Slovak church."

"A *priest?*" Drew-Morris said, screwing up her face. "And how did you know *that* story wasn't true?"

"Oh, I *knew*," Edna said, nodding her head until the skin on her face wiggled like pale gelatin. "Peg told me *herself*. Plus, Choppy would have cut off the priest's private parts—pardon my French, Your Honor—if he ever tried to pull any of that stuff with Peg."

"*Damn right*," Choppy grumbled from his seat. A handful of regular court watchers who had wandered into the courtroom after coffee at Bruegger's chuckled appreciatively.

The judge rapped his gavel to put them on notice.

"You have an *excellent* memory for a woman over the age of fifty," Drew-Morris told Edna, who beamed at the compliment. "What *other* stories did you pick up?"

"Oh, they also said that Lil might've got pregnant from one of the foremen down at Carrie Furnace. I think the leading rumor was that Scots-Irish thug named Ross Burns did it. They said Choppy was too weak to do anything 'cause the guy was his boss."

"That story was a *crock*," Choppy said, standing up. "I would've *decked* Ross Burns and then *castrated* him if he touched my daughter."

"Hold on, sir," the judge said, admonishing Choppy. "I know this is an emotional topic, but you've got to maintain decorum in this courtroom."

Drew-Morris tapped her foot, waiting until the disruption was over and Choppy sat down.

"And how did you know *that* story wasn't true, Mrs. Galovich?" she continued.

"Oh, Peg told me *directly* she was relieved the father wasn't an Irish mackerel-eater 'cause they always have pimply skin," she said.

"What about Mr. Burn's *ears*?" Drew Morris said with a smirk. "Did *they* look like the ones on the illegitimate baby?"

"Oh no," Edna said defensively. "His *chin* might have looked like Marjorie's— a lot of the Scots-Irish have that square chin that resembles a block of wood, just like the *Cro-ats*. But I can say *under oath* that his *ears* bore no resemblance," she said firmly.

Our opponent smiled wickedly. "No further questions, Your Honor," she said.

I sank back into my chair. Choppy looked defeated as he clutched onto Aunt Peg's hand and whispered another useless supplication. I knew that Edna's direct examination rendered useless. Our opponent would have a strong case on appeal if Judge Wendell relied on a single word of this self-contradictory testimony.

Bernie pulled me by my jacket and whispered: "Just keep it calm, Shawn-boy. Old lady Galovich was a throwaway. We'll put in a perfect case once our *star* witness gets here."

I drummed my fingers against the counsel table.

"That's never happening," I whispered back. "Haven't you figured that out yet?"

I swept a pile of papers off the table. "We're done with this witness, Your Honor," I said firmly. "We think she's made her evidentiary points quite clearly."

Edna stepped down from the witness bench, blowing me a kiss.

September 2008

MEMORIES OF CHRISTINE

After court recessed, I went back to my office, where I found J.V. still hammering away at her computer. She looked as exhausted as I felt.

"Look, kiddo, you don't need to stick around," I said. "Tomorrow's witness is in good shape. Why don't you go home and lie down? I'll order takeout, so you and Kalvin don't have to cook."

J.V. was anchored behind the desk in her office, twirling her golden Duquesne Law ring with its distinctive red stone, which she said gave her superhuman powers when working on the toughest cases. An oscillating fan blew her red hair in crazy directions, leaving it tangled and her brow sweaty.

She raised one finger to quiet me and maintain her train of thought. "I'm done with it, boss," she said, tapping out a few more words on her keyboard. "If Marjorie doesn't show up tomorrow, our only hope is to get the judge's head in a different place. I've got all the research done—I'll have the memo for you in an hour. There haven't been new cases on this topic for nearly fifty years. But maybe when Dr. Wade takes the stand tomorrow, you can use this to appeal to the judge's better angels. I'll stick around in the courtroom during her direct examination, so if any questions come up, I can scribble down responses for you."

I flopped into the chair in front of J.V.'s desk.

Behind her on the wall was an Obama-Biden poster with a colorful symbol depicting a rising sun and the coming of a new day. I admired the die-hard optimism of these millennials.

"I think we should just subpoena the old nun," I said, feeling drained from fighting a losing battle. "The hell with what the judge says. And to hell with the nuns' vows of silence. If we got the Sister on the stand and made her share everything she knows, we could probably win this rotten case and avoid any more drama."

J.V. pushed aside her laptop. "Are you serious, boss? Calling that nun would be inhumane and immoral."

I massaged my temple with two fingers. "Well, the whole thing has just become so hopeless," I said. "Sometimes, doing what seems unethical under ordinary circumstances—like forcing a nun to testify—can be justified if it achieves a greater good. Can't it?

J.V. stared at me as if stunned. "Is that really *you* talking?" she demanded.

"Well, I'm just saying . . ." is all I could muster.

"Look," said J.V., not even waiting to hear the next words. "My last email exchange with Marjorie sounded more promising. I'm supposed to talk to her later tonight. I think we can get her here."

"Woah!" I said. "I've been thinking more about this, too. I know we've all wanted Marjorie to come in and tell her story. We gave her a hundred opportunities. Now, waltzing in at the last moment could raise more questions than answers. I vote to have her stay in California."

"C'mon, Shawn," J.V. pushed back. "Marjorie's story is powerful. It's the best evidence we have. Can you really live with yourself if we let these people lose their home? If Aunt Peg got wrenched out of there, I'm seriously worried she'd go to some nursing home and die. They invested everything in that little place. We've got to give this our best shot. That's what the Shawn Rossi I know would *usually* tell me to do, or am I missing something?"

"I'd rather win it *without* Marjorie," I said, unwilling to surrender. "Frankly, I don't trust anything she says anymore. We need the nun's testimony. That's more likely to be our winning strategy. That, plus your new legal angle," I pointed at the screen of her computer. "Why don't you just finish up your memo and head home? You've got to get those boys to bed."

J.V. elevated one barefoot and propped it on her desk. It looked purple and swollen, like a balloon with five toes. "I'm not worried about me—I'm more worried about you and *your* kids," she countered. "I haven't been getting a good vibe about this attitude stuff with Liza and how she and Britt are always fighting. Do you ever really *talk* to them, Shawn? You know, have you ever asked them how losing Christine is affecting *them*?"

I exhaled and repositioned myself in the chair. At least I'd gotten J.V. off the topic of Marjorie.

"I talk to them, sure," I said. "But not about that *exact* topic."

"And isn't it good for *you* to talk about it too, boss?" she asked, navigating the subject judiciously. "Have you gone up there to talk to that Spiritan priest at Duquesne, like we discussed? It would help for you to share this with someone."

I could tell from J.V.'s posture that she wasn't going anywhere. There was no avoiding this discussion, so I closed my eyes and counted to ten before allowing the details to come creeping back into my mind.

It had been just before Easter two and a half years earlier, after we'd celebrated our 15th anniversary, when Christine first noticed something odd and went to the doctor. She'd covered up the pain and nausea while hiding colored eggs for Britt and Liza in the backyard as part of our family's Easter tradition. Later, she watched them find the "lucky eggs" containing Sacagawea dollars under the thornless honeylocust trees she'd planted for each girl when they were babies.

When Christine had called the girls into the family room that night to tell them that she'd have to go to the hospital because the doctors had to remove a growth, the girls seemed puzzled.

"Is that like an operation?" Liza had asked.

"Yes, sweetie," Christine had answered, kissing our youngest daughter's head. "It's surgery, so mom may need you two to be her helpers."

The following week, sitting together in the stark surgeon's office at Magee-Women's Hospital, Christine and I had clutched each other's hands and prayed for positive news. Instead, the specialist had announced that Christine had stage 3 ovarian cancer. The fact that the tumor had attached itself to the liver, he'd explained with clinical matter-of-factness, meant that she'd require immediate surgery.

J.V. took a sip from a bottle of flavored seltzer water on her desk and swallowed it slowly. She knew that this was one topic I didn't handle well. So, she trod carefully. "How did the girls react to everything, you know, after Christine was diagnosed?" she asked. "You've never really told me that part."

I loosened my tie and slouched back. I hated going back to that terrible time.

"They were always happy girls back then," I insisted, feeling almost defensive. "Christine loved doing *everything* with them." I started choking up as I looked away. "After Christine got sick, though, it was like little demons came after them."

Liza had spent much of that time drawing pictures of angels with flowing dark hair and freckles on their faces to look just like Christine. She'd surrounded these images with red hearts and pink flowers that nearly burst off the pages with intense swirls and strokes. Britt, for her part, had served her mom hot bullion broth, one of the only foods Christine could hold down.

But, when the chemo caused Christine's hair to fall out and the skin on her head to turn almost black after the cancer started metastasizing to her brain, all the optimistic talk vanished. For the first time, Britt and Liza seemed frightened to enter their mom's room. At night, Christine's deep, scary coughing filled the house with a sense of dark inevitability.

When her doctors transferred Christine to the intensive care unit at Magee-Women's Hospital, where nurses could watch over her, the girls were almost relieved. We'd take turns with Christine's parents to sit with her. Liza would carry her bag of art supplies, and Britt would plug in her earbuds for our daily ten-hour shifts. Whenever Christine drifted into a zone of twilight unable to speak, the girls would talk about tennis matches or the day's events at school, or we'd hum Mary Poppins songs that Christine had sung at bedtime when the girls were little.

Once in a while, Liza would put down her artwork, rub her mom's arm near the IV port, and whisper with 12-year-old determination: "It'll be okay, mom."

Both girls had tried to ignore the tight nylon cap that Christine had to wear when the tumors had started growing.

In the rare moments when someone wasn't checking Christine's pulse or jiggling bags of fluids, I'd scoot my chair close to her and kiss my wife's lips; they felt dry and inert, but there was still a special warmth that passed between us. I'd listen for the little puffs of air to come from her nostrils to make sure she was breathing easily and say, "I love you more than anything in the world, sweetheart," closing my eyes to savor every second of this intensely personal time.

Then one night, after a long period of quiet, the machines had started beeping, and an alarm had sounded. A young Asian doctor had appeared and thrown open the curtain. In one motion, he'd opened Christine's eyelids, waved his flashlight in her eyes, and then clicked it off.

"In Pennsylvania, she's already legally considered deceased," he'd curtly told a nurse. "If they plan to donate the corneas, we'll have to harvest them soon."

Christine's mom had gasped. Britt was asleep and escaped this moment of horror. Unfortunately, Liza was wide awake. She'd pushed her chair away and ran out of the room. I'd followed her, catching my youngest daughter in the hallway. She was only in grade school; I knew this was *way* too intense for a girl her age to handle.

"I thought she'd be *okay*, daddy," Liza had said, choking on the words.

We'd just held each other until a nurse came and told me that this might be the time to say goodbye.

As I finished recounting this story, J.V. wiped a tear from her eye.

Although I'd been in my associate's office many times, for the first time, I noticed how bare, almost shabby it looked. The only thing on her walls was her framed bar admission from the Pennsylvania Supreme Court and her prized degree from Duquesne Law School; J.V. was the first in her family to go to college, let alone earn a professional degree. The sole knickknack on her desk was a yellow duck her kids had given her for Easter that she kept for good luck.

"Hey, pal," I said softly. "It's not fair to make you listen to all of this. Let's talk about something else. Look here. We've gotta get you some new furniture. This stuff's looking pretty ratty. I mean, you've been practicing law for eight years."

J.V. seemed unconcerned about her office. "Listen, boss," she said. "The day we start worrying about our furniture is the day we oughtta stop being lawyers."

"Well . . ." I started to say.

"Honestly, it's good for *all* of us to talk about this stuff," she insisted, looking directly at me with her puffy face. "I mean, we're a family. Right?"

I nodded my head. I had no choice but to continue: After the funeral, Britt and Liza had gone back to school, attending grief counseling to help them deal with their emotions. But I'd stayed away from other people; I couldn't fight the intense feeling of anger and loss. The person I'd always wanted to talk to most whenever something bad happened in my life was Christine. She'd been my first responder in times of distress. Now, this terrible thing had happened, and I desperately wanted to talk to *her* about it. But that conversation was impossible.

The girls had felt the loss even more intensely as the months passed. "The death of a spouse hits the other spouse like a ton of bricks, but it hits the kids one brick at a time," one of the grief counselors had told me. She was right: There was no mom around to help fix Britt's hair for her first high school dance or to watch her sing and dance in her first production of "The Wiz." There was no mom to witness Liza win a prize at the eighth-grade art exhibit for a painting of a blood-red stream with a fish jumping out of the water, its mouth open like it was gasping for air.

And without Christine's second income, the girls' private academy's bills were tougher than I'd expected. It wasn't as if I didn't have some successful cases: I had one significant estate matter on appeal involving hundreds of acres next to the Rolling Rock Club in Ligonier that was worth a fortune. If the appeals court upheld my victory at the trial level, I knew my client (the manager of a chain of banks in that county) would hit the jackpot, and I could take home a million-dollar contingency fee. But the case had gone all the way to the Pennsylvania Supreme Court, which hadn't ruled on it for over a year—not a good sign. I couldn't pay tuition bills and other necessities with fees that might never materialize. The CFO at the academy had been a saint—he'd offered to cut the tuition in half. But I couldn't bring myself to be a charity case. So, I'd explained to Britt and Liza that the academy wasn't an option without their mom's income, and I switched them over to the public school.

My daughters had seemed stunned at first. Liza, especially, complained. "Why don't we just live in Fox Chapel like grandma and grandpa? We could go to a good school district, plus we could belong to their country club and swim and play tennis whenever we wanted. Why do we have to be stuck in Swisshelm Park and go to a ratty public school and crummy places like the Irish Centre just 'cause you grew up here?"

Increasingly, I started to feel plagued by guilt that I'd been horribly selfish for all these years. I'd indulged myself in my own irrational desire to remain in a sub-par neighborhood just because I'd once had a connection here, working at a nondescript little law firm in town, instead of moving to a better community populated by lawyers and dentists or even to a booming metropolis where I could take advantage of more lucrative opportunities for my family. This grand experiment of living a "noble," understated life, I now realized, may have been a delusion. And a total bust.

I especially worried about Liza. She'd started experiencing mild panic attacks, and the doctors were still working on controlling them. And she'd become increasingly introverted: She even refused to go with Britt and me to the cemetery to visit Christine's grave on Mother's Day or Christine's birthday. Instead, she'd stay curled up on the bed in her room, doing sketches that she wouldn't share with us.

When I'd told my ex-law partner Jim Kennedy that I needed to take some time off because I needed to be with the girls, he'd just drummed his fingers against the phone and said: "Look, Shawn, I feel sorry as hell about Christine. We all loved her to pieces. But you may want to re-think this. If you really care about the *firm*, you might want to come back ASAP. We can't afford to slip any more in our billable hours this quarter. Have you seen the receivables?"

Before he'd finished speaking, I'd slammed down the receiver and typed a letter informing him that I was leaving the firm. I'd told him that he could keep our office space and all the clients he wanted except my Ligonier case. Otherwise, I wanted a no-fault divorce from the place. My only stipulation had been that J.V. would come with me to start my new firm. My secretary, Mrs. McNulty, quit and came too. He couldn't have stopped them anyway. I knew I was getting the best of the bargain.

"That was the best decision I ever made in my professional life," I said to J.V., wrenching myself back to the present. "I'd be up a creek without you, pal. And I couldn't survive without *Mrs.* McNulty either. By the way, did I ever tell you I got an email from Marjorie that same day? I'll never forget it. That message kinda freaked me out."

"Seriously, boss? You held back that vital piece of info from me?"

I rose from my chair and walked down the hall to my desk. I pulled open the bottom drawer and lifted the old snow globe—an artifact from the past—that I kept hidden there. Underneath it was a sheet of paper that I removed. I walked in slow motion back to J.V.'s office and finally slid it in front of her.

"Hmmm," she said, skimming the page. "I'd say your Marjorie friend definitely had a conscious *purpose* in sending this." She read the email partly aloud, but I knew every word of it:

Dear Shawn,

I'm deeply sorry for your loss. I know it must be unspeakably difficult for you and your girls. I realize that I haven't been in touch for a long time, so I'm sorry if this seems out of place. But you've always been so kind to Choppy and Peg, and I wanted you to know we all feel your loss. If I can help in any way, even from out here in California, please call or email anytime. Sometimes talking to a friend feels good in these situations, just like holding someone. Please count me among the people you can turn to. For anything. May God's peace be with you and your family.

With love and my deepest sympathy,
Marjorie
P.S. Please ignore my mother's letter to you about handling her case, Shawn. You don't need that headache on top of everything else. I've told her not to bother you about it again.

Even as J.V. read the email, I still didn't reveal to her an additional aspect of this story. It was this: Just a few days after I had received that email from Marjorie, I had been cleaning out the spare room we had set up as Christine's "sick room" during her final illness, going through cards and unopened Mass offerings she had received, and holding her eyeglasses and other personal items in my hand a final time as if they were relics of a saint. When I opened the drawer in the nightstand to put away stray pens and notepaper, I saw an envelope with shaky handwriting on it that I immediately recognized as Christine's. It said: "My Shawn." Inside was a cream-colored notecard. I could barely open it; my hands were shaking so badly. The writing was jagged and uneven but still perfectly legible. My wife had written: "*It will be good for you and the girls for you to find someone else. Never worry there's anything wrong with it, Shawn. I'll be watching from heaven, and it will make me very happy.*"

I had touched Christine's lopsided signature and the tiny, wobbly hearts she had endeavored to draw around it. And I had burst out crying, alone in that space, and couldn't muster the strength to get up and leave for hours.

I couldn't tell J.V. any of this because there was another half of the story: As I had tucked away the private note from Christine and tried to push it out of my mind in the days following its discovery, I had started to feel an odd sensation. I'd suddenly become keenly aware that I was free to talk to, and be with, *other* women, including women who'd been part of my past. I was ashamed of these unnatural emotions. How long had it been since we'd buried Christine—less than a week?

The worst part was, I had begun to wonder if Christine had somehow known that Marjorie was poised to make a reappearance. I'd certainly thought about Marjorie a few times during our marriage and wondered what she had been doing over the past decades. But I had squelched those thoughts immediately because Christine was the love of my life, and Marjorie was in the past and not part of my life's trajectory. Still, had Christine somehow intuited that Marjorie was lurking in my subconscious? If so, this was both horrible and alarming. Did my wife take her last breaths thinking—or knowing—there was already another woman waiting to replace her? That would be too great a burden for me to carry for the rest of my life.

"I hope this email from Marjorie isn't the reason you're freaked out about her testifying," J.V. said. "That isn't interfering in your decision-making for our clients, is it, boss?

"Absolutely not. It's irrelevant," I said, plucking the printed email from her hands and folding it up to return it to my bottom desk drawer. "C'mon, grab your purse and keys, J.V. You're heading home. Doctor's orders. This stuff is nothing but a distraction. I'm going to get ready for our expert witness tomorrow. If you get me your memo in the morning, I'll be armed with the case law and be ready to try out this new theory of yours."

J.V. looked at me skeptically and began packing up her laptop and backpack full of cases and articles to complete her work at home.

"And I don't think you should be calling Marjorie back tonight, pal," I said firmly. "It's too late. You need to put your boys to bed. And it would be a waste of emotional energy that wouldn't be productive for anyone. That ship sailed a long time ago."

J.V. nodded and headed for the door with her gear. I waited until I heard the elevator in the hallway whisking her down to the garage. Then I went to my secretary's desk drawer, pulled out a form subpoena bearing the seal of the Court of Common Pleas, "commanding the below-named person to attend and testify at the stated time and place as set forth below," and filled out the name and address of the 93-year-old nun.

As unfortunate as this was, I concluded, she was the only person who could bring an end to this painful situation.

Fall 1979 (Sand Steps—Swissvale)

AUNT PEG'S FORTUNE

My second year of law school arrived so swiftly I could barely remember having a summer. Fortunately, I'd earned enough money filing probate papers for Tim Mulroy's downtown firm—commuting from my mom and Aunt Kate's place and spending weekends on Choppy and Peg's couch to visit Marjorie—that I could afford to fly home for fall break. Now, I'd managed to sneak in some time with Aunt Peg alone after Marjorie and her mom had left to grocery shop at Giant Eagle. Aunt Peg enjoyed occasional secretive meetings, as did I; she was a font of wise advice.

"Do you two think you're the first ones to have to deal with all this? Is that what's eating away at you kids, Shawn-boy?" Aunt Peg was seated at the kitchen table, holding my chin and examining me like an ailing patient. "God in heaven, this two-career couple thing isn't really new. Has my Marji been acting funny about it again? I know lots of families where the man and woman both had to work, especially in these little mill towns. Lots of times, there was no alternative. Some people didn't survive it, but most did. God wouldn't hand out something as precious as a family without making people work for it. I'm just an old biddy, but that's how I see it."

Aunt Peg was rarely willing to discuss the period of her life during World War II when she had to work full time and leave Lil at home. But on this Saturday afternoon, she'd ushered me into the kitchen and seemed determined to share her recollections along with a strong Slovak coffee and a slice of homemade sweet bread she called Paska.

"I admit it was harder than I imagined," Aunt Peg said. Her grey hair was neatly coifed, having just visited the hairdresser. Her eyes were bright with vitality. "I saw something very few people got to see, Shawn-boy. It may help you kids; that's the only reason I'm telling you. Don't let Choppy know. He's still private about these personal details."

I already knew from my conversations with Choppy, seated in his basement workshop over a few shots and beers, that he'd joined the Army right after the attack on Pearl Harbor. He'd quit his job at Carrie Furnace and left Aunt Peg and their brand-new baby at home so that he could do his part for America. But I'd never exactly known what Aunt Peg had done to survive this upheaval to their family.

"I knew I needed to help to pay for food, clothes, doctors' visits, and all that stuff," she said, looking out the window to make sure Choppy was still watering the sidewalk. "So when I saw an advertisement in The Pittsburgh Press calling for women to apply for jobs in the mill, I took a trolley to Braddock, and I got offered full-time work at the Edgar Thompson mill," she said, lifting her chin with pride.

"I bought a pair 'a steel-toed boots and got a good-paying position unloading coke cars up on a trestle. Can you imagine an old broad like me doing that, Shawn-boy?" Aunt Peg asked, sipping her coffee.

"It's hard to picture you with work boots," I said with a chuckle.

"Plenty of other ladies stepped up, trust me," she said. "My friend Janet Keane joined the YWCA Industrial Girls to earn a paycheck. She was a tough cookie. It wasn't a glamorous life; those flashy pictures of Rosie the Riveter weren't *nothing* like the real daily life, Shawn. But I could operate a sewing machine, so I figured, 'What the hell.' I could handle most of those machines. And I got damn good at it, too."

"My best friend Edna Galovich—you know Edna. She took a job at the War Production B project at the Heinz Plant on the North Side. They converted the whole cereal floor into a place for assembling glider planes. Can you believe that?" Aunt Peg shook her head. "You should've seen Edna when she came home at nights after ten-hour shifts. Her hands were bloody from nailing strips to those glider hulls."

"So, what did you do with the *kids*?" I asked, getting to the key question. "The whole bunch of you had little babies. It seems impossible."

"You had to take your plan about how you were gonna raise your family and toss it out the window," Aunt Peg said matter-of-factly. "It was a whole new deal."

Aunt Peg replenished my coffee from a Pyrex pot. She paused and scratched at her temple as if summoning a distant memory. "We all made do; that's all I can say, Shawn-boy. Some girls took turns with their sisters or cousins—they'd work six months, then watch the house for six months. Some girls left their babies with their neighbors. Everyone treated everyone else like family. That's how it worked. It was a helluva thing. And when Choppy got his leg blown up in that D-Day business, it was tough, I'll admit it," she said with a glance out the window. "He could barely walk. Once he got home, he was laid off for a whole year. He had to make trips to the Veterans Hospital every day. But none of us complained. I hated leaving Lil with so many people to take care of her. I wished I could have done it all myself. But that wasn't in the cards."

Aunt Peg removed a loaf of Town Talk bread from the fridge and knocked it against her countertop to see if it had thawed enough for tuna sandwiches.

"Don't get me wrong," she said, wiping a hand on her apron. "Life in towns like this wasn't always pretty. But when there were problems, we rallied together. There was something about a place like Swissvale that made people watch out for each other. It wasn't just about figuring out what was in it for themselves. There was something *bigger* they cared about."

Aunt Peg put four slices of bread aside. The toaster would thaw them out.

"That doesn't mean we weren't mistreated and disrespected for sticking together in our little communities with our customs and traditions," Aunt Peg quickly added. "Oh yeah, there were people around us who called us all sorts of terrible names—Wops, Dagos, Micks, Polacks, Croats, Krauts, Hunkies. In our household, we never allowed it. When people don't understand you, they tar you with labels that expose their ugliest fears. That comes from ignorance, Shawn. We just stuck together and ignored them. That was part of our secret.

"We all worked together as a community," Aunt Peg said, "no matter what our nationalities or colors or different customs were. It's no good being mean to other people. What the hell does that accomplish? The opposite feels much better.

"Maybe it looked like we were poor bohunks, as some of those fancier people called us. But we had a magical network in place, Shawn-boy," she continued. "Everyone was trained to help each other out in the mills. So, they did the same at home. That's what made it work. It's amazing to think about it now. We helped each other with the cooking, even with the kids' schoolwork. We had close friends and family chipping in without asking. I look back and ask myself—how did we pull it off? Today, you'd have to be a damn millionaire to do all that. That's what Choppy always says, and he's right."

Aunt Peg walked over, staring out the window at the row of Insulbrick-sided homes beside her own, then kissed me on the forehead.

"I'm sharing this secret with you, Shawn-boy, because you're a very special person in our family."

Aunt Peg stared into my eyes as if she could peer into the future with some magical omniscience. "This is between us, okay? Marjorie doesn't need to know about our little talk. But maybe it will help both of you kids. Sometimes, Shawn-boy, you have to settle for *less now* to get *more* in the long haul. Do you understand what I'm saying? I may be an old Slovak lady, but I'm a hundred percent sure on this one."

Aunt Peg wiped her hands on her apron. She looked around, her eyes lighting up as if with a thought. She hustled into the living room, then returned, cradling something. I recognized it immediately: It was the old snow globe that I'd seen on the shelf of their corner cabinet, collecting dust. As Aunt Peg held it up, I could see a big chunk missing from the wooden base. Inside the globe was an array of structures depicting a skyline, unmistakably Pittsburgh, from some time in the past. "Some people never liked it because it has that rusty-looking blast furnace in it, but I think the scene looks beautiful," the old lady said, admiring the glass sphere. "Marji played with it as a girl and dropped it down the basement steps; that's why it's missing a hunk of wood. But I've always kept it. Choppy gave it to me when we were first married."

Aunt Peg held it out. "I want you to have it, Shawn-boy. It will be good to keep it with you when you're up there at Harvard. That way, you can remember what home looks like."

"It's really cool, Aunt Peg," I said. "But I couldn't possibly take it."

"It's yours. *Please.* Everyone keeps trying to pitch it in the trash anyway because it wobbles—even Choppy. I've had to salvage it a dozen times," she insisted. "So it would make me happy if you took it, Shawn-boy. It's fun to stare at it sometimes. You can imagine what comes next."

———

After Marjorie returned from shopping, we went for a walk and took the path to the Sand Steps, ducking under dense sticker bushes and side-stepping poison ivy. It was a good place to find some privacy. The Sand Steps were made of crumbling sand and tiny stones, a form of homemade concrete fashioned a century earlier so men could take a shortcut to the train tracks and mills along the river.

"What were you and Aunt Peg talking about in the kitchen when I got back from Giant Eagle?" Marjorie quizzed me.

"Nothing," I fibbed. "Just catching up. She was showing me some recipes in her Slovak cookbook. I love that Paska."

"You two looked guilty," she said, scrutinizing my face.

"*Watch out,* Rad!" I interrupted, grabbing Marjorie by the arm and pivoting to another topic. "Careful of the rocks. Don't go sliding down the hillside into the river. I didn't come home to see my girlfriend eaten by a giant *carp.*"

I'd forgotten after a year in Massachusetts how beautiful Pittsburgh could look this time of year—a wonderful union of nature's beauty and the steel mills' impenetrable strength.

The smell of Pittsburgh in the fall was more than just the odor of decaying leaves. It was a sweet, woodsy, intoxicating aroma from a mingling of decaying bark, acorns, and crab apples that smelled like fresh bottles of cider. In the backyards, vegetable gardens of eggplants, zucchini, spaghetti squashes, and tomatoes emitted an aromatic, basil-like odor into the wind, bringing all of these olfactory pleasures together like a grand outdoor banquet.

Just over the hillside from the Sand Steps, the Monongahela River seemed to be searching for a new rhythm. It was no longer a place for summer pleasure craft with men and women casting for carp or river bass near the bend at Skeetersville.

Instead, coal barges and tugboats pushing supplies into the mills were the river's sole occupants. During the Homestead Steel Strike in 1892, the Pennsylvania militia had camped here on the hillside because it provided a sweeping vista from which to observe the entire valley below.

Since Marjorie's mother was laid off from the Switch—again—this spot over the river was the best place to find some privacy and absorb its breathtaking views.

We pushed our way through mountain laurel into a clearing where old-timers had hauled up discarded railroad ties to construct a bench where they could sit and have a leisurely smoke or chew.

"If I ever die prematurely," Marjorie said, as we slid into our secret spot, "I want Nied's Funeral Home to bury my body down here with a poster of Jimi Hendrix to remind me of you." She lay back in a pile of leaves. Her overalls and Dickie jacket crunched against the lush mountain laurel bushes.

"If you die prematurely," I said, allowing myself to savor the autumn air, "forget about Hendrix. I'm diving into the hole with you."

Marjorie laughed at this self-serving pledge of fidelity. We'd long since patched up our misunderstanding from Christmas break of the previous year. Marjorie seemed playful and passionate about our relationship again, especially when we could be together without her mother hovering around us. But she became more serious whenever we dipped our toes, cautiously, into the topic of the next step in our relationship.

The U.S. Steel Homestead Works, which took up the entire bank across the river, glowed like a red flare, even though it was still mid-afternoon. This huge mill was the same one where Marjorie's great-grandfather had worked 70-hour shifts. These days, it was in trouble due to foreign competition and predictions of another recession. Already, General Motors had cut production of its pickup trucks in Michigan. But the Homestead works, refusing to admit defeat, kept churning out liquid steel in its open hearths to be poured into giant ingots that could be shaped and melted into a thousand indestructible products.

"So, let's forget about the two-people-working thing for now," I said, flinging a handful of leaves at Marjorie's hair. "What do you think is the optimal number of kids, Rad? Not having brothers and sisters was a bummer for both of us. I'm in favor of a ton of them."

"No more than three," she said, shaking out the leaves. Her blonde hair was particularly beautiful in the faint sunlight. "And don't think there's going to be a lot of practice sessions, okay? This is purely business."

"How about we compromise on four kids and a monkey like the Becks," I said, suddenly enthralled with the idea of adding a monkey.

A collection of yellow and red leaves skipped like artwork along the riverbank.

Marjorie placed a hand on my chest and whisked a bug off my Harvard zip-up jacket.

"Wow! This is something new, Shawn," she said, pointing. "You're actually wearing some Ivy League gear. That's a breakthrough!"

"It's practical, Rad," I said. "Check it out. It's waterproof. It can double as a rain jacket."

She let her finger sketch around the "H" stitched onto the pocket.

"After I start my master's," she said, "I want to figure out what's next for *me* so I can feel a sense of accomplishment, too. You've pulled it off, Shawn. My nerd friends in the CS department are gaga when I tell them you go to Harvard Law. I wanna do something *just* as important. So, decisions about having a family are going to take into account my career. I feel I've got to make something of myself. I mean, Choppy and Aunt Peg can't take care of my mother *and me* forever."

I unzipped the jacket and put it over her shoulders. "I'll make enough money that you can do whatever you want, Rad. I never thought we were the kind of people these things happened to. But it's true. So, dream big. Your career can be whatever's important to you. That's what I want to help you achieve, okay?"

Marjorie stared downward at the glowing sheds of the mill.

"We'll both achieve it *together*," she corrected me. "For now," she continued, "let's concentrate on you getting back here soon, so we don't have to keep putting our lives on hold. How about that one?"

A maple tree's "helicopter" seed twirled through the air and fell between us.

"I'm working on it," I said, doing a head-fake, then kissing her directly on her lips. "This firm where I'm working could be the ticket. They like my work. They've even let me do some wills. It's technically illegal to practice law until I pass the bar, but Tim Mulroy lets me do it and signs off on everything. He says once you sit down with people at their kitchen tables and help them out, you understand what practicing law is about. I enjoy that feeling, Rad."

She patted my hand. "They like my work at Respironics, too," she said. "They're paying me to write programs, and my boss says that this could lead to bigger projects. Maybe we have something going here, after all, Shawn. It's like we've got a Pittsburgh plan going on. I wasn't sure that was possible."

"Of course, it's possible," I said, waving away the notion. "It is our destiny." I kissed her again, longer this time.

"Hey Rad," I continued, squeezing my eyes closed tightly. "Did you ever wonder what makes a place like Pittsburgh, *Pittsburgh*? Seriously. What would poets like Carl Sandburg or this new guy August Wilson say if they tried to capture the *essence* of Pittsburgh in words? I'll bet they couldn't do it."

Marjorie lay back, a perplexed look on her face as if this was a silly question. "You mean Isaly's chipped ham? Heinz ketchup?"

"Not just the things you *eat*, Rad," I corrected her. "I'm talking about the *intangible* things that most people can't see unless they really know Pittsburgh."

"Geez, Shawn." A look of puzzlement crept over my girlfriend's face. "I always thought most cities are pretty much the same when it comes down to basics, aren't they?"

"You're kidding me, right?" I sat upright. "Maybe it's because I've been away that I can see it so clearly. Pittsburgh is a way of living, not just a place. That's what makes it so cool."

"I guess so," Marjorie said again, surveying the scene along the river as if searching for the thing I was describing. "I still think chipped ham is a key part of our identity."

I pinched her arm. She was a smart aleck.

"Yeah, well, I'm gonna save up all that material and write a poem about '*Pittsburgh in the Fall*' someday," I said. When I pulled Marjorie against me, leaves stuck to us as if we'd created a magnetic force field. Across the river, the sky was thickening over the steel mill, and the late afternoon fall air was becoming chillier. "I'll capture this whole scene—Joe Magarac's entire empire—so future historians will understand why people like us could never leave. I won't screw things up, Rad. I'll give you everything you can see from this spot in every direction. . . ."

I took her hands in mine. "All you have to do is put up with two more years of me being gone. Then I promise—I'll give you all of this and even more."

She looked at me. "That's really sweet, Shawn," she said.

But as I walked her home and said my final goodbye before heading back to Boston, I thought I saw a look of hesitation in my girlfriend's eyes.

September 2008 (Courtroom)

FILIUS NULIUS (CHILD OF NOBODY)

J.V. hustled into the courtroom ten minutes before our starting time, moving as quickly as possible in her extra-large maternity suit. "Here's the memo, Shawn," she said, catching her breath. "I finally spoke with Marjorie after midnight. She's getting on a plane this morning. We'll have to drag this out till she gets here."

"She's coming now?" I smacked my hand against the table. "I thought I told you not to call her, J.V.! This timing is a day late and a dime short. We're in a position to wrap things up quickly. I already got a process server to serve a subpoena on Sister Benedict. He said he can get her here in a couple of days once the nurses in the motherhouse clear her for travel. We have the legal power to do it. I've had enough of Marjorie's playing games with us."

Bernie jumped up, squeezing himself between us. "Marjorie's coming? That's *great!*" he said, clapping my back. "It's what we've been waiting for, right? What's *bugging* you all of a sudden, Shawn?"

"Look," I said, becoming irritated. "I really don't want to see that woman, okay? Are you having trouble understanding that simple point for some reason?"

"I told her about Choppy and Peg's house being up for sheriff's sale," J.V. blurted out. "It's on me. I couldn't let them lose everything they've worked for without giving Marjorie a chance to fix it. Fire me if you want, Shawn. She needed to know."

I was unable to move. A wave of conflicting emotions overwhelmed me. Finally, I said something I hadn't planned: "I'm *quitting.*"

"What?"

"I didn't think she was really coming. So, I never really thought about what that would feel like. I'm withdrawing from this case now, capiche?"

Bernie grabbed me by the tie. He pulled me to his face. "Are you cracking up on me, man? We still have a shot here. You're not authorized to quit."

I shook him off me.

"J.V. can handle the next witness," I said calmly. "Then do what you want with Marjorie." I poked a finger back in Bernie's chest. "'Cause I'm out of here."

"Are you freaking out here, boss?" J.V. demanded. "You've got that crazy look in your eyes."

"No, I'm not freaking out," I snapped. "This is just too much to handle. So, I'm bailing. You're a moot court champ. You know the case. You can deal with the witness, counselor."

The judge's deputy clerk, Jimmy, had entered the courtroom. Today, he was wearing a double-breasted suit with wide lapels. He began straightening papers on the judge's bench. "We'll be ready in five," Jimmy said, looking down on our huddle. "Judge likes to be prompt."

J.V. threw her bag under the counsel table; two coloring books spilled out. Tears welled up in her eyes. I couldn't tell if it was because our little team was falling apart or because I'd been too sharp with her or because I asked her to take over the questioning of a major witness without any advance warning—or maybe all those things.

"Don't be so hard on Marjorie," J.V. whispered, staring me in the eye. "It's not right, Shawn. We had a woman-to-woman talk last night. There's a lot going on here. I can't share everything with you. And I don't pretend to know everything. But trust me. There's a good reason she hasn't wanted to come."

"She *always* has a reason," I shot back, not even bothering to lower my voice.

"She signed on as a petitioner because it meant so much to her family," J.V. continued, still staring me down. "She figured the case would settle, and she'd never have to testify under oath. There are some things, uhm, she doesn't want to have to answer on the stand. And she's put other plans in motion to spend more time with Choppy and Peg. When I told her about the sheriff's sale, though, she dropped everything and sped things up. You should give her credit for that, Shawn."

I stared at J.V., then at Bernie, and swept my papers off the counsel table. "I'll sit in the back," I said, unwavering. "You're handling this witness, J.V. Then we'll figure out how I can withdraw without screwing things up any worse than they already are."

———

Our witness, Dr. Emma Wade, was a 5-foot-11-inch woman with a Ph.D. in psychology. She had short-cropped hair complemented by large dangling earrings and a high forehead with a look of erudition. At age fifty-four, Dr. Wade was the senior psychologist at South Side Hospital, the first Black woman to achieve that distinction. She picked up her water glass and took a dignified sip.

"I'm satisfied that the witness is qualified as an expert," the judge said. "Let's get on with the questioning. I understand that Ms. Vascov will be handling this witness. She's well known by this court as an able and experienced attorney. Welcome, Ms. Vascov. Let's proceed with direct examination. My wife has me drinking decaf these days, and I get fidgety without the high-test stuff."

"Yes, Your Honor. I'll mark Dr. Wade's CV as Petitioner's Exhibit F," J.V. started to say before the judge chimed in with: "So admitted. Jimmy, slap a sticker on it so that it doesn't get lost like every other damn thing around here."

Bernie patted J.V.'s hand. She got up, tugged the coat of her maternity suit over her belly, and waddled tentatively toward the witness box.

"Based upon your twenty-six years of experience in the field of clinical psychology, Dr. Wade," J.V. began her questioning, glancing back at Bernie and purposely ignoring me, "can you tell the court what impact growing up as a child born out of wedlock might have on an individual like Marjorie Radovich in a mill town like Swissvale during the relevant time period?"

The witness rocked back, totally at ease. This was her hundredth-plus appearance in Orphan's Court. "It's a complex question, but I'll do my best," she said.

"It's my opinion within a reasonable degree of scientific certainty," Dr. Wade continued by using the magic language necessary to constitute a valid expert opinion, "that growing up as a child born out of wedlock in the 1950s or '60s, whether in Pittsburgh or elsewhere—but especially in the context of a blue-collar environment like Swissvale—could cause an individual to suffer serious psychological trauma that might actually exceed the pain endured from long-term physical abuse."

"*Worse* than a physical beating, you're saying?" J.V. asked, following up neatly on the prior answer.

"Absolutely," the doctor said, rubbing her palm with a thumb as if assessing how to drive home her point. "We tend to think of single parenthood and unwed motherhood as unremarkable conditions today because they've become so prevalent in our society. We're desensitized because the United States Supreme Court eventually banned these harsh laws against so-called illegitimates in *Trimble v. Gordon* back in the 1970s, forcing legislators to remove the stigma associated with these births. That's why so many people today don't have a clue how horrible it was. However, the facts are irrefutable. Forty or fifty years ago—especially in an ethnic, deeply religious community like Swissvale or any similar mill town in Pittsburgh—bastardy was a black mark for life, not unlike having a clubfoot or being born a Negro."

Judge Wendell lifted his head.

The psychologist's words matched those we'd rehearsed a month earlier in my office when she'd graciously agreed to a pre-trial session at a discounted rate of $400 per hour. She had a remarkable memory.

"And can you explain to the court, Dr. Wade, what *causes* this sort of psychological trauma from a medical standpoint?" J.V. asked.

Dr. Wade stretched back in her chair like a pole-vault athlete mentally preparing for a challenging hurdle.

"It's as old as humankind itself," she said, her eyes flickering with swift, elevated thoughts. "Society has a ruthless self-interest in ensuring that children are born within certain institutional structures—stable families that tow the societal line. The birth of children who didn't fit neatly into the societal machinery was punished in many different ways. Babies born out of wedlock came to be viewed as sins transformed into flesh . . . *irregulars ex defectu*."

Judge Wendell opened his eyes wide as if readying to ask a question.

"*Irregulares ex defectu*, Your Honor. Loosely translated from Latin, it means 'the deviant product of an irregular sexual union.'" Dr. Wade rubbed her temple as if stimulating the flow of blood to her brain. "It's nothing new at all. From the earliest days, societies enacted laws to discourage bastardy. The Christian church doubled down on it. Unwed mothers occupied the bottom of the darkest barrel in society. It wasn't uncommon for convents to build 'tours,' which were round boxes that spun around on an axis nailed to a door"—Dr. Wade made a sweeping motion to demonstrate the rotation—"so that a bastard baby could be delivered to the nunnery anonymously rather than drowned in a sack."

"In a sack?" J.V. asked, driving the point home.

"Yes, that was the preferred method," the doctor said. "Infanticide became commonplace in many cultures. In my professional practice here in Pittsburgh, I saw many Polish peasant women who'd come here from the old country and faced brutal choices when they got pregnant out of wedlock. These ladies were mentally tortured by it. The ones who did the unthinkable were forever haunted by the superstition that their drowned babies became evil spirits, *topczyki*, who'd poison their food, seep into the water they drank and appear as ugly visions at night."

Aunt Peg stirred uncomfortably in her wheelchair at this word from a distant lexicon. There were several green plastic ports taped to her arm for "meds." She picked away at them, attempting to peel off the white tape.

"And the law?" J.V. asked, easing back toward the counsel table to take a sip of water. "Did the legal system itself disfavor children born out of wedlock in any separate way, I mean, as a historical matter?"

Dr. Wade exhaled as if to say, "how many hundreds of ways do you want me to list?"

"Of course," she said. "Going back to English law, these children, after they became adults, were barred from holding public office or appearing as witnesses in court. They couldn't even be buried next to so-called 'respectable' citizens. Their bodies were given to medical schools to be dissected by students. Even in recent times, they were blocked from meaningful societal participation, including the ability to acquire and transfer property. Should I go on?"

J.V. leaned up against the corner of the counsel table. She kept one hand on her belly as if to hold back the baby from trying to be born during the direct examination. "This tradition of using the law to disfavor children born out of wedlock, doctor, would that have any *long-term* impact on the child as she grew into adulthood?" J.V. pressed her.

Dr. Wade pushed her thumb against her palm, thinking.

"That's an *understatement*," the doctor finally said. "Studies have identified *significant* adjustment problems when these children grow into adolescence. They consistently made poorer showings than their so-called legitimate counterparts when it came to IQ, academic grades, truancy, teacher ratings, the whole gamut. As the babies born out of wedlock grew older, they were apt to internalize their inferior status, making the psychic catastrophe even worse."

"And what about the *mothers* of these children?" J.V. asked with a glance at our client. Lil had slumped down in her chair as if to obscure her location.

It struck me that J.V. wasn't much younger than Drew-Morris. She just wasn't as full of herself. That quality made her even more effective.

"Well, until recently, when society was gradually forced to change its thinking on this matter, giving birth out of wedlock was considered a result of familial ignorance," Dr. Wade said. "Low moral ideals. In some cases, mental abnormality. Consequently, some families disowned daughters who brought this shame upon them. Others attempted to hide the babies or put them up for adoption, which produced its own set of devastating psychological problems. Basically, it was a train wreck for the mother *and* baby."

J.V. scratched her chin, which had an extra layer of baby fat on it. "Train wreck?"

"Yes, and it amounted to the preservation of a caste system," the doctor added. "In this instance, the male was viewed as the superior creature; the unwed female and her so-called illegitimate child were treated as lineally irrelevant, wiping them off the map. It was brutal but quite effective."

J.V. moved in for the kill, going directly to the heart of the case. "And was this linked to the ability of so-called bastard children to inherit property from their biological parents?"

"Very directly," Dr. Wade said, leaning back to formulate her thoughts. "Male dominance, especially within the ranks of state legislatures, assured that property would travel through the *father* of unwed children. The unwed mother and the bastard child were cut out of the loop. Because the bastard child was considered *filius nullius*—child of nobody—he or she wasn't allowed to inherit property from the male line except in rare circumstances. The father walked away scot-free, continuing to plant his seed wherever he wanted, often impregnating other unmarried women or reappearing with a wife and 'legitimate' children somewhere else. Very cruel but, as I say, effective. And tragically, those old rules still apply to wills and trusts created under the old system before the courts banned them. It's unfair and reprehensible, but most state legislatures—even as we stand here in a new millennium—have *still* failed to correct this injustice, probably *intentionally.*"

"So, doctor," J.V. said, positioning herself in front of Marjorie's grandparents for maximum effect. "As a *policy* matter, if an individual like petitioner Marjorie Radovich is the biological daughter of a decedent who owned significant property in the form of a trust fund—"

"That's a blatant leading question," Drew-Morris said, standing up.

"Is there a compelling policy reason," J.V. spoke directly over our opposing counsel, "in *favor* of finding a *judicial* remedy to permit the daughter and unwed mother to inherit from the man who abandoned them?"

Drew-Morris got within a foot of J.V., jabbing her finger in the air. "It's a *loaded* question, judge. It's like asking when you stopped beating your wife."

"Please, let's not encroach on Ms. Vascov's space," the judge said, raising an eyebrow as if afraid Drew-Morris would bump into J.V. and set the birthing process into motion. "I tend to allow latitude in non-jury trials." He nodded deferentially to J.V. "We're always interested in what experts have to say. I'll take it with the appropriate grain of judicial salt."

Dr. Wade sat up in her seat, unruffled, her athletic frame establishing a sudden command of the courtroom. "It's my opinion as an expert with twenty-six years' worth of experience in this field that this is *exactly* why we have courts," she said authoritatively. "If there's substantial evidence that an individual like Mrs. Radovich is the biological child of the decedent, it becomes a legal *and* moral issue. Justice Thurgood Marshall famously said that the only way to eliminate discrimination is to search it out and get rid of it, 'root and branch.' The child born out of wedlock and her mother should receive a fair portion of the estate, *regardless* of the old, unconscionable rules. They've both suffered and paid, in my opinion, *a thousand times* over for whatever monetary compensation the court might give them."

"No further questions, Your Honor," J.V. said. She had completed the direct examination masterfully. A surge of pride welled up inside of me, but my ego prevented me from making any sign toward her. I still wanted to sulk for a while.

J.V. sat down with a self-effacing bow toward the court. "Well done, Ms. Vascov," the judge stated for the benefit of the court reporter. "I wish every lawyer was as efficient and skillful in my courtroom."

"*I* have some questions, Your Honor," Drew-Morris interrupted, her voice suddenly tense. She clearly didn't like J.V. getting this attention. "There are *laws* that are supposed to apply in the courts of this Commonwealth," she said, folding her hands. "Nothing I heard from my opposing counsel changed the applicable precedent unless my hearing is going bad."

Judge Wendell raised an eyebrow. He made a brief note on a piece of paper; a dignified smile appeared on his lips.

"So, *Doctor* Wade." Drew-Morris stepped forward but kept a distance from the witness. "Isn't it true that the laws dealing with bastardy, dating back as far as you want to go, were intentionally designed to foster societal stability? Or are you *opposed* to protecting the institution of the family, ma'am?" Drew-Morris said it in one breath before Dr. Wade could speak.

The psychologist extended to her full height like an umbrella opening to ward off a downpour. "I'd say that bastardy laws were a convenient way for society to sweep its sins under the rug," she responded, without missing a beat. "It threw the unwed mother and her child to the dogs while the father blissfully went along siring more offspring." She glanced at Ralph Jr. and rolled her eyes. "If you call that protecting the institution of family, I suppose it does."

"Now," Drew-Morris's voice became tougher. "You're a scientist, so let's talk about your underlying assumptions. Would your opinion be different, *doctor*, if our petitioner, in this case, *couldn't* prove with a reasonable degree of scientific certainty that she was the illegitimate child of the decedent?"

Dr. Wade searched her mind as if replaying the questions and answers that we'd rehearsed in my office.

"Of course, that might change my opinion," she answered calmly.

"And do you have access to any evidence as you sit here, Dr. Wade, that establishes petitioner Marjorie Radovich is—in fact—the illegitimate child of decedent Ralph Acmovic, Senior?"

"I object to the repeated use of the word 'illegitimate' by opposing counsel," J.V. stated loudly, standing up. "This term is pejorative and demeaning. It's precisely the type of harmful stereotyping that's damaged this family and others like them. There's nothing *illegitimate* about my client or any other person just because they were born out of wedlock." J.V.'s voice was quivering.

The judge scratched his sideburn, appearing troubled. "You make a good point, Ms. Vascov," he said. "While I may agree with you, as a matter of personal opinion, that the word 'non-marital' would be more appropriate, the old legal cases themselves use that term 'illegitimate,' so I'll have to let it stand. Overruled."

Drew-Morris shot J.V. a cocky smile. "You can now answer the question, Dr. Wade," she directed. "Do you have any such evidence that Marjorie Radovich is the illegitimate child of the decedent?"

"No, I'd assumed for purposes of rendering my professional opinion that such a fact could be established." Dr. Wade glanced uncomfortably at Bernie and me. "If that's not the case, obviously, I can't render a fully valid opinion."

"And, Dr. Wade, did you know that the birth certificate in this case specifically indicates that the identity of the father of Marjorie Radovich was *unknown* to her mother?" Drew-Morris moved in for the kill.

Dr. Wade halted. "No, I can't say that I'm aware. . . ."

"Or that Ms. Radovich has not even shown up to testify on behalf of her own mother's case?" Drew-Morris continued.

"*Objection*, Your Honor, nobody said Ms. Radovich isn't coming," J.V. interrupted.

"Thank you, Dr. Wade. No further questions," Drew-Morris announced.

I remained frozen in my chair in the back of the courtroom. I'd known this was a big risk. After that damning birth certificate had come to light, I hadn't been in favor of calling Dr. Wade as a witness without Marjorie testifying first. I'd warned Bernie that this move could backfire.

Drew-Morris approached the bench, stating loudly for the court reporter, "Your Honor, Petitioner has *utterly* failed to demonstrate paternity by clear and convincing evidence. On top of that, it's irrelevant what Dr. Wade says in terms of her personal opinion. The old rules relating to the rights of *illegitimate* children and their mothers still govern trusts created back in this time period. The Pennsylvania legislature, in its wisdom, has never seen fit to invalidate prior case law. Whatever Dr. Wade chooses to opine, it doesn't change the fact that petitioners' case falls apart as a legal matter."

Judge Wendell stared beseechingly at J.V. and Bernie.

"I certainly feel some sympathy for the petitioner and her family," the judge said while straightening his black robe. "But I'm hung up on this point raised by our *distinguished, ahem,* counsel from Philadelphia. Doesn't the whole house of cards fall if you can't prove paternity by clear and convincing evidence, Mr. Milanovich? Ms. Vascov? Dr. Wade's the best in the business. But none of us can snap our fingers and change the case law. What about these old rules that still apply? I don't make the laws; I just enforce them. How can I explain this to the Superior Court if I can't even point to a single case?"

Bernie looked at J.V. as if begging for help. J.V. slowly rose to her feet, holding on to the edge of the counsel table for support.

"The authority is there, Your Honor," J.V. said, pulling out the brief she had completed the night before and handing it to the judge's clerk. "If you read this memorandum, Your Honor, you'll see that early cases going back to the creation of Orphan's Court give you a certain amount of *inherent* power when it comes to evaluating the *equities of a case.* This equity power can *supersede* the other precedent."

Judge Wendell flipped through the brief and puffed out his cheeks as if thinking intently.

"We recognize that the intentions of the deceased ordinarily govern," J.V. continued. "But what about the *living?* What if they were *ruined* by the acts of a decedent who's no longer around to pay the price? That's exactly what these equity cases talk about." Thick lines appeared on Judge Wendell's forehead as J.V. continued. "What about the *girl?* What about the family who never got a dime from this man who preyed on young, vulnerable girls? You heard what Dr. Wade said.

"Lilian Radovich missed out on child support and college tuition for her daughter all those years," J.V. continued, pressing the point harder. "Multiply that out for 21 years, and it's a fortune that Acmovic trust owes her. Plus, Lilian was robbed of a chance to have her own career because she devoted herself to raising a child without a father, which she did at great cost, financially and emotionally. When you tack on psychological scars left on the child and everything she's endured even into adulthood, the damages can't even be measured. If you awarded this entire trust fund to these people, it wouldn't be enough, Judge."

J.V. pushed the red hair out of her face. She was sweating, now. I started to worry that this emotional plea might be taking a physical toll on her.

"Think about your *own* experiences, Judge," J.V. concluded nearly inaudibly. "Remember what Dr. Wade just said. Unless you cut off this sort of discriminatory conduct—*root and branch*—the cancer of these injustices will keep eating away at our system of justice *forever*. This is Orphan's Court, Judge. You can do something different here. Fairness and equity matter in this place more than anywhere else in our court system. Thank heavens that's true."

Judge Wendell looked around the courtroom. He seemed to be examining the place that had been his judicial domain for twenty-one years. He stared at Aunt Peg in her wheelchair, her chin slumped against her shoulder, a slow, thin drool escaping from her lips. His eyes next moved toward Choppy, whose tongue was trying desperately to conceal a chew that he'd snuck into his lower lip to calm his nerves.

Drew-Morris clicked her gold pen, one, two, three times, obviously losing her patience. The judge inhaled, his breath rattling deep in his lungs. "I'll have my clerk pull some of these old cases dealing with equity so I can review them before the weekend," he said. He glanced at J.V. and Bernie, then at me, a tentative look in his eyes. Finally, he muttered, "Proceeding adjourned." The judge then smoothed out his robes one last time and made a beeline toward his chambers, searching for a pack of Kents.

Bernie whispered congratulations to J.V. for a compelling closing. I couldn't hold myself back. I got up, put aside my pride, and rushed up to the counsel table. I threw my arm around my co-counsel and hugged her. "I knew you could outperform Drew-Morris," I said, almost boasting. "You're a far better lawyer than she is. I knew that all along, mainly because you understand this isn't about *you*, it's about your clients."

J.V. looked spent. I was still worried about my associate. Her face was so red and puffy it didn't look healthy. She pulled a juice box out of her bag and stuck a straw into it to get a fix of natural sugar.

"I'm really proud of you, pal," I said, kissing her sweaty cheek.

J.V. looked up, her eyes cloudy with exhaustion, and took a slurp of her juice box.

"Does that mean you're sticking with the case?" she asked, sounding tired. "You need to do it, Shawn. Even after she shows up."

Fall 1979 (Second Year Law School, Somerville)

MARJORIE'S NEW ENGLAND VISIT

Our house on Ivaloo Street in Somerville—where Dobbs, Stick, and I moved in as roommates during our second year—probably should have been condemned by the Somerville Health Department. However, our rent was much cheaper than separate apartments, so that was good enough.

Marjorie sprawled out on the bed, giggling as if she'd eaten some silly pills. "Did I ever tell you I want you to father my children, Shawn?" she asked. I'd surprised Marjorie by sending her a last-minute plane ticket on a "super getaway sale" from US Airways, the new airline in Pittsburgh. Even though it had only been a few weeks since my visit, my yearning for private time together had grown even more intense. And we still had important things to discuss.

"Hey, guys," I said to Dobbs and Stick as they tried to peek in the door. "Can we have a little *privacy*? We need to take a nap." Stick's hair had been trimmed over the summer and grew out in neat layers, making him look like Paul McCartney. Dobbs stood on his tiptoes to look over Stick's shoulder.

"Sorry, Rosey, we can't help ourselves," Dobbs said non-apologetically, blowing a kiss toward Marjorie. "Why didn't you bring this goddess to visit us sooner? When you said she was beautiful, I didn't know you were understating it. This woman could be a model."

The truth was, I was happy that my roommates and girlfriend seemed to hit it off so well. But this was no time for Dobbs to fraternize. I grabbed the doorknob and thrust the door outward, causing it to pop Dobbs in the nose before closing it. I could hear him and Stick retreating into the living room to play Nerf basketball and try to eavesdrop.

Marjorie loosened her golf shirt emblazoned with "Pitt Computer Club— FORTRAN Queen."

"Hand me another Black Russian?" she asked.

"Whoa—slow down, Rad," I said. "We have all weekend. Drink some coffee first."

"I'm on *va-ca-shin*, buddy," she said. "I wanna have *fun* with my boyfriend."

"I know," I said, stroking her hair. "But you don't want to burn yourself out the first day. I want you to see *everything* in Boston."

"Sure, sure, sure," she said. "*Hey*, Shawn, how's that woman doing? You know—*her*. The one who drove you home that first Christmas?" Marjorie squinted at me. "You said she was having some health issues?"

"Erica Welles? I barely see her," I said. "Yeah, she's had some problems. Let's talk about something else."

Marjorie had become limp in my arms. "Put on *Harbor Lights*, 'kay Shawn?" she asked. "That song makes me wanna spend a week on a tropical beach with you. Whad'ya say?"

I cued up Boz Scaggs and stared at my girlfriend, who had clearly downed too many Black Russians.

"That would be the best week of my life, Rad," I said.

She sat up on one elbow.

"So whaddya think about moving to the West Coast?" she asked, squinting as she tried to focus on me. "There's plenty'a beaches there." I could tell she was in a hyper-emotional state from the way she was slurring her words.

"The *West* Coast? Jeez, Rad, I don't know. Is this a test or something?"

"Be honest, Shawn," she said. "It would probably be *terrible* for you, wouldn't it?"

"But just a few weeks ago, you were talking about our Pittsburgh plan," I said. "This is getting me confused."

Marjorie hung over the bed and plucked a pack of Newports from her purse. "That was what I *thought* made sense," she said, tapping a cigarette out of the corner of the pack, then slowly clicking the button of a disposable lighter while eyeing me for a reaction.

"When did you start smoking, Rad?" I asked. "It'll wreck your health. I'm quitting chewing. Tobacco of all kinds is bad news. Just look at your mom."

She winced at the mention of her mother, then inhaled deeply. "I only do it to relax," she said, taking another drag. "I'll be fine after one."

I toyed with the clear-green disposable lighter, flipping it upside down to watch the swishing fluid. As I stared at the liquid, I wondered what caused this abrupt change in Marjorie's thinking and behavior—and why she felt she had to relax. But I had to tread carefully.

"I started thinking about it after you left," Marjorie continued, gauging my reaction with one eye. "I'm just not sure it *really* makes sense for us to stick around in Pittsburgh, that's all, Shawn," Marjorie said, blowing smoke toward the ceiling. "Most people our age aren't stagnating in dying mill towns. They're moving to *growth* areas like Miami or San Fran. That's what Doc Cliff keeps telling me. *God*, he's the coolest advisor ever. He received *three* grants for over a hundred million—did I tell you that? He's a *genius* in artificial intelligence. He says the job market on the West Coast is going bananas. They're making microprocessor chips and integrated circuits out there. After I get my master's, maybe Choppy and Aunt Peg can take care of my mom for a couple of years and give us a little break so we can head out to the West Coast. Wouldn't that be a fun idea?"

I shrugged. "I've been telling the people at Mulroy and Kennedy that I'm interested in coming back to the Burgh and maybe working for them. I'll have to rethink things."

"I thought you were supposed to be *flexible,* dude," Marjorie said, holding my face in both hands as if better to butter me up. "I've been looking at all angles since you came home. Remember what you said? You told me to dream big. Anyway, where does that old plan leave *me* if we split up and I get stranded in Pittsburgh? My mother's been laid off for *five months*. I could get trapped in Swissvale, looking after her with nowhere to go. I have to look out for *myself*, okay?"

"Your mom will pull it together," I said. "We'll make enough to help her out."

Marjorie threw up her hands. "God, Shawn, you're so non-judgmental and nice to everyone it's *ridiculous*. Can't you admit my mother is a head case?"

"I'm okay with her," I put my hand on my girlfriend's shoulder. "She produced a great daughter, right?"

"That's nice of you to say *now*," Marjorie countered, her eyes glazed from too much Kahlúa and vodka. "But what happens when you have big-time options, and you don't feel like being saddled with my family? That's what my graduate liaison told me to be careful of when I met with her last week. We've been lookin' out for *you* for the past three years, buddy. Can't we think about *me* now, too?"

"If you wanna go somewhere else for a while," I said, "I'm totally good with that, Rad. But couldn't you look at something in Philly or Cleveland that isn't on the other side of the continent?"

Marjorie shook another cigarette out of its pack. "I know your mom doesn't get to see you much. If she thinks you need to move back, just *tell* me, Shawn."

I turned back to Marjorie. "C'mon, that's isn't fair. Mom hasn't said a *word* about this," I countered. "Let's focus on where *we* think we should be."

"There are *airports,* Shawn," Marjorie said, fanning her face as if to get more oxygen to her brain. "Wouldn't it be good for *both* of us if we got a fresh start?"

Under my bed, I could hear Walter thrashing his scaly feet against his plastic tub, trying to find a good position. This turtle had no sense of propriety; he made a racket at the least opportune times.

"Yeah, I'm open to that," I said while putting my arm around her waist. "Hey, did you lose some weight, Rad?"

Marjorie stuck the cigarette between her lips. "I just have a lot on my mind at school. And at home." She snapped her butane lighter and stared at the flame as if forgetting where the conversation was heading.

"It's just so complicated, Shawn," she said, veering back to our topic and blowing smoke through the side of her mouth. "Did you know there isn't *one* female full professor in the entire CS department at Pitt?" she asked. "There are almost no women VPs in tech companies. They're all nerdy males. How do you expect women to advance if we aren't given a chance?"

Tears started to well up in Marjorie's eyes. I wasn't sure if they were due to Boz Scaggs, the effects of the super-potent Black Russians that Dobbs had fixed for her, or—more worrisome—the direction our conversation had taken.

"And how do you think it feels to be in a place where everyone knows your family history?" she blurted out. "My mother doesn't act like a parent. She acts like a teenage girl who got pregnant by some goon and still can't care for herself. Everyone stares at us. They know the whole story. Do you know how that feels?"

"C'mon, Rad," I said, hugging her close. "That's not true. You're just imagining it."

"I'm really not," she said, exhaling a deep breath. "But I don't want to talk about it."

"Look, Rad," I said, twirling my girlfriend's hair and nibbling her neck. "I'll do whatever you want. We'll just have to think it through. I mean, we have plenty of time to figure out what's the best thing for *you*—*and* for us."

Marjorie pulled a tissue from her pocket and blew into it. "You're probably right," she said, gradually recovering her composure. "I'm probably just hammered."

"True," I nodded.

"But let's face it, Shawn," she said. "Our generation's gonna have to deal with juggling jobs and careers and babies like *nobody else* ever had to do. It's a crazy world out there, dude." She threw down her cigarette pack and started breathing hard as if she had now overexerted herself.

"Don't start panicking, Rad," I said gently. "We can handle whatever gets thrown our way." I slipped my arm around her. "Remember that day you caught Aunt Peg and me in the kitchen? She was sharing some cool stories about how she and Choppy did it when they were first married. Your mom wasn't around, so she felt comfortable telling me some of this stuff. Her basic message was that they sometimes had to shoot for *less* now to get *more* in the long run. It's brilliant. People in that generation were ahead of their time. Aunt Peg said it could apply to us, too."

Marjorie fiddled with her cigarette case, shaking her head. "I've heard her say things like that," she said. "But I see it differently. I think it's better to get as much as you can *now*, even if it means giving up other things, so it doesn't slip through your fingers. Then you can kick back and do what you really want to do *later* when you can afford it. Doesn't that make better sense, Shawn?"

"Sure, Rad." I tried to sound convincing. "I guess."

Marjorie stared at me. The playfulness had vanished. "I've been given *less* my whole life," she said firmly. "Why should I settle for that again? That's where I disagree with the old Swissvale way of doing things. Why should we sacrifice constantly?"

"Hey, guys. . . ." There was a light rapping on my door. "Sorry to interrupt." Dobbs pushed his head through the crack. His mischievousness was gone; he looked genuinely concerned. Stick hovered behind, tossing a Nerf ball in the air apprehensively. "Marjorie's mother is on the phone. She said it's an emergency; otherwise, we wouldn't bother you." Dobbs handed the phone to Marjorie. "I hope everything's okay."

The lingering buzz of too many Black Russians had numbed Marjorie's senses and slowed down her reflexes. She furtively threw her cigarette case under the bed as if the phone might have eyes.

"I hope this is a real emergency, Mother," she said tersely. "I asked you not to call unless—"

There was a long, disturbing pause.

"Oh my God! I *realize* that, mother, but I can't get home faster," Marjorie said. "For God's sake, slow down so I can think straight. Who's *with* her?"

I heard words like "Braddock General Hospital," "Aunt Peg," "intensive care," and "seizures."

Marjorie handed me the phone and staggered back, pushing me away. She grabbed a pile of clothes and threw them into her suitcase.

"I'll borrow Dobbs' car to take you to the airport," I said. "He'll let me use it in a heartbeat. We'll get you on the first flight out."

Marjorie's face appeared drained of color. I slid my arm around her waist, trying to steady her.

"Can God really hate me *this* much?" Marjorie said. She pushed away my arm and lost her balance, stumbling onto the other side of the room. "He's been crapping all over me since I was born. Now, *this*?" My stereo was playing Boz Scaggs for the third time in a row. Marjorie yanked the needle off the LP. She began sobbing so hard she could barely catch her breath.

"Can you figure out how to come home with me, Shawn?" she asked in a demanding tone. "The most important woman in my life might be dying. I know all this law school crap is important to you, but maybe you can do something for *me* this time."

Fall 1979 (cont'd) (Wilmerding)

THE POMEN SERVICE

Three days had passed before I was able to turn in my moot court assignment, buy a Greyhound bus ticket, and get myself back to Pittsburgh. Choppy and Peg's living room resembled a hospital ward. Edna Galovich—Peg's best friend and next-door neighbor—served as head nurse and chief administrator, scowling as I tracked leaves and germs into the makeshift infirmary.

A hospital bed took center stage in the middle of the room. A portable commode was parked in the corner, emitting an overpowering, acrid smell of stale urine, despite the numerous times Edna had doused it in Tide and ammonia.

"You want any lime Jell-O, hun?" Choppy asked Aunt Peg, circling the bed and dragging his bad leg behind him. Choppy had arranged with his foreman at the Carrie Furnace to take time off to attend to his wife. "Familiar people and places," he insisted, "that'll get Peg fixed up." He rearranged the pillow under her neck. "Jell-O's good for her, ain't it, Doc?" He sought confirmation from Dr. Broughert, Swissvale's all-purpose physician.

"*If* she feels up to it," Dr. Broughert authoritatively said as he shined a penlight into Aunt Peg's eyes. "Don't push it, Choppy. Let her get her strength back. She needs sleep more than anything now."

I stared at Aunt Peg. It all seemed so shockingly un-private: Her nightgown was unbuttoned, exposing her milky-colored chest, and the garment had hiked up, revealing a blotchy network of blue veins. Aunt Peg's white hair lay across the pillow.

"Dear God," I thought, wiping a tear from my cheek. "Why had something like this happened to such a *special* lady?" Next to my mother, she had become one of the most important people in my own life. I had assumed she'd be part of my family, or I'd be part of her family, forever. Seeing her like this was jarring.

Dr. Broughert had diagnosed her with *pneumocystis carinii*, a form of non-bacterial pneumonia often associated with over-exposure to poisons, many of which poured steadily out of the mills. The first week after Aunt Peg's attack would be critical, the doctor said; additional seizures could turn into strokes, which could produce the grim onset of respiratory failure.

"Let her sleep," Dr. Broughert said, patting Choppy on the shoulder. "You've got a long road ahead. Pace yourselves."

The doctor accepted a slice of nut roll from Edna as payment for the house call. He sized up Marjorie, then winked at me. "Your girlfriend's still the prettiest patient I ever gave a tetanus shot to," he said, giving Marjorie a half-hug then buttoning his trench coat. Dr. Broughert allowed his dark, medical eyes to scan mine. "This here's a good family, young man," he said before stepping into the cold. "If you plan to get serious with that girl, you'd better give her what she *deserves*. No making promises you don't intend to keep—especially given what she and her family have been through."

Choppy sat at Aunt Peg's bedside, holding her hand. A mantel clock passed down from Aunt Peg's father swung its pendulum and chimed on the hour, a rich sound that gave this dwelling a feel of nobility.

As Aunt Peg slept, Marjorie sprawled on the floor, pecking away at an Altair computer she and her CS classmates had assembled from a kit. Even with Aunt Peg sick, she needed to key in data for her graduate assistant position to pay for incidental expenses. Choppy and Aunt Peg already were paying for her room, board, and tuition. She didn't want to add to those financial burdens.

"You see the *Post-Gazette* story about Mice McMasters?" Lil asked, clomping into the sick room, sipping a huge mug of hot cocoa. "They found him hanging from the bedroom light fixture. I saw him just a couple days ago upstreet."

"For God's sake, don't talk about that, Lil," Choppy whispered gruffly. "Your mother's lying here half-dead, and you're talking about Mice McMasters hanging himself?" Choppy made a "*zip it!*" motion across his lips. "What if she wakes up and hears you? It might give her another stroke."

Marjorie looked up from her typing and sent a death stare in her mother's direction.

"It's just the *way* he *did* it," Lil said, plopping her wide bottom into a stuffed chair, then flipping open a *Star* magazine. "He was hanging from the bedroom fixture when Tracey came home from her breakfast shift at the Village Dairy. I always knew Mice had problems with drinking and that. But the strike must of pushed him over the edge. Six months without a paycheck must of caused his mind to snap."

"I don't have *any* sympathy for a man who hangs himself, even if there's a strike," Edna said while placing a cool washcloth on Peg's forehead. "Heavens, all of our families have had to deal with it. That's why you join a union—to help you get through these tough times. He shouldn't have taken the job if he's gonna kill himself the first time the company jerks his chain."

Choppy waved the topic to a close. "If Mice couldn't hack a little pressure, he *deserved* to hang himself. He's a disgrace to the United Electrical boys. Now let's drop it so Peg don't wake up and hear about Mice's problems. She got her own."

"It's just the *grotesque* way he did it," Lil said, pressing the issue. "They said he *crapped* his pants all over the floor. Tracey said he was hanging there in his boxer shorts with crap all over the place. Swinging from the ceiling and crap all over the carpet. She just had it steam-cleaned. Can you imagine?"

"Only a pig commits suicide in his boxer shorts," commented Edna. "He could of at least worn long pants and saved Tracey that extra heartache."

"For *God's sake*!" Choppy said, waving his hand to silence them. "Forget about Mice's bowel movements, Lil. Go in there and get some lime Jell-O for your mother. Use the small spoon. We don't want her choking."

———

As Marjorie drove Choppy's red Plymouth past Nied's Funeral Home in Swissvale, I could see a long line snaking out the door. All of these people were there to pay their respects to Mice McMasters and to leave small envelopes of $5 or $10 near the registry book, so Tracey would have enough to pay for food and funeral expenses over the next difficult week (and maybe get her carpet cleaned). Knowing the Swissvale crowd, they were also there to gawk inside the casket to see if rope marks were still visible on Mice's neck, as early sightings from the viewing line had reported.

I turned my face away from the car window and looked at Marjorie as she sped past Nied's. "Who's this guy we're going to see again?" I asked her. "If he shot himself or did something grotesque like Mice, we'll probably have to wait in line for an hour."

"It's just my old gym teacher from high school," she said, lighting a Newport and then pinching it into the car's ashtray. "You can stay in the car, Shawn. It'll be quicker that way. I'll get in and out fast."

The taverns of Swissvale were lit up for a busy Thursday night, unaffected by the presence of death. The Roxy's and the Acorn Club, across from Rudy's House of Submarines, were brimming with patrons, many of them loafing on the sidewalk as they nursed their Iron City beers. Even during times of tragedy, people had to drink.

Marjorie took another distracted hit of her Newport. She rolled down the window and flicked the cigarette out. Then she steered the Plymouth under the railroad trestle, checking her side-view mirror as if looking for ghosts. The Westinghouse plant exhaled thin white smoke as we sped along Electric Avenue underneath the Westinghouse Bridge, which, according to local lore, contained the incinerated remains of two mill workers who'd fallen into a vat of molten iron and got mixed into the steel girders when it was built.

"Who'd you say this dead guy was again?" I asked yet again, noticing how Marjorie's eyes narrowed in the dusk.

"My old gym coach from ninth grade," she said curtly.

"Were you close to him or something?" I asked.

"Nope, not really," she said. "Lori Wertz called me about it. I mean, he was our teacher. I just felt I oughtta show up."

Something was up, but I didn't know what. Marjorie had never said a word about a high school gym teacher who was important to her. On top of that, she'd been unusually short-tempered for the past few days. When I'd pressed her to talk about it, she'd just clammed up and muttered something about PMS.

Arriving in Wilmerding, a few towns away from Swissvale, we pulled up in front of the George M. Tishcko Funeral Home. Massive oaks and maples displaying fiery-red leaves surrounded a white building with fluted pillars and a huge porch. A sweeping driveway led us to a white *porte-cochere*, built to allow hearses to deliver corpses through the extra-wide side door. "I'll just be a couple of minutes," Marjorie said. "You can listen to the radio."

Marjorie left the key in the ignition, turning up "*Stayin' Alive*" by the Bee Gees.

I clicked off the radio. "Disco isn't music," I said, turning it off. "It's *garbage*." I exited the passenger side.

"Please, Shawn, there's no reason for you to come in," Marjorie said. "I *told* you. It'll only take two minutes."

I ignored Marjorie's orders, following her toward the heavy front door trimmed with gold hardware. I had no interest in sitting in the car by myself listening to disco music; I'd come home to be with my girlfriend. A short man with a hooked nose, neat white hair, and other-worldly smile pushed the door open, ushering us into the plushly carpeted receiving room.

"Good evening," he intoned. "Family?"

"Friends," Marjorie replied curtly.

Marjorie bypassed the dark-suited man and found her way to the directory mounted on a gold pole that listed three deceased members of the community laid out in the home's parlors. As she pondered the sign, I looked for a familiar surname. They all ran together in a blur of consonants and harsh prefixes.

"Is this place Croatian or Polish?" I whispered to Marjorie.

"Serbian," the man with the white hair interjected, smiling munificently.

Marjorie wasn't acting like herself. Her hands seemed fidgety, brushing non-existent specks off her sweater, and she wouldn't look at me. She again tried to ditch me, moving deftly inside the rose-colored parlor marked "John Geojkovich." A line of ten or twelve mourners waited to pay their respects to a grim, squat man inside a powder-blue coffin with rubber-like hands gripping a pair of crystal rosary beads. Above the man's head, a two-barred crucifix with distinctive round balls on each prong identified him as a member of the Orthodox Catholic Church.

Marjorie stepped forward in the grieving line. She hadn't bothered to remove her driving glasses.

"You a *friendt* of John's?" a matronly woman in black, either the widow or a close relative, asked her. "He always liked pretty girls."

"Yes, friend," Marjorie whispered. Her voice was so low that I could barely decipher the words. "He was, uh, a very nice man. I'm so sorry to be here."

Before the conversation could go any further, a cleric with a thin white beard and a black robe appeared through the doorway, gripping a smoldering incense burner. Choir members carrying sheet music followed behind.

The funeral director appeared in the archway, hands clasped. "Very Reverend Kovich has arrived five minutes early for the *Pomen*. If you would care to join us gathering around our brother John *Geojkovich*, the Saint Nicholas church choir will lead us in beautiful chants picked out special by the family."

Marjorie hurriedly blessed herself, exiting the room as the procession advanced.

"C'mon Marjorie," I said. "Let's stay. I never saw a *Pomen*."

"That's *disrespectful*, Shawn," she said. "This isn't a *Wonders of the World* exhibit."

"But you said you *owed* it to the guy," I reminded her.

"Just warm up the car," she said, throwing the keys to me. "I have to use the ladies' room before we head out. Okay?"

"I'll wait here," I said.

Marjorie stared at me murderously. "I got my period, all right?" she said, clearly exasperated. She shoved her glasses in her purse. "Unless you plan on changing *your* tampon too, I wish you'd just go warm up the car, Shawn. I'll be out in a minute like I said."

After fifteen minutes, with Marjorie still missing in action, I crept back into the front door of the funeral home to look for her. I knew that girls and tampons often produced odd behavior, but fifteen minutes seemed *highly* unusual.

There was no sign of life near the ladies' room. I passed the rose parlor where John Geojkovich was laid out, still grimacing in his powder-blue casket as the chanting of the *Pomen* continued. I walked down the cream-colored hallway, past the funeral director who observed me with a thin-lipped smile. The halls were be-decked with paintings of Kennywood Park circa 1940s along with charcoal sketches of the blast furnace named Dorothy Six, once the most productive furnace in the Mon Valley, and other steel mill scenes. Hanging on these walls was a historical archive—pieces of the past that preserved meaningful memories for families who would end up here at the end of a gritty life in the Mon Valley. I stopped in front of the entrance to a second room—the lavender parlor—that was nearly empty. Inside, a dark-skinned guy with moles dressed in green polyester pants and a silky disco shirt open at the neck was sitting in a folding chair, a look of boredom on his face. Beside him sat two hardened, middle-aged women in pantsuits and flashy metallic belts snuggly pinching their waists, their faces tough and leathery. A painting of "Noah's Ark" and the Jack Rabbit rollercoaster from Kennywood hung above them.

The man in the casket was thin and ghastly looking. A yellowish-plaid suit hung limply over his bony arms and legs. His face was gnarled and severe, and he had blondish hair that appeared prematurely white from hard living. A rough bump in the center of his nose stuck up from the coffin, like a flag on a battleship.

At the foot of the copper casket was a folded American flag—a customary gift from the local American Legion for any veteran receiving an honorable discharge. The basket beside this flag contained only one or two white offering envelopes, a poor take by Pittsburgh standards.

Off to the left side of the room, I saw Marjorie. The image froze itself into my mind. She was standing immobile, her driving glasses affixed to her face. Her feet were firmly planted on the purple carpet, her eyes staring blankly toward the coffin, keeping a safe distance. The young, dark-skinned mourner with moles on his face glanced at Marjorie and whispered some sort of joke, causing the heavier lady beside him to emit a deep, raspy cough. The room stank of alcohol.

I stepped up to Marjorie. "You know this guy?" I asked, pulling her gently by the elbow.

Marjorie pivoted, glared at me, and immediately headed for the door. "*Of course* not," she said, shaking me off her arm. "I *told* you I was here to see my gym teacher. Are you calling me a *liar?*"

"I'm not saying anything, Marjorie," I said. "Geez, what's eating at you? I'm just asking if you knew this guy."

I swiveled and took a final look at the man in the casket before heading out to catch up with Marjorie, who bolted for the car. Somehow, this week had become even worse than if I'd stayed in Boston *without* Marjorie, which seemed hard to imagine. The skinny, jaundiced man in the coffin looked oddly familiar. Swissvale? St. Agnes's? Somewhere else? The name on the directory with an arrow pointing toward the lavender parlor was completely unknown to me but, under these circumstances, I would never forget it. Spelled out in white letters on the directory was the name: "*Ralph Acmovic Sr.*"

September 2008 (Courtroom)

THE MISSING WITNESS

Judge Wendell wiped away a bead of perspiration despite the fact the courtroom fans were running at full tilt.

"Look, fellows, I've cut you plenty of breaks," he said. "Your plaintiff *still* hasn't shown up. I know you've subpoenaed one of the elderly nuns who worked at the Roselia Home. Frankly, I'm disappointed. I think that's cruel. But we can't wait forever for the nursing staff to clear that poor woman for travel. The court can only delay so long. I'm afraid I have no choice. I'm going to have to call for closing arguments."

I was back at the counsel table with Bernie. J.V. was on bed rest per doctor's orders; they were concerned she might be developing preeclampsia. So, I had no choice. I felt terrible for acting like a jerk in front of J.V. and causing her to get stressed out. I'd resigned myself to face whatever lay ahead.

"You can handle this mess," I whispered to Bernie. "It probably doesn't matter much at this point."

Just then, the wooden door in the rear of the courtroom swung open. Two blonde-haired children dressed in neatly pressed clothes ran down the center aisle looking for familiar faces. Following them was a woman with blond hair dressed in an attractive business suit and cream-colored blouse.

Bernie's face brightened like a Christmas bulb. He turned and winked at me.

"Petitioners would ask permission to allow these children to attend the proceedings," Bernie said. "They're family members."

"The court permits it," the judge stated. "As long as it's okay with the parents."

"It is, Your Honor," Marjorie's voice stated from the back of the courtroom.

I swiveled my chair sideways and pretended not to watch the parade. Through my peripheral vision, though, I could see Marjorie and her children—handsome and nicely suntanned—making their way to the front benches to join their long-lost Pittsburgh family.

The boy, Florian—a good Croatian name that had always been one of Marjorie's favorites—high-fived Choppy and claimed a seat next to his great-grandfather. The girl, Dianna—whom J.V. had told me turned eleven this year—was taller and a couple of years older than her brother. Looking like a doll-sized version of Marjorie, she wedged herself beside Aunt Peg's wheelchair, smoothing down her yellow dress. Her small fingers squeezed her great-grandmother's hand, trying to wake her up.

I tried to ignore the seductive pursing of Marjorie's lips that seemed to be waiting to say "hello." Instead, I looked down at an empty pad of paper and felt myself sweat.

"Your Honor," Bernie plucked the glasses out of his breast pocket. "We call petitioner Marjorie Radovich Pearce. She just arrived on the shuttle from the airport."

"*Objection,* Judge," Drew-Morris interjected. "You already called for closing arguments."

Bernie undid the last button on his glen plaid suit coat. His white mustache twitched with newfound determination.

"Your Honor never said we couldn't put our final witness on the stand *if* she showed up," Bernie said. "I'm happy to go back to the office and type up a motion if you want it for the appeals court. Marjorie Radovich Pearce was *clearly* listed as our final witness, right Judge? Our principal witness is here from three thousand miles away, and we're ready to proceed."

Judge Wendell smiled, nodding his assent.

"No need for a written motion, Bernie," he said. "Your witness came all the way from California to have her day in court. *This* judge always lets justice take its course. Take the stand, Miss Pearce."

Marjorie leaned over and squeezed the hands of both children. She rose and walked with clicking heels toward the witness box. Then she stopped and addressed the bench: "It's just Marjorie Radovich, Your Honor," she said. "No Pearce."

Judge Wendell seemed pleased at this new information. He nodded approvingly. "You get that, Jimmy?" he said to his clerk. "It's just Marjorie Radovich, *no Pearce.*"

As Marjorie passed behind my chair, I felt the wool of her business jacket brush against my back. A spark of static electricity seemed to jump from the fabric and hit me like a mild shock. It caused me to recoil.

As my former girlfriend climbed into the witness box, I purposely avoided looking at her. Bernie allowed his witness to get comfortable, then squeezed her hand as if to transfer his strength to her. He had agreed to handle this witness entirely. I was staying far away.

"Now, Ms. Radovich, I suppose we should start by asking you to tell this honorable court *why* you're late getting to this trial," Bernie stated.

"Yes, I'd like to explain," she answered. "Thank you, Mr. Milanovich."

Marjorie's voice was still remarkably youthful, even mellifluous. I'd imagined she would have developed a deeper, raspier voice if she'd continued to smoke those nasty Newport cigarettes since I'd last seen her. But she'd obviously quit. I swung my chair backward, facing the opposite direction. I knew it was juvenile, but I couldn't help it. After all these years, just as I feared, her presence unnerved me.

Bernie prodded his witness gently: "Go ahead."

"We just sold our house in Northern California," she said. "Our closing was canceled twice because of no-lien letters. My children and I are buying a home in Pittsburgh, so we can spend more time—I mean, we already *bought* a place in the Shadyside area last month. Unfortunately, the deal couldn't be finalized till we wrapped up the sale of our place on the West Coast. I didn't feel that we could afford two trips, Your Honor. Not financially, I mean emotionally." She allowed her eyes to sweep over her children. "But I became aware of some other circumstances and got here as quickly as I could. I apologize for any inconvenience, Your Honor. I meant no disrespect to the court."

In the spectator benches, Choppy mussed up the hair on Florian's head. Dianna kissed "Grandma Lil," who was now blubbering at the news that her only daughter and grandchildren were coming home to Pittsburgh. Even Aunt Peg seemed to stir from her catnap long enough to blink her eyes and form a distant smile as she observed the family jubilation.

"No inconvenience at all," Judge Wendell said, beaming down at our star witness as if happy to be presiding again. "Would you folks like a moment of privacy for yourselves?"

Choppy knelt next to Peg's wheelchair, whispering something into her ear. Peg made a gurgling noise, grinning from ear to ear.

Marjorie started to rise momentarily, then straightened her suit jacket with crisp professionalism. "We're fine, Your Honor," she said, brushing away a piece of blond hair from her face. I couldn't help wondering: 'Was it dyed?'

"We'll have plenty of time to talk later," she said. "Thanks for the offer. That was thoughtful."

The judge rocked back in his chair, smiling and unsticking his robe. He signaled for Bernie to proceed.

"Ms. Radovich, could you please state your full name and address for the record?" Bernie asked.

"Marjorie Radovich. My existing California address is still technically—"

Aunt Peg, suddenly alert, pushed against the arm of her wheelchair as if attempting to lift herself up.

Marjorie looked in the direction of her grandmother. Then she took a breath. "My name is Marjorie Marie Radovich. My principal residence has been Hayward, California, but our new domicile is Bayard Street in Shadyside. I forget the address, Mr. Milanovich. I think it's 4904? I'm sorry."

Aunt Peg raised a palsied arm toward her granddaughter. Choppy had neatly brushed her gray hair for these proceedings. An unmistakable grin now crept over the old Slovak lady's face as spittle dribbled at the corners of her mouth.

"No problem," Bernie said gently. "We'll supplement the record later."

Marjorie opened her mouth to speak. She stopped; then she exhaled so loudly it sounded like a gasp, as if she couldn't hold back the sound of relief. She covered her mouth, obviously embarrassed by the outburst of emotion.

"She's quite an impressive *actress*," a voice stated from across the counsel table. "No wonder the two of you made such a cute pair, Mr. Rossi. For the record, let the transcript reflect that Mr. Rossi disclosed at our pre-trial conference that he had a personal relationship with the witness during his college and law school years, so these two people know each other *very* well."

"Mr. Rossi already disclosed that fact. No need to add anything to the record," Judge Wendell said, frowning at our opponent's incivility. "C'mon, Miss Radovich, let's take a little break here," the judge continued, leaning over the bench like a worried uncle. "You take some time to catch your breath. I'll have Jimmy fix you up with a ginger ale."

He struck his gavel lightly. "Recess for twenty minutes," he said, tapping his pocket to make sure his cigarettes were handy before disappearing into his chambers. "We all could use a timeout."

———

During the break, I ducked into the bathroom to collect myself. My reaction to being in the same room with Marjorie and hearing her voice again was just as bad as I'd imagined. I fiddled with my Blackberry and noticed a voicemail. I held a finger to my ear to block out the noise of two lawyers arguing near the sinks while I listened to the message.

"Hi, Dad-o, it's me." It was Britt. "Things are a little calmer here, thank heavens. I think your talk with The Beast helped. Can't wait till you meet this guy Jarrod from the Chem Club. He's awesome. We were thinking of going to Loews Theatre this weekend to see *Mama Mia*, just the two of us. Is it true you and mom listened to that music when you were young, for real?"

Mama Mia? my brain shouted at me. *A movie in the pitch dark? This girl wasn't old enough for serious dating! Did this guy think I didn't know what the plan was? Maybe I'd pull out the bolt cutters from my workroom when he showed up at the door. That would send the right message!*

I slid out the stylus from my Blackberry, ready to peck out a reply.

"Time to get back to work, Mr. Rossi. Judge doesn't like to wait," Jimmy said, holding open the door to the men's room.

"Jesus, Mary, and Joseph," I replied to Jimmy, invoking one of Christine's favorite exhortations. It was bad enough that a boy two years older than my daughter was trying to spirit her away to a darkened movie theatre to watch a flick about a young girl whose mother got pregnant during a summer filled with flings, and the girl wants to figure out who the real father was. Now, I had to go back into that room and look at Marjorie for two hours straight while conveying an appearance of being relaxed and in possession of my mental faculties, which was the furthest thing from reality.

CHAPTER 29

September 2008 (Courtroom)

ABSOLUTE DENIAL

The paralegal had taken a seat next to Drew-Morris. Even though he looked like he could bench-press three hundred pounds, the muscular young man seemed fearful as Drew-Morris jabbed a finger at him and directed him to organize a pile of exhibits.

"I have a big surprise for Constance and that big goon," Bernie whispered to me. "We're gonna knock them off guard."

"You go for it," I whispered back. "I'm going to sit here and pretend I'm invisible." I sat down, suddenly noticing I was wearing two different colored shoes—one black and one brown. I kept them hidden under the table.

Bernie chewed on the tip of his glasses, then stepped in front of the witness box.

"I'd like to ask you an important question if I could, Ms. Radovich," said Bernie, facing our witness. "How *certain* are you that the decedent Ralph Acmovic Sr. was your father?"

"*Objection,* calls for speculation," Drew-Morris piped up.

"I'll rephrase it, Your Honor. Do you have any *first*-hand knowledge, based on all of those years growing up at home with your mother and grandparents, any *first*-hand observations whether Ralph Acmovic Sr. was your biological father?"

Marjorie rotated in her seat toward the judge. She stole a glance at me, then returned her eyes to Bernie. "Yes, I do," she said. "I had *numerous* conversations about this with my mother and my grandparents, particularly my grandmother, Margaret Radovich"—Marjorie nodded toward Aunt Peg—"beginning at age seven."

I found myself calming down a bit, which caused me to stare involuntarily at Marjorie. Her hair was thinner than I'd remembered, more brown than blond, with gentle highlights. Her skin was almost creamy except for slight age creases around the corners of her eyes. Yet she looked remarkably fit and full of youthful energy—even beautiful.

I scribbled meaningless words onto my pad. I knew there was something terribly perverse about this, checking out Marjorie during a court proceeding. Instead, as she took a sip of water, I tried to discipline myself: I counted to twenty in Spanish, something Britt was teaching me so we could go on a vacation to the Yucatan.

"Ms. Radovich," Bernie said, now on a roll. "You just testified under oath that your grandmother identified Ralph Acmovic Sr. as your biological father beginning when you were about seven. Your grandmother's no longer competent to testify directly. So, give us some context: Did these statements take place while you were living at your grandparents' home in Swissvale?"

There was an uncomfortable silence. I snapped out of my trance—I had only gotten to *nueve*. Now, I realized that Marjorie was staring back at me with a look that bordered on accusatory. It was mortifying; she'd seen me checking her out. I looked away and resumed scribbling with more intensity. After what Marjorie had done to me back then, I didn't want her to think I still possessed even a *hint* of emotion for her. Instead, I sat up squarely in my chair to display lawyerly detachment.

"Did you understand the question, Ms. Radovich?" Bernie asked.

"I'm sorry, Mr. Milanovich. Yes, that's a correct statement," Marjorie said.

"And are you aware of any *other* evidence bearing on the relationship between your mother and decedent that might aid the court in rendering its finding as to paternity?" Bernie asked.

I glanced at Marjorie, who seemed to be hesitating. Finally, she said: "Yes, I do have something that might be of value to the court." Marjorie pulled a pink envelope from her suitcoat pocket. "My grandmother sent me this card the week I moved into the dorms at Pitt. That would have been—let's see, fall of 1976," she said, handing the envelope to Bernie, who handed it to Judge Wendell, who nodded his head and handed it back to Jimmy, who returned it to the witness.

"We introduce this item as petitioner's Exhibit G," Bernie stated.

"So received," the judge declared.

"Can you tell the court what this is, Ms. Radovich?" Bernie asked.

Marjorie's fingers slid a card out of the envelope and held it up for a moment, a wistful look overtaking her face. "It's a Hallmark card from my Aunt Peg—I mean, my grandmother. It's dated September 20, 1976, and is postmarked from the Swissvale Post Office."

"By the way," Bernie said, stroking his mustache contemplatively. "Can you explain to the court why you refer to your grandmother as 'Aunt Peg'?"

Marjorie aimed her eyes at her grandmother in the wheelchair, smiling lovingly. "When my mother had me, she wasn't proud of having a baby out of wedlock," she said, directing her remarks to the judge. "My grandmother pretended I was her sister's baby at first—probably out of shame—and helped my mother raise me. She was *always* 'Aunt Peg,' even after I learned the truth. And she's still the most special person in the world."

Marjorie wiped a tear from the corner of her eye. The judge dabbed his own eye with his handkerchief.

"I see there's some kind of kitten and a ball of yarn on the front of this card," Bernie continued, having earned more points in the sympathy department. "Can you identify the handwriting inside the card?"

Marjorie looked toward Aunt Peg's wheelchair in the front row. Her grandmother smiled as if given strength by some invisible force.

"That's my grandmother's handwriting for sure, Your Honor," she said. "She taught me to write cursive. She always said I had a 'light touch,' just like her. I could pick out her handwriting if you buried it in a stack of a million cards."

The words "light touch" jolted a memory of Marjorie studying in my room at the Semple Street Coop and taking a break so I could give her a back rub to relax her mind before a CS exam. "You have such a *light touch*, Shawn," she'd whispered, with absolute lack of awareness of her own sensuality.

Marjorie abruptly turned to face me from the witness box. She gave me an inscrutable look that quickly turned into a scowl. I plunged back into my note-taking. It was unhealthy to think about physical attributes when it came to Marjorie. She had been part of my distant past. At this point, I lectured myself firmly, any thoughts about Marjorie needed to be confined to business.

"Your grandmother has a nice forward slant. The nuns in Homestead must have taught her well," Bernie continued, glancing at the judge with a smile. "Can you read the words your grandmother wrote inside the card there?"

"Absolutely," Marjorie said, slipping on a pair of half-glasses that made her look like a business executive.

My dearest Marji –
We're so proud that you've taken this step. None of us ever had this opportunity for an education like you're getting. We know that you'll do great things with it.

Marjorie held the card in midair, brushing away a tear.

Now that you're grown up, I thought you should have this. If you don't look your past straight in the eye, it'll ruin you. Your mother and Choppy and I love you more than we could put in a card. You'll realize that someday. You're the best thing that ever happened to this family.
Study hard and brush your teeth whenever you eat Twizzlers at night!
Love always to my girl who's destined for great things,
Aunt Peg.

Bernie stood in front of the witness box. Our star witness had taken off her half-glasses as she struggled to continue. In the spectator seats, Choppy was fighting back tears; he covered his mouth with his handkerchief so nobody could see or hear him blubbering.

"And what's *inside* the card, Ms. Radovich?" Bernie finally asked. "I know it's difficult to talk about this topic. But can you tell the court what your grandmother enclosed?"

Marjorie glanced quickly at Choppy, then at her children. Then she stared at me. This time, I stared straight back at her.

"It's a picture of two people standing in front of the gate at the Union Switch and Signal in Swissvale," she said. "The girl's holding a bunch of flowers. The date at the bottom says 'June '57.'"

"And the picture? Who's in the picture?" Bernie asked, holding up the photo. It showed a buxom teenage girl dressed in short pants and a polka-dotted stretch top, sticking out her chest proudly. The young man beside her, with his arm draped around her shoulder and a lustful smirk on his face, wore black slacks and a white T-shirt with a pack of cigarettes tucked jauntily under one sleeve.

"It's my mother and a man. She can't be more than fifteen or sixteen. He looks older," Marjorie said, putting the picture down and turning away. Marjorie's face had tightened; her entire posture had become rigid. I recognized that look. It was the same look that overtook her when her mother said something mortifying, and she recoiled into herself.

"Do you know who that man is?" Bernie asked in a soft voice.

Marjorie took a deep breath as if counting to ten. Then she slid the picture away from her.

"Aunt Peg told me it was Ralph Acmovic. She said it was the man who was my father," Marjorie said.

"No more questions at this time," Bernie said. "We'll allow opposing counsel to cross-examine but reserve the right to recall this witness if needed."

Drew-Morris approached the witness, a steely glint in her eyes. "So, Ms. Radovich-Pearce—" she started to say.

"My name's Marjorie Radovich. I'm divorced," Marjorie countered.

The two women exchanged a look of disdain mixed with competitiveness.

"Okay, *Ms. Radovich*," Drew-Morris said. "It's nice that you could join us for your trial before it's over." She smiled toward the judge. "You mind if I take a look at the *actual* picture? The printing technology at Kinko's these days isn't perfect, I mean with all of those black-and-white pixels."

Marjorie held the picture in the air. "Contacts are great till you turn forty," she said crisply. "You probably need *bifocals*. Try squinting, and you can cheat."

Drew-Morris snapped up the picture with her fingers. She inspected it at arm's length as if demonstrating the keen acuity of her eyesight. Finally, she placed it in front of Marjorie, this time with the backing of the Kodak photo facing upward.

"Can you please read the words written on the back of that picture?" Drew-Morris asked with a smile like a demure schoolgirl. "I realize *my* eyes aren't so good, so why don't you put on *your* glasses and tell us?"

Marjorie left her glasses on the table. She raised the photo but kept it at arm's length.

"It says '*your Mom*' in the left corner."

"And in the *other* corner?"

Marjorie rubbed a shoulder against her ear as if succumbing to a nervous habit.

"It just says '*him,*'" she answered.

Our opposing counsel put one hand to her ear. "Could you speak up?"

"I said it just says '*him.*' But that doesn't mean—" Marjorie started to say.

"*Hold it!*" Drew-Morris struck a pose as if evaluating each word. "Doesn't that seem curious? The inscription on the photo just says '*him.*' Not 'Mom and Dad.' Not 'mother and father.'"

Marjorie pressed the bridge of her nose as if to relieve some pressure. "My Aunt Peg said—"

"So, this photo does *nothing* to prove your claim, Ms. Pearce," Drew-Morris said. "Where's the hard evidence? I mean, you supposedly lived in the *same town* as this man, right? And you never met the man or got a snapshot of the two of you together?"

"As far as I'm concerned, Ralph Acmovic was dead before I was born," Marjorie replied stoically. "There's no photo of us together because I wouldn't have stood next to that man for a million dollars."

I could see the pain in Marjorie's face that I could tell wasn't feigned. I glanced at Marjorie's two children in the front seats. They were listening to their mother's testimony and seemed troubled by it. Marjorie's daughter was a perfect replica of her mother. She knitted her blond eyebrows and whispered something in her great-grandfather's ear, obviously trying to understand why this strange lady was asking questions that were upsetting her mother.

Judge Wendell tapped his gavel lightly. "You mind if I ask a quick question myself, counselor?"

Drew-Morris yielded. Her confident posture indicated that she knew she was on a good roll.

The judge eyed his own handwritten scribbles. "Just to clarify for the record now, Ms. Radovich. You're testifying that this man Ralph Acmovic *was* your biological father. Do I have it right?"

"I was connected to him by blood, yes, Your Honor," she said. "I wasn't happy with that. Unfortunately, it's the rotten hand I was dealt."

The judge nodded and made a checkmark. "Got it," he said with a wave of his hand. "And you're saying that you never met or saw decedent Ralph Acmovic Sr. yourself? Is that the gist of your testimony?"

Marjorie's face momentarily turned dark. She held up a finger, "one minute," pouring herself a glass of water.

An image flashed into my mind of a long-ago Midnight Mass on Christmas Eve. Marjorie and I were standing in the back vestibule of St. Agnes's church while a drunken man with a hooked Serbian nose was weaving through the crowd. "*Hey Ralph,*" a high school boy had shouted at him. "*Ain't that your bastard daughter, the one with the nice rear end?*"

"Excuse me, Your Honor," I said, signaling for a timeout. "Could I have a moment with Mr. Milanovich?"

As soon as the judge acquiesced, I grabbed my co-counsel's arm.

"God almighty, Bernie," I whispered. "Don't let her answer."

Bernie's body stiffened. "What the hell's wrong with you, Shawn?" he grunted. "You having a mental breakdown here?"

"Look," I hissed through my teeth. "I just want to make sure you know the *answer* before you let your witness open her mouth."

Bernie's face turned a shade of purple. "I've asked her *multiple* times," he said. "She swore she never met the guy. You said you wanted to stay out of this. Why are you trying to screw up my direct examination? This photo from the grandma is the *knockout punch.*"

I started having a throbbing headache. I rubbed my temple before raising one eye toward Marjorie, who stared serenely out the window.

"Look. I swore I wouldn't have *anything* to do with her testimony," I said. "But I wanna make sure *you* know the answer."

"We're in good shape, my friend," Bernie assured me, squeezing my collarbone so hard it hurt.

He stood up and bowed graciously toward the bench. "My apologies, Your Honor," Bernie said. "We had a housekeeping matter to address. The witness can respond to the court's question."

The Orphan's Court stenographer pulled out her scroll of paper and read in a clipped voice:

"*Question—the Court: 'And you're saying you never met or saw decedent Ralph Acmovic, Sr. yourself? Is that the gist of your testimony?'*"

Marjorie squared her shoulders.

"*No,* Your Honor, not that I recall," she answered, adding an evasive qualifier that sounded, to my ears, like an intentional non-answer.

I could detect the muscles in Marjorie's chin flinching.

She continued, "As I've tried to impress on my children, one should not associate with reprobates who think it's fine to assault teenage girls and destroy other people's lives."

"The court has no more questions at this time then," said the judge. "Thank you, Ms. Radovich."

Outside the window of the Frick Building, gray clouds filled the sky like poisonous mushrooms, an ominous prelude to an afternoon storm. Bernie gave our witness a thumbs-up while I swiveled my chair and turned my back on her. It was clear to me that this woman, who professed to be the victim of grave injustice and who'd forced Bernie and me to go out on a limb by using the full power of the legal system to win her case, had ducked the truth to cover up the fact she'd met her father on multiple occasions, both alive and dead.

But why?

September 2008 (Home office)

THE HAPPIEST DAY

That night, having retreated to my home office to decompress, I sank into my chair and closed my eyes. Marjorie's appearance in the courtroom had rattled me terribly. It wasn't just seeing her in the flesh after a year of anticipation. It was also the feeling that there was more to Marjorie's denials than she was letting on. Right now, all I knew was that I needed to stop thinking about this case. And her.

To occupy my mind, I decided to try to pin down the *happiest* day of the 19,000 days I'd experienced since entering the world. Thankfully, lots of possibilities came to mind, which helped distract me from the day's events. One was when we visited the Jersey Shore on a family vacation to Wildwood and saw the Atlantic Ocean for the first time. Another was when my dad and I sat on our porch in 1960, listening to the radio, and heard the exact moment Bill Mazeroski hit his famous home run to beat the Yankees and win the World Series for the Pirates. Two other favorite memories involved sleep-deprived mornings at Magee-Women's Hospital when Christine delivered our daughters and I got to snip their umbilical cords.

I stretched my neck and rocked back into my chair. That's when the answer finally came to me. Of course. At the very top of the list had to be that Friday night, a week after I'd met Christine when I'd driven her out to Aliquippa to meet my mom.

It had been a perfect evening for a trip across the bridge to the North Side and up the meandering Ohio River Boulevard. We'd pulled up to the little two-bedroom house my mom shared with my Aunt Kate when one or both of them wasn't gallivanting around on bus trips with their AARP group. Christine's face had broken into a huge smile the moment the door opened. Even at age 72, Mom was still a pretty, Irish woman with a thick head of reddish hair, meticulously brushed so that it caught a sparkle of color in the hallway light.

I'd been waiting all week to see what happened when they met: It was better than I'd imagined. My mom's eyes locked immediately with Christine's. They touched each other's elbows and laughed, a time-honored female greeting that I'd never fully understood—but I knew it was a good sign. Then they hugged as if they'd known each other forever, flopped down on the couch, and began chatting away as if picking up a longstanding conversation, ignoring me.

The room smelled of an Irish feast. Mom had prepared her specialty—corned beef and cabbage cooked slowly in the crockpot—a meal usually reserved for Easter Sundays or my birthday. Along with this steaming platter came three crystal glasses of sparkling California wine "to celebrate the gift of *special* new friends." Mom had spent the rest of the evening asking Christine about key pieces of her life story and expressing wonderment at "your *beautiful* personality that obviously comes from a great family." Then mom recounted some embarrassing stories of my "gift for mischief-making at the Catholic school without getting caught by the nuns—a miracle in and of itself." As they laughed and popped open another bottle of sparkling wine, my mom and Christine appeared oblivious to my presence. I just watched them and felt my heart swelling with joy for three hours. When it was time to leave, mom kissed each of us in the doorway, and I saw tears stream down her cheeks.

"Don't forget to take your medicine," I'd whispered.

"Don't worry about me, sweetheart," she'd whispered back, brushing away the tears with the side of her hand. "Just worry about that fabulous young lady. She's a *keeper*." Then she pressed me against her and whispered something that I vowed to tuck away as one of those private, incredibly special moments between mother and son. "Listen here, Shawn," she said. "There's no rush, but I can't *wait* for you and Christine to get married and have two dozen grandkids so I can spoil them rotten."

On the drive home, Christine had cuddled up against my shoulder as we passed the old scrap yards along the Ohio River, lit up by giant sulfur lamps. "I'm pretty sure this was the best night of my life, Shawn," she'd yawned, punching at my shoulder to fluff it like a pillow.

"Yep," I'd answered, sliding Bruce Springsteen's new "*River*" album into my cassette deck and playing "*Drive All Night.*" I yawned back. "It was definitely the best."

A few days later, my mom had come into town to meet me for our monthly lunch at the Tic Toc restaurant in Kaufmann's Department Store. As I paid the bill, she'd slipped an envelope into my hand and ordered me to take it without objecting. "It's not a fortune," she said. "But your dad and I saved a long time for this occasion. We couldn't *wait* for you to find the right person." Her eyes twinkled. "He'd be thrilled to see who you picked—and who clearly picked *you*. I'm not rushing you. But *when* you decide to ask Christine, I want you to be able to invite *everyone* you and Christine want. Life's too short to cut corners on the *fun* things. Enjoy every minute of them, sweetheart."

When I tried to slide the envelope back into her purse, she blocked my hand and closed her handbag.

"Your dad and I didn't want our son to throw a *boring* wedding party," she said. "Maybe he didn't get to see you graduate from Harvard, but he'll be watching *this*. You and Christine can invite the *whole* city of Pittsburgh if you want—I mean, *when* you decide to ask her. I wouldn't want to rush you."

Two months later, I'd given Christine a marquise-shaped engagement ring from a jewelry store downtown just in time for my mom to join us for a celebratory dinner before she dashed off on an AARP trip to Lake Chautauqua in western New York. "Now I have something to talk about with my friends for the whole bus ride," she said, sweeping up Christine and me against her so tightly I could smell her sweet perfume.

The night she returned home from that trip, having left Aunt Kate to stay in New York a couple of extra days, my mom died in her sleep of a stroke, her new prescription of blood pressure medicine sitting unopened in her bathroom cabinet.

After arranging to have her body transported to Nied's Funeral Home in Swissvale so she could be buried next to my dad at North Braddock Catholic Cemetery in their chosen plot overlooking the river, I'd spent the day on our couch with the blinds drawn as Christine stroked my forehead, her engagement ring glittering in the dark. I'd steadily cried until she ushered me to bed, put a blanket over me, and whispered, "At least you can be thankful that you had the most perfect mom in the world. I know that may not seem like a consolation right now, Shawn. But she gave you the greatest gift possible. Someday I'd like to do that for *our* kids, too."

I shook away these faraway thoughts and sprung out of my chair: Britt was having her friends over tonight. At least I'd talked her out of going to another movie with "that boy." Instead, I'd persuaded her to have a larger group of friends hang out at our house; I figured there was safety in numbers. Christine's mom and dad, Jane and Cy, had already arrived carrying pizzas from Veltre's and a twelve-pack of Diet Cokes.

My parents-in-law were a godsend. Even though they'd raised their own family amid country clubs and the blue-blooded environs of Fox Chapel, they weren't the least bit stuffy. After Christine died, they immediately stepped up to help. Cy had worked as a senior executive for Westinghouse Electric. But now, he preferred to tuck his neat white hair under a Pirates cap, his favorite work attire following retirement, and cart around a toolbox for spot repairs around our house. Jane, an attractive woman of seventy with the same jet-black hair as Christine (thanks to her favorite hairdresser) and impeccable taste in clothes, usually came dressed in sweatshirts and floppy pants. She'd fix meals, shuttle the girls to tennis practice and volleyball, then clean our bathroom toilets and help with homework in a blizzard of efficiency. It was clear where Christine had inherited her ability to juggle forty tasks.

Tonight, Jane and Cy had taken over the role of party organizers. At times I felt a bit sheepish that I'd allowed them to shoulder so many of my parenting duties. But they had a natural gift for bringing order to chaos.

"Thanks, mom," I said, kissing my mother-in-law on her nose. It made my heart beat faster when she was around; the freckles on her face reminded me exactly of Christine's. "If any of these kids start misbehaving, let me know, and I'll Taser them."

"We'll be fine," my mother-in-law said. "By the way," she added, "Britt invited some of her new public-school friends over to hang out, including the boy you told me about."

I'd been nervous about meeting this guy all evening.

Britt came down the steps. "Where's Liza?" she whispered as her friends started filing in the door. "Can you make sure she doesn't do anything *rude?*"

"She's upstairs," I whispered back. "Don't worry about her. I'll take her up some pizza and check on her."

I grabbed a quick plate with a few slices and headed upstairs, feeling oddly nervous at the prospect of confronting my youngest daughter. She wasn't a little girl anymore. And I knew how she must feel: The new kid at school. No mom. All by herself. The gnawing feeling in my gut was guilt mixed with sadness and something else I couldn't identify.

Liza didn't respond to my knock, so I grabbed the little pin I kept on the ledge above each girl's door to pop open the lock. Inside it was dark. Liza was wrapped in a blanket in the corner of her bed, clutching her guinea pig to her chest.

"I have some pizza—just cheese," I said softly. Liza just slid back farther on the bed.

I stood awkwardly for a moment. "What's up, Punkin?" I finally whispered. "You seem so angry lately, not just at me but at your sister. It makes my heart sad. I know you miss mom. I miss her, too. Real bad. I truly believe she's watching over us and wants you to be happy. And I want you to know I love you and Britt more than anything in the world."

She hid her face in her blanket. Finally, she spoke. "I just feel empty," is all she muttered.

"I know. I really do, sweetheart. It will take a while, but that emptiness will pass," I assured her. "You'll begin to remember mom without being sad. You're so much like her. When I look at you, all I see is her. That's the greatest compliment I could give anyone.

"You're smart and pretty," I said, forging ahead. "You have real talent as an artist." I pointed to a small watercolor of a fish leaping out of the water, propped up on her nightstand. "I never could have done anything close to that when I was your age. I'm really proud of you. And I know your mom is, too."

With that, I walked toward the door, hesitated, and said, "You and Britt are the most important thing in my life. I want you to always know that."

I closed the door on the way out, paused in the hallway, closed my eyes, exhaled, then walked down the steps into a sea of kids I'd never seen before.

As my mother-in-law ushered one group of teenagers into the TV room, Britt pulled a young man toward her and held his hand. "Daddy, this is Jarrod, the boy I've been telling you about."

"Hey there, Mr. R," said a surprisingly normal-looking boy with short hair who wore a neat pair of American Eagle shorts and an ironed Izod shirt.

"Hi there, Jarrod," I said. "Fancy car out there. By the way, how was *Mama Mia?*"

"Fun," he answered, not flinching.

I had hoped that Britt would have kept dating one of the boys at the Academy when I'd transferred the girls to the public school after Christine's death. Sure, I wanted them to have this experience of mixing it up with kids from more modest backgrounds like I'd experienced growing up in Swissvale; I thought that would be a positive thing. But now, it was my *daughters,* and their futures were at stake. Britt actually thought she was dating this boy I knew nothing about from among the horde of public-school kids. I was starting to doubt my decision.

"So, you're starting senior year? Are you planning to go to college?" I quizzed Jarrod, hoping to trip him up.

Brittany elbowed me. "He's been in the honors program every year," she whispered.

"Actually, Mr. R.," Jarrod spoke softly, "my advisor wants me to apply to Hershey Medical School's early admission program—three years in undergrad and directly to med school. We'll see about the scholarship package, but that's my top choice."

This answer threw me off balance. I retreated, saying, "So, I hear Stevie Yates down at Swissvale Auto Parts is your uncle? Good guy. I used to ride the bus with him back when we went to Pitt."

"Yeah," Jarrod answered, munching on a chip. "Uncle Steve told me he knew you when you were dating some girl who worked at the *Pitt News.* He said she was a knock-out blonde who all the guys had a crush on," he said.

"D'you ever see that woman anymore, Dad-o?" Britt interjected, standing on one sandal. "What was her name again?"

"I don't remember, guys," I replied. "It was a long time ago."

"I think it was Margaret or something," Jarrod offered.

I counted to five. That was the one thing I hated about living in a small town like Swissvale: Everyone knew everyone else's business.

"Her name was Marjorie," I finally answered. "My memory's shot now that I turned fifty."

"Do you think we'll ever meet this Marjorie woman, Dad-o?" Britt raised an eyebrow.

Christine's mom leaned halfway over the kitchen counter, craning her neck to listen. Her freckles seemed to be dancing across her face.

"Why would *you guys* want to meet her?" I asked no one in particular.

"She'd probably have some great stories about you, back when you were a *fun* person," Britt answered. "If I posted something on that new Facebook thing, I bet we could find a picture of this babe from an old Pitt yearbook."

"Try it, sweetheart, and I'll cut off your internet privileges," I said, all kidding aside.

"Mom wouldn't have cared," Britt said. "She'd have thought it was *way* cool."

"So would I," interrupted Christine's mother.

Cy took a step forward. He handed his wife a bowl of chips and a jar of salsa to extricate her from this conversation.

"My Uncle Steve wouldn't tell me what happened to her," Jarrod continued, now devouring a bite of pizza. "He said she wasn't like other kids. But he never explained what he meant by that. Uncle Stevie said every guy in Swissvale tried to date that Marjorie girl, but you were the only one she seemed okay with. He said she ended up moving to California real sudden, so nobody ever knew what really happened. Is that true? I mean, if so, it's kind of a sad ending to the story, isn't it, Mr. R?"

"Well, it's really a *nice* ending," Britt interjected, clasping my hand. "Otherwise, my dad wouldn't have met my mom. And I wouldn't have been born, and we wouldn't be a family. Isn't that exactly what you'd always wanted, daddy?"

CHAPTER 3 1

September 2008 (Courtroom)

LAST RIDE TO THE SOUTH SIDE

The next morning, as Judge Wendell tapped his gavel to resume the proceedings, an odd feeling of unsettledness and jeopardy seemed to fill the courtroom. Drew-Morris immediately went on the attack in her cross-examination of Marjorie.

"So, Ms. Radovich, weren't you *slightly* curious to meet your father?" Drew-Morris asked tersely, continuing her questioning. "You've certainly taken a *keen* interest in the man, I mean, now that he's dead."

Marjorie stared directly at Drew-Morris. "I never had a perverse interest in meeting someone who'd ruined my mother's life and abandoned me before I was born," she volleyed back.

Marjorie directed her eyes towards our opponent's feet. Drew-Morris shifted her heels, trying to cover up the tiny green etching of a butterfly on her left ankle.

"So, you're telling me you never saw the decedent when he was laid out at the George M. Tischko Funeral Home in 1979?" she asked. "Would that fall within your definition of '*meeting him during your lifetime*?'"

A fresh image swirled into my head: I could see the ornate vestibule of the funeral home, October leaves blowing across the porch, a brief *Pomen* service, a man in a casket in the lavender parlor, a flag draped over the corner.

I looked at Ralph Acmovic Jr. and suddenly made the connection: He was there that day. The rubbery moles. The smirk on his face. His eyes now seemed to convey a perverse appreciation for the trap his attorney was setting.

Marjorie swallowed as if enduring painful drilling in the dentist's chair. *Now* I understood why she'd waited so long to show up at the trial. The silence seemed to continue forever. Then she said, "I have no recollection if I ever knew where the man was laid out. And, no, I never had a perverse interest in seeing him—dead or alive."

Marjorie glanced at her questioner with steely eyes. "Let me just say this clearly, Ms. Drew-Morris," she continued. "I never considered that man my father, except in a legal sense. I would have *thrown up* if I was ever forced to look at him. Now, that doesn't mean he shouldn't pay my mother every bit of money in that trust fund to make up for his horrible sins. Those are two separate issues."

I squirmed in my seat. Marjorie's answer, once again, was skillfully evasive. If she was willing to duck the truth about this, under oath, what other facts was she twisting in her story?

Our opponent glided over and whispered in the ear of Ralph Acmovic Jr. He stared at Marjorie, checking out his alleged half-sister from top to bottom, almost lecherously. He nodded affirmatively.

Drew-Morris flipped through a pile of papers, whispering something heatedly at her paralegal. Evidently, he hadn't subpoenaed the records of the Tischko Funeral Home that would have included the visitors' book at the viewing. It didn't matter. I knew Marjorie wouldn't have signed the guest book.

Drew-Morris now approached the witness box with a color-coded folder.

"Okay, *Ms.* Radovich-Pearce," she said while removing a document and slapping it in front of Marjorie. "I'm showing you what I've marked 'Respondent's Exhibit 16.' This is your permanent record from Swissvale High School. In section 'C,' look at the box marked 'Name of Father.' So why does *this* document, which was compiled from information supplied by you and your family, state that your father is 'deceased?'"

"I told *lots* of people that my father was dead," Marjorie responded, unflustered. "I wasn't thrilled about telling my teachers that my mother had been impregnated by a low-life alcoholic while she was in high school."

Drew-Morris threw up her hands. She grabbed another piece of paper and waved it. "And didn't you tell your best friend, Lori Wertz, that your father was a Navy pilot who was killed when President Eisenhower sent him overseas to 'beat down a Communist threat?'" she asked. "I have an affidavit from Ms. Wertz, who now goes by Mrs. Lori Rothrauff. She attests that you made such statements on at least a dozen occasions. Would you like to see the affidavit, or is Mrs. Rothrauff a liar too?"

"Lori Wertz would never tell an intentional lie," Marjorie said, turning to the judge. "I have no reason to question her. I made up lots of stories about my father. I *wanted* to hide the truth."

"Speaking of covering up the truth, Ms. Radovich, why would you sell a relatively valuable piece of property in Northern California—if your story is true—to buy a place in Pittsburgh that will be far less marketable?" Drew-Morris asked. "Is this story another ploy to pull at the heartstrings of the judge here when you really have no intention—"

There was a sound of something banging against metal, followed by a violent coughing noise. Aunt Peg's wheelchair slammed against the wooden bench, causing Marjorie's daughter to clutch her brother's arm. Aunt Peg suddenly began grabbing at the nasal tube that fed her oxygen as if trying to rip it out with her hands. The old woman managed to push herself up in her chair, straining at the belt, making a strange guttural noise—"*Home-meh!*"

"Sit down, Peg," Choppy said. "It's okay, *hun.* You're gonna hurt yourself if you don't sit back down in that seat."

At the sound of Choppy's voice, Aunt Peg paused. A deep cough lengthened into a prolonged phlegmy gurgle that she struggled to hack up.

"C'mon, hun," Choppy said. "*Marji's* here! She's staying in Picksburgh with the kids. We'll ask the judge if we can take you home."

Aunt Peg's neck turned sideways slowly. For the first time since the trial had begun, the old woman's eyes appeared oddly clear and alert. They settled on Marjorie in the witness box. Then they turned directly toward me. The old lady grinned, her mouth attempting to form a word. But her body continued to thrash about, nearly bucking itself out of the wheelchair to which she was belted.

"*Jesus God,*" Choppy said, pinning his wife's arms against the armrests. "She's convulsing. Someone get an am'blance. *Jesus,* Shawn, Peg's in trouble. Can't someone *help* us?"

I jumped out of my chair to restrain Aunt Peg's arms. Choppy fumbled around desperately, looking for something inside the medication bag. He pulled out a bottle and a plastic dropper, then filled it, jamming the dropper into his wife's mouth and squirting some red liquid into it. Aunt Peg spat the medicine onto her dress and then clamped her teeth closed, blocking Choppy's effort to drive the plastic dropper into her mouth for a second time.

"C'mon, *Midge,*" he cajoled. "If you take some of this here medicine, it'll stop the convulsing so we can get you home."

Marjorie leaned over my shoulder and gently massaged her grandmother's hand. Choppy loosened the top buttons of Aunt Peg's blouse so it wouldn't constrict her breathing. Suddenly, with crystal clarity in her eyes, the old woman stared at me, then she cocked her head toward Marjorie, smiling so broadly that the excess medicine spilled out the sides of her mouth.

"Take the medicine, Aunt Peg," Marjorie whispered in her grandmother's ear. "Listen to your Marji. We're *moving* here. We'll be here all year round now. I'll bring the kids over whenever you want, every day of the week. We're all together; our whole family is here now."

A team of paramedics banged through the courtroom doors, their bags of instruments knocking against the counsel table. Already, Aunt Peg seemed subdued, her chest gasping in short gulps.

The EMTs strapped the old woman onto a gurney and carried her out, her head facing the rear of the courtroom. The high Slovak cheekbones were fixed with a look of calmness and unwavering pride as her eyes blinked one last time.

Marjorie gathered up her children and their jackets. They stared at me, their eyes large and frightened. She briefly paused as if debating whether to introduce them to me, but instead, she pushed her children out of the room behind the army of paramedics.

Choppy limped as fast as he could, trying to keep up with the gurney as it banged down the hallway. He caught up and placed his hand gently on Aunt Peg's check, his tears dripping on her pillow. I stood in the hallway, my arms at my side, watching them crowd into the service elevator that led to the building's front entrance on Grant Street.

Minutes later, I could hear the siren as the ambulance fought against rush-hour traffic. Looking out the window, I saw the ambulance make a U-turn in front of the courthouse, then speed in the direction of South Side Hospital to the same red brick building where Peg Sotak had been born eighty-two years earlier. I knew, even before the sound of the siren vanished as the vehicle crossed the Monongahela River, that this would be her last ride across the bridge.

Bernie and I waited nearly two hours in the courtroom, debating whether to go to the hospital and offer the family support.

As the courtroom clock struck four o'clock, Jimmy emerged from the judge's chambers carrying a Totes umbrella. Nodding toward Bernie and me, he tacked the court's daily calendar onto the door before locking up for the night. The bold print on top confirmed that going to South Side Hospital was now pointless.

It said: **"Petitioner Marjorie Radovich et al. v. Estate of Ralph Acmovic Sr., No. 87 of 2008. Closing arguments to be postponed, subject to further notice of Court, due to death in the family."**

Fall 1980 (Third Year Law School, Somerville)

JEALOUSY AND DISTRUST

The boredom and sense of isolation during the third year of law school caused us to retreat to the basement on most Thursday nights. It was the best place to start the weekends early. This night's impromptu party in mid-November was meant to celebrate the fact that Dobbs had received two rejection letters from big firms in New York (he had zero interest in working at a big corporate firm) and one call-back from a political consulting firm in Washington (his first choice after graduating). The party consisted of a case of beer, generic Star Market pretzels, and a ping-pong tournament that had no beginning or end. Stick kept slamming the ball deep toward the water pipes hoping Dobbs would crack his head on them and forfeit. Cheating was an essential part of our ping-pong games.

"I got winners!" I called.

Stick had cranked up Steely Dan's *Deacon Blues* on our basement stereo. I had to shout over the noise to get their attention.

Outside, sheets of freezing rain hammered against the cellar window.

I straightened the red Izod sweater Marjorie had bought me so I'd look more like an Ivy Leaguer. Recently she seemed intent on having me *look* like a successful Harvard Law graduate, so I'd fit the role when I got out and joined the professional world. I'd never felt comfortable wearing preppy clothes, so I'd surgically removed the green Izod alligator with scissors, leaving only a faint shadow above the pocket. Marjorie would never notice.

There was a loud rapping on the front door as hard soles clicked across the upstairs floor.

"Hey, Pittsburgh-boy," Dobbs said, turning down the stereo. "I think your *other* main squeeze is here." He shouted upstairs: "C'mon down, Erica. Your buddy Shawn can't make up his mind about which job to take. He's worrying about it so much that he's giving everyone colitis."

A wave of light perfume preceded Erica as she navigated the cellar steps. She stood at a slight slant as she unzipped her rain slicker and shook herself off, mumbling, "*bwwr, col.*" Erica wore oversized powder-blue corduroy pants and a heavy Liz Claiborne sweater, an outfit baggy enough to obscure the contours of her body.

"Hi, S-s-Shwam," she said, her lip drooping and a dribble of saliva glistening on the right side of her mouth. "I hear you guyz'r havin' some kinda party to cel'brate Dobbs' rejeg-shins. Less break open the beers. I'm a firss-class *reject;* I oughta fit in perfectly."

Erica settled onto our basement couch, straightening her right leg with both hands.

I walked over and plopped down a foot away from her. I didn't want Stick and Dobbs spreading gossip, but I also didn't want Erica feeling worse about herself. I'd never known twenty-four-year-olds could have strokes. But, according to the doctors at the Harvard Medical Center, it could (and did) happen to Erica. And now, she had become largely isolated. Most of the Ivy Leaguers, even women's libbers, had been offended by her air of superiority before this calamity. Now, it was hard to repair those broken relationships. Lanny, Erica's classmate from Chicago, had transferred to the business school to earn a joint J.D./MBA, admonishing us that "lawyers don't earn any *real* money." So, Erica had few friends left. As she leaned closer to me on the couch, I gave her a quick kiss on the cheek to make her feel welcome. Her skin felt cold.

"We'll leave you kids alone," Dobbs said, sliding his paddle on the table and giving a thumbs up. He seemed pleased that Erica had latched onto me as her new friend—a surprise to all of us. For all his bluster, Dobbs seemed to have a personal interest in everyone in our class and was particularly troubled by Erica's situation, wanting her to become *better*. He and Stick headed up the steps and clicked off the basement light as if we were high schoolers on a date. "Hah, hah!" I shouted after them. "Real funny!" There was no response. I could hear them banging around pots in the kitchen to make popcorn. There was still enough light coming through the cellar window from neighboring porch lights for me to see Erica. She clearly *did* think it was funny.

"Nice Izod, S-Shawn," she said. "Where's the alligha'dur?"

I touched the spot where there was nothing but a serpent-shaped shadow. "It must have fallen off," I said, then quickly switched subjects. "Did you get your hornbook to review corporations yet? It boils down to a few key rules. You can pull a B if you nail down the basic elements, Erica."

"I can't concen-tate like before. An it's a prol'lem writing with this damn thing," she said, holding up a withered hand. "Don't ever hava' stwoke, S-s-Shawn. It's hell on your self-a'teem."

The slight aphasia that impeded Erica's word retrieval made it difficult to follow her at times. It was only when she slowed down her speech—as the therapists were teaching her to do—that I could understand all the words. Other things were also off-kilter—even her hair, which was neatly groomed on the left side but largely uncombed on the other. She made a deliberate movement with her lips, trying to form a smile.

The principal cause of the stroke during our second year had been "hereditary factors." Her mother's side of the family had a long history of embolisms at a young age. This congenital weakness likely had been exacerbated, doctors had concluded, by Erica's use of birth control pills and her smoking cigarettes as a weight control strategy. But none of these factors alone, they added, would have normally caused a healthy 24-year-old woman to have this kind of "cerebrovascular" disaster. That explained why the Harvard Health Clinic, they said, had found no underlying health issue during previous visits—including the night she'd lost her balance and I'd driven her to the clinic to be checked out. The specialists concluded that the main exacerbating factor was almost certainly Erica's penchant for "recreational drugs," including cocaine, the use of which had begun in college but had reached a frenetic pitch in law school, escalating after her relationship with her boyfriend in Chicago became a mess.

Tests confirmed a "grade-3 bleed." It could have been worse, the doctors said; she could have been permanently paralyzed. But it certainly could have been better. Erica was able to return to classes during the mid-second year with the help of professional tutors, physical therapists, and speech therapists. If she worked at it diligently, they told her, she might be able to graduate only a year behind our class.

"You mine-if I haff *one* dr-rint, S-Shawn?" she asked me. "Uh, I'll promise not-ta ge' bombed."

"I thought the doctors said no alcohol with your medication?" I reminded her.

"One dr-rint wouldn't huwt, right?" she asked.

"I'll get you some apple juice," I said, patting her leg.

While I was at it, I pulled out an old Chi-Lites album. In Swissvale, we'd grown up on Motown and R&B. Tonight was a perfect night for reliving those memories. I'd lost the album with "*Oh Girl.*" So, I put on "*You Got to Be the One,*" one of the sleepers Marjorie and I had discovered in the record pile. I'd always told her that this should be the theme song for a spectacular movie about the triumph of love over everything in its way.

In the dark, Erica noisily sipped the last of her apple juice.

"You ready to get a cab pretty soon, Erica?" I asked. "One apple juice is probably enough," I said, half-joking. "You should get some sleep, so you're fresh when you tackle corporations tomorrow."

Erica shook her head sideways, meaning "not yet." She rearranged her sweater, causing flickers of static electricity to shoot like sparks in the dark.

"Stick sez you-ur sill freaked out about, uh, which jo-ob to pick? God, Shawn, you wor-ree too much," she said, dabbing her mouth with a Kleenex.

"I'm just worried about taking the *wrong* job, Erica. Or winding up in a place neither me or Marjorie wanna be," I said.

Erica exhaled loudly, taking in air through her open mouth. "Mar-zie or *I*."

"That's what I meant," I countered.

"Are you sure you're *lissen-en* to what *she* wants, Shawm?" she asked.

"Of *course* I'm listening, Erica," I said tersely. "Cripes, you think I'm dense? I just can't decipher what she's *saying*. One minute she's telling me I should come back home to Pittsburgh. The next minute she's talking about moving to the West Coast or even Texas, where one of her friends took a job at some computer company. She actually told me we should 'jump on whatever train takes us to the best option at that moment, hold our breath, and see what happens.' She said I shouldn't get too hung up on getting tied down to one *place*. What's wrong with picking a place, Erica? My brain's scrambled from thinking about this stuff."

"Did you as't the question diret'ly?" she continued.

"Meaning what?"

"Didn't you learn *anything* in trial moot court class, Shawm-with-a-w?" Erica said. "Ask the question' *diret'ly* of the witness. That's the only way for a good lawyer to know the *true* answer." Erica tilted her head.

"I keep asking her what *she* wants me to do," I said. "But she just keeps being evasive."

"*Hmpph*," Erica said, then abruptly announced: "I hafto go-a bath-oom."

Erica straightened her right leg and made her way through the darkness to the basement john hidden behind a wooden partition. After a long interlude followed by the flushing of the commode, I could see Erica maneuvering herself back toward me. Her hip bounced against the ping-pong table; she was still having trouble gauging locations and dimensions with any precision.

The smell of her perfume seemed more powerful as she tucked her crooked hand into her sweater. Then she fell gently onto my lap, making a slight gyrating motion against my thighs, and exhaled contentedly.

"C'mon, Erica. We can't do that," I said, pushing her away.

"That wuzza *joke*, Shawm," she said. "Loosen up!"

The stroke hadn't impaired Erica's sense of humor. "Right," I laughed.

I helped ease her onto the couch. "What about *you*, Erica?" I asked. "If you keep working hard, you should be on track to graduate next year. What comes after that?"

She propped herself against my shoulder, breathing through her nose.

"Y'know my folks got divorced last year, right?" she said. "Dad was goin' on work trips and having aff-airs with other women, dam *bas'sard*. He wants me to move back to Chi-cago, but there's no way. I'll pro'ly just move to New Yor', whatta' hell? New Yorz' a good place. I wanna do my *own* thing, not something that *jerk* wants. Mom supports me. I toll' her she can move there *with* me." Erica forced a smile.

"But here's my *real* dream, Shwan-with-a-w. One I never toll' *anyone* before," she said, inching closer. "I wanna handle *bid,* I mean *big* cases and solve *big* prom'lems. I wanna be *so* damn suxessful that no one even *notices* I'm a woman. You think tha's possible? I mean—even with *this?*" She held up her clenched hand in the dark.

I slipped an arm around Erica, rubbing her lower back on the side that was afflicted. "A bull-headed person like you? Absolutely. Now, stop jabbering so much and chill out."

After a few minutes, she began snoring loudly.

In my head, I heard the soothing beat of "*Rolling Down a Mountainside*" by the Main Ingredient and pictured listening to it while lying with Marjorie on the couch at the Semple Street Coop. It was incredible how music could trigger such a precise memory and bring back such good feelings.

"It's definitely possible, Erica," I whispered, taking her hand and straightening out the fingers. It made me sad to see her in this state. But even as she slept, with one lip drooping sideways, there was a firm look of determination on her face. "I know you'll do exactly that," I whispered to her.

———

"*What the hell?*"

The basement phone was clattering on its sixteenth ring before I knocked it off its cradle. Based upon the darkness of the cellar and the absolute stillness of the house, I judged it to be two or three in the morning. Before I could locate the receiver on the floor, though, Erica's good hand beat me to the mark.

"Hello?" she said sleepily.

She held the phone to her ear for a good ten seconds before blurting out: "I hear all abou' you Mar'gee. You're a lucky woman! S-s-sure, Shwam is right here. He was, uh, jus' *sleepin* here with me. Hold on."

Erica covered the receiver, nudging me in the side.

"Pretty coinc'idal, huh, Shwam?" she said, extending the phone to me with her afflicted hand. "We were jus' talking 'bout Mar-zie." Then Erica's voice halted as if she realized that she might have done something wrong.

I took the phone. "Hello. Look, Rad, there's nothing weird here," I said. "I just fell asleep after a ping-pong party."

Static pounded in my ear like a drummer tapping out quarter notes. It took ten or twelve beats before Marjorie spoke, "So now I understand why you're always in such a hurry to get back to Boston, Shawn." After five additional beats, the line went dead.

I sat there holding the phone in the air, recognizing that my already screwed-up relationship with my girlfriend had just turned into a bigger mess. I asked myself: Did Marjorie distrust me out of some weird, unfounded jealousy? Was it possible she didn't know how much I cared about her? Or was she looking for a reason to dump me and move on?

Erica held her knees and curled her fist, shivering from the cold air seeping through cracks in the basement windows.

"Can-yu-oo call uh cab, Shwan?" she said. "I think I bettuh geh' home."

Winter 1981 (Third Year, Somerville)

CALL TO MOM

As winter blew into Boston, the weekends became the worst times for me. For some reason, all the most beautiful women at Harvard seemed attracted to Dobbs, which bedeviled me and made me jealous because he was constantly going out on dates. Stick had friends from Nebraska who had moved nearby to attend grad school at Tufts, so they had a routine of getting together for Cornhuskers games or heading to bars in Boston on weekends to meet women. I would finish the dishes and wander down to the subway station at Harvard Square, sometimes buying a *Sports Illustrated Swimsuit Issue* at the Out-of-Town Newsstand when I was sure nobody I knew was watching me. I'd shove the brown bag under my coat, stealing quick peeks at the photos on the subway car—Red Line to Green Line, Green Line to Boylston. Here, Boston Public Garden offered a refuge for people with no purpose on lonely Saturday nights.

The famous swan boats at the Public Garden's pond were out of commission this time of year, pushed together and parked under a bridge like lonely birds hibernating from the cold weather. I'd watch the ice skaters do figure eights around the pond while hockey players knocked around pucks on the far end. By nine o'clock, as a winter moon settled over the scenic spot, couples would make their way onto the ice, lacing up skates, laughing, running onto the frozen pond, holding each other's hands. That would be my cue to leave, walking toward the Arlington subway stop and leafing through the magazine on the deserted ride home.

On the way through Harvard's campus, I'd stop at the Aiken Computation Lab, a red brick building in the Yard that housed machines marked "PDP-10." These giant computers allowed people at "centers of excellence" like Carnegie Mellon University in Pittsburgh to communicate with Harvard and a handful of research nodes around the country. To supplement her paid internship at Respironics, Marjorie had begun a part-time job at CMU through her advisor, Dr. David Cliff, which gave her free access to the ARPANET. As she explained to me one night on the phone while we devised a plan to get me hooked up too, the ARPANET was a communications system developed by the military so that foreign enemies couldn't "knock the whole system out during a nuclear attack."

Under the pretense of doing legal research, I'd gotten permission from the CS department to communicate with Marjorie during the late shift when the Harvard computer geeks sat slumped in their chairs and pecked at their computers.

After logging on, I'd compose a quick paragraph to Marjorie. The PDP-10 would hammer out a series of cryptic codes as it sent my message bouncing through the ether-world. If I was lucky and Marjorie was at her station at CMU, a message would come bouncing back to Harvard. I'd scoop up the paper spewed out by the machine, scan it quickly, then carry it home to study the words in private.

Her latest message, sent on a cold February night after I returned from the subway, was particularly maddening. It ended by saying: *"Respironics said they're going to offer me a job. But Doc Cliff says to hold out. He says MIT up there in Boston is starting to get a lot of action as a CS hub. He has connections up there. Also, there are a lot of new tech companies on the West Coast. This is going to have to be your choice, too, Shawn. I'm not telling you what to do. We're just going to have to keep an open mind."*

Marjorie had added a stinging P.S. to the message: *"I prefer not to hear about that Erica Welles woman anymore, either. If she has such terrible health problems, why isn't she home instead of hanging out at your house all night? Enough said."*

Stick had stayed home and was hanging out in the living room this night, messing around with his guitar. He was strumming the chords to *"Best of my Love"* by the Eagles, which only made me think of Marjorie—and miss her more. I finally pulled the telephone by its cord into my bedroom and called my mom. She was the best person I knew for helping to sort out impossible situations.

"Shawn," she'd asked me immediately, "Is that you? This is a Friday night. Peak rates still apply. Is everything all right?"

"I know it's a Friday, mom," I'd said. Hearing her voice had been remarkably soothing. I could have put the phone to my ear and just fallen asleep for an hour, comforted by it. "I just wanted to tell you I love you and wish you an early Happy Valentine's Day. I guess I couldn't wait till tomorrow."

I could picture my mom in her room at my Aunt Kate's place, probably wearing curlers and watching the ten o'clock news. She was undoubtedly staring at the phone with suspicion. Mom was no dummy.

"Oh, sweetheart, I appreciate that," she said. "But if something's bothering you, you've gotta tell me that, too." The soothing Irish lilt in her voice confirmed that her "mom antennae" were up: She could always intuit when I was hurting.

I closed my eyes and remembered sitting on her lap as a little boy snuggled up on the window seat atop the radiator in the dining room, feeling an absolute sense of security as I rubbed the smooth diamond on her ring. Being in her presence, commanding her full attention, was the closest I ever came to a feeling of pure safety no matter what was going on around me.

I now spilled out everything about the recent mixed signals I was receiving from Marjorie and the frustration I felt because I had no idea what my next step should be.

"She's getting a job offer at Respironics," I vented. "It's only twenty minutes from her house, and the pay's good. This programing work is right up her alley. But now she's talking about Boston and even the West Coast as a destination. Am I nuts?"

"Listen, baby," my mom had said in a voice that was both comforting and parental. "I never want to be a *buttinsky*, but it sounds like you kids need to make sure you're on the same page about the *big* things. When your dad and I fell in love, we just knew we were meant for each other. That was it. From there, we let everything else fall into place. It's not supposed to be this hard. That's what I worry about."

"Maybe each of you can't have *everything* you want, sweetheart," she continued. "But if you follow your hearts, you should end up in the right place. That's how your dad and I always looked at it."

"I appreciate that mom," I said. "I totally agree. I've gotta pick a law firm, and it can only be in one place, not five. I *thought* I knew what we wanted, but Marjorie's bouncing us around like a ping pong game. We supposedly had this settled. Aunt Peg and Choppy even had a room scoped out for a spare nursery, for whenever the time comes. Not that anybody's rushing things, but that's always been the plan."

Mom seemed to pause for a minute before speaking. When she did, her voice had that tone she used when she was weighing every word. "We love Marjorie; you know that sweetheart," she finally said. "But did you ever think you two may be going in different directions? Are you sure all of this is *her* plan? Are you positive you're listening to her?" She paused again. "I'm just afraid you could end up getting your heart broken, sweetheart. I'd never want to see that happen to my son."

"I sometimes think she's envious of this Harvard stuff," I interrupted, ignoring her last comment. "Every time I talk about my friends up here, she gets weird about it."

"Oh, Shawn, that's not fair." Mom halted that line of argument. "Your dad and I taught you to think the best of people. Marjorie's a lovely person. Can you blame her if she wants to have the same opportunities as you? A little competitive spirit is a good thing. Isn't that what you like so much about her? Of *course*, she wants to make her own mark. And let's be honest, you do talk a lot about your classmates, including that woman from Chicago—is it Erica?"

As usual, mom had outflanked me. "I know Marjorie's a great person," I replied. "I want to do what's best for her. So, what's my next move? I have no clue."

"Well, first you have to figure out what *you* think is important to do with your *own* life," mom said gently. "You can't help Marjorie figure out anything if you don't know where your own heart is pointing you."

My mom's voice became soft. "Do you ever think about the lessons your *dad* taught you, sweetheart? He's been gone almost three years. I miss him every day, just like you do. But he gave us lots of wonderful examples of how to live. Just close your eyes whenever you need him and ask for his help. He's still listening, Shawn."

I usually resisted praying to dad—it seemed selfish to turn to him only when I needed favors. But tonight, at mom's insistence, I exhaled loudly and relented. When I squeezed my eyes shut, I could see my dad perfectly, as if he were living flesh and blood: He was relaxing on the couch, shoes off, chewing a Bic pen, and scratching out formulas for his latest project at Kopp Glass. He looked up and caught me trying to sneak in TV time, watching F-Troop instead of studying as mom had instructed.

"You'd better always listen to your mother, Shawn," he said, his voice steady. "She's the person who brought you into this world and made your heartbeat. Always show respect to her, son. The same goes for everyone else in our family. Friends and neighbors fall into that bucket, too—they're the other half of our family. Always put them first. Don't let other things get in the way."

I kept my eyes closed and saw him as a tall man with thin hair that had turned from black to steel gray. I marveled at how strong his hands were when he placed them on my shoulders. He had walked into my room. I was a teenager. The time frame was obvious because my mom made sure I laid out my clothes for the next day—a regular routine during high school years.

"Make sure you get down on those knees of yours, Shawn," he said, "and say a prayer of thanks for everything God gave you today."

I was always a little embarrassed that he talked to me this way as if I were still a child, especially with my mom standing there.

"Yes, sir," I said.

"Because every day is a gold coin that you need to spend doing good things for other people."

"I know, dad," I could hear myself saying. "You told me that a hundred times."

He looked at me with steady eyes that communicated a special connection between us.

"Well, that's because you need to think about how you plan to spend that gold coin tomorrow, Shawn," he said, giving me a kiss. I could feel the bristles of his beard against my face. Even though I considered myself too old for that, it still felt comforting. "Because we never know when it's our last one, son."

I held that image for one more moment, savoring it. Then I opened my eyes and snapped back to my phone conversation. I'd already ordered Valentine flowers as a surprise for my mom from the florist in Harvard Square. They were due to arrive the following afternoon. So, there wasn't much more I could say without spilling the beans. And I didn't want to risk getting too emotional and letting her hear the warble in my voice.

"Thanks for the advice, mom," I said. "It helps a lot. I'll think about what dad would tell me to do if he were up here with me."

Then I hung up and curled myself in the bean bag chair in my room, listening to "*Stay With Me Tonight*" by the Iron City Houserockers and feeling a tiny bit more hopeful that I could turn things around if I remained true to myself. I pulled open my bottom drawer, pushed aside some T-shirts, and extricated the old snow globe that I'd kept stashed there since Aunt Peg had given it to me. I shook the glass sphere and watched the white specks swirl around its tiny buildings, houses, and blast furnaces meant to represent some past version of Pittsburgh. If I figured out the right thing to do for me, I told myself, which in turn would allow me to do the best thing for the people I cared about most, this situation with Marjorie would work itself out neatly.

September 2008 (Strip District Café)

AMAZING CAFÉ

Aunt Peg's wake and the funeral had created a week's hiatus from trial—a terrible way to get a break.

J.V. had insisted we use the time to organize files and create "to-do" lists to prepare for her impending maternity leave. I'd pushed back, reminding my associate that she was supposed to be on bed rest. But she'd insisted, saying that her preeclampsia symptoms had subsided and "my blood pressure will shoot through the roof if I don't organize these cases before I leave." I appreciated J.V.'s hyperactive efficiency. But I was still feeling drained emotionally from Aunt Peg's sudden death and saddened that I never had a chance to say goodbye. I also didn't want to risk my associate jeopardizing the baby or herself.

To put all of this out of my mind, I'd decided to take J.V. out for breakfast. It was a good way to relax while talking about things. It was also better than dwelling on this recent sadness and the fact that I'd soon be on my own for two months once J.V. left to have her baby.

"Would you like another decaf latté, ma'am?" asked a thin waiter with tattoos on both arms.

"Sure, just a teeny one," J.V. said. "My doctor says I can't have anything that even *smells* of caffeine."

The Amazing Café in the Strip District was J.V.'s favorite breakfast spot. Attached to a yoga studio, it featured coffees with peace signs drawn in the foam, omelets whipped up from brown eggs laid by chickens that had never consumed pesticides, and an assortment of organic vegan specialties. J.V. was in the process of demolishing a plate of organic French toast topped with roasted flax seed and drenched in blueberry compote and syrup. She'd also ordered a side of honey-cured bacon made from pigs raised at a local farm in Butler. At the moment, J.V. seemed ready to scarf down anything—including the table.

"Here's a printout of our active case files," she said, handing me a binder as she bit into some toast. "The ones with yellow sticky notes are the ones I'm principal attorney on. I've reassigned each case; don't try to mess with it, Shawn. You need to delegate more to Alison. I know this is still a temporary deal. But her career was almost ruined by that unethical register of wills and Drew-Morris. Alison deserves a chance to rebuild a client base. Give her more responsibility, Shawn. She'll rise to the occasion."

I inspected the giant brown binder with color-coded tabs. This was going to be a hellish maternity leave.

"How long's your break again?" I asked.

"It's not exactly a break, boss," she said with a hint of exasperation.

"Oh, right," I replied.

"Don't worry," she tried to reassure me. "The last two times, I didn't even take six weeks. Remember how Christine drove me to Somerset so I could handle that will contest for you after Cam was born?"

"Yeah, that wasn't my finest moment," I said. "Take six-and-a-half weeks this time. I can tough it out."

"By the way, Shawn, I just finished this estate—the one with the red sticky. It was for a lady from the church on Polish Hill. The poor thing's sister died, and she has emphysema." J.V. pointed to the flagged page in the binder. "I wasn't going to say anything, but I did it for free. She gave us two nut rolls and an apricot roll. You get half."

I nodded. "Sounds like a fair deal," I said, approving of my associate's good business judgment.

"And while I'm on leave, Uncle Billy said he wants to have you over for beer and pizza once a week to check on you," she said. "That's non-negotiable."

As Pink Floyd's *Dark Side of the Moon* wafted through the Amazing Café speakers, a banging noise disrupted the tranquil scene. J.V.'s boys Terrell and Cameron had bombed through the door, dragging Alison and a tall young man behind them.

"Do you have our markers, mom?" the little one asked. The boys wore matching Spiderman T-shirts, carrying mocha Frappuccinos from Starbucks and sticky treats from Peace, Love, and Little Donuts.

"Some dude at the coffee place gave us Mister Rogers Neighborhood coloring packs," Terrell said. "He says Handyman Joe comes there for egg-and-cheese breakfast sandwiches sometimes." J.V. swept the boys into her lap, mussing their hair. Terrell, the oldest, favored his dad with frizzy hair and skin that was unmistakably black. Cameron had lighter, caramel-colored skin and a tinge of red in his hair, like J.V.

"I'd really better go, Shawn," J.V. said as she searched for her purse. "I don't feel comfortable leaving the boys with other people. It isn't fair."

"C'mon J.V., you deserve a pre-baby break," I said. "Besides, you *told* me we need to delegate more to Alison."

J.V. had convinced me to hire Alison part-time while she (J.V.) was on maternity leave. Today, it was clear I had made the right decision. Alison wore a business suit with a list of "to-do" items in her hand to discuss after breakfast. With her was a male au pair, or "bro-pere," as Alison called him. He was a mature teenager from her church who'd agreed to help J.V. because the boys' school had an in-service day. A tall boy from Germany, he was armed for battle with a towel slung over his shoulder to mop up spills and messes.

"The boys are having a *blast*," Alison said, giving a thumbs-up. "Fränk just needed their colored markers to finish their project. Once they get busy, I'll jump onto that conference call at ten, then meet you to go over our list, Mr. Rossi."

J.V. pulled out a massive bag of art supplies from her purse and handed them over. "No drawing tattoos on yourselves, guys," she said. I noticed that her belly had become the size of a beach ball, and her eyes were puffy.

"Is it gonna be a boy or girl?" I asked, keeping it quiet.

"We've decided to surprise ourselves," she said. "I'd love to have a little girl, you know. But Kalvin's chromosomes only seem to produce crazy little boys."

The waitress, a sleeve of wild tattoos adorning each arm, delivered a second order of honey-cured bacon.

"God, Shawn," she said as she scarfed down a piece in one bite. "I feel like I have ADD. I can't *focus* worth a damn. It's my own fault. I waited to do this kid stuff *now* so I could get started in my career. Nobody told me how *tired* I'd be. I told Kalvin that he's shut off after this one."

"You're just sleep-deprived," I said, rubbing J.V.'s hand. "I'd give a million bucks to be back to where you guys are."

"Right," she said. "You and Christine were smart enough to stop at *two*. I don't know how we'll pay for these little buggers. Jesus, Shawn, that full-day Catholic kindergarten will *bankrupt* us next year. Oh yeah, I probably didn't tell you this, boss. Kalvin had an interview over this new Skype thing, and it went well. He got a job offer in the IT department at Northwestern. We're thinking he'll probably need to take it, and I'll stay here for now with the kids."

I choked on my flourless crumb cake. "Northwestern's in goddamn *Chicago!*" I blurted out.

"It'd be a *big* break for Kalvin," she said defensively. "He finished his master's from CMU, for God's sake. I've been hogging all the attention. That poor guy deserves some recognition for a change." J.V. pushed away her organic French toast. "It's not ideal. Kalvin has a cousin he can rent a room from for a year or two until we can afford a house there, so it won't be a big hit financially. Realistically, it's inevitable. How are we gonna get the boys to college on *one* salary? And with the new baby coming, we're going to burst out of our house. We'll need a bigger place with more bedrooms. Mortgage payments and taxes will just keep going higher."

I slid my stool closer. "Commuting marriages *suck*," I said. "Most of my friends who've done the long-distance thing have ended up getting divorced or wanting to slit their wrists. And what do you mean, you're going to 'buy a house in Chicago?' C'mon girl, you're not allowed to move to freaking Chicago. You're too important to me here."

"That's nice of you to say, boss." J.V. jiggled her foot under the table, something she did when she was keyed up. "But if we've gotta move to Chicago, we've gotta move to Chicago. I'd just have to find the right place where my kids would be okay. It wouldn't be a problem for you—I'm easily replaceable. You've got a great reputation, Shawn. You can find someone far better than me. There are Harvard Law grads who would snap up the position in a second. It won't be a loss for you, believe me."

"C'mon J.V." I shut her down. "I *care* about you guys. Don't even talk like this."

The skinny waiter offered to pour fresh coffee for me. I waved him away.

My associate stared at me so long it felt uncomfortable.

"You *care* about me?" J.V. said as her eyes grew red and her voice warbled. "Why waste your time, boss? I'm exhausted. I'm fat. And I do a *half-assed* job at everything!"

I looked over at a table of women in stretch pants who'd just come from a workout at the yoga studio. They'd stopped eating their omelets to stare at us.

"That's not true, J.V.," I said, lowering my voice. "You do a *great* job. And you're only *temporarily* big."

As she started sobbing louder, I fumbled to pull a hankie from my pocket.

"And my dad doesn't just have *PNEUMONIA!*" she blurted out. "The specialist found a spot on his lung. Now he has to have chemo. Mom and dad helped watch our kids when they were babies, and I ignored *them*. Now, I'm *responsible*. We'll have to be able to afford a house in Chicago that's big enough for them to move in with us. This is going to be a horrible year, but we'll handle it."

"Jeez, J.V., why didn't you *tell* me about your dad?" I asked. "I could've let you take some time off."

"You can't help me, Shawn," she said, blowing her nose into my hankie. "My life's in *shambles*. I'm even late for *daycare* most days. I'm a total screw-up. I can't even be on time when *other* people are watching my kids."

The yoga ladies were now intensely checking out J.V.'s pregnant belly and glancing at me with incriminating eyes.

"You want another confession, Shawn?" J.V. asked, her face radiating a stew of emotions like a giant mood ring. "I actually sneak out of the house when mom's with the kids and go to the car wash, just so I can be alone. Isn't that *pathetic*? It's the only place my damn cell phone won't work. I *abandon* the kids with my 70-year-old mother so I can go to the freakin' *car wash* to get a break. I need to see a shrink."

"That's not so weird," I said, knowing it was weird.

"Look, I know you're my boss, and I shouldn't be telling you this, but my hormones are *out of control* right now, and I need to get this guilt off my chest," she half-sobbed.

"C'mon, sweetheart," I said, taking J.V.'s hand while scowling at the yoga 'neb-noses.' "You're just stressed out from wanting this baby to come. After you have a chance to rest up during this maternity leave, you'll feel perfect. And we're going to figure out how to make things work out for you and Kalvin here in the Burgh, I promise. I'm going to make it my mission."

J.V. used a sleeve to brush a tear from her cheek. "I'm glad I found you as my mentor, boss," she said. "I got lucky on that one. I'm really grateful."

"There's no reason to be thanking anyone, J.V.," I said, handing her my nap-kin. "That's what makes Pittsburgh 'Pittsburgh,' isn't it? Did you ever think about why people like us stick around this place?"

J.V. sat up, her splotched face seeming to regain its composure. "That's an easy one, Shawn," she said, laughing as she dabbed her eyes. My associate gazed out the window at shoppers and produce workers hustling along the sidewalks of the Strip District. "It's the intangible stuff. Nobody's *snobby* here—there's no hierarchy, right? Like Josie, the waitress at the Duquesne Club. Think about it. She's on par with the CEO of U.S. Steel, who eats lunch there. One big-shot corporate VP was rude to Josie and yelled at her, so they kicked him out."

"Yeah!" I high-fived her. "That guy deserved it."

"And the *informality* is another thing, Shawn," J.V. continued, dabbing her eye with my napkin and perking up. "How about that neat couple who just hired me for their big estate planning project? They own a baking supply company in Carnegie that went global. They're multi-millionaires now. But guess what? They told me they shop for their toilet paper in bulk at Walmart!" J.V. threw her hands up as if to say, 'who knew?' "On weekends, they do volunteer work at local church camps. Total humility. You'd never know they were rich. That's what makes Pitts-burgh, Pittsburgh for me. It's the *invisible* things. Kalvin always says that, too. . . ."

"*Mommy, mommy, MOMMY!*"

J.V. sprang from the chair and catapulted toward her youngest son like a preg-nant gold medalist as every patron in the café froze. Cameron held out his left arm as if it was paralyzed.

"*Mommy, mommy, MOMMY!*"

J.V. swept the little boy into her arms.

"What's the matter, sweetie?" she said. "Mom's here. Please *talk* to me."

"*Look!*" he said, pointing to a bright red mark the size of a bead on his forearm.

"*Oh my God!*" exclaimed J.V., holding up her son's limb and turning it sideways like a surgeon determining a diagnosis.

"That's a *ladybug*, Cameron," she said, touching it gently. "Haven't you seen one of those before?"

Cameron shook his head. "Nope," he said. "Is it like a *VW bug?*"

He kept his arm rigid, gawking at the speckled bug as if he'd discovered one of the great wonders of the world.

J.V. adjusted her maternity skirt and knelt.

"They eat bad insects that suck the juice out of Mommy's flowers in the garden," she said. "Do you know how *lucky* it is to find a ladybug this time of year, sweetie? This one has *lots* of spots. It's just a *little* guy, like you."

Fränk, the bro-pere, hurried back into the café dragging Terrell, who was punching away at his Gameboy. "Sorry he got away," he said. "This boy's like a wriggly salamander."

J.V. stood up and pushed the hair out of her eyes. "It's not your fault, Fränk," she said to the bro-pere. "I appreciate the help."

As J.V. stood there with her sons, a cozy little pod, the ladies seated beside us smiled and whispered "how cute!" as the boys wrapped themselves around their mom and pinched each other's arms. J.V.'s face flashed a look of relief. I realized something, staring at them, which had never occurred to me before: No matter where she went, J.V. always had to be conscious of the fact that she was the matriarch of a mixed-race family and needed to make sure her sons were safe in their surroundings.

"Thanks for breakfast, boss," J.V. said, turning to me. "These boys are gonna take M-O-M home. Alison can cover the conference call at ten, and you should be all set."

Now that the "crisis" was over, the gawking yoga ladies returned to their food.

"Sorry, I'm such a *nut case*, Shawn," she said, planting a solid kiss on my cheek. "I'll be fine once this baby gets here. Thank heavens I work for an *understanding* person like you."

She handed me the thick binder and gathered up the boys' gear.

"There are still a few things that worry me about going on maternity leave right now," she whispered so Alison wouldn't hear. "One is that Drew-Morris lady. We can't let her win, Shawn. The more she pushes the envelope to get what she wants, the more she gets away with it. There's something up with that woman. I just can't put my finger on it. I have a terrible feeling in my gut about what she might do next.

"And I feel even worse about Choppy and Peg's house. I've tried everything, but I've failed to stop it." J.V. wiped a few tears from her eyes. "It breaks my heart. That little house and neighborhood are all that ever mattered to them." She took a deep breath. "But I think you should withdraw the subpoena of that poor nun, Shawn. Bringing her into court would be cruel and immoral. There's no way Choppy and Aunt Peg would want that. That poor Sister is too old to handle the stress of this. And who knows what she can actually add that isn't tossed out as hearsay? You'd be hurting someone who was quietly helping young women in dire straits, and she clearly doesn't feel comfortable talking about it. That's not who you are, boss. You always stood for something bigger than that."

J.V. kissed me on the cheek. "I've invested everything in you and what you stand for. Don't disappoint me on this, boss."

September 2008 (Swisshelm Park Home)

BRITT AND LIZA'S NIGHT OUT

The end of the week couldn't come soon enough. I was never good at pretending to work when I was distracted. J.V.'s impending maternity leave had me rattled: I hadn't run the law firm by myself for years. At least things seemed calm at the home front—for now. Until recently, walking into my own home often felt like walking on eggshells. But there had been several consecutive days without a battle.

"See ya, Dad-o," Britt announced as she swept past me at the kitchen table. I was eating alone again—a frequent occurrence on Friday evenings. "Jarrod's taking me to get frozen yogurt. Then we're playing Taboo at Jimmy Kambic's house. He'll have me home by midnight."

"Eleven o'clock," I said emphatically.

"Eleven forty-five," she volleyed back.

"Done," I said. "Tell Jarrod I'm watching him. He'd better not try to go parking with my daughter or smoke blunts at the playground."

"Don't worry about *me*, Dad-o," Britt said. "It's the *other* daughter you need to control. You put no limits on her. Maybe you need to take a parenting class."

As I hustled into the hallway to kiss Britt, she'd already made a call on her pink RAZR flip phone and slid out the front door. At least her outfit looked appropriate: It buttoned up to her neck and covered her shoulders. That much was a relief. I heard a car door slam and the roar of a powerful engine as the car pulled away.

A second set of footsteps tiptoed down the staircase. From the timing and deliberate movement, I knew I was in trouble.

Liza looked me right in the eye as if daring me to tangle with her. She was wearing a blue shirt that clung to her skinny body and exposed her entire midriff, and her jeans looked like bleach had been dumped across them in random splotches. She appeared to be wearing a push-up bra, flaunting curves that didn't naturally belong to her. My fourteen-year-old daughter's hair had a bright pink streak at the forehead that dangled like a pink windshield wiper. For the first time, I also noticed there was something gold protruding from her belly button.

"It's a bellybutton ring, Shawn," she said, preempting the question on my lips and daring me to engage. "I got it today at the mall with a couple of dudes from my class."

I counted to ten. I could play the game, too.

"So, where you going tonight, Punkin'? Do I need to pick you up?" I asked cheerily.

"You always ask the same question," she said, with an edge to her voice. "You treat me like a *two-year-old*. BoBo's mom is taking us for sushi, and then a bunch of us are watching a Redbox movie and sleeping over at Jee-El's for her birthday, 'kay?"

"Who's BoBo?" I asked. "That's not a real name."

Liza curled her lip. "No *wonder* none of my friends like you," she retorted. "It's my personal choice who I hang out with. Isn't that called the First Amendment? Why do you always feel the need to butt into my life, Shawn? Do I ask *you* where you're going every minute?"

"I'll probably go out for gas, and then I'll be hanging out to do emails. If you need a ride, just call," I told her, still not satisfied about BoBo's identity but unwilling to begin another skirmish. "Maybe you should wear a jacket. It's supposed to rain."

"Right," she said, clearly not intending to do anything I suggested. "Okay, Shawn."

"You have a good night, Punkin'," I said, caving. "Don't get in trouble, or I'll ground you for a year."

I was a terrible parent. But I was a dad with a fourteen-year-old daughter who had a severe attitude. I was fighting for survival.

At that moment, a VW Bug of the sort I hadn't seen since the 1970s pulled up. At the wheel was the mother of a kid I didn't know. Liza got into the back seat with a group of teenagers who were staring ahead with zero affect on their faces. I waved goodbye from the doorway as the Bug backfired and pulled away, carrying my daughter off for another Friday night of teenage activities in unknown places. If I'd tried to stop her, it would have erupted into a shouting match, and Liza might have stayed over at an undisclosed house for days. At least we had a fragile détente.

As I fell onto the couch, I almost wished Christine's parents had come over tonight; Jane and Cy were far better at parenting than me. They also were pleasant company. I would have enjoyed having a Rob Roy with them at the kitchen table like we used to do when Christine was here. Her mom, in particular, made my heart jump with joy because Jane had many of the same mannerisms as her daughter, including the same giggly laugh that made the freckles on her nose dance when we swapped stories of Britt and Liza's latest infractions.

It was far too early to attempt to go to bed. I still found it strange to close my eyes and fall asleep by myself. And I had a hard time migrating from my side of the bed to the other. Every night, I tried to keep Christine's side neatly made and undisturbed. That meant the less time I spent thrashing around in the bed, the better.

I trudged into my study and reached for an old cigar box on the top shelf of the closet. I usually avoided any temptation to indulge in these memories, but I was alone tonight. The little cardboard box had a pink band across it with the words "It's a Girl!" A coating of dust showed how long it had been since I'd extricated it from its hiding place.

A neat label marked "Letters" was stuck to the side. Christine had always been a big fan of letter-writing and was a fastidious organizer. I opened the clasp. The faint smell of Bazooka bubblegum wafted from the box. Inside, the envelopes were neatly stacked, starting with the oldest first, and wrapped with a rubber band. But the handwriting on the letters was mostly my own; Christine had saved every letter I'd written to her during our first year of marriage as a sort of time capsule of our early years together. The one on top was when Tim Mulroy had sent me to explore opening a satellite office of our firm in Florida. There were lots of old, wealthy Pittsburghers who'd retired to the Gulf Coast communities, and Tim said, "This could be a golden ticket for you and Christine. I'd like to make something special happen for you two." It had been an exciting time. If all went as planned, we would merge with a larger Florida firm to double our receivables; I would help run the new Sarasota office, and my salary would skyrocket.

I pulled out the next letter with my chicken-scratch writing. I remembered sitting next to a little swimming pool in Sarasota wearing Ray-Bans and flowered swim trunks, writing this letter on a yellow legal pad as I sipped a Corona. It said:

My dearest sweetheart—

Things are going great again this week with a couple of big potential clients and a super meeting on the merger. It's incredible how many opportunities exist down here. I can't believe Tim is making this happen—he's using all his contacts to give me this chance. He said we reminded him of him and his wife when they were just starting out. We always thought life revolved around Pittsburgh, but like your dad said, we could probably have a MUCH more glamorous life down here. My buddy Dobbs has his main office in Raleigh-Durham for political work, but he just opened another office in Orlando for his consulting gigs with IBM. It's only a couple of hours away. He said it's a blast. I've already checked out a little two-bedroom place a couple of blocks from the beach we could rent. It has a pool and palm trees out back and a deck for parties! How cool is that?

I smiled at the image of the palm trees and cerveza coupled with the dreamy memory of Christine visiting for a whole week right after that letter. It had been the ultimate in romantic adventures. I'd been on cloud nine for weeks, scoping out neighborhoods and envisioning a lifetime of tropical frolics and daiquiris on the deck of a home near the blue waters of the Gulf. But all of that had changed in one trip to the mailbox.

I pulled out the next blue envelope with Christine's beautiful, calligraphic printing on the front, remembering how my heart had danced when *this* letter arrived.

I unfolded the notepaper as if handling a priceless artifact. It read:

My Dearest Shawn—

It was wonderful spending time together and seeing your new digs in sunny FLA. You sure looked nice and sexy with your shirt off! I'm proud of everything you've done, and it's certainly nice to know that we have great options—living by the beach on the Gulf Coast sure wouldn't be a bad life! And Tim is like a saint watching after us like this.

But here's a new twist. I bought a pregnancy test kit yesterday and—hold onto your chair!—you're going to be a daddy!!! I've been keeping it quiet, so I don't jinx anything. But when I told my folks, my dad said: 'That's the best news ever, sweetheart. You'd better tell Shawn to get his fanny back to Pittsburgh. The experiment's over—with grandkids in the picture, you're not allowed to leave town!' So, it looks like we were destined to start having babies and build our life here in the Burgh, after all. It may be a less glamorous existence than other places, I guess, but we'll be near our families and the people we love most who will want to hang out with our babies, too. You can't buy that for a million bucks, so I think it's a good investment. I know your little law firm in the Burgh isn't as glamorous as the Sarasota firms surrounded by palm trees, but you'll be able to do a lot of good for people using your talent, and that's a special gift. You should share it generously.

Don't worry about getting into a rut, OK? I figured it out: The secret to life is getting into a rut that you LOVE. I think maybe that's what God's telling us now. . . .

Can't wait till you get home, Shawn, so we can keep working on those babies!

Love you forever,
XXOO Christine

A tear dripped down my cheek. I wiped it away so it didn't smear the precious blue ink.

For a long stretch, I sat in my chair, clutching the cigar box, until I eventually fell asleep. Then sometime near midnight, the phone rang, startling me awake. The voice on the other end conveyed this was "all business" when the person asked for the "parent or custodian of Eliza Rossi." I could hear emergency radios and scanners squawking in the background.

"This is her dad," I said.

"Mr. Rossi?" the voice said. "I'm recording this conversation, sir—my name's Sergeant Lavella, Pittsburgh Police, zone four station. Sir, your daughter's been picked up for underage consumption of alcohol. About forty minors have been rounded up at a party in Greenfield that was outta control. Some of them are in bad shape down at Mercy Hospital getting their stomachs pumped."

"Is Liza okay?' I interrupted.

"Like I said, sir, there are forty kids down here," he said. "I'm just calling parents off the list. I'm not sure who's in the hospital and who ain't. You'll have to call the front desk to check out the status of your daughter once we get them all processed."

"Look, sergeant, I know the drill. I'm a lawyer," I said, trying to sound authoritative. "I'd just like you to check that list and see if my daughter Liza's okay. She sometimes needs special medication."

"Look *yourself*, sir," he said tersely. "Everyone's a lawyer around here. Your kid's no different than everyone else's. We got shootings and prostitutes and druggies OD'ing. We don't run a daycare center dahn here. I was told to go through the list, and that's 'zactly what I'm doing. If your daughter had a little parental control and oversight, maybe she wouldn't be in police custody, and we wouldn't be having this conversation. Am I right about that, sir?"

Outside, the rain was pounding so heavily that I had trouble seeing through the fogged windshield.

I sped up Commercial Street and through two red lights, cutting past the fringe of the business district in Squirrel Hill where high school kids were still loitering in front of a Dunkin' Donuts. I finally arrived at the zone four police station, a brick fortress surrounded by squad cars set back from a residential area on Northumberland Street. I pulled up against the curb. Inside, bright lights stung my eyes. In the waiting area, a throng of parents shouted at the desk sergeant, demanding service.

"Hey, Shawn, your kid get swept up in this dragnet, too?" Bruce Marsh, a lawyer who now worked at Jackson Rhodes, stepped up to me. "Christ, I knew I shouldn't have let Brucie associate with those lowlifes from Swissvale. That's why I sent him to the Academy. I'm gonna kick his rear end from here till Sunday when I get my hands on him."

Jackson Rhodes was a Chicago firm, but Bruce had helped set up the firm's new Pittsburgh office and was now making a fortune in securities work. I'd spent time with him when he'd served as president of the school board at the Academy. We'd discovered he was a remote cousin of Lanny, my law school classmate. They certainly shared some family resemblances.

"Lanny wanted me to tell you 'hi' next time I saw you, Shawn," he said. "He's making obscene amounts of money running a hedge fund. He says he hopes you're eking out a living here; he said to call him if you ever need a loan. That guy's hilarious."

"Tell *Laniard* I'm doing great," I said.

Bruce narrowed his eyes. "I should've never let my kid hang out with those punks from the *hood*. I ought to ask the cops to let me go in there and knock their heads off myself."

The last time I'd seen him, Bruce was a hefty fellow who wore oversized suits from Brooks Brothers. Tonight, the man seemed emaciated. He wore gold bracelets that nearly flew off his wrists as he waved his hands in my face.

As if reading my mind, he said proudly: "Bariatric surgery, Shawn. I look like a million bucks, don't I?" He twisted and turned to show off his body as if displaying a prize horse.

"Like I said, this pisses me off. If Brucie gets in trouble with these lowlifes and gets a criminal record, he won't be able to go to law school," he said. "This school district's gone down the crapper with all these Black kids and Asians. I'm not biased; I'm just speaking facts here. Word to the wise, Shawn: Get your daughters' butts outta that public school and back to the Academy. It's a cesspool down there. *Look* at these people."

He paused and pointed a finger at me. "I know you don't have a wife anymore to keep your head on straight, Shawn. But listen guy, *you'll* be responsible if your kids get into trouble."

A cluster of parents surged forward like ticket holders trying to storm the gates of a rock concert. A female dispatcher in Pittsburgh Police garb—Lucy Cicero, whom I'd known from Swissvale since kindergarten—waved me over to her corner. It was a relief to see a familiar face. She dragged me down a hallway to speak privately.

"Your daughter's in the room down this hall, Shawn. She's a little scared but fine," Lucy said. "From what I can tell, that Marsh boy was the one who bought the alcohol for these kids. He's a spoiled brat, like father like son. Don't be too hard on her, Shawn. We did the same thing. Remember hanging out on Rocky Cliff during senior year? I had a long talk with her and made sure she's okay. She's a good kid, Shawn. I think your daughter might have learned a lesson here."

"Thanks for watching out for her, Lucy." I made sure nobody was watching and gave my friend, decked out in a police uniform, a hug.

Lucy squeezed my hand. "You'd do the same for me, bud."

I walked down the hall where Lucy pointed and entered the room. In the holding cell, two dozen teenagers huddled on benches like prisoners in a maximum-security facility. One girl was vomiting into a bucket. At the sound of hard shoes, they all leaned forward, gasping a prayer that someone had come to get them.

Liza cowered in the corner, leaning against the wall with a boy's jacket thrown over her shoulders. Her clothes were soaked from the rain, making her look like a wet rat. Next to her was a familiar face.

"Oh my God, it's *you*?" I asked.

Jarrod, Brittany's alleged boyfriend, recognized me and extended his hand. "Hey, Mr. R," he said in a subdued tone. "Glad you got here."

"Don't come near me *or* my daughters again; you got it?" I said, pushing his hand away. "You're nothing but Swissvale trash. I should've known."

Liza rushed up and hugged me. Her mascara ran down her cheeks, and her exposed midriff with the bellybutton piercing looked absurd in this setting. She shivered from the cold; her lips were blue. Instead of a defiant, mouthy daughter, she'd become a scared, skinny kid with goofy pink hair who desperately needed her dad.

"Oh, daddy, I wasn't even *drinking* that rotgut," she said. "BoBo said this party would be cool, so me and my friends decided to go check it out. Then the police came when that guy threw a couch off the fire escape, and one dude took a swing at the cop, and that's when they started handcuffing people. It was like *horrible!*"

"Let's go, Punkin'," I said. "I gotta sign you out so we can get you home."

"What about Jarrod?" she asked, tugging me backward.

I turned and looked at the boy with the crewcut. I took the jacket from Liza's shoulders and whipped it back at its owner.

"Jarrod's parents can deal with him," I said. "Only one criminal per parent, Liza. We're done hanging out with reprobates like him."

Back home, after making Liza some hot Ramen noodles to calm her down and making sure she'd taken her anxiety meds, I sat on the edge of the bed, holding her hand until her teeth stopped chattering. "Punkin, you scared me to death," I whispered, squeezing tight so that I could feel the warmth of her little hand. "My heart almost stopped when I saw you all soaked and scared in that jail cell." She looked up and gazed directly into my eyes, locking her brown eyes tight onto mine for a moment and smiling faintly, just like she'd done when I'd put her to bed as a little girl. It hit me at that moment that this was the first time we'd connected in that way since Christine had died. My lip began to quiver, but there was no need to say anything else. In seconds my youngest daughter fell asleep.

Britt had somehow managed to get home on her own. Across the hallway, I could hear the loud banging of Britt throwing shoes on the floor. When I walked into her room, Britt was sitting in the dark, shaking.

"I know it's hard to find out that your boyfriend's not a good person," I said to my daughter. "But I suspected that about Jarrod from day one. It's better to get rid of him now. You deserve better than a *troublemaker* like him."

I put my hand on Britt's shoulder. She yanked it away.

"So that's what you think, Mr. Lawyer?" my oldest daughter said, glaring at me. "I guess people like you who went to Harvard are so smart you know *every-thing*, right? That's your *problem*, dad. You never listen. You don't really know *either* of your daughters, do you?"

"You'll get over it, Britt," I said. "There are a lot of better boys out there."

"Right, let's just write him off as public-school trash," she glared at me. "*News-flash*: Jarrod went over to pick Liza up at that party 'cause she called my cell and said it was getting outta control. We were playing Taboo at Jimmy Kambic's. He wasn't anywhere near that place. He only got picked up by the cops 'cause he went down there to get *your daughter* out of that rat hole, to get her home safe. Jarrod was looking out for *your* baby, dad. And now he probably won't get into medical school, thanks to the fact you left him there. Aren't you proud of yourself, Mr. Big Shot Harvard Lawyer?"

September 2008 (Lincoln Club—Part II)

JUDGE WENDELL'S PROPOSAL

The Lincoln Club, once again, was almost empty. For multiple reasons, I wasn't looking forward to another "private" conversation. It was risky business. This time, I had parked three blocks away so that nobody spotted my car.

Nearly a week after Aunt Peg's funeral, it was clear we now faced the end game of our case.

"Don't worry, Judge," I said, slugging down a shot chased by a mouthful of beer as Petey collected our empties. "I've decided against subpoenaing the nun—if that's why you called us here. My associate J.V. talked me out of it. Tell the Sister to offer up a rosary of thanks to her."

The judge settled back and lit up a Kent. "That's good to hear, Shawn," he said. "That was out of character for you. But that's not why we're here. By the way, I want to remind you, fellows, this is purely a *social* visit. I'm not wearing my robe, see? It's just a conversation among friends. Hey, this presidential race is really tightening up, isn't it?"

"You were right, Warren," said Bernie. "I think this Obama guy could actually win."

"Next I'd like to see a Black mayor of Pittsburgh," the judge said, nodding. "That would be a miracle, too."

I suddenly remembered that I hadn't responded to an important message from my daughter.

"'Scuse me, gentlemen," I said. "I gotta hit the restroom."

Inside the men's room that reeked of stale toilet-bowl cleaner, I checked my Blackberry that had been buzzing inside my pocket. I scrolled down to read the message. It had been several days since the police station incident. Britt was talking to me again:

Dad-o,

Had an awesome paintball session with Jarrod today. I think he's gotten over the recent traumatic events. L's not a bad kid. She just seems desperate for attention.

Hey, it would be nice to have you around more, like you really live here??? Having a lawyer-guy dad isn't what we ever wanted. I mean, you're the only dad we got. I think we could both use some TLC. And you should probably find another LADY friend, too, if you catch my drift. I put some cool passionflower herbs from a store in Shadyside under your pillow. The lady said that'll do magic! TTYL.

B.

I fiddled with the buttons on the gadget and punched out a response:

B—Just talked this morning to the police and cleared it up—the report's gonna show Jarrod came to help a minor LEAVE the party. They're sending him an official note of thanks. That kid's all right. And I promise to be home more— just have to finish this case.

XXOO

Dad-o

"Lawyer-guy dad?" I whispered to myself as I staggered back to the table. "God, when did *that* happen? I want just to be *dad*."

"It was a damn shame about the grandmother," Judge Wendell was saying as I sat down. He knocked down the remains of his Rock'n Rye, chasing it with a swig of Iron City beer. "I remember her from the *Croat* Club years ago. She was a spunky gal, a gen-u-ine Pittsburgh article. Why do the good ones keep dying off, Bernie? Damn, they'll be reading about *us* in the obits pretty soon."

Bernie turned to the judge. "She had a helluva turnout, Warren. That line at Nied's Funeral Home went all the way down to the Swissvale Fire Hall. Lots of guys from the Carrie Furnace came up to be there for Choppy, even those who could barely walk. There were flowers on one side of the casket from the union boys and flowers on the other side from the old management guys, just like the good old days. The whole town shut down out of respect. Lil got so many dinners from the neighbors that they didn't even fit in the fridge. It was quite a send-off for old Peg. I just worry about what comes next—I mean, for the family."

I squeezed my eyes shut, fighting off the buzz from too much alcohol. My eyes began welling with tears as an image from the past week appeared and haunted me: Marjorie was helping Choppy down the aisle of Visitation Church in Rankin. Choppy's leg was dragging as he limped behind Aunt Peg's casket draped in a creamy pall with yellow roses on top. Behind them walked Marjorie's two beautiful children, whom Aunt Peg and Choppy had seen only for a couple of weeks each summer. The children held each other's hands as the organist sang *Panis Angelicus*. Lil, assisted by a second cousin, followed in a wheelchair so that she didn't collapse.

I found myself getting choked up. I was going to miss Aunt Peg, I realized, almost as much as I missed my mom.

"What's happening with the mortgage situation on the house?" the judge asked. "I got your fax on that. Has the bank backed off yet? Surely, Peg's death should make them feel a shred of compassion for these people."

Bernie shook his head, downing a fresh shot. "The sheriff's office just notified us they listed the property for sale. They served Choppy with the formal complaint right after the funeral. A date's been set for next month." My co-counsel tapped his shot glass against the table. "I spoke with Choppy. He's resigned to leaving the house. He said now that Peg's gone, there's no point going into assisted living in Turtle Creek. He's looking at the old Swissvale school building that was gutted and turned into rental apartments. They take Section Eight housing so he can get a government voucher that will make it doable. It's not ideal with so many stairs and no air-conditioning, but he says he and Lil can manage. He said the most important thing for him is that they stay in Swissvale. He wants to be able to walk to his old neighborhood and see his friends. That's where the guy wants to be for whatever time he has left. He wants that for Lil, too, so she can have a familiar, stable place to live when he passes on."

We sat in silence. I felt uncomfortable being here. Besides the professional jeopardy it was putting all of us in, it reminded me how hopeless every aspect of our case was.

"You know, fellahs," the judge finally said, looking us square in the eye, "my reputation means more than any other worldly thing. I took an oath when I became a judge, and I'm not gonna do anything that's even *remotely* inappropriate."

Judge Wendell tapped his cigarette against a plastic ashtray. He examined our faces gravely as he chose his words carefully. "I've never rigged a case in my life, and I'm not gonna start now, especially with my judicial career almost over. My next stop is at the pearly gates to meet my maker, so I've gotta be on good behavior." He blew an emphatic smoke ring into the air.

"So, we've gotta follow the rules even though the results can be harsh, you hear me?" He watched the thin smoke dissipate in a plume toward the ceiling. "I can't ignore the law and evidence, even though I know this Radovich family is probably suffering terribly here."

Petey delivered some pickled eggs and Bressler's deviled crabs—"ballast for the belly," as the judge called it. He swapped fresh beers for the old ones.

"This family is really good people," Judge Wendell continued reflectively. "That Marjorie girl's a sweetheart. I'd put the moves on her *myself* if I were forty years younger and didn't have a pacemaker. Can't figure out why anyone would let her go," he said, raising an eyebrow in my direction. "But the evidence just isn't there. At least nothing that's admissible. The mother and daughter stand to benefit financially, so their testimony alone isn't enough. There needs to be some independent corroborating evidence, and it just never materialized. That picture from the grandmother came close, but it was still inconclusive. Sometimes that just happens."

I scarfed down a Bressler's deviled crab that had far more breading than crab. I doused it in hot sauce so I could at least taste it.

"But I'm having trouble sleeping at night," the judge said, "because this whole thing isn't sitting right with me. I feel a kinship to you, Bernie, and to these people you're representing." Judge Wendell now downed a shot of Imperial whiskey and chased it with a sip of beer. "That's what's gnawing at me."

Judge Wendell, I knew, had grown up in Rankin among the cluster of Black families who first established their presence in the mill towns during the Great Strike of 1919. That's why he and Bernie—who had grown up on the hillside just blocks away in that same half-square-mile borough on the banks of the Mon River—had such a special bond.

I also knew a little about Judge Wendell's personal story from Bernie. As Bernie had recounted it, the judge's parents, Livingston and Vervy Wendell, were well-educated and had migrated with family members to Rankin in the early 1900s. Mill owners had sent bounty hunters down South, paying them to load Black workers and their families into boxcars with the promise of good wages and free board up North. When they arrived in Pittsburgh, conditions were horrible, especially for Black workers, but there was no turning back. So, Livingston promptly set up a doctor's office and served the town's Black families and anyone else who needed medical care. He and Vervy were unable to have children no matter how hard they tried, so they devoted themselves to taking in any unsettled family members who needed assistance.

"Tell Shawn that part, Wendell," Bernie motioned him to continue. "Tell him about Rosie. That part breaks my heart."

The judge's eyes shifted back and forth. He looked uncomfortable all of a sudden.

"Well, I can only repeat what my mother told me," the judge said, not looking at Bernie or me. "I can't verify it, but this was the story, Shawn. I had a cousin named Rosie Harper, a beautiful girl. She came up here when she was fifteen to live with an *aunt*. After a while, she moved in with my parents because they had more space. With my mother's help, Rosie took a job doing washing and cleaning at a fancy house in Squirrel Hill." Judge Wendell's hand seemed to shake as he lit up a smoke.

"Only the mister of the house, some White guy who owned a dry goods business in town, he forced my poor cousin to have sexual congress with him," the judge said. His voice became strained. "But what could a Negro girl say back then? Right? I mean, the guy was White, and he wanted her company. That was that.

"So, when Rosie became pregnant that winter," the judge continued, "that White guy shipped her off to a secret location in the city to have the baby without telling her parents. These places guarded the identities of the girls fiercely. Of course, mixed-race babies were particularly frowned upon; they usually ended up at county orphanages or used as cheap labor. So, as soon as this baby was born, my mother said poor Rosie bought a one-way train ticket back to North Carolina. According to my mother, my cousin was never heard from again. She just vanished."

"Again, this was just the version of events my mother told me," the judge added with an odd look. "I'm not swearing it's the truth."

The judge said his parents told him they had looked around frantically for Rosie and eventually determined she had stayed at a place in the Hill. "You guessed it," he said. "It was the Roselia Home—the same place where your client Lil stayed."

According to his mother's account, his parents had driven there immediately and personally begged the nuns to help them find their niece's baby so that they could give it a loving home. But the sisters couldn't find a newborn baby *anywhere* in Pittsburgh who matched the infant's description or his date of birth. Tragically, the baby was lost for all time, just like its mother. But miracles did happen, the judge went on. According to the story, Vervy had discovered she was pregnant just weeks later, and Warren was born later that year. Even though they were older parents, that joy had helped Livingston and Vervy mend their hearts.

"My mama used to tell me, 'Warren, you're born to be something special.' She'd say, 'Someday, you're gonna be something important and help break this cycle of injustice that caused people like poor Rosie and her baby to have no chance for a normal life,'" the judge recounted, inspecting the bottom of his glass while swirling its contents.

"My father was sickly the whole time I knew him," the judge said softly. "He suffered a bad heart attack one morning and died in our house. A couple years later, my mother moved us from Rankin to the Hill District. And right away, she got herself a job at the Roselia Home. Barely made anything, but it seemed to give meaning to her life. She could've earned a lot more as a nurse for the county health department. But, instead, she worked nights as a cocktail waitress at the Crawford Grille, keeping us afloat so she could work as a substitute nurse at that Roselia Home. She always took care of the 'special needs' babies, the same ones your client talked about. That was her passion. She said they need more love than ordinary babies. And she did it till the day she died."

Judge Wendell dabbed his eye with a hankie.

"It was the only thing that seemed to mean anything to her," he finally said. "But she never told me why. That's why I've been wanting to find that nun who used to work at the Roselia Home for so long." The judge glanced at Bernie with a pained look on his face. "This case gave me the chance to do that."

Bernie remained silent, giving the judge a moment to compose himself.

"And I went to see her again," the judge blurted out. "The administrative nun I found at the mother house in Greensburg—Sister Benedict, who's now Sister Mary Jo? I spent a Sunday afternoon clearing up some things with her. It really helped me, personally, to finally do that."

"That's fabulous!" Bernie interjected, eager to shift back to the topic at hand. "When you spoke with the Sister, what intel did you get from her about *our* case? I sympathize with your family's story, but did she share any clues or evidence that we can use for our case?"

The judge looked around evasively. "Look, fellas, I'll be honest, that nun worked with my mother side-by-side for years. I needed to talk to her man-to-nun, okay? It was pretty intense. I needed her to answer some things, just so I could have a sense of closure," he said. His eyes seemed transfixed on a distant point. "I got some answers, but I can't get into that. It's too personal and private. But I didn't risk getting that old Sister off track by discussing anything else. We didn't talk about your case."

Bernie smacked the table. He didn't look pleased.

"But I have another idea," the judge said, lifting a finger so we'd hear him out. "Maybe it will help make up for this bad situation, at least a little bit. It tears me apart to know these people will probably lose their home that they worked for their whole lives." He wiped the corner of his eye. "They'll get screwed royally *again* when all they did was try to live honorably. Lord knows they've done their best."

"That young woman associate of yours, Ms. Vascov, she said something powerful that really stuck with me," the judge added. "It's not often a young lawyer comes into my courtroom and causes me to re-think everything. You ought to hang on to her, Shawn. That young woman has a helluva future."

"I agree with that one, Judge," I replied, not knowing where this was heading.

We sat, waiting. I took a cautious sip of Rock'n Rye.

"I keep thinking about what she said about the equity powers of the court," the judge continued. "There's no way I can just hand your people a chunk of the money when the cases don't support that. But I started thinking maybe there was another way to skin the cat. Isn't that what your associate said—there can be equitable solutions that aren't spelled out in the precedent? Isn't that why they put a robe on me? This family doesn't need to go through hell again," the judge added, puffing on his Kent, "not weeks after the most important woman in their lives just met her maker."

Judge Wendell twirled his wedding ring. "And don't worry—I'm plenty troubled by the way this Drew-Morris lawyer has been using my courtroom to stoke this sexual harassment nonsense against you in the media, Bernie. I understand she has some kind of angle here. But that's another topic."

"I'll handle that one myself," Bernie said, patting his friend's hands as if to allay his concerns. "I won't need any favors. I'll prove it's false. I have a way to do that, if necessary. It's just no fun to have your reputation trashed unfairly."

"I didn't expect I'd need to do you any favors, Bernie," the judge said, folding his hands serenely on the table. "And anyway, that's not why I called you here for this, ehm, social visit."

Bernie removed his gold-rimmed glasses and wiped his eyes. He stared at the judge.

"Let's get to the topic that brought us here," Judge Wendell said. "My visit to that old nun at the mother house caused me to do a little soul searching. I've been tossing it around in my head, sorting it out. So, here's what I'm willing to consider. When you show up for the final settlement conference, I'm open to sitting everyone down and giving you a shot at salvaging a smidgen of money for this Radovich family. Maybe it will at least be enough to let Choppy and the daughter hang onto the house for now. It's gonna be extra tough on them with poor Peg gone. But we've gotta play by the rules. Ms. Drew-Morris has to recover the *full* amount of the trust fund, even though that's a tough pill to swallow. It would be a breach of my judicial oath to steer a *penny* of that fund away from her. But I may be able to use my good name with the folks at Mellon Bank to see if we can get a small measure of recompense for the family. That's why we *build up* our reputations, fellahs—to help people when they need it the most. If I talk informally with the right people at Mellon Bank's trust department, they might agree to waive part of their own fee. They collect on a sliding scale that works out to about three percent. I'd only be willing to ask them to consider waiving about twenty thousand bucks. It's a relatively small chunk. But it'd be enough to cover the family's costs and maybe put enough money in their bank account to square things up with the mortgage company. These poor people had their lives devastated by this Acmovic's guy's behavior. And I really believe he raped that poor Lil as a girl, even though they can't prove it. If I explain the circumstances to the Mellon folks, maybe I can even get them up to thirty thou. Who knows? I've sent them a lot of guardianships and trusts over the years, and I've never asked for a single thing for myself. If I request they cut the family a break on this one because it's the right thing to do, I think they'll consider it seriously. You can't bring that Sister in to prove your story's legit. That's unfortunate but it shouldn't knock you out of the batter's box. These Mellon execs will take me at my word if I tell them we need to improvise to make sure justice gets done here."

Bernie and I looked at each other, astounded. Judge Wendell was known for trying to work out fair solutions; he was a "people person" who cared about letting "little people" exit losing cases with a modicum of dignity. This idea he was proposing was creative; it wouldn't technically violate any ethical rules because Drew-Morris and her client would get every cent they claimed they were entitled to receive. Yet if he could persuade the bank to cut its fees—totally discretionary—this would give Choppy and Lil a few dollars to stabilize their situation.

"If we could really get them thirty thousand," Bernie repeated the number as if entranced by it, "that would go a long way to help these folks keep the house and move on. At least they wouldn't be hurt even *more*."

I swallowed long enough to open my Eustachian tubes to make sure I heard all of this correctly.

"This case made me realize a few things myself," the judge said, pausing. "But this isn't the right time to get into that." He stared into Bernie's eyes as if communicating something.

"It's just the *right* thing," Judge Wendell continued. "It's not perfect. But you've gotta agree to play by the rules. I hate to say it, but Ms. Drew-Morris won the case on the *law*. I can't undo that." The judge sucked on his cigarette thoughtfully. He looked around to make sure nobody was eavesdropping.

Bernie's chin rose. "This means we won't get any attorney's fees, Shawn. You realize that?" he said to me, cutting to the chase.

"If it's good for Choppy and Lil," I said, "I'm in."

"Good. We're all on the same page," the judge said. He turned to me. "You're gonna need to play a *special* role with this Marjorie woman, okay, Shawn?"

"Hold on, judge," I raised my hand to stop him. "We have an agreement that only Bernie and J.V. deal with her. I've stayed away from being involved with this woman in *any* way in working on this case. I don't feel comfortable doing it."

"Heavens, Shawn," the judge said with a soft chuckle. "You knew her *well* back when, right? She doesn't bite, as far as I can tell."

"I've got a personal conflict," I said. "I'm going to recuse . . ."

The judge slid his arm around my shoulders as he interrupted my protestations. "I've been in this business for a long time, son," Judge Wendell said, a kindly look on his face. "Sometimes doing what's *right* is complicated. You've got to trust me on this. If we're gonna work this out and make sure we don't violate any rules, you've gotta be our guy in the middle."

The judge saw Petey and slid a fifty-dollar bill on the table—an exorbitant tip. Petey's eyes nearly popped out as he nodded and accepted this treasure, then hustled over to split this largess with the wait staff so they could all go home with crisp bills in their pockets.

We cut through a side room once reserved for women, back when the Lincoln Club had been an all-male establishment with just a small area where ladies could go and be shielded from their husbands' rough lifestyles. Tonight, it was filled with old Croatian men in dark caps and women with tired looking faces pumping quarters into a video-poker machine that blinked and pinged with the faint promise of a payoff.

As we walked past, I dropped a twenty-spot into the bucket of an old lady with big ears and flecks of excess skin on her eyelids—"Slovak beauty marks" Aunt Peg used to call them. The woman placed her hand on my cheek as if bestowing a silent blessing.

"Are you sure we should do this?" I whispered to Bernie as Judge Wendell retrieved his jacket. "We know our *basic* story's true. The judge even admitted it. Maybe we should stand and fight. We both know Marjorie's been lying. I still can't figure that one out. But this isn't about her. I keep thinking about Choppy and Lil. What if we cut this deal and give away something that *legitimately* belongs to *them*?"

Bernie pushed open the side door to face the chilly South Side night, helping his friend up the steps. The two men locked each other's arms as they walked toward their cars parked in spots reserved with two folding chairs in front of the Lincoln Club.

"What belonged to your ex-girlfriend's family was taken away a long time ago," Bernie said, turning in my direction and tugging up the collar of his jacket. "Maybe you were the luckiest one in all this, Shawn. Maybe she knew *exactly* what she was doing when she left you and ran off to California, way back when. Did you ever think of *that*?"

C H A P T E R   3 7

March 1981 (Florida)

SPRING BREAK ESCAPE TO DAYTONA

During spring break of third-year—our final year—my roommates and I decided to go on an irresponsible fling before graduation.

Mulroy & Kennedy had offered me a position as an associate in its firm. I needed to decide in two weeks. Marjorie's offer at Respironics had a nice salary attached to it, so this seemed like an easy choice. But nothing was easy with my girlfriend these days. She'd gotten a lead on a position in San José with a company that was developing "personal computers," something she said was "hot." There was also a start-up company making computer chips in San Mateo. To hedge my bets and expand my options beyond Pittsburgh, I sent out applications to a dozen California firms. As much as I pushed her, Marjorie continued to give me zero guidance about her preferences.

So, to send a message of my own, I chipped in with Dobbs and Stick to rent a car and join a group of our 3L classmates on a spring-break trip to Daytona Beach. Dobbs had helped organize the whole trip; he'd also set up an interview with a political consulting firm in Orlando—an offshoot of the firm he'd interviewed with in D.C.—to talk about a post-graduation job. I knew this trip would stretch the last dollars of my student loan money, but I needed to let Marjorie know that I wasn't just sitting in Somerville pining away for her with no life of my own. It was time for her to tell me what *she* really wanted so I could make my next step.

In one maddening message she'd sent on the ARPANET the previous week, Marjorie had written:

> *"Shawn —You need to do what's best for YOU. You're a hopeless Pittsburgher. It doesn't make sense to move three thousand miles to California just because you think it may be positive for ME. Here's the bottom line: Leaving Pittsburgh may be contrary to your internal makeup, and I don't want to be the person*

who causes that. Just make the decision you think is best for YOU, and the rest will work out for us, however it's supposed to work out. M."

"We met them first, Dobbs!" I shouted.

"They weren't even interested in you guys, Rossi." Dobbs stared at me belligerently.

"We bought them four sloe-gin fizzes," I countered. "That cost us twelve bucks."

We trudged across the sand under the illuminated sign of "Big Daddy's" nightclub. It was two o'clock in the morning—closing time for all bars in Daytona Beach. Most of our 3L classmates had scored plane tickets courtesy of their parents' credit cards and were arriving the next day. Dobbs, Stick, and I had saved money by renting a 1970 Chrysler Imperial from Rent-a-Wreck, into which we threw coolers and a pile of gear before pulling out at midnight and driving a thousand miles from Boston to Daytona. As co-organizer of the trip, Dobbs got to split a free hotel room with a Law Review nerd who coordinated the airline's reservations; that complimentary room would start the next night. Stick and I couldn't afford the extravagance of a hotel during the prime rental season. So, we'd brought our sleeping bags and were planning to crash on the couch of any young ladies we could meet. This pair of seniors from the University of Delaware would have been perfect. They even had a spare sleeper sofa. Dobbs had screwed up everything.

We climbed into the car, banishing Dobbs to the back seat. We'd been warned that it was illegal to sleep in cars here, a rule which the police enforced strictly. "We're hosed," I said.

Stick pulled out and headed up the stretch of beach road. After a while of aimless driving, he took a sharp left and drove into a residential area lined with darkened palm trees. The street sign was marked "Seaview Avenue."

Across the street was a partially built house constructed on wooden stilts to withstand hurricanes, framed out and sided in raw lumber but still missing paint and shingles. A big white sign out front swung in the breeze, illuminated by faint moonlight. "Another Daytona Home Constructed by R. Gold Associates," it said.

"We can't go in there," Dobbs objected, sinking into the backseat. "We'll be disbarred before we even graduate."

"Do you have another option for us, Dobbs?" I growled at him.

We quietly slid out our sleeping bags from the back. Stick looked like a great blue heron as he craned his neck and tiptoed across the street. Along the side yard, he found a door for the work crew with an orange warning sticker on it. Stick removed the Harvard ID from his wallet, jiggling it into the crack in the door. Finally, the latch unhooked.

"Welcome to the Seaview Hotel," Stick joked, extending his arm like a bellman.

It was pitch-black inside. We had entered a big open space, most likely the living room-to-be. Stick threw down his sleeping bag.

"This is as good a place as any," he announced. Before we'd arranged ourselves, there was a loud rattling above us.

"Who's down thur'?" a voice called out.

We shrunk against the wall. A flashlight clicked on and played itself across the room. A piece of wood slid sideways in the ceiling to reveal the face of a hippyish guy with sun-bleached hair.

"No problem with y'all stayin' here," he said, grinning widely enough to show several teeth were missing. "I'd come down to visit, but I gotta git to *work* tomorrow." He laughed so hard at that inside joke that it sent him into a coughing jag. With that, the man extinguished the light, slid the trap door closed, and vanished.

We spread our sleeping bags down on the floor, still covered with sawdust.

"You're reimbursing me if someone slits my throat and steals my traveler's checks," I said, pointing to my sock and directing my ire at Dobbs.

When I finally fell into a restless sleep, it seemed to last only an hour or so. A deep, guttural voice awakened me. My eyes popped open; I could see Dobbs and Stick sitting upright. Next to Stick stood a big guy weighing at least two hundred fifty pounds and wearing a leather jacket with his arms crossed over his chest. He was holding a motorcycle helmet.

"So, I'm guessin'," the guy said in a Southern voice that emanated from his big belly, "that y'all'd like to purchase some trinkets for your girlfriends." He pushed up his leather sleeve and displayed, on his wrist, a glistening assortment of gold and silver bracelets interspersed with some watches.

The guy seemed particularly attracted to Stick, eyeing his long hair up and down. "Hey, let yo' freak flag fly, right brother?" He touched the hair lovingly. "How 'bout this forty-carat bracelet?"

"No thanks," Stick said, pulling his hair away from the biker. "Maybe next time."

The bald guy scratched his massive head, which resembled a sunburned billiard ball. "How 'bout some *weed* then?" he asked, reaching into a side pocket and surveying each of us. "It's good stuff, directly from Jamaica."

Before any of us could answer, the trap door above slid open. The voice this time seemed to have an urgent tone to it. "Cops out front, dude. They must've spotted your *cycle!*"

Our biker friend bolted from the room, fumbling his way through the darkness. We could hear the unsticking of a door somewhere at the rear of the house. Then we heard a loud thud that sounded like a whale landing on the beach.

At the front door was a loud rapping of knuckles on wood accompanied by stern voices. Above us, we heard a collection of bodies crawling across the rafters like rats escaping a fumigation.

Stick, Dobbs, and I grabbed our sleeping bags and headed down the darkened hall in the same direction taken by our motorcycle friend. A back door swung open.

"There's no back porch," Stick whispered.

"What's your point?" I demanded.

"I'll sacrifice myself," Dobbs said. "Getting arrested isn't an option."

Dobbs took a running start and leaped out of the open door. We could hear him thump to the ground, apparently in one piece. Stick and I followed, jumping feet-first and landing in a thick clump of tropical shrubs and cactus bushes. It felt like I had a hundred needles stuck into my sunburned skin, which made me shriek with pain. Stick slapped a hand over my mouth. He led us through adjoining backyards, where we hid behind a storage shed until we felt it was safe to circle back to the Chrysler. Then we drove along the Daytona strip and found a 24-hour diner where we could drink coffee until sunrise when it was legal to go sleep on the beach.

"Thanks for a perfect night," I said to Dobbs, staring into the bottom of my coffee mug.

Dobbs ignored me. He shook his head to keep himself awake. "Hey, I heard Erica's coming on a late flight tomorrow," he finally said. "Maybe you'll get lucky and land a place to stay if you play your cards right, Rossi. I heard she has some kind of fancy joint on the beach."

I leaned against the mini jukebox at our booth. It was playing Southern rock songs like Freebird repeatedly. My brain felt as if it had turned to jelly from exhaustion. "I can't even keep one woman happy," I said. "I'm staying as far away from Erica as possible. You can be sure of that."

———

Stick and I slept on the hotel room floor shared by Dobbs and the Law Review nerd for two nights. It was generous of Dobbs to take pity on us and share, but it was a horrible place to be stranded. Most of our 3L classmates sat on their balconies, wearing sunglasses, studying for final exams, and soaking up the sun. Stick and I were forced to be nomads, living out of our backpacks with no space of our own. On the fourth day, we wandered down the beach with masks and snorkels looking for a spot to swim. That's when we ran into Erica.

"Hey, Shawn-with-a-w—is 'at-ou?" Erica asked, squinting through her sunglasses. "Someone toll' me you and Stick were here somewhere. Where are 'oo staying?"

"We're crashing with Dobbs, watching our budget," I said, oddly comforted by a familiar face—even Erica's. "Are you guys here all week?"

"Jus'sa few days," she said. "My dad's business par'ner owns a condo a couple miles from here. We just drove down lookin' for the Har-verd people. Someone said you might be near, uhm, by."

Erica's speech sounded remarkably improved. Physically, too, she looked better than I'd remembered.

"D'you guys wanna join us?" Erica asked.

"Sure," I said, nodding toward Stick. "The snorkling's no good here, anyway."

Stick and I spread our towels on the sand. We weren't about to complain. Erica's sister was as attractive as she was—in her early twenties, blond, dressed in a sheer one-piece bathing suit. Erica wore a two-piece tropical flowered bikini that clung to her body with surprising shapelessness. Her left leg was still slightly atrophied from her stroke, skinnier than the right. But otherwise, she looked remarkably intact. She rolled over and asked me if I'd apply suntan lotion to her back. As I rubbed on the tropical lotion, Erica turned and gave me a coy look—just like the "Erica Welles of First Year" before her stroke.

The first wave of college students had descended onto the long stretches of white beach, carrying plastic coolers, Frisbees, beach blankets, kickboards, and little portable boomboxes with silver antennas. They walked with flip-flops across the sand, still wobbly (obviously) from a late night of drinking cheap beers and shots at the discos and clubs. Boomboxes blared *Funkytown* and *The Pina Colada Song* from multiple directions. One group beside us, kicking up sand as they played volleyball with no net, was decked out in matching yellow shirts embossed, "I Survived Spring Break '81."

"You guys wanna get a drink atta' hotel?" Erica asked. "Much quieter there. Celeste has'r car."

The Shores Resort and Fitness Club, where Erica and her sister were ensconced, was a shiny new hotel occupying a prime spot overlooking the Atlantic Ocean at the front and the intercostal waterway at the rear. A cluster of coconut palm trees surrounded the enormous pool, and calypso music played from dueling speakers. "This looks like a freaking paradise," I whispered to Stick.

We settled into white wicker chairs, slaking our thirsts with tall, pink rum concoctions in stemmed glasses. Erica's doctors had given her the okay to drink alcohol "on special occasions" now that they had reduced her medication dosage. As Stick and I floated in the pool to enjoy the cool water and hot sun, Erica and her sister watched from their chairs on the veranda, downing more rounds of exotic drinks.

"*Great daiquiris!*" Erica said as she and her sister slid out of their chairs. "Led' us show you our place. There's penty 'a room if you wanna crash wid' us."

The scent of strawberry rum punch punctuated Erica's breath.

"You wanna check out the views of the intercoastal?" Celeste asked Stick, sliding her arm into his.

"Sure," he said. Erica's sister was petite and sophisticated looking. Stick was growing a stubbly beard and looked twice her height. They appeared oddly matched but happy as Stick loped beside his new date, trying to stretch his arm downward to reach her waist. They disappeared into an open-air "community space" that looked out onto the ocean.

Erica and I had reached the elevators. She stood there awkwardly, waiting for me to signal our next move. I knew that her left leg couldn't sustain weight for too long, so waiting here until Stick and Celeste returned wasn't an option. I said, "Hey, let's check out your place. They'll be able to find us."

The sprawling condominium suite was on the top floor with stunning views of the turquoise ocean. Blue umbrellas and Tiki huts dotted the beach below.

"It's good to get offa feet," Erica said, sitting on the edge of a stuffed chair. The room was impeccably furnished. She kicked off her sandals and wiggled her toes.

"Whew!" she said. "That's nice a-yoo to let a cripple bring you back to her place, Shawn-with-a-w. I haven't felt this relaksed since before I got sick. It feels great to be *normal*."

"You're *not* a cripple, Erica," I said. "For heaven's sake, don't say that stuff."

"*For-mul* cripple," she laughed and twirled her toes as if they were regaining their circulation. "Check out this waterbed in 'ere," Erica said, standing up abruptly and weaving her way into the adjoining room. "Pretty cool, huh?"

The waterbed could have held four people. A colorful painting of Mayan pyramids gleamed from above the headboard. Erica touched a sleek tape deck, and it began playing the new *Earth, Wind & Fire* album. She fell backward onto the bed and flapped her arms like she was paddling in the ocean. "Try it, Shawm," she laughed.

I sat down at the edge of the waterbed next to where she lay. It struck me that this Erica was much different from the over-the-top Erica I'd known during our first year. Her self-importance and sarcasm had melted away; we could now talk as friends and equals. It also struck me how surprisingly beautiful Erica looked in this uncomplicated setting, sprawled out in her flowered bikini.

"So, what's Mar'ji doing these days, Shawn?" she asked as if it were the most natural question in the world. "You don't tawk 'bout her much anymore. I mean, is everythin' okay?"

I folded my sunglasses and set them on the end table.

"Sure, everything's great," I said. "I don't keep track of Marjorie *every minute*, you know. She's finishing her master's in CS at Pitt. She got a job offer in Pittsburgh, but she's checking out northern California, too. I get confused trying to figure out where her head's at sometimes, Erica. But I'll be seeing her soon. It'll all work out."

"Northern California?" Erica cocked her head. "I thought you guys settled on Pipps'burgh?"

"Yeah, that's what I thought," I said. "She keeps changing the options. I *want* to be a team player. I just can't figure it out, Erica. She laid out two different options last week—Pittsburgh or the San José area. She just won't tell me what *she* thinks is best."

Erica propped up on an elbow. "Well, Shawm-with-a-w, if she's giving you different options, maybe she wants *you* to pick the one she has in mind. Women don't go around wearing a sandwich board adve'tising what they want. Maybe she wants *you* to know the right answer and pick that one."

"Jeez, that seems unfair, Erica. I'm not a mind-reader. What if I get it wrong?"

She moved her face closer. I could smell coconut oil on it. "Going back to Pipps'burgh sure sounds like the right thing to do *for you*, Shawm. You just have to make sure it's the right thing for Mar'ji at this moment, too. You may have to shelve your plans and go somewhere else for a while till she works through what's good for *her*."

"That's a smart way to tackle it," I said, nodding and feeling mellowed out from the rum punch. "I've got a plan to cover it no matter which option Marjorie decides."

I jiggled one flip-flop. "So, whatever happened to your boyfriend from Chicago—that med student?"

"Joel Rick-ards?" Erica laughed, causing the waterbed to swish with rubber waves. "He married that lil' *slute*." Erica's right hand curled involuntarily toward her chest. "That's fine. It would have been a nuc'uler dis-aster if we ended up together."

Erica wiped away a bead of perspiration. A ceiling fan whirled above us.

"No matter what you and Mar'ji decide to do right now, I'm glad you're thinkin' a going back to Pipps'burgh, event'chly, Shawm," she said. "That's a cool move, doin' something you care about in your hometown."

"You'll do great at that firm in New York," I said, returning the compliment. "One more semester will be over before you know it. Look, your dad didn't even think you could *make* it at Harvard Law. You've sure proven he was full of crap. You're making it in the big leagues by going to the Big Apple."

"I do get satis'fashin knowing I proved that SOB wrong." She smiled.

"But listen," she continued. "You're gettin' id right, Shawn. I wish more people had the guts ta' do thad. Thinking of a way to give back your talents in Pipps'burgh is the right thing to do."

"It's just a little estates firm, but I'm pretty sure it's the right choice," I said. "But I applied to a bunch of firms in San José too, just to keep my options open. If that's what Marjorie decides is important for her, I'll make it happen. Just like you said. We can do whatever she wants for a while."

A single lamp on the nightstand provided a dim source of light with the room-darkening curtains drawn. The light faltered for a moment, probably from someone in another unit overloading the circuit with too many appliances. I considered making a quick wish, but I suppressed that foolish impulse.

"I think that's a smart compromise, Shawm-with-a-w," Erica said, rocking herself in the waterbed gently as *Kool and the Gang* played on the tape deck. "Getting rooted to a place that's important to you is a smart move. In twenty years, you'll have somethin' most of us will *never* have."

The sharp buzz of the rum punch seemed to be relaxing its grip. I was finally starting to feel at ease.

"Well, New York is a *cool* place to practice law," I said, returning to a safe subject. "Getting an offer from the Ruppert firm is a helluv'an accomplishment, Erica. Nobody will even *remember* you had this slight setback."

Erica smiled, understanding my awkward attempt at a compliment.

"I plan to make the *bess* of it," she said, pushing her hair from her face. "I probably won't find a man dumb 'nuff to marry me af-fer *this*." She held up her clenched hand. "But I have a *different* goal, Shawm. I wanna run my own firm someday. I wanna prove a *woman* can do it. At'll be my prize. *Yours* will be even better. But that'll be mine."

Erica reached over toward the lamp, giving it a flick of the button. "It feels won'nerful to get the light outta your eyes. You ever feel that way?" she asked innocently.

Then Erica whispered, without even a hint of immodesty: "It would be nice to lay with yoo for one night, S-Shawm-with-a-w. I feel like I can trust you. I know you have someone else, and it's probably in'propriate. But you make me feel like everything will be okay someday."

I didn't move for a minute. Two minutes. Then I fell backward beside Erica, causing the waterbed to undulate from the waves. We ended up face-to-face, staring at each other. Erica's skin smelled of perfume and saltwater.

"Most guys in the law school look 'it me like I'm some kinda freak after my med'cal problem," she said, clutching her hand. "*I* used to be the girl always fending off guys. I'm that *same person*, Shawm—I mean Shawn. I think I still gotta sharp int'lect. I've got urges like any twenty-five-year-old woman with a helphy libido. . . ."

"You're *incredibly* attractive," I said, shushing her. "You've got nothing to apologize for. You hear me, Erica?"

"Like right now," she leaned into me. "Even after all that talk about Mar'ji, I feel like gettin' naked with you. Is that so wrong? We're here a thousand miles away from everyone else, and that's how I feel. It is bad to tell you that?" It was obvious Erica was drunk from the rum punch. I was, too.

"Of *course* not, Erica," I said, placing my hand on her cheek. It felt warm. "Jeez, that sounds tempting. But I made a *commitment* to someone. I'm already thinking about buying a ring when I get back so me and Marjorie can get engaged. I've gotta respect that commitment, right?"

"Marjorie and *I*," Erica corrected me. "And yes, I re'spect you for that. I just wan'ned to tell you how I felt. If you don't feel the same way, I can handle that."

I rolled over on my side and tried to stop my brain and fend off the feelings of temptation creeping into it. How was I supposed to *stop* myself?

"It's not that," I finally said, turning toward her. "Look at you. You're sexy as hell, Erica. And I kinda feel the same way. But I've gotta *control* myself."

Erica rolled over and turned up the stereo a notch so that *Earth, Wind & Fire* now filled the room with the sound of horns and the steady beat of percussion.

"Whatever happens here," Erica said softly, "I'd never say anything. You unner'stand that—right, Shawm-with-a-w?"

June 1981 (Boston and Pittsburgh)

GRADUATION SURPRISE

"Why don't you hang around for another week, Rosey?" Dobbs asked, looping his arm around my shoulder and hugging me. He was getting extra sentimental these days. "C'mon, it's wrong to skip graduation. All the roommates need to leave at the same time."

Dobbs had taken a job with the big-time political consultant he'd visited in Orlando, working on campaigns in Florida and back home in North Carolina. Stick was heading to Chicago for a job in the public defender's office. We would now be hundreds of miles apart.

"Can't stay, Dobbs," I said. "I have to get back by Saturday. Family stuff, you know?"

"Right," he deadpanned.

"Seriously," I said. "My mom called yesterday, and her legs have been swelling up. She and my Aunt Kate don't feel up to the trip. What's the point of attending graduation without family?"

"How's Marjorie?" Dobbs asked, still adept at cutting to the chase.

"She has her last CS final coming up," I said, shifting my feet. "She can't come either."

"I mean, how are *you* and Marjorie?" Dobbs persisted, his voice revealing genuine concern. "I'm worried about you, bro."

"You want to know the truth? I think she knows what happened in Daytona," I answered, jamming a small chew of Copenhagen under my lip. Snuff didn't agree with my stomach these days. Part of it may have been guilt rather than the snuff. Even though things hadn't gotten completely out of control with Erica, they'd gone far enough that I knew Marjorie would intuit it; she had a sixth sense for these things. The moment I said a word about our spring break trip, she'd detect the guilt in my voice and feel hurt and betrayed by my lapse of judgment.

"Don't beat yourself up over it, Rosey," Stick interjected, trying to pep me up. He was carrying three cups of beer and wearing sunglasses with a black fedora. He'd shaved his beard and now sported long sideburns like Elwood from the Blues Brothers, his favorite new theme movie. He'd already learned the chords to "*Sweet Home Chicago*" from that flick and put down a deposit on an apartment in the Windy City. His mother had arrived after driving across the country to pack him up, attend our commencement ceremony, and head back with Stick so he could start studying for the Illinois bar exam. She'd made pork tenderloin sandwiches and raisin pie for lunch. Stick was primed and in a mood for celebrating.

He fell backward into our group beanbag chair, sloshing beer all over the three of us. *KC and the Sunshine Band* was pounding from the speakers below, shaking the walls. We were throwing our final bash, and guests were already arriving downstairs.

"You can write it off as a meaningless drunken fling on vacation," he said, coming to my defense. "Any woman can understand that men are stupid and guilty of youthful indiscretions. From what I heard, it sounded like you didn't even *consummate* anything with Erica. That's what Celeste said. Anyhow, Marjorie will never find out unless *you* blab. Everyone knows you're still in love with your hometown honey. Why spill your guts when it doesn't change how you feel about *her*?"

"She knows," I said, staring at the moon rising over the rooftops in our Somerville neighborhood. "Or she will." Most of the homes were occupied by elderly residents who, luckily, would soon be going to bed and wouldn't hear our stereo once we cranked it up. "Anyway, I've got to get home right away. Marjorie said she wants to talk about a new opportunity, and I've got to be there face-to-face so I can figure out how to make it work, whatever it is. The main partner at my firm in Pittsburgh is a cool dude. He said he understands how important this is to me. He's willing to let me go with Marjorie for a couple years, if that's what we need to do, and keep the position open for me. I've got to hash through all of this stuff with her. But I've made up my mind—I'm going where she goes."

Dobbs clamped a big hand around Stick's neck, then mine. He cracked a big smile that revealed a set of handsome, Chicklet-sized teeth and pulled us together like brothers posing for a family portrait.

"I'm gonna miss busting your chops, Pittsburgh-boy. It's hard to believe three years vanished so fast," he said, linking our arms together. "We'll have to watch out for each other the rest of our lives. Even if you skip graduation and don't see me give the commencement speech. . . . Didn't you hear I got picked to do that?"

"No, Dobbs, nobody told me." I rolled my eyes. "Of course, you goof, we stuffed the ballot boxes and got everyone to vote for you twice!"

Stick took his Harvard cap and stuck it on Dobbs' head as if he were crowning him king of the graduating class.

"Yeah, I really wish I could be there to hear your soaring oratory," I said, "but I'll attend when you're sworn in at the White House. That will be an even bigger party."

I planted a kiss on Dobbs's big jaw. It felt like kissing a horse. "I always knew you were a sentimental, dude," I said, grabbing one of Stick's beers and holding it up in a toast. "So, I guess you're right—the three of us are stuck with each other. Forever."

A few days later, I climbed out of a People's cab on Semple Street in front of the Coop, clutching a rose wrapped in green cellophane. The Pitt campus was nearly deserted by this time in June except for a scattering of students who needed to make up failing grades on their final exams by taking summer courses.

I waited for over ten minutes. A man on the porch next to our old apartment, likely an outpatient from Western Psych, eyed me suspiciously. After checking my watch, I shouted at him, "Have you seen a girl—I mean woman—with light brown hair? She's supposed to be here."

"I didn't see nothing," he said. "I don't talk to girls with light brown hair, man. Picksburgh Police say they'll bust me next time I do that."

One of the petals from the red rose fell to the sidewalk. "*Damn*. Now what?" I said. My voice sounded strangely off-key, even to my ears. "Either she already came here and went back to her dorm 'cause I was ten minutes late, or else she's late getting back from Aunt Peg and Choppy's place."

I sprinted a half block down Forbes Avenue.

Brackenridge Hall was part of the brown-brick dormitories on Pitt's campus next to the Student Union, with ancient fire escapes that looked like dizzying catwalks. The early June breeze blew white curtains in and out of windows, indicating the rooms housing RAs in the summer.

I squeezed behind the bushes and anchored one shoe onto the brick ledge, shimmying upward until my eyes were at window level. Two white curtains danced from their curtain rods, propelled by an invisible fan. A lava lamp that I recognized from Marjorie's old dorm was bubbling its colored light on an end table. She was in there.

"*Phew,*" I said. "She must be around."

I hoisted myself up another brick. From this spot, I could see the flickering of a television. It was possible, I told myself, that she hadn't received my last ARPANET message. That computer was bad *mojo*. Often, days elapsed between her trips to CMU; so, it was impossible to tell when she had read them. Another possibility was that Marjorie intentionally decided *not* to show up to extract some concession—maybe she wanted to commute for a year until we decided which city was best. Or perhaps she was still so confused she couldn't commit to a long-term plan yet. I had prepared myself for any of these possibilities. I'd work out whatever solution was best for her.

I fell back into the bushes and dusted off my shirt. The rose in the green cellophane had lost three more petals; now, it looked like a red nub on a stalk. I fluffed up the cellophane wrapper and stood at the front entrance of Brackenridge Hall, pushing my hair back into place before ringing the buzzer.

"Stupid campus cop. Come on, man!" I muttered to myself.

There was no security guard at the front entrance—just an empty pizza box and a half-consumed can of Pepsi on the desk. I walked into the lobby where six oscillating pole fans were blowing around stale air to combat the stifling summer heat. The door that led into the maze of dorm rooms was propped open with a book to let the air circulate. I slipped inside; the security person must have left for a bathroom break.

I paused, sliding my hand into my pocket. The velvet case was still there. I had made a stop in Boston and purchased a pretty quarter-carat ring. It wasn't the biggest one in the world, but it was all I could afford at the moment. I knew Marjorie would disapprove of spending money we didn't have. Once I started earning steady paychecks at the law firm, we could go shopping for a proper engagement ring. It was important for her to pick it out herself.

I walked down the hall to Marjorie's door, wishing I could see through the thick wooden door, and knocked firmly.

There was no answer. I knocked again louder.

After the fifth time, I could hear the television turned down. There was a scrambling of activity inside the room as if someone was pushing the furniture into place. Finally, I could hear footsteps.

"Hi Rad, I'm glad you're here–" I said, spreading out my arms to hug her as she opened the door.

Marjorie's blue-green eyes looked startled, like a cat caught with a partially eaten canary in its mouth. I was caught off guard, too: This didn't look like the person I'd dreamed of for months. Her face was tight, exhausted-looking, even unattractive.

"My God, Shawn," she said, looking around. "You're supposed to be in *Massachusetts*. I thought you were joking about skipping graduation. Are you seriously missing your Harvard Law School commencement? I thought your friend was giving the commencement speech."

I couldn't formulate a single thought or utter a single word. My mouth remained frozen in place.

Marjorie shifted her feet. She lowered her voice to continue. "I sent you a message on the ARPANET on Wednesday. You're supposed to meet me at Aunt Peg's *next* Sunday for dinner; you're *not* supposed to be here yet. I thought we should talk in private. Didn't you check the ARPANET? My message was very *explicit*."

"I'm sick of the damn ARPANET," I said, sliding the jewelry bag into my pocket. Then I held out the stubby rose in its green cellophane. "I wanted to see you. *Today*."

Marjorie wore green hospital scrubs that she had obviously purloined from Pitt Medical Center. On top, she wore a loose CMU T-shirt with no bra underneath. She was holding a stack of computer programming cards, a pencil in one ear. In her free hand was a smoldering cigarette with a long ash dangling from the tip.

Another set of footsteps emerged from inside the suite. A middle-aged man with a spray of gray hair at his temples strode into the room with a *New Yorker* magazine in one hand and a coffee cup in the other. Our eyes locked momentarily. Smiling obtusely, he took an unconcerned sip from his coffee cup, then allowed his gaze to drift to the pathetic flower in my hand.

"Shawn, this is my adviser, Dr. David Cliff," Marjorie said. "This is my, uhm, friend, Shawn Rossi. He just finished his degree at Harvard Law. He's heading back up there *right now* for graduation."

The man exposed a bright, white smile of the sort perfected at the Ivy Leagues. He took a lingering sip of java.

Marjorie tugged at her scrubs to pull them up securely. She glanced over her shoulder at the interior of her dorm, where the television flickered. Her face seemed to assess whether there was enough room for all of us—and just what our conversation might be if we went in there. The cigarette ash on her Newport broke off and dropped like a bomb to the floor.

Marjorie's eyes appeared red and puffy, caught in this unwinnable predicament. Finally, she took two barefooted steps closer to me, so close that I could smell the fresh menthol cigarette on her breath. She clenched the stack of computer cards firmly. Her voice was low but firm, a tone usually reserved for speaking to her mother.

"There's something I have to tell you, Shawn," she said. "It may not sound *ideal* right now. But someday, you'll understand it was the right thing for *both* of us." She stared at me. "I'm moving to Stanford to get my Ph.D. in computer science. David just got recruited to run the CS department out there. He's asked me to go with him."

"So I'm going," Marjorie said. She slowly closed the door without giving me a chance to respond.

I stood in the doorway, stunned and utterly speechless. Eventually, I turned, retraced my steps down the hallway, stumbled onto Fifth Avenue, and collapsed in the grass in front of the Cathedral of Learning. I couldn't breathe.

September 2008 (Orphan's Court)

THE CONFRONTATION

From the window of my corner office in the Koppers Building, I watched a ribbon of fog from the Monongahela River swirling over the streets below, giving the storefronts a magical sheen. Fifteen stories below, a young woman unlocked the doors of Crazy Mocha and dragged a cart of pastries inside. Across the river, the Duquesne Incline was making its first run down the hillside from Mt. Washington, transporting young professionals wearing suits and sneakers down from their lofty apartments to work at a growing array of digital marketing firms and high-tech startups that had sprung up downtown.

Directly below my window on Sixth Street, a PAT bus driver wearing a Steelers jacket helped maneuver a woman's wheelchair onto the bus's handicapped ramp.

After all these years, I still couldn't articulate why I was so attached to this city that, in the eyes of some, was still a sooty, rusted-out industrial town whose time had passed. Maybe I'd deluded myself for all these years and squandered away my career and my family's future for something that *I* wanted to believe in but that didn't exist any longer. Staring out the window, though, I still couldn't deny that I felt a sense of excitement and pride at what I saw. Red kayaks bobbed in the Allegheny River that used to be too polluted for swimming. The new African-American Cultural Center stood as a tribute to Pittsburgh playwright August Wilson, who'd set his epic plays in the Hill District of his youth. Across the Roberto Clemente Bridge, the newly-dubbed North Shore, once occupied by the former Clark Bar factory and Heinz 57 plant, was now home to the cool PNC Park (for the Pirates) and Heinz Field (for the Steelers). And the old Volkwein's music building on the North Shore housed a museum for hometown pop artist Andy Warhol. There were still amazing things—new things—going on in this town. But, it was sad that other people—including my daughters—couldn't see what I saw.

Mrs. McNulty walked in from the hallway, having started a pot of coffee, and sorted through the first bundle of envelopes from the mailroom. "Here's one from the Pennsylvania Supreme Court," she said, holding out a brown envelope with trepidation. "I don't know that you want to look at this one today, *Mr. Rossi*," she said, appearing genuinely sad to be the bearer of another piece of bad news.

I slid the judicial opinion from its envelope. It was about the big Ligonier estate case that I'd been banking on for years to inject a hefty fee into the firm's coffers. I flipped to the last page and stared at the final words: "Decision of the lower court reversed, judgment for objector."

"Looks like we lost the big one, Mrs. McNulty," I said. "Why not? I've lost everything else recently."

Mrs. McNulty took the envelope, threw it on the conference table, then kissed me quickly on the cheek. "I don't care what those PA Supremes say," she said, looking me squarely in the eye. "You're doing good things, and I'm glad to be here with you." She eyed up a candy wrapper on the floor. "Even if you're a slob sometimes, Mr. Rossi."

At the Orphan's Court entrance, a county police officer waved a lawyer through the metal detector. Another officer, wearing the white latex gloves of a surgeon, dug through a female lawyer's briefcase and accordion files.

As I pulled my Blackberry from my pocket, I noticed a message from Britt. That was odd: She usually didn't text when she was at school. I scanned it:

Dad-o-

Mom's friend Beth Gahara stopped over last night with stuffed shells. She told us the ladies think you're 'hot.' What about that?

Is that lady still in town U knew in college? R we gonna meet her? Maybe you could bring her for pizza tonight. Grandma seems interested in checking her out too. Send a text and let us know if we can do something to celebrate after you win your big case. You're awesome, dad-o.

"You're up, Mr. Rossi," the police officer said. I tossed the Blackberry into a plastic bin like a hot potato.

Next, I emptied my pockets and walked through the upright barriers, triggering the alarm.

"Sorry, Mr. Rossi. Step around the corner," the officer said. "Take off your shoes and belt. They'll have to wand you."

I jerked to a halt when I noticed Marjorie sitting on a wooden bench, slipping her feet into a pair of black dress shoes. Her skirt was hiked up several inches, revealing a few inches of skin above her knee.

"You go first, sir," I said, guiding an elderly man toward the bench.

Marjorie's head jolted up. She saw me and blushed. "Good morning, Shawn," she said. "How's your family doing?" I turned away and receded into the knot of county police officers performing searches. By the time I left the security area, she was gone.

I stepped behind a pillar and pecked out a quick message on my Blackberry:

B—Don't think pizza with the lady from Calif. is good idea—she's still in a state of mourning for her grandmother. Maybe another time? Let's pick up some burgers after work with you and g'ma and g'pa from Big Jim's. Your dad needs some TLC right now, I think.

I pushed the transmit button, watching the message dissolve into a flickering cloud of pixels.

———

The door to Judge Wendell's chambers was open. Jimmy hustled us into the conference room, arranging an electric coffee pot and a tower of Styrofoam cups on the conference table that the judge used only for special occasions. Jimmy looked exhausted, with circles under his eyes.

I patted him gently on the back. "Hey, Jimmy, you need to get some rest." I slid him a Starbucks gift card from my wallet. "Get something for yourself. And pick up a drink for Ronald on the way home."

"Thanks, Mr. Rossi." Jimmy accepted the card, looking almost teary-eyed. "We have that big picnic coming up this weekend. But I think I'll skip it and chill out. Ronald's been up all night with his asthma; that's the problem. It's gotten real bad. So I really couldn't go anyway."

Jimmy's partner, Ronald, had sporadic health issues; that part was true. But I also knew it weighed on Jimmy that he never felt welcome to bring Ronald to public events like the clerks' annual picnic at North Park. "Don't ask, don't tell, we don't wanna know!" his co-workers would joke about his lifestyle.

Jimmy listlessly arranged folders at the judge's desk. Bernie stepped beside me. "Let's hope this goes as planned," he whispered to me.

Judge Wendell walked into the room, an American flag pinned on his lapel. Today was the seventh anniversary of the 9-11 attacks and the whole courthouse was on heightened alert.

"So, gentlemen and ladies," the judge said, nodding toward Drew-Morris, who was folding and unfolding a napkin. "This has been a helluva sobering week." He dumped three Sweet 'n Lows into his coffee and stirred. "Sorry for the extra security and body frisks, folks. Homeland Security put us on orange alert today. Those terrorist operatives get worked into a frenzy on anniversaries like this, and every threat needs to be taken seriously."

We all nodded solemnly.

"So, folks," Judge Wendell said, nodding at Bernie and me as if to send a signal while sipping his coffee to make sure it was sufficiently sweet. "We're at the end of the road on this Acmovic Trust. We can walk in there and give closing arguments. But why kid ourselves? Why not sign these here releases—consent to a judgment for Ms. Drew-Morris? Let's get the whole mess cleaned up today, so we don't have to drag it out in the court of appeals, right?"

"For *once*, I'm in complete agreement, judge," Drew-Morris said, closing her fists. "This should've happened months ago."

"We recognize there are certain, *uhm*, weak spots in our case, Your Honor," Bernie said, placing his bifocals on the table. "It's a tough pill to swallow, but I respect your judgment. Under these circumstances, I might recommend that the Radovich family sign full releases and relinquish their rights to the trust."

Drew-Morris allowed a smile of superiority to slip through.

"But I'd also like to explore whether there's a way to get the bank to cut its fees so that the family can put a tiny bit of money in their pockets," Bernie added. "That would be the fairest result, Your Honor."

Bernie was sticking to the plan we had hatched at the Lincoln Club the night before.

Drew-Morris' drink nearly went down the wrong pipe.

"I'm not agreeing to any reduction in the bank's fees," she said. "I don't want these people getting a penny. If the bank reduces its fees, my client deserves it all. It's still coming from the trust fund."

Judge Wendell folded his hands serenely. "I don't know how you do things in Philly, *Ms.* Morris," he lectured. "But we always look at ways to resolve cases *fairly*, even if we've gotta think outside the box a little bit. The bank's entitled to its fee as a matter of law. Nothing prevents it from waiving as much of that as it wants. This proposal wouldn't hurt you or your client at all."

"No deal," Drew-Morris said, clicking her fingernails against the chair. "I'd rather go into the courtroom and give my closing argument so that these people lose on the *record*. And then I'll petition for fees for *vexatious* litigation."

The judge ignored this comment.

"Mr. Rossi, I understand Ms. Radovich is camped out in Jimmy's office," the judge continued. "You've known this woman the longest. Take these papers here . . ." he said, fishing through his folder, ". . . and explain the facts of life to this Marjorie gal. Tell her she'll be giving up any right to the trust itself, but I'm willing to make a plea to the bank and ask for some consideration on their fees to let her mother walk away with a few dollars and a little dignity. Be nice and see if we can't get her to fold up her tent for the good of all concerned. Maybe you should use my clerk's library. It's good and private in there. Spend some *quality time* with this lady. You're a talented lawyer. Get her John Hancock so I can treat you all to a nice, boxed lunch and call it a day. I'm buying."

Turning his head so our opponent couldn't see, Judge Wendell nodded solemnly toward Bernie and me.

"I'm not interested in having lunch with you people," Drew-Morris said, becoming agitated. "I have some personal issues to deal with back in Philadelphia if you don't mind. Of course, you don't know what it's like to have an ex-spouse making your life miserable."

The judge lifted his head. "I'm sorry to hear that, Ms. Drew-Morris," he said, appearing genuinely empathetic. He touched his fingertips together patiently. "I'll try to be sensitive to your situation and get you home as expeditiously as possible. To that end, it seems *everyone* in this room would benefit if Mr. Rossi spent *all* the time he needs with his client. If we want to get you on a plane to Philly, we want Mr. Rossi doing what it takes to get her to sign these papers allowing your client to receive the remaining trust fund distribution in full."

He smiled serenely and turned back to me. "So, Mr. Rossi, I'll have Jimmy set you up in the library. It's nice and cozy in there," he said, punching buttons on the phone. "Can I freshen up your coffee, Shawn?"

"No thanks, Judge," I said as I stood up, gripping my folder. "I'll be back *real* soon."

———

The cramped library attached to Judge Wendell's office was a vestige of pre-computer days when *Fiduciary Reports* and *Atlantic Seconds* in bound form were still part of dispensing justice in the Commonwealth. Now the books were mere decorations, their bindings unraveling, because that line item had been stricken from the Orphan's Court budget with the advent of computers and digital cases.

I squeezed into a narrow wooden chair. Over the din of a photocopy machine, I could hear a brisk rapping on the door.

"Judge said to leave you and Ms. Radovich alone here in the library, Mr. Rossi," Jimmy said. "Buzz, if you need anything."

My heart was starting to pound out of sync, a feeling I hadn't experienced since my earliest days of law school when I worried the professors would call on me in class.

Marjorie walked in and pulled up a chair across from me.

"Shawn, first I want to say I appreciate you're doing all of this," she said, waiting for me to raise my eyes, which I refused to do.

"Are you okay?" she asked when I said nothing. "Sorry if I caught you off guard downstairs." Marjorie appeared slightly uncomfortable being in the position of having to initiate this conversation. Yet, she also seemed to have a calm self-assuredness that came with holding positions of importance in the fast-moving world of high-tech companies.

I breathed deeply before sneaking a peek at her through my bifocals. Up close, Marjorie was unusually attractive for a woman who had recently turned fifty. She was wearing a rich blue business suit. Her blondish hair was short and nicely high-lighted to cover up a smattering of gray hairs. The slight bump on her nose added an aura of Eastern European beauty. After all these years, I'd finally realized that the bump didn't come from her mother's Slovak side.

"No, I'm fine," I said, twirling the gold wedding ring I wore faithfully. "I've got these release papers; I'm supposed to get you to sign them. It might be best for Choppy and your mother. Did Bernie talk to you about any of this?"

"Whatever you and Bernie say is the right thing is fine," she said. Marjorie's eyes were open, direct. I'd forgotten how alluring the hazel-green color was. "Choppy's biggest worry was always paying for a nursing home for Aunt Peg. That issue's moot now. I'll make sure Choppy and my mother get taken care of. I found out about the mortgage foreclosure from J.V.—she's a keeper, by the way. I'm working with the bank to take over the payments. Choppy has no vote in it. Lots of those loans were for my education anyway. We're getting it resolved. *You* do whatever you think is best at this point."

All of a sudden, the person looking back at me wasn't a fiftyish woman but a freshman college student at Pitt gazing coyly from across a library table as she toiled over calculus homework.

"I have *lots* of things on my mind right now, but we'll get through it," she continued, checking my face for a reaction. "Anyway, how are Brittany and Eliza?"

The mention of my girls' names nearly knocked the wind out of me.

Marjorie smoothed her cream-colored blouse. "I've read the newspapers online whenever you've had a big case the last couple of years," she said. "I wasn't stalking you, Shawn. I just needed to know you were okay."

"We're all fine," I said quietly.

"I saw that picture of your family when you did that Make-A-Wish fundraiser back when Christine was still, you know, okay," she said. "She was a beautiful wom-an, Shawn. And those girls are heartstoppers. They have your eyes."

I lifted my head, remembering my daughter's last text pressuring me to invite Marjorie over for pizza. That was downright outrageous.

"The girls are great," I said. "You'd get a kick out of them. They're bull-headed little things. Christine's parents are a huge help. And just because I'm unattached doesn't mean I don't have an occasional date."

I clamped my lips shut. *Where the hell did that come from?* I dropped the folder containing the releases onto the table, trying to signal a shift in topics.

There was a light rap on the library door.

"Judge wanted me to ask, can I get you two any hot beverages?" Jimmy said, peering into the room. "Plus, we got Dunkin' Donuts from the jury down the hall. They're just a day old. Not stale at all."

"Not me. My stomach's upset," I said. "You need anything, Ms. Radovich?"

"I'm fine, thanks, Jimmy," Marjorie said. "By the way, I like that suitcoat. Very dapper."

"Thanks," Jimmy said, beaming at Marjorie. "My partner picked it out at Kaufmann's close-out sale. He has a good eye for awesome deals." Jimmy smiled and drifted out as silently as he'd appeared.

"Look, Shawn," Marjorie said, straightening her skirt. "It was a traumatic thing for me back then. Okay? I just need to say that. Please don't make me feel any worse about it."

I suddenly felt my blood pressure shoot up.

"It involved things that you couldn't possibly have understood," she continued. "I had to make a decision, and I've lived with that decision ever since. I can't apologize for leaving; that wouldn't be honest. I did what I needed to do."

I sat back in my chair. Silent. Then I just blurted it out without having time to filter my thoughts: "So you were shacking up with that adviser, and that's why you left. Isn't that the Reader's Digest version?"

Marjorie looked as if I'd slapped her in the face. "Doc Cliff? How's that relevant *now*, Shawn?" she asked, unusually defensive. "That was thirty years ago."

Jimmy returned suddenly.

"Judge says he'd like you to come back in five minutes, Mr. Rossi. Bring the paperwork with you," he said, giving me a quick thumbs-up. "Your pal from Philly says she can't wait anymore. She wants to call the question."

I stood up without looking at Marjorie, then walked out the door.

September 2008 (Judge's Chambers)

NO DEAL

"What we get accomplished in there, Mr. Rossi?" Judge Wendell asked, leaning across the conference table. "You have the releases signed so I can call the bank folks, and we can try to wrap this case up? I promised Ms. Drew-Morris we'd get her back to Philly. You got documents inked and ready for a notary?"

I stared blankly ahead. Marjorie's words played through my head as if on a loop.

"Mr. Rossi?"

My head jerked up. "No, Your Honor," I said. "Nothing got signed." I dropped the papers onto the table. "I didn't have a chance to talk about it. Frankly, this is *her* problem."

Three sets of eyes blinked at me.

"*I can't apologize for leaving.*" The words kept looping around in my head.

Drew-Morris smacked her hand against the table.

"May I consult with my co-counsel, Your Honor?" Bernie said, grabbing my elbow and dragging me into an adjacent photocopy room.

"What the heck are you doing here, my friend?" Bernie demanded. The smell of stale tobacco on his mustache assaulted me. "This is our *one* chance to help the family and let them walk away with a little self-respect. Don't *screw it up* just 'cause this girl did a number on your head when you were a young guy. Get over it, pal."

"Sorry, Bernie," I said, shaking my head to clear my brain. "There's a lot of stuff getting me confused here. I need to have some time to process it."

"The judge is going out on a limb to do the right thing," Bernie pressed forward. "We've got an *obligation* to help Choppy and Lil get a tiny measure of justice here."

I nodded my head.

Bernie straightened my tie, nudging me back toward the door. "Once we get things straight with the judge, you go out there and *get* her, tiger."

We returned to the conference room, marching in lockstep.

"Your Honor," Bernie began. "Mr. Rossi informs me that his sit-down with Ms. Radovich hit a little snag. Not surprisingly, talking about these events is opening a lot of wounds. But he'll take another stab at it. He's confident that she'll—"

"*Emotional, my ass!*" Drew-Morris said, knocking over a cup of coffee. She had a strange look in her eyes like a person who had become paranoid. She began stuffing papers into her litigation case. "I'm outta here, boys. Go ahead and *try* to write an opinion explaining this stunt, Judge. We'll see who gets the last laugh on appeal."

"*You* hold on, Ms. Drew-Morris," the judge said, speaking louder than usual. For the first time during our trial, his face appeared angry.

"I don't know what's come over you, but I don't like it. Maybe you have some personal issues, but that doesn't justify disrespectful behavior. I've been handling cases since you were in diapers, ma'am, and I don't have much patience for ill-mannered lawyers with dubious clients—regardless of the circumstances," he said, leaning across the table. "As far as I can tell, your client's father never earned a *nickel* of this trust fund. Now he's buried in someone *else's* coffin, so *he* doesn't get a vote. *Someone* impregnated Lilian Radovich when she was sixteen. I'd lay five to one odds it was your guy, Ralph Senior, just from the feeling in my bones. If you push me too hard, I'll have to take my time ruling on the case and see if plaintiffs come up with any new evidence that fills in the missing pieces. I could drag this out for a year if I wanted. You don't want that, do you, young lady?"

Drew-Morris stepped backward, stung by this blast of vitriol.

"I'm giving you the chance to walk out of here, take a cab to the airport and tell your colleagues back in Philly you kicked butt out of these Pittsburgh lawyers. You get a full recovery. What more can you and your client want?" The judge stood up erect, making direct eye contact with our opponent and maintaining his judicial composure.

"I don't agree to any deals," Drew-Morris said, glaring back. "If there's more money in that trust fund, my client deserves it."

The judge paced around his desk several times as if to weigh his words carefully. Finally, he said: "Now, Ms. Drew-Morris, I want you to listen up for a final time. I'm gonna do this for your own good. I'm gonna walk over here, pick up the phone and call the President of Mellon Bank. I've known Mark Haibach forever. He's an honorable fellow, and he'll know I'm making this request because it's the right thing. The bank's entitled to its fees, and you have no standing to object if he waives them. It won't impact your recovery at all. But it will help let this family get some closure. Maybe the Mellon folks will throw in a little extra sweetener to cover the family's pain and suffering. That would be a good ending. It would be the right thing to do."

Drew-Morris tensed her jaw. "I don't want these people getting a penny," she replied. "It's a matter of principle. No deal."

The judge sat back in his chair and stared for a long time in the direction of the Hill District. Then he turned around, saying: "I've made my decision. And I don't appreciate it when lawyers tell me how to run my cases. I'm just trying to think outside the box to achieve a fair result. That's why I took an oath to seek justice when I donned this robe. And any lawyer who takes her duty to the legal profession seriously would feel the same way."

The judge picked up the phone from his desk and punched in a number. "Hi, Elaine. This is Judge Wendell from Orphan's Court. Could you see if Mark Haibach's in? We're hoping to resolve a big trust matter. I just wanna ask for his help so we can wrap this up fairly."

The judge nodded his head and cupped a hand over the phone. "*He's there,*" he whispered to us. "They need to pull him out of a conference with his VPs. Just one minute."

I stood up as if drawn by an irresistible urge and walked out of the room. "Is she still in the library, Jimmy?" I asked.

The clerk shrugged his shoulders. "Miss Radovich? Oh, yeah. Judge didn't say anything about letting her go."

I pushed open the door and entered without knocking. Marjorie was seated at the table, flipping through a copy of Stephen Ambrose's book on the Lewis & Clark expedition.

"Did you know Merriweather Lewis started his trip in Pittsburgh, Shawn?" Marjorie asked, inserting a napkin as a placeholder. "There's *a lot* of history I never knew or appreciated about this town."

"Look, Marjorie," I said, not amused by her effort to avoid the elephant in the room after decades of dodging it. "We don't need to pretend we have amnesia about what happened. Maybe you don't regret walking away and screwing up my life. But I got past it, and I married a beautiful woman, and even though she's gone, I'm good now. So, please don't try to breeze into town *again* and mess everything up for me. And please don't talk about what a great goddamn town Pittsburgh is after being gone for thirty years."

Despite the decades of our separation, I was confident I could predict the words Marjorie would offer in response. I was right.

"The last thing I wanted to do was mess up your life, Shawn," she said.

Then she took a breath and added something I hadn't expected: "I *did* have a fling with Doc Cliff. I'm not going to lie about it, okay? The night you sent me that message saying you were moving back to Pittsburgh and taking that law firm job, I just had a total breakdown. I *wanted* you to come with me to California. You probably don't believe it; I wanted that more than anything in the world. But I couldn't let myself be *selfish,* and I didn't know how to *ask* you without making you do something against your own interest. That's when it happened with him."

This news felt like a slap in the face. I stepped away from her.

"So, you had a fling with this guy and followed him to the other side of the country, even though you knew it would wreck our plans and ruin my life?" I said sarcastically. "Wow! I'm glad you finally shared that news with me."

Marjorie slumped back in her chair. She pulled up her knees, holding them against her.

"Look, Marjorie, I didn't mean to put it that way," I started to say.

She clutched her knees and sobbed silently, openly displaying her pantyhose, any concerns of modesty out the window.

Marjorie wiped a sleeve against her cheek. Even in a state of distress, she was still beautiful.

In that instant, I felt a powerful urge to kiss her. Instead, I placed a hand on her shoulder. She reached up and squeezed my hand. Her fingers felt moist.

"The crazy part was that I kept pretending it was *you*. Isn't that a big joke Shawn?" she said. "I needed *someone* to be with. It was a scary time. Stanford was an attractive option. When that admission letter arrived, I was flattered, and it made me more confused than ever. I needed someone to be with. I needed someone to hold me after being alone for so long. *He* was there." She looked directly into my eyes. "Like most men, he was happy to do the favor. But he knew he was just a stand-in for the person I really wanted to be with. It wasn't hard for him to figure that out. He was just a temporary security blanket. He was someone I knew. I was scared to make the move alone. There was never anything permanent about it."

"It doesn't matter anymore," I said, not wanting to relive any of this.

"There's *more* to the story," she continued, almost defiant. "You *asked* me, so now I'm telling you the whole sick thing." She forced our eyes to reconnect. "I missed my period right before you came back from Harvard. I thought I might be pregnant. That part completely unhinged me. Can you imagine me repeating my mother's stupidity? California wasn't *far enough* to escape to. So, I panicked and accepted the offer from Stanford without talking to you. It wasn't really about Doc Cliff. I just couldn't imagine hurting *you* like that. And my family? I mean, after what my *mother* put all of us through?"

Marjorie squeezed her eyes shut and put her hand over her mouth.

"Like I said, Marjorie, it's ancient history now," I said. "I didn't come in here to—"

"And I'm not going to ask *you* about that Erica woman," she interrupted, looking at me, her eyes filled with tears. "I have too much respect to do that to either of us. So please don't say a word about it, Shawn, because it will make me cry, and I don't want to do any more of that."

I sat mute. Checkmate.

Marjorie stood up, adjusting her skirt. When she caught me staring, she moved toward me hesitantly and brushed back a strand of my hair. She looked directly at me.

"I wanted to come back from day one. But it was impossible," she said. "I needed to go as far away as possible to shed some things that I couldn't shake here. I also needed my own career and identity. If I would have stayed, I would have just resented my mother and you, and I couldn't do that. I'm glad you stayed here and did what you did. I'm proud you did that, Shawn. And as much as you may dislike me now, if I could do *one* thing this second that'd make me feel good, I'd put my arms around you and ask you to hold me for a week. But that's not going to happen, right, attorney Rossi? 'Cause you have every right to be angry at me. Not to mention the fact that I'm a mother, and *you've* got two teenage daughters, and it wouldn't get us anywhere."

Marjorie withdrew her hand and picked up the Lewis & Clark book as if to make sure we didn't do anything rash.

I briefly reconsidered the idea of inviting Marjorie home for pizza but concluded that idea was madness.

"So why did you even come back? I mean *now?*" I asked.

"You're a smart Harvard lawyer, Shawn," she said. "I'd assumed you analyzed your ex-girlfriend and figured that out."

I rested both of my hands on her shoulders and stared into her eyes in search of clues. She didn't blink. I realized that being able to analyze Marjorie correctly had always been a challenge. As much as I thought I understood her, it dawned on me that maybe I hadn't listened carefully enough to her.

There was a firm knock on the door. "You still in there?" Jimmy asked, poking his head into the room. "Judge says he needs you, Mr. Rossi. He's got the Mellon president on the phone. They need to ask you a couple questions."

———

Judge Wendell calmly leaned back in his chair inside the conference room, cradling the phone receiver between his shoulder and ear. "Mark Haibach's on hold," he whispered. I could hear Muzak playing on the other end. "I think it's gonna fly. Your client okay with this plan before we draw up the papers, Shawn?"

Drew-Morris paced the floor like a trapped animal, her face muscles tight and her eyes harsh as they darted in my direction.

"I think Ms. Radovich will sign whatever we tell her is fair," I said. "Go ahead and type it up, Judge. Bernie can go back in there and get her signature."

The first notes of the national anthem jangled from inside a muffled hiding place. Drew-Morris stopped pacing and reached into her handbag. After studying her Blackberry, she stepped out of the room.

"I think we can get the family to accept this, Mark." The judge returned to his conversation with the Mellon bank president. "Get your folks to fax us over something. We'll stay here till we get the papers inked."

The conversation stopped abruptly as Drew-Morris reappeared through the doorway, looking like a woman with a new mission. *"Hang up the phone, Judge,"* she commanded.

"I wasn't finished thanking Mr. Haibach," Judge Wendell said, leaning forward in his chair and signaling her to lower her voice. "Can you show a little respect here, Ms. Drew-Morris?"

"I said *hang up* the phone," she repeated, every muscle in her body appearing tight and in command. "I *know* that you fixed this case."

The judge's face turned almost white. "Call you back in a minute Mark, I got a problem on my hands," he said.

Bernie and I leaned closer to each other, fearing that a nuclear bomb was about to drop.

"Okay, listen up, gentlemen," Drew-Morris continued, glaring at us. "I have a friend in the corporate legal department at Mellon. He blew the whistle. Thank God there are a *couple* of reliable people in this crummy little town. I just got the inside story. The bank's lawyers knew about this deal *yesterday*. Turns out a couple of VPs admitted they got the initial contact a couple *days* ago at a certain judge's request. The whole deal's a *setup*. There's obviously been *collusion* to fix this case."

Judge Wendell leaned forward in his seat. This senior jurist who'd spent his life building a sterling reputation in public service, the first African American in Pittsburgh to be named "Man of the Year" by the Chamber of Commerce, was now accused of rigging a case. And on the face of it, the facts seemed damning.

"Look, here," Bernie said, struggling to stand. "The judge didn't do anything wrong, Ms. Morris. It was an honest effort to do the *right* thing. He only contacted the trust folks to see if they'd give up some of their fees. That's well within his equity powers. He made clear you'd still recover the full amount." Bernie was almost pleading now. "I know it can be twisted out of context. *Jesus*, it was probably poor judgment to have a conversation about this without including you. But there's no collusion and nothing *illicit* about it. In fact, it was *my* idea. We'll drop the whole proposal and have Ms. Radovich sign the release. I'll pay every penny of her costs outta my own pocket."

"We're not signing *any*thing," our Philadelphia opponent replied, her shoulders thrown back, neck muscles flexing. "First, I'm swearing out a complaint in front of the Disciplinary Board. You just admitted to having *ex parte* communications with the judge. I plan on proving that you and Mr. Rossi were colluding to fix the case. First, you hid evidence. Now, this. Not good, Mr. Milanovich. Next, I'm driving to Harrisburg to file charges with the Judicial Inquiry Review Board. *You two* won't be practicing law," she said, aiming a finger at Bernie and me, "and *you'll* be out of the judging business by month's end," she said, shooting a condemnatory look at the judge. "The Judicial Inquiry folks don't screw around with case fixing. Equity powers or not, I'll push for the *maximum* sanctions. You'll be forfeiting your pension, *Your Honor,* but I didn't make the rules. I'm just a lowly officer of the court doing my duty."

Jimmy opened the door without knocking and walked briskly toward his boss. "Sorry ta' interrupt, Judge," he said. "There's a lady on the phone says she's the managing partner of Miss Drew-Morris' firm in New York. She says it's *urgent* or I wouldn't interrupt. The lady sounds important."

Drew-Morris turned away with an authoritative pivot. "Be right back, gentlemen," she said, taking two brisk steps toward Jimmy.

"Nope, it's not for you, Miss Morris," Jimmy said, clearing his throat. "The lady says she wants to talk to Mr. Rossi."

September 2008 (Judge's Chambers)

NEW YORK SUPER LAWYER

In the years since she'd graduated from Harvard Law School a semester after the rest of us, Erica Welles had built a highly successful boutique firm specializing in high-stakes estates and corporate litigation with satellite offices throughout the East Coast. The American Bar Association had ranked her firm of Sidney, Welles & Rupert as one of the top twenty trial firms of its kind in the country—an agile alternative to New York's stuffy blue-stocking firms. Erica's star had risen many times over due to winning massive jury verdicts, serving as president of the New York Bar Association, and steadily climbing to the pinnacle of a lucrative profession.

Shortly after Bernie and I had filed the case, I'd figured out that the Philadelphia boutique handling the *Acmovic* litigation was a satellite of Erica's firm. But I'd avoided mentioning this connection to Erica's young partner during our prickly pre-trial conferences. Drew-Morris, I assumed, wouldn't be amused by my cozy Harvard connection to her boss. And it was awkward for other reasons: I hadn't seen Erica in years—ever since she'd appeared at a law school reunion in Cambridge before I was married, spending the night at the party getting bombed on cosmopolitans. We'd ended up at my hotel room at the Harvard Square Inn because I didn't think she could safely maneuver back to her fancier hotel across the river. Erica had sprawled on the bed and told me her life had been "sucked away by cut-throat litigation work and billable hours" and that she'd never be able to have a child unless she went for artificial insemination because "I can't trust the genes of most of the men I know." She then asked, hanging over the bed thoroughly intoxicated: "Would you be interested in being the donor, Shawn-with-a-w? It can be a no-holds-barred deal. You won't get many offers like this!"

"I'm flattered," I said, draping a spare blanket over Erica and putting her to bed. "But I think I'll stick to having babies with Christine after we get married."

After I'd tied the knot with Christine the following year, it no longer seemed appropriate to invite drunken women into my room to have these types of discussions. So, I'd carefully avoided reunions and one-on-one encounters with Erica. Whenever she made business trips to Pittsburgh and called me at work, I carved out time to chat and stay updated with her life and career. But, when she asked about getting together for drinks, dinner, or a quick Pirates game, I pulled out the standard excuses that I was "doing a deposition" or "preparing a witness for trial" or "heading home to help the girls with homework because there's a test tomorrow." Erica and I still spoke on the phone three or four times a year and stayed in touch by email. Yet, I had avoided rekindling anything that could be interpreted as an "intimate" relationship because it would have been awkward on too many levels.

Now I held the phone to my ear and wondered: *Was my real reason for avoiding Erica all these years jealousy?* I'd tutored this woman in corporations after her "health issues" and gave her pep talks about doing "something productive with her life." Now, Erica had turned into a phenomenal success while I managed a no-frills firm in an economically depressed town. Had I subconsciously been consumed by envy? Or, more likely, had I been afraid that she'd figured out the truth about *me*—that, by the standards of her and most people in our Harvard class, I was largely a failure?

I couldn't avoid facing Erica. It had probably come as a shock to her. Drew-Morris had probably informed Erica that she'd discovered "serious breaches of professional conduct" by the judge and lawyers in this case, including a soon-to-be-disbarred lawyer named Shawn Rossi. At this point, Erica probably made the connection and believed every horrible thing Drew-Morris had relayed was true—that Bernie and I had agreed to throw away our professional integrity in return for a little cash in our pockets. No matter how completely I tried to explain it, she'd never believe the truth—that this was an honest effort to get a few dollars for the Radovich family, who had suffered too much. Nor would Erica ever know that, despite the lack of evidence, I was confident Marjorie was, in fact, the daughter of Ralph Acmovic. That proof would die with a few tight-lipped nuns who would never testify.

"*Yes?*" I said into the phone, keeping my voice lowered.

"Hello, Shawn-with-a-w," Erica replied, her voice sounding surprisingly relaxed as if she were perfectly happy to be talking with me. "I'm worn out from all this 9/11 anniversary stuff. It's emotionally draining. I was just looking over the files last night and put two-and-two together that you were in this case. Has Constance beaten you up yet?"

Her voice maintained a commanding yet mildly humorous tone with no hint of the impediment that had once afflicted her speech. She had quashed those demons a long time ago, just like she had knocked down every other barrier to success. The sound of her voice was pure Erica.

"We put on a decent case, Erica," I said. "The facts just weren't with us, I guess. In fact, now I'm a little worried that maybe we . . ." I peeked into the conference room. Was it possible that Erica didn't know yet?

"You didn't call back when I was in Pittsburgh to give the keynote at the Academy of Trial Lawyers' retreat last month, Shawn," she interrupted me, her voice scolding. "God, all this September eleventh anniversary stuff is bringing back too many horrendous memories. It's good to talk to a friend."

I stretched the phone cord into the hall closet. It was an awkward time for this conversation.

"I've been thinking about you for weeks, Erica, honest," I said, keeping my voice low. "I saw your interview in the *Times*. I know this must be tough for you."

She exhaled. "I'm looking out the window right now, and this whole thing still freaks me out," she said. "There's a cloud of dust down there where they're digging the new foundation where the Twin Towers used to be, and I think about that day . . ." Erica became silent. "At least Dobbs has been doing things right in Congress. He hasn't been spouting off sound bites about '*remembering our 9-11 heroes*' to make himself sound like a goddamn patriot. Most of these politicians turn my stomach. They have no clue what it felt like to have lost someone that day. It's all about political posturing for them."

"How's your family doing?" I asked gently.

There was silence. Erica's voice revealed no hint of emotion.

"Celeste's hanging in there," she said. "It's already been seven years, but she's still recovering from the fact those damn terrorists decided to blow up the *one* building in eight million where her husband worked. We're doing our best. We're still working through it. Can we talk about something else? I try not to go back there. How are *you* doing? And how are those beautiful girls, Shawn-with-a-w?"

I closed my eyes: I could picture Erica perfectly, perched on a chair in her swanky Manhattan office. From the photos I'd seen of her in the *ABA Journal*, her hair had become reddish instead of blonde. She now looked like a well-coifed power-lawyer who easily navigated the highest echelons of corporate and political life from coast to coast as she jetted around the globe.

"My girls are great, Erica," I said. "One of these days, I'll bring them to the Big Apple. They're actually sassy like you. You'd love them." I tried to laugh. "It's still a little weird, but I'm coping. I miss Christine every day. I never expected to be single again."

"By the way," Erica interrupted. "I was surprised *as hell* when I saw you were representing your old flame, Shawn-with-a-w. Don't let it mess with your mind. Are you paying attention to me? It was good *and* bad back then. Accept the fact and don't freak out over it. You and Christine made something amazing together. You should be thankful for that every day."

I rapped my knuckles against the closet door to make it sound like someone was summoning me. "*I'll be right out!*" I said purely as a way to end this uncomfortable conversation and the shame that went with it.

"Gotta go in a minute, Erica. Hey, did you hear Stick was appointed the head federal public defender in Chicago? He cut his hair and looks like a darn TV attorney. My associate saw him on the news and told me he's downright handsome. Wow, that's my man Stick. And how about Dobbs kicking butt in Congress? He made a good choice when he settled back down in North Carolina. Who would've ever thought it? The polls have him ahead by twenty points over his challenger, so he should be golden. We're really proud of him."

"Yeah, I've donated a fortune to Dobbs's campaign," she said. "He deserves to win. Even before he went to Congress, his company was off the charts. Who would have pegged Dobbs as a business genius? He got behind the design of DVDs in the nineties, lining up investors for IBM before anyone else imagined you could put movies on a little disc of plastic. He earned his millions fair and square. And he has the political moves like nobody since Ronald Reagan. But don't change the subject on me, Shawn. *Look*. I drive a new Jaguar every six months, and I have a timeshare in Cozumel. A lot of us have made money, but I'm still jealous as hell of you. It would *kill* me to see you throw all those great things away that you and Christine built together just because your old flame walked back into the movie."

"No need to worry about that, Erica. I'm *already* throwing them away," I said with a nervous laugh. "I wish I would have sold out and moved to New York or a gated community in Florida like everyone else in our class. At least I could have earned buckets of money and given Christine and the girls what they deserved before the whole plan went up in flames."

"Heavens, Shawn," Erica said, clearly annoyed. "Am I really listening to *you,* or is that your downer twin brother? Last I checked the definition of success, it had *your* picture on it, my friend. Don't you realize you're a living version of the American dream, Shawn-with-a-w? Most of us would walk on broken glass to be in your shoes. You've got your own little firm where you can make a difference. You live in a place you love. You have two beautiful girls who adore you. What am I missing here?"

The phone emitted a loud call-waiting beep on Erica's line. She ignored it. "I've got a conference call, but it can wait. Let's get down to business," she said. "I reviewed the pleadings. So, what's your take on this case? Was this Ralph Acmovic guy really your ex-flame's old man? Or is this just an effective snow job by a Harvard-trained lawyer who still knows how to write a dynamite brief? I'm talking off the record here. Give me the real scoop, Shawn-with-a-w. Anything you tell me *can't* and *won't* be used against you."

I recognized the rich irony here. "No chance of violating *my* rights, Erica," I said. "We got ourselves into a box on this case. Your partner Constance is going to take her pound of flesh, and I don't blame her. We probably pushed the envelope too far here. I admit it looks suspicious as hell. We thought we were doing something good for the family. We thought there was a way to work around the usual rules to make justice work in a *practical* way. Only she caught us, and she's going to paint it in the worst possible light. I probably should have anticipated this. Now we're in hot water, and it's our own fault."

Erica's voice still displayed no emotion. She maintained the demeanor of a skilled card player with a concealed trump card. "So, did you ever ask Marjorie the question?"

There was a loud rapping on the closet. "You still in there, Mr. Rossi?" Jimmy asked. "Judge wants to sit everyone down and see if he can't make peace with Ms. Drew-Morris."

"No, I *didn't* ask her, Erica," I said, whispering. "Where's *that* supposed to get me?"

"You're this woman's *lawyer*, Shawn-with a-w," she said. "Didn't you learn anything in our trial tactics class? You have to ask the question *directly* of the witness. It might be good for *both* of you to know the truth, I mean, from this woman's *own lips*. Is your old flame still around?"

"She's in the judge's library ten feet away," I whispered, checking to make sure the door was shut. "But that's nuts, Erica. We're almost *positive* this Ralph Acmovic guy was her father. But the evidence we need doesn't exist anymore. The poor nuns who handled her birth are either dealing with Alzheimer's or can't help us. Even *Marjorie* hasn't been able to prove it with anything concrete. And she's been ducking the truth about some *obvious* things. She's making it worse, and I just don't understand why. But there are *lots* of things about Marjorie I never figured out."

"I'll wait here with my cell turned on, Shawn," Erica said. "Call me back when you find out what *she* has to say about this. If she's twisting the truth, she deserves to get called on it. But if she's hiding something for *another* reason, that may change the equation. It's your job to find out."

"I don't think that's a good idea," I said, glancing at the door.

"Don't be nervous, Shawn-with-a-w," Erica said. "How can you represent your client if you don't ask for the *facts*? This lady doesn't intimidate you just because you had the serious hots for her three decades ago. *That* isn't the problem, is it, Shawn?"

"*Nobody* intimidates me, Erica," I said, feeling intimidated.

"Good. Then suck it up and confront this Marjorie-babe directly," Erica said, her voice now softened. "Face the facts, Shawn-with-a-w. Your life will always include the person you *thought* you'd make a life with and the one you *did* make it with—there's no reason to be ashamed of that. It's actually kinda nice. And it doesn't change just because Christine's gone. You hear me?"

A pair of knuckles rapped loudly at the closet door. "Mr. Rossi, Judge says we gotta sit down with that Drew-Morris woman and try to get a peace treaty worked out before it turns *nuclear*," Jimmy said. "What are you doing in there?"

"I'll have to call you back," I said to Erica, hanging up the phone.

I pulled Jimmy into the closet and closed the door. It was pitch black in there. "Tell the judge to *stall* Drew-Morris." I pressed a finger to the clerk's mouth, *shushing* him. "Tell him that this managing partner lady in New York is chewing me out. Tell him I'm shouting back at her into the phone. Say whatever you gotta say, Jimmy. Just get me a couple minutes."

"But the judge says . . ."

"I understand, Jimmy. But this is our last chance to work something out, and I need a little time."

Jimmy moved closer to me until I could see his baggy eyes. He nodded resolutely. "It's not fair how they treated that poor mother and baby, Mr. Rossi," he whispered. "I didn't realize how bad it was for people like that. I wanna help."

"Thanks, Jimmy," I said, grasping his hand and squeezing it. I steeled myself, preparing to return to the library. "Just get me five minutes. I need to go talk to my client."

Before I left the closet, I punched the number into my Blackberry. After ten rings, J.V. answered. I began talking so fast she seemed unsure if this was a crank call.

"Look, J.V.," I restated. "This is me talking. I know this isn't ideal timing, but I need your advice *now*. Bernie and I did something stupid, okay? It could get us disbarred, and the judge kicked off the bench. I need you to troubleshoot this with me."

"That's seriously you, boss?" J.V. said. It sounded like she was breathing hard. "I'll try to help, but I'm kind of limited here."

"I'm hearing lots of background noise. What the heck's going on?" I asked.

"That's Kalvin's digital stopwatch beeping. We're in the car on the way to the hospital," J.V. said, trying to catch her breath. "I'm in labor, Shawn. I'm supposed to be timing my contractions." She paused and groaned. "What is God's name did you and Bernie do? Did you subpoena the nun and kill her?"

"Can I scribble down a few questions and get Jimmy to fax them to you?" I begged her. "I don't have time to tell you the whole story. Marjorie's in the room next door. I've gotta frame a few questions that pin her down. I need to know her level of certainty that Ralph Acmovic was really her father. I need your help, pal. We could lose our whole firm if I screw this up."

The noises on J.V.'s end became louder and more chaotic. Car doors were slamming. Voices were issuing directives as if they were shouting right into the phone. I could hear Kalvin pleading with J.V. to sit in a wheelchair.

"I think I'm out of time, boss," she said. "They want to wheel me to the delivery room in, like, two minutes. I think the nurse is gonna seize my phone."

J.V. paused long enough to exhale in loud puffs; it was clear she was trying to suppress the pain of her contractions. "Just ask for the *truth* and take the high road, Shawn. Isn't that what you always taught me? They're making me get off, now. This baby's coming in a hurry, Shawn. That has to be my priority. You can handle it, okay?"

"Take care of yourself and that baby, J.V.," I insisted. "Don't worry about any of this. Yes, I'll handle it."

"Please say a prayer it's a *girl*," were the last words my associate uttered.

After listening to the sound of silence, I dropped my Blackberry into my coat pocket. Then I walked into the library.

As Choppy had reported them to me, the relevant facts were much as I'd pieced together from my own snooping. After she'd abruptly broken off our relationship and moved to the West Coast, Marjorie had enrolled at Stanford and completed her doctorate in data visualization. It was there she met and married a fellow Stanford grad student named Michael Pearce. Even though she'd been recruited heavily by Respironics to return to Pittsburgh and offered a prestigious fellowship at Carnegie Mellon as part of the package, she'd turn down those offers in favor of part-time gigs in Palo Alto. Through the connections of her adviser, Dr. David Cliff, Marjorie had been hired by a small up-and-coming tech firm in San Mateo. She'd worked on satellite image processing during the early stages of that industry and became well respected in the field.

Once Marjorie had enough seniority, she and her husband decided to have a family, and she gave birth to two babies in a short span of time. "That girl could get pregnant as fast as the guy sneezed," Choppy told me during our pre-trial meetings at his house, which I told him was too much information. Marjorie and her husband had bought a modest home in Hayward—across the bridge from San Mateo—where they could afford their own place. They had put their kids into private daycares and schools, adapting to the easygoing northern California lifestyle but plunking most of their paychecks into daily living expenses.

At first, Choppy and Aunt Peg had put on their game faces, telling their Swissvale friends that they were "thrilled" Marjorie had found such "incredible opportunities" on the West Coast. "They'll make a bundle of money and then transfer back to Picksburgh," Choppy would say. But gradually, Choppy and Peg came to realize there was nothing "temporary" about this situation. Marjorie and her husband were "house poor" because the cost of living was so high, and plane tickets were a luxury. Choppy started complaining that Marjorie was being held "like one of those brainwashed Moonies" three thousand miles away from Pittsburgh with two beautiful great-grandchildren whom they rarely saw, except for summer vacations when they were allowed to stay for a few weeks to play kickball in the streets and experience a "normal" Swissvale childhood.

Choppy also grew to dislike Marjorie's husband, who "couldn't even operate a screwdriver." This guy, Choppy lamented, didn't seem to care about household chores, childrearing responsibilities, or other marital duties. Choppy turned out to be right; in truth, Michael-the-husband admitted that he disliked any distractions that took him away from his computer terminal. He particularly got annoyed by Lil's frequent calls and emotional meltdowns and health crises that required Marjorie to spend hours on the phone resolving her mother's insurance problems and addressing her constant neediness.

One night over dinner at a Polynesian restaurant, Michael asked Marjorie for a "mutually agreeable separation," which was northern California parlance for a no-contest divorce. He bought motorized go-carts for both children so they wouldn't have hard feelings and signed over his half of the house to Marjorie to avoid a court battle. Then he joined the migration of computer entrepreneurs to the new software and high-tech opportunities in Denver's suburbs.

The part of the story that remained a puzzle to me, though, was why Marjorie hadn't pounced on this opportunity to move back home—something she'd told Choppy and Peg she had dreamed of doing for years. All I could conclude was that she was a woman who had plenty of excuses but was in no rush to rejoin her first family.

It wasn't until after Aunt Peg's funeral that J.V. had shared with me that Marjorie had been taking steps, for months, to plot her return to Pittsburgh with the children.

Ironically, it had turned out to be "too little too late," as Aunt Peg would have said.

"I've gotta ask you a couple of questions, Marjorie," I said, walking into the library and closing the door. "I'm talking to you *off the record* now. I need some honest answers this time, no matter what issues still exist between us."

CHAPTER 42

September 2008 (Judge's Chambers)

MARJORIE'S DARK SECRET

I pulled up a chair, keeping my distance.

"I've *tried* to be truthful, Shawn. I hope you've seen that," Marjorie said while she reached for her purse and snapped open the pocket as if looking for cigarettes. Instead, she pulled out a Vitamin C lozenge and began sucking on it. "I suppose you still don't know me very well, even after all this time. Is that where we are, Shawn?"

"You missed a whole week of trial, okay?" I said. "That story about the no-lien letter was a nice try, but there are *fax machines* in California, Rad. We've all stuck our necks out on this case. We deserve some better answers."

"*Nice try?*" Marjorie said, her eyes displaying hurt. "Look, Shawn, I thought this might be my chance to show my mother that I *felt* something for her, okay? It's not easy, but I'm trying to get over our history. And reading these depositions had been a real eye-opener for me. My mother is a lot braver and did far more for me than I ever knew. Now the most important thing, in *her* mind, is winning this case so she can buy herself a fancy car and get her own apartment—mainly to show everyone she's *worth* something as a person. I guess she needed to prove to Swissvale that she wasn't still a sixteen-year-old girl with loose morals. Can you blame her? *Plus*, I wanted us to recover *something* so Choppy and Aunt Peg could move to a nice assisted living facility where they'd be safe and comfortable. They refused to take money from *me*. This lawsuit could have given them exactly what they needed. That *was* the plan. But then it all got shot to hell when we lost Aunt Peg. God always figures out a way to screw over my family. I should have expected it."

I maintained a professional distance. Her explanation was plausible, but there were some gaps in the narrative.

"I never knew my mother went through what she did," Marjorie continued, "not just at the Roselia Home. I mean, the whole deal. It wasn't easy reading those depositions, but I'm glad I finally know the whole story, Shawn. I've treated her like a dumb big sister my whole life. I'll probably never be able to fix that, but . . ."

Marjorie's lip began to quiver.

"So, let's talk about the facts here," I jumped in, trying to maintain a strict lawyer-client conversation. In truth, I had the urge to put my arm around Marjorie and feel the contour of her body again. I suddenly felt sorry for her and wanted to comfort her. But I realized that would be wildly inappropriate. "Moving from Silicon Valley to buy a place in Pittsburgh isn't an everyday occurrence, Marjorie. Why are you coming back *now*?"

"It's not that complicated, Shawn," Marjorie said, extricating another Vitamin C drop from her purse. "I made a nice salary as a VP, but the stress is a killer, and most of the money went into paying the ridiculous mortgage. I don't get to hang out with my kids *nearly enough*. Plus, I miss the technical work. CMU offered me a position as project lead to help develop cameras for cars that will drive themselves. I thought it would be a cool opportunity."

I raised my eyebrows. This job sounded somewhat far-fetched.

"It can really work," she insisted, her voice growing more excited. "They developed prototypes in the '90s that I've seen in action. I'll work on the vision piece. There'll be cameras on the top of these vehicles that look in different directions to avoid collisions. It's a great technology."

"You must be even crazier than *me*," I interjected. "You're willing to leave California to take a risk on *that*?"

"Swissvale's always been important to my kids, Shawn. They've come here since they were babies. They just haven't had a chance to spend enough time here. I have enough money from the sale of my place to take care of the mortgage on Choppy's house and make some long-overdue updates. I want to add a little apartment for my mother so she has her own space and put in a nice backyard patio for Choppy to have cookouts with his buddies where he can set up his Auto-Croat." Marjorie exhaled. "I should have done this a long time ago. I wish I could have done it for Aunt Peg, too, years ago. But Pittsburgh wasn't ready for a female computer scientist back then, and it definitely wasn't ready for me." Marjorie lifted her eyes. "Now I think it is."

I was silent as I tried to process this story.

"It's not like I've hated California," she continued as if unburdening herself. "Some people end up with the love of their life; some don't. That's how things play out. You're lucky you found Christine. My marriage was fine, but that magical romance you found never happened for me. Still, I have no regrets about it. I got two fabulous kids who complete my life. My ex isn't a bad guy; he still cares for them. I've made decent money. But now I'm ready to get off the train, Shawn. I feel I can succeed at something important here. It's as simple as that. I think we're all ready to do that. There's always time for another chapter, isn't there?"

I took a deep breath. It was a lot to absorb.

"Okay. Let's say all that's true," I finally said. "There's an even *more important* question I've gotta ask you, Marjorie." I stood up, paced around, and addressed her as a lawyer. "How *sure* are you that Ralph Acmovic *really* was your father? I need to know the truth. Give me some *percentages* here. Nothing you tell me will go outside this room. I have my own guess, but now I need to know because we've run out of time."

Marjorie slid down in her chair as if weighing whether she could crawl under the table and escape completely. She bit at her Vitamin C lozenge until it cracked.

"Look, Shawn, there's *one* fact not even Aunt Peg or Choppy knew," she said, squeezing her eyes shut. "And it's going to *stay* in this room, understand? Maybe it wasn't right to get you sucked into this case, but I wanted to give my family a chance. I was hoping you and Bernie would pull it off—even though I had information I was never going to give to you."

"*What information?*" I asked loudly, expressing my exasperation.

Marjorie sat silent.

"Look, Marjorie, if you've got something you're holding back, you owe it to *everyone* to tell us, including your mother. She's about to lose big-time if you play games and withhold key facts."

I kept my eyes fixed on my former girlfriend. I knew if I maintained eye contact, she'd eventually crack.

Finally, she did. "Why do you think I didn't show up to testify, Shawn?" Marjorie looked to see if anyone was listening at the door. "I was hoping you could win the case without me so they couldn't ask me questions about this kind of stuff."

She pulled out a tissue and wiped it across her nostrils. "Dammit, Shawn. This wasn't supposed to be how it ended."

I kept my eyes trained on Marjorie. She remained stock still. Finally, she looked back at me and said in a challenging voice, "*Fine.* If you ever tell anyone, I'll deny it. Here are all the sick details. I met Ralph Acmovic when I was fifteen. He *told* me he was my father. So, there it is. I know it from the bastard's own mouth. Sure, I could go into that courtroom, testify about every disgusting fact, and even bring in someone who could corroborate it. But I'll never humiliate myself by admitting it because that would be even worse than the day I was forced to see that pervert with my own eyes. So, that's where this game ends, Shawn. *Do you hear me?*"

"So, the guy admitted he was your old man?" I prodded her. "What's the big deal? Just get up on the stand, tell the truth, and it will be over in ten minutes."

Marjorie took a deep breath as if struggling to maintain her composure. "There was more than that," she said, her voice almost shaking with anger. "I've never told anyone these details in my life, Shawn. If you repeat them, I'll deny the whole thing and never speak with you again. Do you understand me?"

The summer after their sophomore year in high school, Marjorie told me in a halting voice, she and her friend, Lori Wertz, had treated themselves to French toast and sausage at the Village Dairy—their special outing on Saturday mornings. They'd just settled into a corner booth with their first cups of tea when a skinny man with a protruding nose and blondish hair styled in a bad Rod Stewart cut pushed himself into the booth next to them.

"Ain't you Maggie Radovich?" the man had asked.

"We're having a private conversation," she had replied. "We'd like to keep it that way."

"You'll have a conversation with *me* if I tell you to," the man said, coughing wickedly. "My name is Ralph Acmovic. Didn't your mother teach you to respect your old man?" The hacking sound had turned into a laugh.

"My father's dead," Marjorie had shot back. She hadn't allowed herself to look up from her plate.

The man had lifted his nose into the air and scooted closer to her. "Well, *I ain't dead*," he said, touching his arm to indicate living flesh and blood. "You're even sweeter than I pictured you, Maggie. You got big boobs like your mother. I still remember them sweet things when we were at Kennywood."

Lori had jumped out of the opposite side of the booth to summon Augie Randazzo, the Village Dairy's manager. Before she could find him, though, Acmovic had slid his hand on Marjorie's bare leg, just below her cut-off shorts, and attempted to caress it with his rough fingers, coughing with delight. "You're as sweet as candy, Maggie," he had said, sliding his fingers under her cut-offs. Marjorie had shrieked. He had pinned her inside the booth and kept pressing himself against her.

Out of the kitchen, Augie had emerged with a butcher knife. He'd grabbed Acmovic by both arms and dragged him along the tile floor, banging his head against the booths as they exited the Village Dairy. "You touch that girl again, Ralph, I'll have the Swissvale cops bust your head open *after* I cut off your pecker," Augie had shouted, wielding the knife to emphasize his point. "She doesn't deserve to be within a thousand miles of a monster like you."

Augie had dumped Ralph onto the sidewalk, kicking him for good measure. The disheveled man played possum until he was able to scramble to his feet, bolting down the street and—as soon as he was at a safe distance—shouting obscenities over his shoulder.

"Just for that, you'll never get a nickel out of me, you little slut!" Ralph had yelled. "Even though my old man says we oughtta leave you some of his cash, he's weak in the head. I'll stick it to you just like I stuck it to your MOTHER!"

Marjorie had remained frozen in her booth at the Village Dairy, shaking and drinking her tea until she could steady herself enough to walk home. Augie had said he wanted to call the Swissvale police so she could swear out a complaint, but she'd begged him not to do it. She had left only after Augie and Lori had promised they'd never discuss the events of that day, not as long as they lived.

"I went to see a shrink about it when I got older," Marjorie now said, staring at me blankly. "I'd have *nightmares* about that day. It was just a short encounter—but I *still* feel such a sense of *shame*. And *disgust*. How could this guy who claimed to be my father try to molest his own daughter? What kind of pervert would do that? And the thing that kept haunting me was the thought that half of my genes are from this guy. You'd think I could've put it behind me, Shawn. But it was tied up with so many *other* things in my childhood—being a bastard child wasn't so easy, especially in a place like Swissvale. I guess I just couldn't shake it."

"I'm so sorry, Marjorie," I said, ashamed that I'd made her disclose this dark secret.

"I didn't want to lie about being at the funeral home," she said, shaking her head as if shamed. "But I just went to that place to make sure he was really dead."

"I told my kids I *never* met my father," she continued. "That's the only truth I ever want them to know, Shawn. Can't you respect that and help me here?" Marjorie pushed the hair out of her face and stared pleadingly at me. "After I talked things through with the shrink, I promised myself that degenerate would never get the satisfaction of having me admit that I knew him or had laid eyes on him—or that he even existed. That's the *one* thing I still have over him that allows me to keep my dignity. And it allows my kids never to have to carry those burdens like I did. So, if you go back to that judge and try to make me tell that story under oath, I'll have to deny it and turn on you and Bernie, which would kill me. But I'd have no choice. This lawsuit isn't worth it to me. The whole damn trust fund isn't worth it. For me, the experience of having that sick predator grope me was worse than being born his bastard baby in the first place."

Now it all made sense: Marjorie's avoidance of any discussions about her father since our earliest days together; her fear of settling down in Pittsburgh where her screwed-up history would come to light; and her refusal to come home to testify because she knew, eventually, she'd be forced to fill in details about her father that she wanted to forever expunge, for her own sake, and so that her children never had to hear them.

"I *never* met the man. Do you hear what I'm saying?" Marjorie repeated firmly, her lip trembling. "That's exactly how we have to leave it. Do you hear me, Shawn?"

September 2008 (Judge's Chambers)

THE TRUST

The judge's deputy clerk ushered me back into the conference room.

"I spoke with that managing partner from New York again," Jimmy announced. "She asked if I could put you all on speakerphone."

I sat down, fidgeting with my pen. Bernie and Judge Wendell remained mute. They appeared even *more* stressed now that management from New York was getting involved. Gripping a yellow notepad, Drew-Morris stood above the phone like a young military commander watching over her prisoners. Jimmy punched in the long-distance number.

"Yep, Ms. Welles? I have Judge Wendell and all the lawyers here like you asked," he said.

Erica's voice filled the conference room with authority. "I hope everyone's doing well this morning. Pardon my intrusion, Your Honor," she said, clearing her throat. "So, did you find out any facts for us, Mr. Rossi?"

I hesitated, staring at the speakerphone. "I can't say, Erica," I said.

Drew-Morris took a belligerent step toward the speakerphone. "What's this *Erica* stuff?" she demanded.

"He knew me when I was young and voluptuous, Constance," Erica stated crisply. "Don't worry. He's harmless. Shawn probably wouldn't even lay a hand on me if I flew to Pittsburgh and *threw* myself at him. The guy doesn't know how to take advantage of *anyone*. So, tell me, Shawn-with-a-w: Is our decedent really this woman's father? You aced trial tactics at Harvard. Did you get an answer on direct?"

"He's the father," I said, staring at the speakerphone. "But we can't use the evidence, Erica. We're done."

"You're telling me you *asked* the question?" she repeated.

"Of *course*, I asked it, Erica," I said. "You think I'm a *total* wimp? The answer's a *ninety-nine percent* 'yes.' I have rock-solid information that corroborates the family's story. But we can't use it, okay? It would hurt some people who don't deserve to be hurt. I'm not gonna do that—under any circumstances. So, if you can call off the dogs, Erica, it would mean a lot to me. We screwed up. If Constance doesn't file disciplinary charges, we'll sign the releases and give her *everything* she wants."

"Ninety percent sure she's the daughter?" Erica persisted.

"Ninety-*nine*, Erica," I answered. "We cut some corners. I'm ashamed of that. But our instincts were right. Maybe we can't legally prove paternity. But she's Ralph Acmovic's daughter. I guarantee it. The guy *admitted* it himself, but I can't get into the details. There are some, *um*, personal considerations we've got to respect. Trying to put the facts on the record would devastate some people I care about. So, it looks like we've run out of options."

There was a buzz of static on the other end. The speakerphone hummed for a minute. Then Erica's voice cut back in:

"Settle the case for two million, Constance," Erica said crisply. "That's a third of the trust corpus, a million less than what the woman would have received as the man's daughter."

The young Philadelphia lawyer stood up, pointing a finger at the speakerphone.

"Are you out of your mind, Erica?" she shrieked. "You must have missed the news flash: I have these guys boxed in. I can prove they had ex parte communications and then set up this deal with the bank president. Who cares about their intentions? I can make a solid showing that they were trying to fix the case. They don't have a way out. On top of that, I'm holding the ace card. Ralph Junior won't sign off on the deal, no matter what you say. Their local rules *require* his signature." She glanced at Judge Wendell, smirking at the irony of this statement.

"I'm not talking about the local rules," Erica said, her voice tough, intractable. "I'm talking as managing partner of the firm, Constance. I said *settle* it."

Our opponent pressed her face close to the speakerphone. "Maybe you can pull rank on me, Erica. I get it. You're my boss," she said, speaking directly into the device. "But you still have to convince my *client* to sign the papers. Good luck."

Erica clucked her tongue. "*Gracious*, Constance," she said, sounding like a mother admonishing her child. "I didn't spend my life building this law firm so that some two-bit scammer like Ralph Acmovic can make *my* decisions. I wasn't thrilled when you took this case in the first place. Now we have to deal with it. Let's see what the fee agreement says."

There was the sound of papers shuffling on the end of the phone and the hum of an adding machine clicking out some calculations.

"You established a fee that works out to be forty percent of the total recovery," Erica began. "Very aggressive, Constance, you learned well. When you subtract out-of-pocket expenses, it looks like our firm's entitled to just under two million. So, we'll take another couple hundred thou from firm assets, then write the whole thing off as bad case intake. No matter what your client decides, I have final say over the firm's finances. Or am I missing something? It won't hurt you to have a slightly smaller draw this month, will it, Constance?"

"*No* way, Erica!" Drew-Morris said, squeezing her fists together and trying not to lose her cool with her boss. "You're sending the *wrong* message if you allow this Radovich woman to rip off the system, not to mention this parochial judge and a couple two-bit Pittsburgh lawyers who have serious ethical issues. I *refuse* to throw this case."

"I'm not talking about throwing a case, Constance," Erica said evenly. "I'm talking about making a *business* decision to settle this matter because I believe it's the right thing for the firm. I'm the person paid to make those decisions, aren't I? Don't worry, I'm happy to call the client and get his consent. That guy just wants the money. He doesn't care about the intra-firm budget details. He's got too many ethical problems of his own that could land him in jail if we make a stink about it. Frankly, he'd throw you under the bus in two minutes, Constance. You should learn that before taking on clients like this in the future.

"And, *speaking about ethical issues*," Erica continued, "I don't want to get into this in *great* detail on the phone, Constance, for privacy reasons. But your paralegal came to see me last week when he was in New York. Nice looking guy, I'll give you that. Too bad you cast him aside after squeezing him dry. The poor kid spilled his guts, told me everything."

Drew-Morris froze.

"Abusing a legal assistant is a shameful thing," Erica said. "Making him work eighty hours a week is bad enough. But trading sexual relations for promises that you'll give a young employee an associate's position after he graduates from law school, that's downright unconscionable. It's abusing your position of power in the workplace. I think they call it *sexual harassment* under Title VII, Constance. Plus, he told me you instructed him to cover your tracks in that affair you had with the register of wills down there—Rick Rankin? Sounds like a real peach of a guy. We don't need to earn fees that way, Constance. It doesn't impress anyone here. Submitting false information to perpetrate a fraud on the court is pretty serious stuff, Constance. We'll now have an obligation to conduct an internal investigation. It seems mighty close to a disciplinary code violation in New York *and* PA."

"*Jesus H. Christ*," Judge Wendell uttered, blessing himself. Bernie lifted his eyes toward heaven.

Drew Morris's face began twitching so violently it looked like she might be having a seizure. Huddling over the speakerphone, she cupped a hand over her mouth and whispered, "I sued this Milanovich guy first; I have the upper hand. My employment discrimination lawyer, Lance Laughlin, says I can sue for retaliation if he tries to expose any of this."

"*Forget* it, Constance," Erica said, her voice loud and clear. "Laughlin's a bottom-dweller in the profession. We're not using someone like him to pervert the legal system. Our firm's *reputation* is at stake. And your paralegal told me you're developing a problem with oxycodone. I know that you tore your ACL a few years ago, but this kind of dependence isn't normal. It worries me."

"Maybe I should catch a plane to New York so we can talk this over," Drew-Morris said hurriedly. "I swear I can . . ."

Erica cut her off. "Yes, we'll need to get together right away, Constance," she said. "We'll have to deal with these issues through the firm's ethics committee. They'll be reasonable if I can confirm that you're getting professional treatment. I know some good people at Lawyers Concerned for Lawyers. They'll be able to help. And we'll have to return any fees you improperly diverted from that young attorney. What's her name—Alison Varanti? Richard told me the whole story. You've lost your sense of balance, Constance. This kind of risky behavior could really hurt you. It could ruin your career. We'll have to address it immediately."

"Look, I admit I've been under a lot of stress. The expectations of making partner and my situation with my so-called husband have been brutal. It's not easy being a professional woman these days, Erica. Everyone told me that I had to bring in money to advance myself in the firm," Drew-Morris said, now on the defensive. "I was just doing what I was told."

"Heavens, Constance," Erica replied. "That's not how you bring in revenue. Your generation wants to go from Point A to Point B too fast, and most of the time, that just leads to cutting corners. That's not what our profession's about. You have to earn it the right way. I'm going to make it a priority to mentor you personally. That will be my promise. I made mistakes like this one time a long time ago. I understand how it can happen. Right now, we've got to clean up this mess."

Drew-Morris didn't move. This dressing down by her boss seemed to have paralyzed her.

"Let's get one final thing straight," Erica stated calmly over the speakerphone. "I'd never even *consider* asking you to throw a case. That's not in my genetic makeup. I'm directing you to *settle* this matter, so neither of us has to go to sleep tonight with a guilty conscience. It's a good result for the client. He's lucky to be getting his full share of this trust, and he'll know that. Anyway, I've made the decision, and I'm telling you how we're going to resolve this. Don't you work for me, Constance? Or do I have it backward?"

"*Incredible,*" Judge Wendell stated, wiping his brow and straightening the American flag pin on his lapel. "I didn't know you people did things like this in New York."

"We *don't,*" Erica's voice crackled back over the speakerphone. "But if *Shawn Rossi* tells me this woman is the heiress of Pittsburgh who deserves to inherit the whole damn city, that's good enough for me." Her voice sounded confident like the old Erica of many years ago. "He's one of the few people I've ever met whom I can trust, and I mean *completely.* So that's how *I* choose to do business."

Drew-Morris picked up her yellow pad and packed it in her briefcase slowly, her hands shaking.

"I don't want to be humiliated," she said, whispering into the speakerphone. "I'll do what you're telling me. I'll switch my ticket to JFK and meet you tonight." She pressed her face closer to the speakerphone, her voice trembling. "Will you really try to help me, Erica?"

"Absolutely," the voice replied. "Let's wrap up with these folks first."

The judge lit up a Kent and took a prolonged puff as if trying to inhale the entire smoke at once.

Erica's voice broke up for a minute, becoming stronger and then fainter as if moving from one location to another in her office.

"When I look out this window, Judge," she said in a crackly voice, "I stare at that big hole in the ground, and I keep asking myself: What the hell are we trying to preserve here? Isn't *that* the real question we should be asking ourselves as members of our profession?" she asked.

The cell connection faded out, and Erica was gone.

September 2008
(Magee-Women's Hospital, Oakland)

THE KEY

Bernie and I paced the waiting room floor at Magee-Women's Hospital, two blocks away from my old apartment on Semple Street. We sank into ergonomic chairs, waiting till the desk nurse signaled that we could enter J.V.'s room. I gripped a bouquet of helium balloons and slid a gift box with a bow onto the seat next to me.

"I guess we could've lost our licenses," I said, wiping my forehead. "I feel rotten that we let the judge risk his *own* reputation, even though he's the most honorable guy in the world. We probably shouldn't have let him take a chance like that for *us*."

My co-counsel, still in a state of disbelief, stroked his mustache with one finger. "Warren didn't do it for *us*. He did it because he knew an injustice had to be corrected," Bernie said. "Root and branch. His meeting with that old nun was the turning point."

"The old nun at the retirement home? How did that change anything?"

Bernie put a finger to his lips as if preserving a secret. "Let's just say there was more to the story about his mother working at the Roselia Home than he told us," Bernie said. "What he repeated to us was the story he'd always been told by his mother. But he suspected there was more to it. The other night after we left the Lincoln Club—when we walked to his car? He took me into his confidence and spilled his guts."

"More to the story?" I asked, looking around the waiting room. There was nobody else within earshot.

"That story about the niece who gave birth to a baby and mysteriously vanished? Warren confirmed with Sister Benedict that story was made up by his parents to protect him. Since Vervy is long gone and the nun is preparing to meet her Maker, she was willing to share the truth with him," Bernie said. "He found the Sisters after reading our depositions and finding out their identities. Sure enough, some of them were the same ones who worked with his mother. Incidentally, he found his mother was so devoted to the Roselia Home she was almost considered an honorary nun. Warren implored the administrative nun to come clean with the facts because the story he'd been told never added up. The nun relented and spilled the beans. Warren's real birth mother was Rosie, the girl who disappeared. She was Vervy's *daughter.* The poor girl got pregnant from some White guy in Squirrel Hill who paid her to clean his house. That part was true. She was still in high school. She was ashamed and afraid her parents would be ruined if the neighbors found out. So, she ran away to the Hill District, where a pastor arranged for her to stay at the Roselia Home. After the baby was born and put up for adoption, she left the Roselia home, wandered down to the river one night, and jumped off the West End Bridge."

"That's horrible," I said. "The girl died?"

"It wasn't until the body was found in the river and the coroner determined that the girl has just delivered a baby that Livingston and Vervy discovered what had happened to their daughter, but they still didn't know where she had been hiding all those months," Bernie explained softly. "The poor father was already sick with worry over the girl's disappearance. When they found her body, he had a breakdown and nearly died of a stroke.

"But Vervy wouldn't let it go. She'd lost her daughter, and now she knew her grandbaby was out there. She drove around the city and checked every home for unwed mothers until she discovered Rosie had been holed up at the Roselia Home. The nuns were sympathetic. The whole situation was tragic, and Rosie had been a sweet girl. The baby—Warren—had already been sent to the orphanage. But those nuns helped Vervy find him. She got him back."

"After the father died of a heart attack a few years later from all the horrible stress, Vervy picked up young Warren, moved to the Hill District where a mixed-race child would be more accepted, and raised Warren as her own."

"Let me get this straight—the person Warren spent his life thinking was his *mother* was really his *grandmother*?" I asked, still trying to wrap my head around it.

"Yes, and fortunately, she was a strong enough woman to hold it all together," Bernie said, adjusting his spectacles. "Vervy died owning nothing. She worked three jobs so Warren could get an education and do something important with his life. And she tended to those babies at the Roselia Home. That was her calling in life after losing her child and living through one tragedy after another. So, the more Warren learned of the truth from these old Sisters, the more he felt he had a duty to do something here, Shawn. He'd been afraid to face some of these issues until this case gave him one last chance to deal with the truth. It was *his* choice to go out on a limb to get some measure of justice for the Radovich family. Not ours."

The desk nurse stepped into the waiting room. "You're the visitors for Ms. Jaime Vaskov? She and the baby are ready to see you. Be sure you scrub your hands with *plenty* of hand sanitizer, especially if you're gonna touch the infant," she said, eyeing my fingernails.

I grabbed the balloons, carefully picked up the gift box, and spat my gum into a tissue.

"Bernie, you mind if I go see J.V. first?" I asked. "I've got something special I wanna give her. It'll only take a minute."

"No problem," Bernie said, giving me a wink. "I need to find the gift shop and buy a box of pink bubblegum cigars."

The room was dimly lit. A bassinette in the corner had an identification card listing the name of the baby (Jessica), sex (female), weight (eight pounds, two ounces), and the name of parents (Jaime and Kalvin). A computer beeped at a steady pace, keeping track of vital signs.

J.V. was resting with her bed partially reclined. Cuddled in the nook of her arm was a brownish baby wearing a knitted beanie. The infant didn't have the same black hair that J.V.'s other babies had when they were born. Instead, she had wisps of orange hair peeking out from underneath her hat.

"*Wow*, she's a *baby doll*," I said, kissing J.V. on the forehead. "Good job, mom." The tightly wrapped bundle made a bleating noise at my touch.

"Thanks, boss," J.V. said. "She looks like me, huh? We're calling her Jess. Named after my grandma. Thank heavens we *finally* got a girl. I wasn't sure Kalvin's chromosomes were up to it."

J.V.'s husband was snoring loudly, sacked out in a chair next to the bed. He wore green hospital scrubs with his neat cornrows tucked into a hairnet. He'd been working two jobs all week to get ready to take some personal days off. At the sound of my voice, he opened one eye.

"I heard you didn't faint, Kalvin," I said, giving him a thumbs up.

Kalvin uttered an incomprehensible sentence and instantly fell asleep, trying to get a catnap before the boys arrived with their grandparents to wreak havoc.

"Let him snooze," J.V. said gently. "The poor guy's fried. And thanks for the balloons, Shawn. I feel like it's Christmas in September. It's another one of the *best* days of my life."

Settling myself onto the corner of the bed, I stared into J.V.'s eyes. She looked tired but almost radiated with maternal energy as she clutched the little bundle in her arms.

"So, Allison texted me some crazy message that you and Bernie got two million bucks for the Radovich case. What the heck happened?" J.V. asked. "Did someone exert super-human powers to force Constance to do it?"

"Kind of," I said, smiling. "It's a long story. I'll save it for when we can sit down together and drink lots of wine again."

"I mean, that's *unbelievable*, Shawn," my associate said, freeing one hand and mustering a little thumbs-up.

"Yeah. I wish you could've been there when Constance surrendered," I said, now happy to boast. "The guy from the state employment discrimination agency already contacted Bernie's office and let him know Constance withdrew her sexual harassment complaint *with prejudice*. She's barred from ever re-filing it. Basically, she's had to publicly eat crow. I can't wait to see *that* story in the paper tomorrow."

J.V. hiked herself up in the bed.

I added nonchalantly: "Hey, what all did Marjorie tell you about her real reasons for not coming?" I asked. "How did you know she had a legit reason? I should have put more stock in what you told me."

J.V. paused, twirling her hair with one finger. "I'd be violating a confidence if I talked about that," she answered cagily. "I'm taking the Fifth."

I reached up and rubbed the pink foot of the baby, which had wriggled free from the blankets. The little brown foot twitched then withdrew and pressed itself against the warmth of J.V.'s stomach.

As J.V. adjusted the baby's position, I caught a perfect view of the tattoo on her wrist, depicting three blue shooting stars blazing across her skin. "Hey, you'll have to add a *fourth* star on there," I pointed out. "It'd better be *bright* pink. She's gonna have to stand up to all those boys."

J.V. laughed and patted the baby's rear end.

"If she's anything like her mother, that's a foregone conclusion. By the way," I said, taking a deep breath, "I brought something for you and Jess." I cradled the gift box in both hands and held it out.

J.V. opened the box and carefully pulled out the object from the folds of white tissue: It was the old snow globe, with a scene of a past Pittsburgh inside it, which Aunt Peg had given me an eternity ago.

"I *love* it, Shawn," J.V. said, holding it up and shaking it, so that snowy sparkles danced inside the sphere. She inspected the little chunk missing from the base. "This looks really old. It's so cool."

"I wanted you and Jess to have it," I said. "Aunt Peg gave it to me at a special time. Now, this is your time."

J.V. did a double-take. Underneath the base of the globe was taped a freshly cut key. "Hold on, it's not safe to leave this on there, she could swallow it," she said, peeling off the key. "And what message is this supposed to be sending me, boss? I know I gotta get back to work. I talked to Kalvin about cutting my maternity leave to four weeks. I don't want my boss thinking I'm a *slacker* just because I had a baby."

"You're a *wild woman*," I said, scooting my chair closer to her. "That's what I love about you millennials. You're a little flaky, but you're *intrepid*. Don't even *think* about coming back till after you take your full eight weeks. But after you come back, I want you to have *this*."

I held up the key she'd removed from the globe's base. "It's a master key to the office," I said. "I'm giving you half of the firm, J.V. I still wanna keep a few of my big clients. But you're taking over everything else."

J.V. patted my hand. "That's sweet, boss," she said, humoring me. "*Someday,* I wanna buy-in as a partner, even if we have to leave the city for a while. That's my ultimate dream. But that's not gonna happen till we get our kids through school. Let's be realistic. We can't even afford *daycare* for these little monsters."

"Clean the wax outta your ears, girl. I said I'm *giving* half of it to you," I said. "You can telecommute and spend some afternoons at home; you need to carve out time to do homework with your kids. And you've gotta keep an eye on your folks, too. Maybe you can buy a bigger house where they can stay whenever they want. There's only one stipulation: You and Kalvin are never allowed to move to Chicago. You guys are Pittsburghers."

J.V. stared at me as if she'd swallowed a hallucinogenic drug. "Kalvin has never wanted to leave, Shawn," she said, her lip trembling. "He broke down and spilled his guts right after Jess was born when we were alone. He has no desire to leave. This is our home. He loves his IT work at Community College, and he has a chance to teach a course at Duquesne; that's always been a dream for him. Northwestern may be a big name, but he feels he can do more here. We want to build something *together.* But we're going to earn it ourselves. We don't want any handouts, boss."

"This isn't a handout," I corrected her. "You *earned* this. And it's exactly what I want."

J.V. blinked her swollen eyelids, still not processing it.

"We'll call the firm '*Rossi and Vaskov.*' And we'll need someone to be your senior associate," I continued. "Maybe Allison will apply."

J.V.'s husband smashed a pillow over his face; our voices were interrupting his sleep.

"But I've only been out of law school eight years, Shawn," J.V. said. "I'm not qualified to be half owner of my own law firm."

"You don't get a vote," I said. "I'm *investing* in you, J.V. I'm getting too old to do this crap forever, and, besides, there are lots of other things I wanna do. Like, I'm going to that Jimmy Buffet concert in Florida with Dobbs and Stick next month and drinking some margaritas. It will be like a second spring break. Only we'll be able to afford a hotel this time—I'll tell you that story sometime. By the way, I just got an opinion from the PA Supremes on that Ligonier property case. After ten years of work on that sucker, they reversed my big win—we won't get a nickel. That's how this business works. But the guy I represented called and said he was super impressed with my work. He said I was 'tenacious.' How cool is that? Anyway, he's hiring our firm to do the trust work for all ten of his banks. He said it's a seven-figure account. Can you believe it, J.V.? We'll have enough work to keep us busy for years."

"What about the girls?" J.V. protested. "You need to save money for them. They'll have college bills and weddings to pay for. You can't be reckless about this."

I waved a hand, dismissing her. "When Christine got sick, she set up a trust for the girls' college and grad school. She was always thinking ahead. This new business for the banks will pump plenty of extra money into their trust account. We'll be in good shape. Christine always said Britt was destined to be a businesswoman like her, and Liza would be a bull-headed lawyer like me. She had an amazing ability to look into the future. The girls will be able to do whatever they set out to do. Christine probably pulled some strings up in heaven to make this happen, so we're good. Kalvin can start taking over the IT work at the firm, too. He's experienced enough to do it. I want you and Kalvin to inherit the same thing Christine and I were lucky enough to inherit. It's the only way all of this can continue, right, J.V.? Just don't kick me to the curb when I become an old geezer who wears a suit coat over his shorts."

J.V. held up the baby and pressed her to me. Then she began blubbering like a baby herself, her motherly hormones now kicking in. The smell of the baby's skin against me brought back a burst of happy memories: I could picture being in the hospital with Christine, wearing my scrubs at the births of each of our two daughters. It was like a delicious freeze-frame of the past. I squeezed my eyes shut and savored the images.

"You and Kalvin will figure it out," I whispered to my new partner. "You've gotta think of yourselves as *one* unit. If you settle for less sometimes, you end up with more in the long haul. I think that's what Aunt Peg once told me."

J.V. blinked.

"It's all about redefining success," I said, squeezing her arm. "I think *you* were the one who told me that, *partner*."

September 2008 (Grant Street)

THE ENCOUNTER

Bernie and I rode the bronze elevator from the seventeenth floor of the Frick Building to the lobby, our litigation cases swinging weightlessly at our sides. A stream
of nattily dressed lawyers and accountants clicked across the Carrera marble floor.
Another day's commerce had come to a close. This group of young professionals
would now go home and prepare for the next cycle just as their predecessors had
done for a hundred years since Henry Clay Frick had built this grand building as a
testament to profit and power.

"You got something good accomplished in this one, Shawn," Bernie said, holding out a pack of Doublemint gum to offer me a stick. "You pumped a helluva lot
of billable time into this case. But a good family finally got what it deserved. Maybe
Lil can get her apartment and buy herself that pink Caddy she's always wanted so
she can start over again at age sixty-seven. It's better than never having that chance.
You gave her a new life, my friend."

"We beat the odds on this one, Bernie," I said. "I guess the system worked in
a crazy way."

My co-counsel gripped my arm. "I won't tell Choppy that your firm under-
wrote all the costs. *Or* that you turned down your fee," Bernie said, chewing at
the edge of his mustache. "We can certainly play around with the math, so the
Radoviches don't know. But are you sure you don't want at least a hundred grand? A
little cash right now would let you send the girls back to the Academy. You're gonna
catch hell from J.V. when she finds out you gave away a fortune."

I patted his shoulder. "To heck with the Academy," I said. "The girls are making good friends at the public school. That Jarrod's gonna be a star. He's a *super* guy.
I may have lost the Ligonier case, but I have some other things cooking. Christine's
watching out for us, Bernie. The girls will be fine. So will the firm. I already talked
this over with J.V. She's good with waiving our fee so that the Radovich family

can get the whole kitty. Just don't go telling everyone in the bar association, or they'll think I went mushy in the head. Some things you just do for yourself. Okay, counselor?"

Bernie's eyes twinkled. "Your mentor Tim Mulroy would be proud of you," he said. "But I can't promise you'll pull this off, that's all I'm saying."

I stopped at a flower vendor's kiosk in the corner of the lobby run by an elderly woman who'd emigrated from Korea and raised her own family in Pittsburgh. She'd been in business since I'd first started practicing law. It occurred to me that I might be seeing someone to whom I wanted to give a nice bouquet.

"Hey, *sweetheart!*" she said, throwing up her arms. "Where you been the past few months?"

"Busy in court," I said. "But I still think about you every day, Esther. How's your son doing?"

"He made dean's list last semester at CMU and just started sophomore year," she said. "He's happy as could be. You get extra greens for remembering."

I lingered to pick out a bunch of flowers that still had plenty of unopened buds, then watched Esther wrap them in shimmering cellophane after layering in a handful of baby's-breath. "You want a bunch too, Bernie?" I asked.

"Not me, Shawn," he said, chuckling. "It would make my wife suspicious. Don't forget, I was accused of being a *harasser.*"

I pulled out my wallet and extricated a fifty-dollar bill, feeling in the mood to give an extravagant tip.

"This is for you," I said, sliding the bill into Esther's hand.

"Looks like some nice lady is gonna get *lucky* today," she called after me, blowing a kiss.

Having arranged for a celebratory lunch at the Common Plea the following week, Bernie and I twirled through adjoining revolving doors, heading in opposite directions.

"You know what, Bernie?" I called after him. "This case reminded me why I wanted to be a lawyer in the *first* place."

He stopped on the sidewalk and gave a thumb's up.

On Grant Street, a red Plymouth Valiant pulled up to the curb and flashed its blinkers. Marjorie and her two children, each clutching a big M&M cookie and bottled juice, were about to climb in. She'd told me they were going to walk around town and get treats; it was perfect timing. Choppy laid on the horn and motioned a bus to go around him while Lil rolled down the front window and waved, a huge bag of Doritos in her hand.

Marjorie took a step toward the car door then yanked her children back onto the curb when she saw me.

"You guys," she said, waving them toward me with a copy of the latest *Rolling Stone* magazine in her hand. "I want you to meet someone you've heard a lot about.

You never had a chance to say hello to Mr. Shawn Rossi, did you? Wipe that gunk off your hands before you shake."

I knelt and peered into the faces of Dianna and Florian Radovich-Pearce, who wore their casual clothes for this expedition. Dianna was shorter than my girls, with blonde hair pulled back in a scrunchie. Florian had darker features and a mischievous smile.

"Your great-grandpa says you guys like soccer," I said, hiding the flowers behind my back with one hand while I shook each of their hands. "I'll bet my daughter Liza and her buddies would let you play pick-up ball with them. They go to Frick Park every Saturday."

"That would be *super cool*, Mr. Shawn," Dianna said, pulling a pen from a pint-sized purse along with a small spiral notebook. "If you write down Liza's info, we'll IM her. We're free this Saturday, right, mom?"

On one knee, I scribbled down the email address and cell number. Then I leaned secretively toward the two children: "Hey, you guys don't *really* know who I am, do you?" I asked. "I know you saw me in the courtroom. But I never really introduced myself."

"Oh, sure, we know who you are," Florian said as he wiped melted chocolate on his pants while checking to make sure his mother didn't see. "You're the friend who mom said stayed in Pittsburgh and did something cool."

I leaned closer and whispered: "People always say great things about lawyers *after* they win their cases."

"Oh, no, Mr. Shawn," he said earnestly. "She told us that a long time ago. We know all about you. We even know about your dog Plutarch and how he threw up that time when he ate the paint at your apartment."

My face reddened. "That place was unsanitary," I said. "Don't *ever* live in a dump like that when you kids go to college."

I reached into my pocket and handed them two little boxes containing folding robot-like reading lights that I'd picked up at a tech fair in Market Square.

"*Awesome,*" Florian said. "Maybe I can sell it on eBay."

The children clutched their gifts as Marjorie ushered them into the back seat. They gave two thumbs up, and Dianna yelled: "Have Liza check her IM when she gets home!" I touched Marjorie's arm for a moment as if stopping a dramatic movie to insert a final, crucial scene. My thumb crinkled against the cellophane that Esther had wrapped around the bouquet, which I still was holding behind my back.

"Could you step over here for a second?" I asked her.

Marjorie and I moved into an alcove outside PNC bank, shielded from view. Dressed in a snappy yellow jacket over her court attire, a blade of sunlight illuminating her face, she looked more stunning than ever.

"It sounds like you guys are really staying," I said, still feeling nervous being alone like this. "Let me know how we can help, okay, Rad?"

"We're fired up and ready to go," she said, blocking the sun out of her eyes. "I can make a decent living here. I know I haven't stayed in touch with many friends, but Lori Wertz and her family are nearby in Youngstown. She already helped me do my house hunting. And there are plenty of folks in Swissvale I want to connect with again. All of that stuff about my mom and our past seems like it popped and disappeared like a faded, bad dream. I feel I finally can deal with it now."

"Hopefully, your kids will like it, Rad," I said, mildly apologetically. "It's not San Fran, but they'll find fun things to do."

"What the heck are you talking about, Shawn?" Marjorie put her hands on her hips. "You've got all *kinds* of cool new stuff here. We're going to the Andy Warhol Museum tomorrow. I used to buy piano music in that old building when it was Volkwein's. And I want to check out the Rangos Omnimax Theatre in the Science Center, then go to the markets in the Strip District and get cheesesteaks at Primanti's. C'mon, dude, this is *better* than the West Coast. Around here, you don't even have to wait in line. Just don't tell everyone these secrets or the whole world will want to come to the Burgh. That would ruin everything."

I eyed my ex-flame from top to bottom. "Who would have thought it?" I asked, shaking my head. "I think you're still a darn Pittsburgher."

Marjorie laughed at that one. I had smoked her out.

"Look, Rad," I said, lowering my voice and still clutching the flowers behind my back. "I admit that I'm pumped up from that win. Right now, I could imagine that it would be fun to go off to the William Penn Hotel and have a wild affair with you and see what happens." Marjorie looked stunned. "But that probably wouldn't be a good move."

Marjorie's eyes sparkled, alive.

"As my kids would say, '*That would be gross*,' right?" I said.

"We're both grown-ups with families," Marjorie agreed, nodding her head soberly. "We're not college students anymore, Shawn. And *you* are a widower. I respect that." She paused, touching my suitcoat sleeve, before withdrawing her hand. "It'd be interesting, I'll admit it. But it wouldn't be appropriate for two people who haven't even seen each other for thirty years, right?"

"Right," I said.

"Anyway, we aren't defined by those kinds of physical attractions anymore, are we, Shawn?" she asked seriously.

"Nope, we really aren't," I said, looking around. The Plymouth wasn't in view.

Impulsively, I leaned over and kissed Marjorie directly on the lips. "I just wanted to do that for the hell of it."

We stood looking at each other for a long minute. Marjorie didn't unlock her eyes. Then she caught me by surprise, standing up on her tiptoes and initiating a long kiss of her own. "I'm glad you did," she said. "Otherwise, I'd have had to do it *for* you, Shawn. We needed to clear that up."

All afternoon, I'd been thinking about everything Marjorie had told me in Judge Wendell's library. It had hit me like a pile of bricks that my resentment after she'd left for California was mainly my fault. She'd figured out, back then, that we were destined to take separate paths, which was necessary for me as much as her. I just hadn't heard what she was trying to tell me. I realized, suddenly, that my life would always be defined by a fundamental truth: I'd loved Christine more than any person I could ever love in the world. I'd been a good husband and dad. Now, it was okay to think about new possibilities without feeling overwhelmed by guilt. Frankly, I still wasn't sure if it was too soon to date. This part might take a while to sort out. I knew that I was a vastly different person than I was thirty years ago. So was Marjorie. We both had pasts and futures, which would always be part of each of us. And that was a good thing.

I felt as if I could read Marjorie's thoughts at that moment. Throwing inhibition to the wind, I popped the question: "You think you might wanna get together sometime, Rad? I know it's been about thirty years. But I feel like I know you a lot better now. And you've taught me some things about myself—better late than never. Now that this trial is over, I could probably squeeze in some time if you're game for it. I think I'm free for the next ten weekends."

"How about this Saturday?" she asked. "I think I can get a babysitter for the kids. I mean, just in *case* we end up staying out late. I'm not saying we *need* to do that."

We laughed simultaneously before Marjorie kissed me a second time, directly on the lips, then ducked out of the alcove and climbed into Choppy's car, wedged between her son and daughter. She slammed the door, then rolled down the window and motioned to me as if she'd forgotten something, her face that of an efficient businesswoman's.

"Also, we'll need a good lawyer on that Carrie Furnace Museum project to give us advice, Shawn. It's *pro bono*. I'd like to sign you up."

"No problem, Rad," I said. "I get bored earning *gobs* of money on cases like this." I waved to the group inside the Plymouth. "Also, if you need a *real* job here in the Burgh, let me know so I can help. That job at CMU working on cars without drivers sounds far-out."

"That's what you said about the ARPANET," she yelled back. "Look how that worked out."

Choppy tooted the horn, then gave a second longer honk to ward off stray buses and cabs that might cut in front of him in the chaotic downtown traffic. Lil turned around in the front seat, sharing her bag of Doritos with Marjorie and waving. The car navigated slowly toward the Parkway East ramp in the direction of Swissvale.

September 2008 (Grant Street)

THE NEXT CHAPTER

I strolled down Grant Street feeling free of any deadlines or commitments. I stopped to stare in the window of Mellon Bank Tower at nothing in particular. From the direction of the Koppers Building, I saw two forms rushing toward me, ducking through cars to bolt across the street. The girls gasped to catch their breaths. "*Dad-o?*"

"Hey guys," I said. "Geez, you're actually on time!"

Brittany and Liza grinned simultaneously, pleased with themselves that they'd met a deadline for once. They seemed to be getting along, like true sisters.

"*Hey*, dad," Liza said, dressed in clothes and accessories that appeared uncharacteristically normal. "What were you doing back there with that lady?"

"We saw that woman stand up on her toes and kiss you." Britt pulled me toward her, making a dramatic show of maintaining confidentiality. "You're *too* hot, dad."

"Honest, girls," I said, straightening up. "That was just what old people call a '*friendship kiss.*' I swear it felt like kissing your mom's Aunt Linda."

"Aunt Linda? *Gross!* Spare us the details," Britt said.

"Actually, it was much better than Aunt Linda," I said. "But don't rat on me."

"We won't say anything to grandma," my oldest daughter said, punching my arm. "Just don't make a habit of it with *too* many ladies, or we'll sing like two canaries. When my old boyfriend tried to do that, I almost *decked* him."

I stared at my two daughters. They looked beautiful in their casual fall skirts. Their dark hair bounced from their shoulders in soft waves, which meant they'd taken time to use the curling iron. I couldn't take my eyes off Liza: My skinny daughter still had a pink streak in her hair and a tiny nose piercing. But Britt had obviously assisted with hair and makeup, giving Liza a chic-teenager look. She even wore lip gloss, the first time I'd seen that since she had played dress-up as a little girl.

"Hey, you girls look *gorgeous*," I said, changing the topic from the kissing episode while I was still ahead. "I never expected you two would stop fighting long enough to get down here so quickly. You got my text message. Am I a *techie* or what?"

They eyed each other, then laughed at me. Britt whisked flecks of invisible lint off my suit, straightening my power tie, which had slipped sideways.

"We went over to the cemetery to visit mom earlier today," Britt said, matter-of-factly. "We figured it would bring you some good luck. That little honeylocust tree looks beautiful, daddy. Its branches are getting bigger and bigger. I swear mom could see us while we were standing there. It was really special to be there together, right sistah?" She slung her arm around Liza.

I stared at my two girls. They weren't really girls anymore, I realized. They were growing into beautiful young women, just like their mother. And it struck me that despite the occasional issues, we were an amazing trio.

"Hey guys," I said, "I'm thinking I might cut back on this law firm stuff a bit. I'm tired of fighting lawyers over money all day long. Anyhow, J.V. is going to step up and become an equal partner in the firm. She's ready. I know my cooking sucks, but grandma can teach us some of mom's recipes. We'll do it together. There's lots of cool stuff I'd like to do with you guys."

"Paintball," said Liza. "I know it looks like a gross mess, but most kids just soak their clothes in the sink later. It doesn't do any permanent damage."

"Done," I said.

"Cosmic bowling," Britt chimed in. "Jarrod likes cosmic bowling and wings— the hotter, the better. I think you owe him big-time, Dad."

"We'll go whenever Jarrod wants," I replied, shaking Britt's hand to make that deal official. "I was a jerk. We'll fatten him up with as many wings as he can chow down, so he forgives me. And we'll bowl all night till the sun comes up."

"Have you been smoking pot, dad?"

"No pot necessary," I said. "I'm just tired of being a boring lawyer-guy. I even checked out that place over on the South Side you've been talking about, Lize."

I unbuttoned the sleeve of my shirt and pushed up my suit jacket, holding out my forearm.

"*My God!*" Liza and Britt touched the spot. "Are these things for real?"

On my wrist, I displayed four tiny stars, no bigger than droplets of rain. There were two slightly bigger ones, one red and one blue, trailed by two smaller red stars.

"That's mom and me," I said, pointing. "The other two are you girls. J.V. made me go over there last week and try it out."

"Were you creeping on me?" Liza demanded.

"What do you mean?" I asked, pretending not to get her point. The truth was, she was right. I'd gone to the dumpy tattoo parlor only because I wanted to see how bad it would be if Liza carried out her threat to get one. While I was there, the guy talked me into doing a test run. It was harmless; it also was the "temporary" kind that wore off in a week. But I didn't plan to tell my daughters until I milked it for everything possible.

Both girls burst out laughing as they inspected my wrist. "Shawn, I think you've flipped out," Liza said. "I love it. So, can I get one now? One of my friends got a massive Japanese eel on her ankle. It's way cool."

"We'll talk about it later," I said. "But don't even *think* of getting a full-body tattoo. We're not going crazy here."

Before I could get my arms around both girls to hug them, Christine's parents crossed the street, hurrying to catch the "walk" signal. I almost didn't recognize my father-in-law today. Cy had donned a blue blazer for this occasion and had combed his white hair neatly like a business executive. Mostly, I couldn't tear my eyes away from Christine's mother. Instead of the usual sweatpants and grungy shirts she wore for cleaning the house, Jane was wearing a classy black outfit with sparkly trim and a matching jacket. She had the same dark, curly hair as Christine that bounced along her shoulders as she walked.

"*Wow*, you look *fantastic*, mom," I said. "You're both dressed up so nice. I feel bad. I was just going to get some burgers to go."

Cy slipped his parking receipt into his pocket. "We thought we'd show you we still knew how to clean up, son," he said with deadpan delivery.

Christine's mom eyed me up and down as if inspecting my attire. I tried to stand with one shoe covering the other, but she caught me immediately. Her eyes focused on my light brown shoes that clashed egregiously with my grey pinstripe suit. She shrugged her shoulders as if to indicate that I was still hopeless.

"There's nothing wrong with getting spiffed up to have a little party at home, is there?" my mother-in-law said. "We just wanted to meet our son to celebrate."

Christine's mom pushed her hair away from her face in a gesture that reminded me exactly of Christine.

"You oughtta take a month or two off to recharge, Shawn," she said. "You need to have some *fun*."

The whole family stared at me, almost daring me to argue.

"Maybe I *will*," I said, throwing up my arms. "Since everyone seems to care so much, maybe I'll just go and do it. Anyhow, I think I just invited someone out. It's just Marjorie Radovich—the person I was representing? It's not exactly a date. It's more a friendship thing. But I'll probably need to go shopping for a new shirt. Can you guys help pick one out? I don't want to humiliate the whole family."

"Good," Jane said. "That's what we like to hear. I'll spring for it and don't even try to go to Sears."

"By the way, mom," I said. "Marjorie and her kids are moving back to the Burgh. She's taking a position at CMU. She volunteered to set up some sort of high-tech archive about steel history, and she wants me to do the legal work. I'm thinking about doing it, just so you know."

Christine's mom snapped open her purse and applied some ChapStick to her lips. "Your pal J.V. told me Marjorie was getting a place here and moving back days ago," she said. "It's about time."

I froze in my tracks. J.V. had shared privileged attorney-client information and told my mother-in-law before she even told me? That seemed totally unfair and unprofessional. But I knew better than to utter a word. My mother-in-law was only five-foot-six, but she was still a force to be reckoned with.

"They don't have any money in the budget," I went on, returning safely to my point. "So if I help Marjorie out with this project, there won't be any pay."

Christine's mother studied my eyes. She looked at me, up and down (pausing when she got to my shoes), inspecting me with a disarmingly beautiful smile. It had been a while since I'd seen that look in full bloom.

"*Of course*, Shawn," she said, pulling me by the tie towards her. "That's why my daughter married you. You're absolutely ridiculous. If you're asking permission from your wife's mother, you can't *possibly* be a wild philanderer."

Brittany and Liza high-fived each other. "Wow, dad's a *super* hottie," Britt said. "He's in demand!"

"I want to meet this Marjorie gal, anyway," Christine's mom said. "After you two get reacquainted, maybe we can all go out for pizza. Speaking of old flames, Mrs. McNulty called before we left to say your friend Erica Welles contacted your office from New York. She asked for our address to send a check. Mrs. McNulty said it was for your work on *this* case that you'd turned down. She said your Erica friend said you've *got* to take it; it's 'non-negotiable.' Are we in the Twilight Zone here, Shawn? Why is *Erica* paying *you*?"

I shrugged my shoulders. My mother-in-law grabbed my chin and stared into my eyes.

"Were you doing legal work without billing for it, again?" she asked. "Tell the truth; otherwise, I'll choke you."

"Just a little," I confessed. I could never lie to Christine's mom.

"Mrs. McNulty said they had quite a chat. She reported that Erica told her you were the only guy she ever had a crush on in law school," she said. "How many women did you *date* back then?"

"Zero," I said. "I was saving myself for your daughter."

My mother-in-law let go of my chin. "That's the right answer," she said. "I'll look forward to meeting her, too. Mrs. McNulty said this Erica woman sounded like a firecracker. She already invited me and the girls to visit her in Manhattan. She said something about meeting the editor of *Rolling Stone* and seeing the new *Mary Poppins* show on Broadway. I think that's a fabulous idea. These girls need to learn to become sophisticated travelers. You can come, too, as long as you don't try to cramp our style. If you want to go out with Erica too, that's your business. We'll go shopping on Fifth Avenue and stay out of your way. But you only get one day. The rest of the time is ours."

Christine's mother pulled the black jacket over her shoulders. "So now that we have all that business over with, we need to celebrate your big victory," she said. "I want to know all the details. It sounds like you pulled off a big win."

"Oh, yeah," I said. I couldn't resist some more bragging. "No Philadelphia lawyer can out-maneuver me and Bernie. Especially not someone from Penn with an ankle tattoo."

My mother-in-law nodded her head. She'd tolerated stories of my courtroom prowess a thousand times over the years, never acting bored or dismissive. As she smiled at me, the freckles on her nose caught the last sunlight reflecting off the Mellon Bank Tower. Staring into her face, I saw my wife Christine as clearly as if she were standing there with me.

My mother-in-law interrupted my thoughts by winking at me. "The girls and I are staying at cousin Jill's this weekend for a ladies' night out, so it's good timing for you to have Marjorie over for dinner," she said. "I even put a bottle of champagne in the fridge in case you're thirsty. Now that we've worked that out, can we get something to eat? We're all starving."

The first autumn leaves swept across Grant Street in a gust that mingled with the fragrance of the nearby rivers. That smell of Pittsburgh in the fall was always intoxicating. It struck me that this same smell had sustained generations of people in this town built upon the collective dreams of thousands of immigrants who'd come here to build something special. Even though I realized that might seem simple by some people's standards, it still seemed priceless to me.

"Hey, Liza, that's cool that you get to stay at Jill's," I said, kissing my youngest daughter on her forehead. "She always spoils the young ladies in the family *big time*, especially once they turn fifteen. I know that you're not much for fingernail polish and hair extensions, but humor her. You'll probably come back with a new phone case and a flashy dress for homecoming to dazzle all the boys at school. Just don't let Jill spend *too* much. That woman's out of control."

Liza almost managed to blush, an unusual sight. "Maybe I'll ditch the bellybutton ring before I go shopping with her," my daughter said. "Whatya think about that, Shawn, I mean, daddy?"

Britt winked at me.

I shook the bouquet of flowers in my hands so they'd appear fresh and slid them into my mother-in-law's hands. She looked at me, her eyes sparkling with surprise as if this were the first time anyone had given her an arrangement quite so beautiful. Squeezing her finger to convey a message that I knew only she would fully understand, I dropped my briefcase and pulled together my family into a tight pod, feeling warm and safe.

Beyond Pittsburgh's glittering skyline, I could see a tiny coal barge pushing its way up the Monongahela River, hewing closely to the bank. It was headed toward Homestead, Swissvale, Rankin, and other towns nestled in the valley, where Andrew Carnegie's last remaining steel mills still belched smoke and rumbled through their cycles as they had for the past century.

Together, we walked down Grant Street, heading over to Big Jim's for giant celebratory hamburgers and piles of fries to go. Then we climbed into our two cars, parked side-by-side in the garage.

And we went home.

ACKNOWLEDGMENTS

———.◆.———

Many friends thought I was crazy for sticking with this project after scrapping and re-writing numerous earlier versions. Yet, working on this novel over a period of decades and finally completing it—in between writing non-fiction books, working full-time and living life—has been rewarding, uplifting, and energizing. Its completion was made possible only through the support, encouragement, good humor, and patience of many friends and collaborators. At the top of that list is Tara Bradley-Steck, whose bed and breakfast my wife and I visited when our children were little, only to get engrossed in discussions with Tara and her husband, John, about home repairs, writing projects, and books-on-tape. Tara, a former AP bureau chief and journalism professor, ended up reading innumerable drafts of the novel and contributed her vast editorial and copy-editing expertise to make the finished product far more polished than I could have accomplished otherwise. Peggy Blocky Eiseman, my friend since kindergarten days at St. Anselm's in Swissvale and now my trusted assistant, did a Herculean job typing and revising as I readied this novel for its unveiling. Of course, she's from Swissvale, so she conquered each task effortlessly! Another St. A's friend, Michelle Keane Domeisen, assembled her intrepid book club—comprising 14 women of different backgrounds, ages, and professions—to read multiple versions of the manuscript and offer their insights. The book is immeasurably better thanks to the world's best book club! My friend Alison Sulentic, a Harvard-trained lawyer who previously taught at Duquesne Law School and now practices in Texas, pored over successive versions of the novel, offered creative plot ideas, and helped develop key characters. She also had a bolt of inspiration and imagined the snow globe on the cover, which was such a great idea that I promptly wrote it into the story!

My Harvard Law School and Somerville Bar Review friends—including Rex, Mark, Joel, Rick, Steve (MAD-KID 5), and a long list of close friends who spent Thursday nights together—helped bring to life the fictional Harvard characters in the book. (They also read drafts during the COVID-19 pandemic, joined in on raucous Zoom gatherings, and made useful suggestions so I wouldn't get in trouble!) A special thanks to Connie Sadler, no relation to Constance in the story, who had the brilliant idea of adding a map to the front of the book to sketch out the key locations in the story. My Pitt News friend from an eternity ago, publisher/author extraordinaire Jess Brallier, hated early versions of the book but kept reading until he finally relented and agreed the current version was worthy of publication. Other friends and confidantes who read drafts and to whom I'm grateful include Bob Cindrich, Tom Hardiman, Maureen Lally-Green, Max King, Linda Hernandez, Rhonda Hartman (we deeply miss her), Joy McNally, Maggie McKay, Alison D'Addieco, Bill Generett, David Conrad, Nicholas Perrins, John Furia Jr. (my late uncle and world-class writer/producer who was an inspiration to me and gave me steady encouragement during the earliest versions of the novel), Nancy Gormley Pfenning (my sister), Leslie Kozler (my sister-in-law), Annemarie Hall Gormley (my daughter-in-law), and others who wished to remain anonymous to avoid self-incrimination.

Editor Patricia Mulcahy read a prior draft and provided excellent guidance about point of view and other writing basics that were new to a first-time novelist. June Devinney at Duquesne Law School worked on many earlier versions of the novel; without her, it would never have taken shape. And Dee Paras (wife of Harry-the-Greek) contributed to polishing those chapters. Anne Burnam (formerly on the board of Autumn House Press) contributed her exquisite editorial advice to an earlier draft. Mel Berger, my world-class agent at WME for my book "Death of American Virtue: Clinton vs. Starr," offered encouragement as I embarked on a work of fiction after years of toiling away as a writer of non-fiction. Joanne Rogers, the beloved wife of iconic Pittsburgh figure Fred Rogers (of "Mister Rogers' Neighborhood" fame), became a friend who cheered me on, volunteering to read the novel and write a blurb for the jacket. Sadly, Joanne passed away with the novel still sitting on her coffee table before she was able to read it—but her kindness and friendship will be an enduring treasure.

The team at Sunbury Press (and Milford House Press) has been extraordinary from the start. The publisher and founder, Lawrence Knorr, is a visionary in the literary/publishing field who has taken a small independent press in central Pennsylvania to national prominence. I'm indebted to him for his support and enthusiasm for this project. My editor, Abigail Henson, contributed her keen proofreading eye and excellent editorial judgment in navigating this special book project to a conclusion. She has enormous talent and will do great things as a writer and editor. My thanks also to Marianne Babcock (executive assistant), Joe Walters (marketing expert), Crystal Devine (book designer), and others at Sunbury for their extraordinary work.

My longtime Swissvale/Pitt News friend and collaborator, Matt Kambic, did his magic by creating a beautiful piece of artwork for the cover as well as the map that graces the inside of the book. Now an accomplished artist, writer, and publisher living in New Zealand, Matt adds a creative spark and sheen to any project he touches. I'm grateful that he was willing to Zoom across time zones and work on this book project while juggling writing a play and a hundred other artistic projects. He is truly one of the great Pittsburgh artists!

The Sisters of Charity, one of the most amazing groups I've ever encountered (who kept me in line during grade school and high school at St. A's in Swissvale), graciously contributed information about the Roselia Foundling Home, a true beacon of hope for many young pregnant women during a bygone era in Pittsburgh. I also benefitted from long chats with attorney Marty Hagan and others involved in the hidden world of Orphan's Court, where I was lucky enough to practice law in my early legal career. It was here that I learned about the harsh treatment suffered by unwed mothers and "illegitimate" children under laws that existed until relatively recently, which piqued my interest and led to the creation of the central plot and characters in the book. Also, thanks to Dr. Cyril Wecht, a great friend and Pittsburgh treasure, who provided insight on exhumation, DNA, and related topics in crafting the story.

My brothers and sisters and their spouses—Bill and Rosie Gormley, B.J. and Cindy Gormley, Nancy and Frank Pfenning, Susie and Mark Hogan—and my nieces, nephews, and new generations of offspring, are partners in every project. They've walked the streets of Swissvale and Edgewood, where this novel took shape, and absorbed shelves of books at the C.C. Mellor Memorial Library along the railroad tracks on West Swissvale Avenue, allowing the aspirations and dreams of Elena and Bill Gormley to take flight.

My Kentucky kinfolk (including plenty of colonels) and my New York/Furia family have been a constant source of laughs and encouragement in my life; they have also taught me a lot about the gift of storytelling. Similarly, my wife Laura's Ringwood, N.J., family—including Joe Kozler, Beth and Mark Scarpato, Amy and Tom Maxey, Leslie and Bryant Kozler-Wesley, and our fabulous nieces and nephews from Laura's side of the family tree—are a rich part of my great fortune.

Jack McGinley, our intrepid chairman of the board at Duquesne University, graciously allowed me to keep tinkering with this book project on nights and weekends for relaxation and mental stress relief while carrying out my full-time job of running a major university. He and the entire board, Spiritan Congregation, cabinet, leadership team, faculty, staff, students, and alumni at Duquesne University have been a source of pride and inspiration to me each day. It's impossible to imagine having a better or more meaningful job than serving as president of Duquesne University of the Holy Spirit. Proceeds from the sale of this book will go to a fund for Duquesne students dedicated to honing their skills in creative writing as we shape writers and thinkers to carry the torch forward into future eras.

Finally, my wife Laura, and our children and their spouses—Carolyn and Brian Wehrle, Luke and Annemarie Gormley, Becca and Kyle Nolan, and Maddy—are the most significant sources of love and pride in my life. They've lived through every stage of the gestation of this novel, provided me with daily reason to keep forging ahead, and proved that Aunt Peg and Choppy were right: Family is more valuable than any of life's more fleeting riches. It's to them that I dedicate this book.

ABOUT THE AUTHOR

KEN GORMLEY is president of Duquesne University in Pittsburgh. A lawyer, constitutional scholar and author, Gormley's work has earned him national and international acclaim. His book "The Death of American Virtue: Clinton vs. Starr" (Crown 2010) was a *New York Times* bestseller and was selected as one of the top non-fiction books of the year by the *New York Times* and *Washington Post*. Gormley's first book, "Archibald Cox: Conscience of a Nation" (Addison-Wesley 1997), won multiple book awards.

Earlier in his writing career, Gormley received the first Rolling Stone magazine college journalism award for feature writing, chronicling adventures including setting a Guinness World Record in brick carrying and wrestling a bear.

"The Heiress of Pittsburgh" is Gormley's first work of fiction. Over thirty years in the making, it speaks to a subject that is universally relevant. A love story about people, places, and simple virtues that flourished in working class towns and ordinary communities that once built America, this beautifully-crafted novel provides hope that precious qualities of the past can be recast to create a rich new future; but only if success is boldly redefined.

Gormley has appeared on NBC's Today Show, MSNBC's Morning Joe, NPR's Fresh Air, multiple PBS and BBC documentaries, and hundreds of television and radio shows in the United States and worldwide. His work has appeared in The New York Times, The Washington Post, The LA Times, Politico, HuffPost and numerous other publications. The former mayor of his town in Forest Hills, Pennsylvania—a small community outside Pittsburgh—he lives there with his wife and family.

CPSIA information can be obtained
at www.ICGtesting.com
Printed in the USA
BVHW031722111221
623818BV00003B/13